Contents

FALLEN BROOK SERIES BOOK 3

Jennilynn Wyer

Romance Author www.jennilynnwyer.com

Copyright

Broken Butterfly by Jennilynn Wyer

ISBN: 979-8500863188

This book is a work of fiction. Names, characters, businesses, places, events, brands, media, and incidents are either the products of the author's imagination or are used fictitiously. The author acknowledges the trademarked status and trademark owners of various products referenced in this work of fiction, which have been used without permission. The publication/use of these trademarks is not authorized, associated with, or sponsored by the trademark owners. Any resemblance to actual events or persons, living or dead, is entirely coincidental.

Cover Design By: Jennilynn Wyer

Cover Image from Shutterstock / Canva

Proofread By: Paul W.

Copy Editor: Ellie @ My Brother's Editor

Formatting By: Jennilynn Wyer

Beta Readers: Julia, Lisa, Landi, Maegan, Rita, Samantha, Kelly

WARNING: The Fallen Brook Series is a mature High School & Young Adult, New Adult & College, and Contemporary Romance with mature content, sexual content, foul language, and possible triggers (violence, reference to traumatic events). Recommended for ages 18+.

Connect with the Author

WEBSITE | FACEBOOK |
INSTAGRAM | YOUTUBE

TIKTOK | TWITTER |
GOODREADS | BOOKBUB

AMAZON | BINGEBOOKS | NEWSLETTER

email: jennilynnwyerauthor@gmail.com

SUBSCRIBE TO MY NEWSLETTER
for news on upcoming releases,
cover reveals, sneak peeks,
author giveaways, and other fun stuff!

Synopsis

"Speechless!! Thank you Jennilynn for writing one of the best series I have ever read. I fell in love with each and every character. The story was filled with love, heartbreak, happiness, hope and second chances. This third and final book to the series was perfect! I'm not going to lie, the ending broke me in more ways than one. I have a book hangover after this!" -Julie David

One man will claim her. One man will own her heart. One man will save her. And one man will break her.

Fallon

Jayson, Ryder, and Julien have loved Elizabeth since they were kids. They grew up together. Shared their lives together. They were a family. Elizabeth's choice almost tore them apart. Then one horrible night forever changed their lives and Elizabeth was taken from them, only to return over a year later a different person. That's when things got interesting.

Elizabeth has always been my obsession. My fascination. She was the light to my dark. When her life exploded once again, she came running to me for help. Stupid girl.

You see, I have a secret. One that could destroy her.

Elizabeth thinks she's broken. She thinks I can help fix her.

She doesn't realize that I am as broken as she is.

She doesn't realize that I am the villain in her love story.

Elizabeth

Fallon was the only man who could save me when my life fell apart. I wish I knew he was also the only man who could break me.

"This series ripped my heart out. I don't think I've ever read one that affected me like this one did." - Amazon reviewer

"This is love like nothing that I have ever read. Original, complex, emotional and amazing...This story is a journey of the best kind." - Sharon, reviewer

Reader's Warning: Broken Butterfly is Book 3 in the Fallen Brook Series. It is a steamy romance full of angst, emotion, and suspense, and told in multiple POVs. Book 3 takes place in college and beyond and contains scenes that may be triggering (violence and reference to assault and abuse, foul language, suspense, and death). Sex/sexual intimacy in the book is consensual. Recommended for mature readers aged 18+. Please note that even though there are multiple love interests, it is not a RH.

The Fallen Brook Series

Book 1: All Our Next Times
Book 2: Paper Stars Rewritten
Book 3: Broken Butterfly

...

"WOW!! This book was better than the first! I need more. Everything about this series is addicting. I need to know what happens next. Highly recommend!!!" - Just One More Chapter

"This is one of the best series I have ever read!!!! The cliffhanger is an omg moment. I can it wait for book 3. Jennilynn is a new author.so glad I came across this series!!!!" - Cady - Amazon reviewer

"Captivating from the first paragraph! Book 2 in this series is even better than book 1. The character development is spot on, and the chemistry between Elizabeth and her boys leaves the reader wondering how it will all end. Wyer does a great

job capturing the change in Elizabeth as she grows from a somewhat passive teenager in book 1, to a confident woman in control of her own life in book 2. You will love this book and will eagerly await book 3!" - Amazon reviewer

"This series is so good - one of my top favorites. I can't wait till 3rd book I need to know how it ends! The cliffhanger has me waiting anxiously. Take my word for it and read this series!!" - Jennifer, Goodreads reviewer

"What a page-turner! Book 2 in the Fallen Brook series does not disappoint! I'm so invested in these characters." - texasgirl, Amazon reviewer

"I could not put this book down. I love the story-line and the plot twists. I'm rooting for Elizabeth and Ryder. I can't wait for book three." - Lisa, Amazon reviewer

Dedication

To all my Jennifers, Kelly S., and my awesome mother/daughter duo, Rita and Maegan.

Your enthusiasm for this series and love of the characters made it all worth it!

Prologue

Elizabeth

Last night, I remembered everything. Last night, I lost everything, too.

My name is Elizabeth Penelope Fairchild. I am nineteen years old. I was born on March 5, 2002. I am the daughter of Ann and John Fairchild. The older sister to Hailey Fairchild. The mother of Elizabeth Ann Jameson. My family was murdered over a year ago. I was brutally attacked and barely survived. I was in a coma for two months. I woke up with no memory. I found out last month that I had a daughter. Then I found out she was gone before I even had a chance to meet her or hold her.

I grew up with three boys. Jayson and Julien Jameson, the brown-haired, silver-eyed twins that would crawl through my window at night; and Ryder Cutton, the dark-haired, amber-eyed rebel with a heart of gold. We had been best friends since elementary school—until we were more. I loved all three of them, but I fell in love with two of them.

Jayson was my first boyfriend. But even when I was with Jayson, my young, conflicted heart was drawn to Ryder. I know that must sound awful and selfish. Jayson was all my firsts, but then Ryder was too. Doesn't that sound confusing? But, for me, it's my truth. See, there was my life before the attack, and then there was my new life after. Jayson was before; he claimed my heart when I was a girl. Ryder was after; he owned my heart when I was a woman. In truth, Ryder has always owned my heart my entire life. And last night, I fucked it all up.

Let me explain.

After that horrific night over a year ago—the night I lost my family and my memory, the night that shattered my life apart—a distant relative of my father's, Daniel, and his husband Drew, took emergency guardianship over me. They carried me back to their home in Seattle, Washington and hid me in a private medical facility. Thirteen months ago, I woke up from my coma with no memory of the first eighteen years of my life. Three months ago, I left Seattle to attend college at Carolina University, drawn by a pull I did not understand, where I came face to face with Ryder, Jayson, and Julien—the boys who were my childhood best friends. The boys I grew up with. The boys I fell in love with. The boys I had no memories of. They had been searching for me, desperate to find me for over a year; to find out what happened to me. And then, *poof*! There I was in the same town, at the same university, as the three of them. A miracle, right? Perhaps fate?

It's funny how life plays out sometimes. I think the ancient Greeks had it right with their belief that the Fates controlled everyone's destinies. Those fickle Fate bitches. They've been pulling the strings of my life and tying them into twisted knots. Soon after I returned to North Carolina, I ran into Ryder by chance while on the CU campus. I'm positive the Fates made sure it was no accident. Then Jayson and Julien came barging back into my life, literally. We've spent the last three months getting to know one another again, becoming friends again, existing in the new normal of New Elizabeth, the girl with no memory. Jayson struggled with his jealous anger because I was no longer the girlfriend he knew. Julien struggled with his guilt because he thought he failed me. Then there was Ryder. New Elizabeth fell deeply in love with Ryder.

And then last night happened. My memories came back. The one thing I was afraid of happening, did. You would think that regaining my memories, remembering the old Elizabeth, remembering my family, the people, places, and events of my life, would be a good thing. Fuck no. It was the worst thing that could have happened to me. I don't want to be Old Elizabeth. I despise Old Elizabeth. The boys had been telling me stories of our life together, hoping it would help bring my memories back. From everything I heard about Old Elizabeth, all I saw was that she was a selfish girl who was weak and let others make choices for her. And I never wanted to be her ever again. I liked New Elizabeth. She was strong and capable. She didn't say she loved one man while pining for another. New Elizabeth told it like it was and stood her ground. New Elizabeth gave all of her love and her whole heart to Ryder Cutton. New Elizabeth had a good group of friends. She enjoyed new things and new experiences. New Elizabeth liked to curse and drink and have fun.

I'm pretty sure the Fates are laughing their asses off right now. They are probably in hysterics, looking down at me as I drown in the misery of my greatest mistake. The mistake I made last night when I fucked Jayson like the world would end if I didn't. These stupid goddamn memories! New Elizabeth is so in love with Ryder, but Old Elizabeth's memories came back, and those memories were filled with her love for Jayson.

When I woke up this morning and felt Jayson's arms wrapped around my sore, naked body, I hated myself. If I could have unzipped my skin and crawled out of it, I would have. Instead, I slipped out of his bed and searched for my clothes. On the floor, I found my phone along with the tattered remains of my shirt and yoga pants. I quietly opened a couple of Jayson's drawers and found a T-shirt and some sweatpants, which I hastily put on. I unlocked and opened his bedroom door. Old Elizabeth started screaming at me not to leave. She wanted to wake up in Jayson's arms and look into his metallic-gray eyes. I told her to fuck off. Once I reached the kitchen, I saw some paper and a pen left on the counter. I took them and used them to write a note.

"Jayson, I'm sorry. Last night should never have happened. – Elizabeth"

I folded the paper in half and wrote Jayson's name on it, then placed it on top of the coffee machine. I caught my reflection in the shiny stainless-steel surface of the refrigerator. Jesus, I looked a mess. I hadn't taken a shower since yesterday morning. I smelled like Jayson, rain, sweat, and sex. I scowled at my image.

"I hate you," I hissed at the reflection of Old Elizabeth staring back at me. Then I left.

So, here I am now, standing in the parking lot outside of the boys' condo. I don't care that

I am barefoot or that my long hair looks like a knotted, tangled bird's nest. I search the parking lot for my car but then remember that I ran here last night. I ran here in the rain. *What the fuck, Elizabeth*?

I look down at my phone. I open the settings and am about to turn off my location sharing so the boys can't track me, when I notice that it's already turned off. When did I do that? I know I had already uninstalled the location-tracking software that Daniel and Drew put on it, but I always keep my phone's location sharing on so Ryder, Jayson, and Julien can find me. Why? Because I have been having a lot of what I call 'memory blackouts.' When my memories started to resurface over the past few months, they would incapacitate me, turn me into a hyperventilating zombie. The boys feared for my safety. They worried that I could be driving or out and about when one of the episodes hit, so they turned my phone's location sharing on as a way to find me if that ever happened.

Old Elizabeth must have turned it off last night when she got to Jayson's. Wouldn't want her night-long fuck-fest with him to be interrupted. Goddamn bitch. I sound absolutely crazy, even in my own twisted and tumbled mind, but I feel like two different people are warring inside my jumbled brain. I can't deal with the texts and missed calls right now, so I power off my phone again and begin to walk. I walk for a mile. I get stared at by several people. One mother who is out for a walk pushing her child in a stroller, sees me and turns around to walk the other way.

After a half hour, I'm finally at my destination. I don't know why I'm here. What the hell am I thinking? *It's because you're not thinking*, I tell myself. You fucked up, Elizabeth. You just destroyed everything good in your life. You deserve every ounce of pain you're feeling right now.

I raise my hand and knock on the dark oak door. It smells like wood cleaner. Who the hell polishes their front door with wood cleaner?

A guy I don't recognize opens the door and looks at me. I know I look like crap. I'm wearing Jayson's clothes which hang loosely on my smaller body. I must look like an unwashed lunatic to him.

"Can I help you?"

The door swings open wider and the man I came to see steps out. Relief pours through me.

"Kitten?"

"I need you, Fallon."

Chapter 1

Jayson

My dreams are filled with Liz. Last night, her memories returned, and I got my girlfriend back. We screwed like animals. I devoured every inch of her and then went back for seconds, thirds, and fourths. We didn't talk. We didn't speak. We just fucked. Once one orgasm ended, we would go after the next one. We couldn't stop. We had over a year to make up for. It wasn't until sunrise that we fell into an exhausted sleep.

As I slowly wake, I stretch the soreness out of my body and can feel the evidence of bite marks and scratches over my back and chest. I don't think I've ever been happier. Before I dozed off a few hours ago, I had my arms wrapped around the love of my life. Liz is my soulmate. She's my forever. And last night, she came back to me. I don't know how long we've been asleep, but I'm suddenly fully awakened by pounding on my front door. I turn over to grab Liz but she's not in the bed. The pounding on the door gets louder and I hear Ryder's voice. Where's Liz? I hear the front door open. Ryder still has a key, and he lets himself in.

"Jay, you here?"

My bedroom door is cracked open and I panic. Liz is probably in the kitchen making coffee or sitting out on the balcony. I rush to pull on some sweatpants and a shirt.

"Jay?" Ryder shouts again, the sound of his voice closer as he walks down the hallway.

I open my door all the way. "What?"

"Jesus, you scared the crap out of me," he says.

"Being woken by someone pounding your door down isn't much better," I reply.

"Sorry about that. Have you heard from Elizabeth?"

I peek down the hallway half expecting to see her. I step out and close the door to my bedroom. It smells like musk and sex.

"Why?"

"Fuck!"

"Ryder, what the hell is going on?"

"She wasn't at home last night when I got back from the track. She never came home. I've been driving all over town. She's not answering her phone. I've tried calling Fallon. I don't know how to get in touch with Meredith or Trevor, so I went to campus this morning and searched every place I thought she might be. I even called the police, but they said she had to be gone for twenty-four hours before I could file a report. Jay, where the hell is she?"

I walk around the condo, looking for Liz. Ryder follows me wondering what I'm doing. *Liz, where are you? Did she sneak out?*

"Jay, I'm worried."

"Ry, she's fine," I assure him. Liz was with me in bed a few hours ago.

"How can you be so sure? Weren't you the one who pointed out what could happen to her if she had another memory blackout? She could be hurt for fuck's sake!" he yells at me. "Her location tracking is turned off. Why the hell would she do that? She promised to keep it on so we could find her in emergencies."

That's a good question. *Where the hell are you, Liz?* It's then I see the piece of paper with my name on it sitting on top of the coffee pot. The paper is folded like a tent, my name is written in large block letters. Ryder sees the note at the same time I do but gets to it first.

His face morphs into furious anger. I rip the paper from his hand.

"Jayson, I'm sorry. Last night should never have happened. – Elizabeth"

"What happened last night, Jay?" Ry's voice is hard and threatening. I think he already knows.

"Liz's memory returned," is all I get to say before Ryder punches me in the face.

Chapter 2

Elizabeth

One good thing about Fallon is that he knows when not to ask questions. He takes one look at me standing on his frat house doorstep and grabs my arm, pulling me inside. A dozen of his fraternity brothers silently watch as he leads me upstairs and into what I assume is his room.

"You look like shit," he tells me as he shuts his bedroom door. He grabs a rolled-up towel from a shelf and throws it at me. "Bathroom is through there." He points to the doorway located adjacent to his dresser.

I hold the towel close to me, hugging its softness, wanting to feel something good to help replace some of the bad. I nod at Fallon and walk on blistered feet across the wood floor and into the tiled bathroom. I turn the shower on to the hottest setting it will go to and step under the spray without taking off the ill-fitting clothes I arrived in. I pray the hot water will scald my skin until it peels off. If it doesn't, I will rub every inch of my body raw until it does, needing to get the smell of sex with Jayson off of my skin. I don't realize I'm screaming until Fallon flings open the bathroom door and rushes in.

"What the fuck, Elizabeth?"

I'm not used to him calling me by my given name. I've always been "kitten" to him. He reaches for the shower handle and turns the temperature down. "Jesus," he hisses when he looks at me. Some of my skin, the parts not covered by clothes, are bright red, and thin trickles of blood create a path of rivulets from the broken blisters on my feet to the shower drain. Fallon steps inside the shower with me and turns me around to face him, not seeming to mind that his clothes are getting drenched. I look up at him with desolate, beggar's eyes.

"Going to tell me why you landed on my doorstep?"

No, I'm not, so I don't answer him. He's not supposed to ask questions. He's not supposed to care.

Fallon sighs then reaches for a bottle and squirts some of its contents into his hand. He lifts my heavy, long hair and massages the lather through each strand. I close my eyes and step forward to grab his waist, laying my forehead to his chest. Fallon takes his time with my hair, making sure to rinse it thoroughly so no shampoo remains. He reaches behind me and turns the shower off. He uses the towel to rub my hair dry, then takes my hand. The soggy clothes on my body drip water all over his floor, but he doesn't say anything. Fallon tells me to sit down on the seat of the toilet and I obey. He takes out a first aid kit from his bathroom cabinet and wordlessly tends to my blistered feet. I watch as he walks into his bedroom and takes a couple items of clothing out of his dresser and lays them on his bed. He comes back inside the bathroom and lifts me up in his arms to carry me the ten feet to his large, king-sized bed. Setting me down on the bedspread, not caring that I am also getting it wet, he lifts my bandaged feet, carefully slipping a sock on each, before picking up the folded clothes and placing them in my hands.

"Put these on," he tells me.

I follow his directions like a child does a parent. Fallon opens his bedroom door and steps outside, giving me some privacy. I strip the wet fabric off, gingerly walking back into the bathroom and placing the garments in the sink and put on the clean ones Fallon gave me. The cotton shirt and pants soothe my scalded skin. I can tell how expensive the cloth is just from how it feels. I trundle back over to his bed and lie down. The scent that lingers on his sheets smells like lemon, ginger, and bergamot. How the hell do I know what a bergamot is? I do. It's a type of orange.

I hear the bedroom door click open and then close. The bed dips beside me and Fallon lies down at my back. He pulls me into his arms and rests his head against mine. "It's going to be okay, Elizabeth."

"You always call me kitten," I mumble.

"That's because I'm an asshole."

If I didn't feel so utterly destroyed, I may have chuckled. "You're not an asshole, Fallon."

"A lot of people would disagree."

Old Elizabeth would agree with that. She would never have come to Fallon for help. She would never have allowed him to touch her. Old Elizabeth was both wary of and cautiously fascinated by Fallon.

I roll over and look at him. We are almost nose to nose. I take in his crystalline blue eyes. They are a unique color of blue, almost like the blue of arctic ice. His sandy-blond hair is disheveled and sticking up at the top, and his lower jaw is covered in a day's growth of dark blond stubble.

"I never thought I'd see the day when I got Elizabeth Fairchild in my bed."

"I take it back. You are an asshole."

We lie quietly and stare at each other for a long time.

"Secret for a secret?" he asks me. I nod yes.

"What happened?"

"My worst fear."

"Inflatable tube guys?"

This time I do chuckle. "No. The other one."

Fallon's eyebrows scrunch up as he thinks. I lift my finger to the creases and smooth them away. "I remembered."

He goes rigid next to me. I would never have been able to tell if I wasn't lying so close to him. "What did you say?"

"My memory came back. I remember everything."

He swallows a few times. "What do you remember?"

"Everything."

"Elizabeth, what happened?"

I roll over onto my back, not able to look him in the eye when I say it. “I slept with Jayson last night.”

He curses a few times. “Why the fuck would you do that?”

I burst into tears.

“Shit. Elizabeth, stop crying.”

I cry harder. He curses some more.

“It’s her fault!” I finally say.

“Who?”

“Old Elizabeth. I hate her. I didn’t want her to come back, but she did. She’s ruined everything!”

“You know that you sound crazy as fuck right now.”

He’s right. Perhaps I have lost my mind. I suck in a deep breath and wipe my face.

“I swear on my life, I love Ryder. I would never hurt him, Fallon. Never.” When Ryder finds out I slept with Jayson last night, he will never forgive me.

“Then explain it to me. How could you fuck Jay when you say you love Ry?”

Fallon hit the nail on the head with that one.

I did fuck Jayson. There was no making love at all. It was pure, animalistic fucking.

"When the memories came back last night, it's like I became another person. I had no control anymore. It's as if someone else had taken over my body. Holy shit, Fallon! I remember everything. I remember what happened *that* night. My fight with Jayson. Going to Ryder. Coming home."

I touch my tattooed-covered scars on my side. "I can feel *His* breath on my skin. The way the knife slid easily into me. I can see my parents. I remember what *He* did to Hailey!" I scream, not able to bear the memory of what happened to my sister.

I jump off the bed and start throwing anything I can get my hands on. Glass items, cologne bottles, papers, and books crash into the walls and onto the floor. Fallon tries to grab me, but I twist out of his hold and start punching and slapping him just like I did to Jayson last night. I'm so angry. I want to hurt something. I want someone to hurt as badly as I do.

Fallon catches my fist and twists my arm back behind me. The sharp tug of pain spurs me on, and I kick him. He lifts and flips me over onto the bed, then lands on top of me, pinning me down. I growl up at him and he smashes his mouth down onto my lips. The shock of his mouth on mine stops me cold and sobers me up instantly.

"Fallon, what the hell?" I screech, bucking up to throw him off me.

Fallon grins down at me. He *fucking grins* and I still my movements. "It made you stop, didn't it?"

He lifts himself up. I want to smack the smirk off his face at the same time I want to hug him. He's right. The kiss brought me back to reality and dried my tears. I'm still angry, though. I'm still destroyed.

"What am I going to do, Fallon? How can I face Ryder after what I've done?"

Fallon pulls me to a sitting position. "What do you want to happen?"

I scrape my fingernails over my thighs, needing to feel that slight sting of pain on my skin. I'm briefly reminded of the marks Hailey tried to hide from me that morning in our bathroom. "I don't know," I reply, heartbroken and lost.

It's the truth. My mind is having an internal battle between what once was and what is now. I already know I'm about to do the one thing I promised Ryder and Julien I would never do again. It's going to break my heart and hurt the boys deeply, but until I can get a grip on which Elizabeth will prevail, I need to stay away from all three of them. Not just for their sake, but for mine as well. And knowing what I have to do just makes everything seem that much worse now. I swore to Ryder that if my memories returned, it would not change things between the two of us. I promised Julien that I would never leave again. And knowing I will not keep those promises shreds my already tattered heart even more. I thought I couldn't break any more than I already have, but I was so wrong. *Poor little broken butterfly.*

Fallon scrutinizes me for a long minute, then appears to make a decision. "Stay here. Do not leave this room."

I flop back on the bed and grab one of Fallon's pillows. I want to tell him I have nowhere to go. I can't go home because Ryder will be there. Fallon leaves the room and closes the door behind him. My body and mind finally agree on one thing—total exhaustion. Within minutes, I'm asleep.

Fallon

I leave Elizabeth in my room and go downstairs. A few of my frat brothers stop talking when I round the corner to go to the kitchen, but when Matt spots me, he elbows Jacob beside him, and they both grin.

"Damn, Fallon. You're the only guy I know who can get pussy express-delivered to him on a Friday morning. That chick is definitely a screamer." Matt laughs. He thinks he's being funny.

"Want to repeat that? I didn't hear you."

Jacob stops laughing and steps away from Matt. Jacob knows how I am. He knows who I am. Everybody on this damn campus knows. Matt, however, apparently doesn't. He's one of the new freshman initiates. He'll learn who I am, what I am, soon enough.

Matt chuckles again and opens his mouth to speak, but I'm in his face before he gets a chance to utter his first syllable. I grab the front of his shirt and slam him against the refrigerator. The heavy appliance rocks back into the wall then settles.

"Fallon, what the hell?" he yelps.

I sneer at him, baring my teeth. "The first mistake you made was talking to me like we're friends. We're not friends, Pledge. I'm the king of this castle and you are *nothing*. The second mistake you made is that you opened that smart-ass mouth of yours. The worst mistake you could have ever made was talking shit about that girl."

I release my grip on his shirt, then deliver a punch to his gut that sends him to his knees. I place my foot on his chest and push him down to the floor, holding him in place, not caring that he's struggling for breath or that his face is turning red.

"You will not look at that girl. You will not talk to that girl. You will not come near that girl. Do I make myself clear?"

Matt gasps a few times then nods his head yes. I look around at all of the other fraternity brothers who have gathered around or are standing in the doorways that lead to the kitchen. "Do I make myself clear?" I repeat, looking at everyone. "Now get this fucker off my floor and out of my sight."

I grab the items I want from the pantry and walk out to the back patio deck. It's late morning and the autumn sun is bright today. The temperatures are nice and cool. I reach in my pocket and grab a stick of gum. Why did I stop smoking again? A glance up to my bedroom window answers that question. Popping the gum into my mouth, I take out my phone.

Me: Her memory came back. We need to talk.

I hit send.

My little kitten came crawling to me for help. She may come to regret that decision. I open the contacts on my phone, scroll to the one I need, and press call.

"Fallon, thank God. Have you heard from Elizabeth?"

"Hey, man."

Ryder has always been that guy for me. Even though he's a year younger than I am, I look up to him like a reverent little brother would an older brother he idolizes. Ry's had my back far more times than I can count. There's nothing I wouldn't do for him. I know Jayson, Julien, and Elijah have never understood why we're friends. It's none of their goddamn business.

"Elizabeth is missing. Please tell me you've seen her."

I can hear the panic in his voice. The worry. My boy has always loved Elizabeth. I hate what I'm about to do to him.

"Ry, I've got her."

"Thank fuck! Where are you? I'm on my way."

"Nah, man. That's why I'm calling."

"Fallon, stop messing around. I'm worried sick. You don't know what has happened."

"I know what happened," I tell him.

"What? How?"

"She's messed up. She needs time."

Elizabeth thinks she's broken. She thinks I can help fix her. She doesn't realize that I am as broken as she is. In a fucked-up way, we're perfect for one another right now.

"Fuck that! She needs me," he shouts into the phone.

"Not yet," I calmly tell him, hoping he understands. I hear a loud exhale on the other end of the line. I wait.

"She ran back to him last night," he says, and I can hear the defeat in his voice.

"No, *she* didn't." Her past ran back to Jayson, not Elizabeth. I never could stand that pompous asshole.

"Fallon, I just got her back. I can't lose her again. I love her too damn much. I can handle what happened last night with Jay. I can accept it. What I can't handle is losing her. I just want her back," he states with desperation.

He's not going to like what I say next.

"I'm taking her away for a while. She needs time away from you, Jay, and Jules. She needs time to decide what she wants."

"I swear to God, Fallon—"

"Ry, listen to me. Deep down you understand what I'm trying to tell you. I won't let anything happen to her. I promise. I'll protect her with my life."

"Shit! Fuck! No way, man. You're not taking her away from me!"

"You need to trust me." He's silent for a long minute.

"What about her classes, Fallon?"

"I've got it covered."

More silence.

"I want to talk to her. Put her on the phone."

"No," I tell him.

"Then I'm coming over."

"We won't be here."

"Goddammit, Fallon!"

"If you love her, Ry, let me do this for her. Give her the time she needs."

I know he'll do the right thing.

"I don't like this one damn bit," he finally says.

Good. He shouldn't, but I know he won't stop me. He and I could always say a page's worth of thoughts in just a few words. If he pushed me to bring her back, I would. I know he won't because he truly does love her. He wants what's best for her even if it hurts him. It's one of the reasons why I admire him.

"Fallon, please tell me that she's okay."

"She's in a real dark place right now. If pushed, she might not come back from it. I can give her the time and help she needs to deal with everything."

Ryder exhales again. "If anything happens to her, I will hunt you down myself. Fuck, I'm going to regret this. Call me tonight and let me know how she is."

"I'll be in touch," I say, and hang up.

I walk back upstairs carrying the bottled water and banana I got from the kitchen pantry. Matt and the other frat brothers have wisely retreated out of sight. When I open my bedroom door, I see Elizabeth curled up in my bed, fast asleep. I put down the water and fruit on the table next to my bed and sit down in the armchair across from where she's sleeping.

I laze back, propping a knee on top of the other leg, and watch her sleep. Her face is relaxed but I can tell she's dreaming from the way her body twitches and jerks. She has always been the most beautiful girl in the world to me. She's always been my obsessive fascination. I would love to be inside her head right now, to live in her mind's chaos. I'm fucked-up like that.

I feel my phone vibrate and I see a reply to my earlier text.

Unlisted: Can't talk now. I'll call you later.

I hear Elizabeth moan, then gasp as her eyes fly open, her green eyes wide in alarm. She blinks a few times when she sees that it's me sitting across from her. "Fallon?"

"Hey, kitten."

She sits up and rubs her eyes. "How long was I out?"

"Not long." I point to the water beside her on the table. She picks it up, twists the top off, and guzzles half of it. "We're going on a trip," I tell her, and her face fills with confusion.

"What?"

"We're leaving. Get up."

"Leaving for where?"

"Consider it an extended vacation. Trust me," I tell her.

"Fallon, I have no clothes or shoes."

I rise from the chair and hold out my hand to her. Elizabeth looks up at me with a scowl.

"I have classes, Fallon. I meet with a therapist twice a week. I can't just up and leave."

"*Trust me.*" My eyes never waver from hers as I keep my hand outstretched in front of me.

It takes a few minutes, but she finally takes my hand without another word.

"Oh, kitten. We're going to have so much fun, you and I." The devil inside of me grins.

Chapter 3

Day 1: Finding Myself

It Begins...

Elizabeth

I truly have lost my ever-loving mind, I think as I follow Fallon down a short, narrow flight of stairs on a yacht we just boarded. I know I've already said it today, but what the hell am I thinking?

Fallon opens a door and leads me into an expansive, stately room that resembles a luxury hotel suite. A queen-sized bed filled with pillows of various sizes sits at one end of the room with a full entertainment center directly across from it. The TV is mounted on the wall. An elegant wood desk, a dresser, and a small love seat and coffee table finish the room's furnishings. The room is decorated in muted shades of dusty blue and gray.

"There's a selection of clothes and shoes in

that closet that should fit you," he tells me. "We'll pick up whatever else you need along the way."

I open the small closet and find a myriad of colorful blouses and skirts. There are also tailored slacks and dresses. I finger the fabric of one of the blouses. It feels like satin. I turn to Fallon. "Whose clothes are these?" If he says they belong to his mother, I'll refuse to wear them. That's just fucking creepy.

"They're my sister's. She's shorter than you, but I think most of her stuff should fit."

"Wait a minute. You have a sister too?" It wasn't that long ago I found out that Trevor was his half-brother. How many secret siblings does this guy have?

"Another result of my father's numerous affairs. It wouldn't surprise me if I had dozens of half-siblings scattered around the globe I don't know about."

"Wow," is all I can say.

Fallon leans a shoulder against the doorframe and crosses his arms. "You'd like her. She lives in Madrid. I go see her about once a year and we sail the Mediterranean together for a month during the summer."

"What's her name?"

"Tatiána."

I catalog that bit of information for later. Fallon straightens and walks away from the door. After he leaves, I lock the door and remove a few garments from the closet and lay them on the bed. Next, I investigate the contents inside the dresser drawers. I find a selection of sleepwear, underwear, bras, garters, and socks. I grab the items I need and throw them on the bed next to the clothes. Slowly turning around in a circle, I take everything in, while continuing to question how I got here.

After we left Fallon's frat, he drove us to a marina. Just like this morning, people stopped what they were doing and stared. Fallon was dressed in dark charcoal trousers and a nice sweater. I, however, was still wearing the sleep clothes he had given me and a pair of men's slippers. We must have looked like the oddest couple. He walked me down a long dock then stopped in front of an enormous yacht.

"Holy shit, Fallon," I said in disbelief. "Is this your parents'?"

"No, kitten. It's mine. Come on." Despite my newfound curiosity, Fallon practically had to drag my ass onto the boat.

"What am I doing here?" I had asked him while watching several crew members walk around

doing whatever people do to get a yacht ready to set sail. One of the crewmen approached me carrying a tray with prepared drinks. He greeted me by name and asked if I needed anything. I declined. This was insane. I tugged on Fallon's arm.

"Fallon."

"Give me your phone, kitten."

"What?"

He reached out, palm up, waiting. "Give me your fucking phone."

"Not a chance in hell," I told him.

"You want to find out which Elizabeth you're going to be? I'm giving you that chance. Give me your phone."

"Why do you need my phone, Fallon? I need to call Ryder, Jayson, and Julien and let them know I'm okay."

"Already took care of that."

"What? When?" He must have done it earlier when he left his room and I fell asleep.

"Kitten, you came to me for help. I'm helping. You might not understand how right now, but you will. The first thing you need is time and space away from Ry, Jay, and Jules. You can't do that if you're texting and calling them at all hours every

day. Now, put your goddamn phone in my hand or I will take it from you."

"Jesus! Fine! Here." I slapped my phone into his hand.

"Good girl."

Another worry popped into my head. "Fallon, I have classes I can't miss. I'm already a year behind."

"Also taken care of. Will you just shut up and fucking trust me?"

That's when he takes me down the stairs and into his sister's stateroom, which is where I'm currently standing.

Once I finish circling the room, I decide to take another shower—a proper one this time. The various shampoos and soaps smell like flowers. After I'm done, I take my time getting ready. Finding a hair dryer, I blow dry my hair before piling my thick blond mass on top of my head in a loose bun. Next, I try on several items of clothing until I find a blouse that I like. The trousers are all too short for me, so I choose one of the longer skirts. Fallon was correct about Tatiána's stuff being my size. Other than our apparent height difference, most of her clothes fit me. There's a light knock on my suite door.

"Miss Fairchild? Mr. Montgomery would like

for you to join him up on deck."

I open the door to find an impeccably dressed man standing in front of me. "Hi," I say, unsure of what to do.

"Good day, Miss Fairchild. My name is Robert, and I will be your personal concierge while you are on board. If you need anything, please do not hesitate to ring me at any time by pressing the number seven on any phone you find on board." I catch a faint British accent and want to ask him where he's from but decide not to. I give him a polite smile in greeting.

Realizing he what he said about the phone, I eye the phone in my room and Robert follows my gaze. "Mr. Montgomery also wanted me to inform you that the phones on board are pin-locked and you will not be able to call out unless you have the code, which he has informed the staff you are not to have. Also, the laptops and computers on board are password-protected."

I make a silent, internal growl aimed at Fallon. *Asshole.*

"Please follow me." Robert offers me the back of his hand like we're about to walk out onto a ballroom floor to waltz. As we walk, he points out various rooms to me. Fallon's suite is right next to mine, which makes sense if I'm staying in the one his sister uses.

Robert escorts me to the upper deck. I look around, taking everything in. We're already sailing in open water, the marina now a tiny speck in the distance. The late afternoon sun is sinking toward the horizon. It's absolutely breathtaking. I wish I could take some pictures, but Fallon has my phone. The breeze is strong and whips some of my hair out from my bun. The wind feels crisp and cool against my skin. I breathe in and smell the salt of the ocean. Grasping the top railing, I lean over to watch the small white caps form along the side of the yacht as it trails through the rippling Atlantic waters.

"I've got it from here, Robert," Fallon says from behind me. Robert quietly slips away. Fallon comes to stand beside me, his hands shoved into the pockets of his trousers.

"You look beautiful," he tells me.

Not knowing what else to say, I tell him thank you. I breathe in the open ocean air once again. Instead of the heavy saline smell of the ocean I detected before, the air now smells like freedom.

"Ready to find yourself, kitten?"

The setting sun makes his sandy-blond hair look almost burnt umber. "I'm trusting you,

Fallon. Don't make me regret it."

He gives me one of his classic Fallon smirks and slings an arm around my shoulder, pulling me into his side. He places a kiss to my temple like a protective older brother would a little sister he adores. Fallon is a complete conundrum to me. He can be a foul-mouthed loud jerk, but like now, he can also be tender, sweet, and caring. For some strange reason, I like all his sides, even the asshole-ish ones. With his arm around me, we stand together near the railing and watch the sun sink until the stars come out.

"So, are you going to finally tell me what your plan is?" I ask Fallon.

We just finished dinner, which was excellent. I told the chef about my dairy allergy and preference for gluten-free, and he whipped up a gorgeous allergen-free chocolate cake with raspberry drizzle just for me. That was after we enjoyed a selection of grilled fish, chicken, roasted vegetables, and salad. I hadn't eaten anything since yesterday, with the exception of the banana Fallon brought me this morning, so I was ravenous. Now we're back out on the top deck enjoying an IPA and looking up at the stars.

"In about two days, we'll dock near New York so I can take you shopping for some new clothes."

I think my mouth drops open. "Fallon, you're not buying me clothes and I'm not taking your money."

"Kitten, who the hell do you think you're talking to? You should know by now that money is not an obstacle for me. I have millions. A few clothes and shoes are nothing. Besides, you have to do what I say. It's in the contract you agreed to."

I mouth the word "asshole" at him, and he gives me a cocky salute with his beer bottle. It would be nice to have some new clothes and not have to wear his sister's.

Knowing I'm zero for like a thousand at winning arguments with him, I relent. "Alright, new clothes. Then what?"

"We'll stay in New York City for a couple of days, take in the sights, see a show, do the normal touristy things."

I have to admit, a part of me gets excited about the thought of touring New York City. I've never been there before.

"And then?"

"And then it's up to you where we end up."

"Are you serious?"

"Operation 'Finding Elizabeth' has begun. Where you go, I follow…but I'm still in charge. So, where do you want to go?"

"Fallon, this is too much. I'm just a girl from a small town in the middle of nowhere. You don't even know me that well. Why are you doing this for me?"

He narrows those pale blue eyes at me. "Where do you want to go?" he asks again.

He's not going to answer me. "You are so frustrating!"

For the third time, he asks, "Where do you want to go, Elizabeth?" He drinks his beer while watching me. Waiting.

I bite my lip and look at him, so many thoughts and possibilities run through my head.

"Elizabeth, I'm serious about doing this for you." His phone rings and a strange expression crosses his face when he looks down at the screen. "Sorry, I've got to take this," he clips and gets up.

I lean my head back on the deck chair and

scan the night sky. I can see so many stars. You never realize how much of the night sky you miss out on when you live in a town. The night sky is usually obscured by light pollution from streetlamps and buildings. Gazing upon the star-filled expanse above me makes me think of the night Ryder took me out to his quiet place where we danced under the moonlight. I remember the night of my first date with Jayson when he lit up our tree and we perched on top of one of the branches as we cuddled among the fairy lights. God, I already miss the boys so much. But there's my problem in a nutshell; the reason I ran to Fallon for help. The old and new parts of me are battling for control inside my mind, leaving me yearning for both Ryder and Jayson. This insane idea of Fallon's is my chance to decide who I want to be and who I want to be with once and for all. Will Old Elizabeth win out, or will I choose the new life I've been creating with Ryder these past several months?

I stand up to stretch my legs and walk around. Fallon's yacht is gorgeous. He let me explore it a little before dinner. I think tomorrow morning I'll try out the fitness room. I'm so used to running with Julien in the mornings that I'll probably be up before five anyway, so I might as well. I stroll around the deck and see Fallon walking back, his head down.

"I said I'm handling it." He looks up and sees

me. “Look, I’ve got to go,” he tells the person on the other end and hangs up.

“What if I want to go to Europe?” I call to him as he slowly approaches.

“Done.”

This guy. I could probably tell him to buy me a tropical island and he would give me the same response.

“Which city?” he asks.

“London. Paris. Venice.”

“Okay.”

I scoff at his easy acceptance. I continue, “Reykjavik. Amsterdam. Barcelona. Sydney.”

“Fine, even though Sydney’s not in Europe.” He smirks. “We can take the family jet. I’ll call and get it ready. We’ll fly out of JFK.”

“I will never be able to pay you back.”

“I would never ask you to, nor would I let you.”

“There’s something I’ve been wondering, Fallon.”

Fallon stops in front of me, the wind ruffling his hair in every direction. “And what would that be, kitten?”

"Why me?"

Even though I had tried to ask him something similar to that earlier, I don't think he was expecting me to ask again, point blank. *Why me*? Two words. So simple yet packed with so much meaning.

He takes a lock of my hair and rubs it between his fingers. "I could say that it's because you're Ryder's girl and I owe him one, which means that I'm being a good friend to him by helping you. Or I could say that I'm a nice guy who sees someone in trouble and wants to help out of the kindness of my heart. Instead, I'll give you a partial truth because you wouldn't be able to handle the whole truth."

I snort at his last words. "You did not just semi-quote *A Few Good Men* to me."

Fallon chuckles for a second when he realizes that I'm right, but then plows on. "Why you, you ask?" he casually questions while twining the lock of my hair around his finger and giving it a slight tug to bring my face closer to his. "Because Elizabeth, Ry and Jay aren't the only ones who want you."

I literally gasp in surprise. "Fallon, you can't say things like that to me."

"Too late. I just did."

Holy shit. Either Fallon is just messing with my head, playing those cat and mouse games he loves so much, or Julien may have been right about Fallon's interest in me. I flip back through my memories of Fallon and I decide it's best to assume he's just toying with me. Besides, I have too many other things to concern myself with other than Fallon's maybe, not-really-sure desire for me. The guy is a total man-slut who has had sex with who knows how many girls from both my school and his, and who knows how many more at CU. The fact that I was never interested in him would be like dangling chocolate cake in front of a starving person, making him want me because he could never have me. So, I do the only thing I can at this moment. I ignore his remark.

"I have one condition, Fallon."

"Name it."

"You have to either call or text Ryder, Julien, or Jayson every day, so they all know that I'm okay. Otherwise, turn the boat around and take me back."

Fallon narrows his eyes at me, but I stand firm on what I want. "Deal."

"How can I trust that you'll keep your word?"

"Because New Elizabeth would kick my ass if

I didn't."

A grin splits my face. "Damn straight. Now challenge me to a game of pool so I can hustle you." I noticed a gyroscopically-controlled pool table in the game room earlier. Fallon barks out a laugh.

"You know what, kitten? I have a feeling that we're going to have a fucktastic adventure together. Tomorrow is Halloween. I hate that I don't get to see you in a sexy kitten costume, but I've made plans."

I spin around, arms wide. "Fallon, if you've forgotten, we're on a boat in the Atlantic. I doubt we'll be getting any trick-or-treaters."

"Still doesn't mean *we* can't have fun."

Fallon

Me: Kitten made me promise to text one of you assholes every fucking day. You're the winner only bc I like u best.

Ry: <middle finger emoji>

Ry: How is she?

Me: Scared and confused. She loves you. She hates herself. I think she may have a split personality.

Ry: Don't tell me that. I hope you're joking.

Me: Her words, not mine. She says Old Elizabeth and New Elizabeth are battling it out. I'm half expecting her head to start swiveling around in a 360.

Ry: That's not funny. Is she ok?

Me: As good as can be expected. I made sure to have a doctor on board just in case.

I told Robert to act like one of the crewmen so Elizabeth wouldn't be freaked out.

Ry: I hate hearing that. Anything at all comes up, you head for port or get her helicoptered out and take her to a proper hospital immediately. Even if you think it's minor.

Me: I got it covered. She's safe with me.

Ryder goes silent for a minute, but I see the little dots dancing that tell me he's typing a reply.

Ry: She promised me that nothing would change between us if she ever got her memory back. She promised all of us she would never leave again. Why couldn't she come to me? Why did she run?

Me: You, Jay, and Jules are the problems right now. She needs distance and time to set-

tle and make a decision. Being around u three would just fuck her up more. U guys would be fighting over her like rabid dogs and making things worse.

Ry: I would never hurt her.

Me: U wouldn't mean to, but u would. U, Jay, and Jules would be in her face, pressuring her 24/7. I'm Switzerland in this scenario.

Ry: Help her, Fallon.

Me: I will. You might not like my methods though.

Ry: I trust you.

He shouldn't when it comes to her.

Ry: Tell her that I love her.

I don't reply. Instead, I turn my phone off.

It's one in the morning but I'm too amped up to sleep. As I walk out of my room to go up to the deck and sit for a while with a tumbler of scotch, I hear high-pitched mewling cries and whimpers coming from Elizabeth's cabin. I'm very familiar with those sounds. They were the theme songs of my childhood. Elizabeth is having nightmares. I hesitate briefly outside her cabin door before continuing my way up the stairs.

Chapter 4

Day 2: Finding Elizabeth

Halloween in the Atlantic

Elizabeth

"You can't avoid me, you know."

"I can try," I tell myself.

"It won't work. I'm you and you are me. There's no two ways around it. Our memories are back, and you can't deny me anymore."

I'm sitting in a dark room filled with fairy lights, a mirror in front of me. I glare at my reflection because it's not really my reflection. She is me. Old Elizabeth. And she's not happy.

"I want to go back. I want Jayson," she tells me.

"Well, tough shit," I snap at her.

"He'll come for me. You'll see."

"I don't care."

"Why are you making this so hard on us?"

My fiery green eyes blaze at her. "You never could decide who you wanted. Jayson or Ryder. I made the final choice. The right choice. I chose Ryder. You never could do that. You can't have both. You were selfish thinking that you could."

"What about Elizabeth Ann?" she taunts. "She was Jayson's. We belong with him."

"Don't you dare bring her into this. I love my daughter."

"You can't fight history, New Elizabeth. Everything we are and have been belong to Jayson."

"That's not true. I was making a new life for myself. I was happy. For once in my life, I was truly happy. You could never say that. You could never be happy loving two men. Being with one man while wanting another."

Old Elizabeth throws back her head and laughs and I want to smack her. "You will never find true happiness with Ryder. You're deluding yourself if you think you can. Jayson will never let me go."

"You're a bitch," I tell her. "A weak, selfish bitch. I'm a different person now. Stronger. I know what I want."

"Do you? Open your eyes and see, Elizabeth."

Those words send chills down my spine. "What?"

My reflection sneers at me. The eyes of my reflection turn heterochromatic, one blue and one brown. It's not my voice I hear anymore. It's His.

"Don't you see, Elizabeth?"

A thick hand strikes out of the mirror, those dual-colored eyes sparking devil fire. The hand grabs my throat and I start to choke.

"It's always been about you, sweet Elizabeth. Hailey was a poor substitute for you, just like your new life is a poor substitute for Old Elizabeth's. You will never win because she and I will never let you go."

"Kill her," Old Elizabeth chortles. "Set me free. Let me go back."

"No!" I scream. "I don't want my old life back!"

A knife appears in my hand. It's the same one He *used on me that night. As his fingers continue to tighten around my throat, I stab blindly at his arm with the knife. I will never allow him to hurt me again. He's taken too much from me already.*

"No!" I scream over and over again. Old Elizabeth is screaming now too, our combined voices creating a sonic blast that shatters the glass of the mirror. Then everything goes silent. It's just me sit-

ting in the dark room. Alone.

I wake suddenly to tangled sheets around my head. No wonder it felt like I couldn't breathe. Shit. I haven't had a bad dream like that in a while. Sleeping in Ryder's arms usually kept them at bay. At least I don't have to listen to my asshole neighbor pounding on the wall, telling me he'll call the police if I didn't quiet down.

Knowing I won't be falling back to sleep anytime soon, I decide to get up and go to the fitness room to burn off some excess energy. I change into some leggings and a T-shirt I find in Tatiána's drawers. Her shoes are too small for me, so I'll have to go barefoot or wear socks. I opt for socks. I slip out of my room as not to disturb Fallon since his room is next to mine and make my way up the stairs. As I enter the main area, a man's voice startles me.

"Can I get you anything, Miss Fairchild?"

"Holy crap, Robert. You scared the bejeezus out of me."

"May I ask what a bejeezus is?"

"Sorry. It's a figure of speech where I come from. It means you scared the mess out of me." I walk over to where he's sitting. "I noticed your accent."

"Born in Surrey, about thirty minutes outside of London. However, I have lived most of my life in the States."

Robert is still dressed in his crisp attire from earlier and it makes me wonder if he ever gets to rest like a normal person or if he has to be on call all the time while we're on the boat.

"I couldn't sleep, so I was going to go work out for a while in the fitness room," I tell him.

"If you need anything, just pick up the red phone mounted on the wall next to the door in the fitness room and press number seven."

"I remember. Thanks, Robert. Hey, Robert? May I ask you a question?"

He lays down the newspaper he was reading. I hadn't noticed him reading it when I walked in because he scared me half to death. He loses a bit of his stiff rigidness and relaxes slightly. He looks like a dad would, sitting at a table with a newspaper in hand. My dad would have had a guitar pick instead of a newspaper, but it doesn't stop the pang of longing that stabs through me at the thought. I would give anything to see my father again, have him hug me in that certain way only dads do that make their daughters feel cherished, loved, and special. Robert must see something on my face because he motions for me to take a seat with him at the table.

"What questions may I assist you with, Miss Fairchild?"

"Please, call me Elizabeth."

"As you wish," he replies, and I giggle.

"*Princess Bride* reference," I explain when he gives me an inquisitive look. Then he nods in understanding, a small curve tipping his lips. "How long have you worked for Fallon?" I ask him.

"I have worked for the Montgomery family in one capacity or another for about twenty years."

"So you know Fallon well?"

"As much as an employee knows an employer when they've worked for them for an extended period of time," he replies.

"You must be used to him bringing strange women on board then."

"Actually, Miss Elizabeth, from the gossip of the staff that is circulating around, it appears you are the first woman, other than his sister, that he has ever brought on board. You are causing quite a stir."

That shocks me and my mouth falling open

tells Robert so.

I lean forward on the table. "I'll let you in on a little secret, Robert. I had amnesia. I had no recollection of the first eighteen years of my life. My memories returned recently. It's really hard for me to connect what once was with what is now. I remember Fallon from high school, but my old memories of him are nothing like what I know of him now. It's very confusing."

I have no clue why I told a total stranger that. Maybe it's because Robert reminds me of my dad.

"I cannot imagine what you must be going through," he says kindly. "May I ask you a question, Miss Elizabeth?"

I sit back. "Please do," I tell him.

"Why are you here with Mr. Fallon?"

"Let's just say that right now, he's my life preserver. Without him, I would have already drowned. Bad analogy, I know, since we're on a boat in the Atlantic."

"Very true." He chuckles. "I hope Mr. Fallon is able to give you what you need."

I consider that and say, "I think he's the only one right now who can."

"Very well, then." He reaches over to grab a pack of cards at the end of the table. "Have you ever played cribbage before?" he asks.

"Actually, yes I have. I love it."

"Excellent," he says. "No one on this bloody boat plays and I usually wind up playing Solitaire by myself." Robert hands me the deck of cards to shuffle and pulls a beautifully crafted wooden cribbage box out of a drawer in the table. Ah, this is a game table. Cool.

"What's going on?" Fallon inquires as he saunters in. His hair is windswept, and he brings with him the smell of the ocean.

My gaze sweeps him from toe to head. "I thought you were asleep."

"Nope. I screwed up my sleep rhythm a long time ago. Usually up all night, and then sleep most of the morning."

"That's not good for you."

"Yes, Mom," he yawns and sits beside me. "What are we playing?"

"Cribbage. Want me to deal you in?"

"Yeah. Might as well. Robert, can you call the kitchen and get some coffee brought up?"

I slap Fallon's arm. "Fallon! Leave the poor

man alone."

"It's not a problem, Miss Elizabeth."

"Not at two in the morning. Where's the coffee maker? I'll go make it."

"Kitten, sit your ass down."

"Don't tell me what to do. I can make coffee if I want to."

"Not while you're on my boat. The only thing you need to do is rest and relax."

"Fallon, for Christ's sake. It's just coffee."

Poor Robert is standing idly by, waiting patiently, his formal posture restored. Fallon, however, doesn't care that we have an audience. He leans over to get in my face.

"You're having nightmares and not sleeping. You need to rest to get better." How does he know I had a nightmare?

"Were you spying on me while I was asleep?"

That cocksure Fallon smirk makes its arrival. "No. You were loud enough that I heard you through the door, if you must know."

Robert slips away while Fallon and I glare at one another.

"What did you hear?"

"Enough. Now stop fighting me on everything. You're supposed to do what I say, remember?"

"Oh, please." I roll my eyes, then acquiesce.

"Thank you."

"You're not welcome."

"Happy Halloween, kitten."

Well, shit. "Happy Halloween, Fallon. And thanks for caring," I sincerely tell him.

Chapter 5

Day 3: Finding Elizabeth

New York City

Elizabeth

Anyone who has read *Under the Tuscan Sun* or *Eat, Pray, Love* knows the romanticized tales of women who travel around the world to find themselves. That's how I feel right now. A woman preparing to travel the world to discover who she really is. But first, this woman needed some clothes.

I learned something new today as a result of five hours of nonstop shopping through New York City. Fallon Montgomery is a clothes whore. The second thing I learned today is that he has impeccable taste. He picked out most of my new clothes and shoes. I didn't care. It's not like I could really say anything since he was paying for it. I refused, however, to let him choose my underwear and bras.

We're staying in a penthouse suite at one of those swanky hotels near Central Park. We have our own elevator and a five-person staff. I'm having trouble believing this is real life, but then again, Fallon grew up around all this pampered, rich bullshit every day. How can people take this kind of wealth for granted? As an idea forms, I drop my pile of shopping bags on the bed and go find Fallon.

"Hey, Nutter Butter! Where you at?"

"For fuck's sake, come up with another nickname that doesn't sound so fucking stupid," I hear him yell back.

"You call me kitten, jackass, so deal with it."

I found out yesterday during our Halloween fun on his boat that Fallon has an addiction to peanut butter candies. After that, the nickname came easily. Fallon surprised me with his Halloween scavenger hunt. He hid things all around the boat for me to find using clues and a map. I'm pretty sure all the stuff I found was his. I am now the proud owner of tons of candy, an iPod, a men's I Love NY T-shirt, a six-pack of beer, a dirty romance novel (not sure if it was his or Tatiána's), and a sex-toy—I didn't ask. Yeah, he got a kick out of that one before I threw it at his head. We spent the rest of our Halloween on the boat enjoying scary movies and sitting out on the deck again watching as the boat docked. As we prepared to disembark, I hugged Robert bye, and thanked him for his kindness. Then, Fallon escorted me to a car that was already there waiting to take us to our hotel.

"Hey, Nutter Butter!" I open a door but no Fallon. The penthouse suite is four-thousand square feet and takes up two entire floors of the hotel. I got lost last night trying to find the bathroom after we checked in.

"Marco?" I shout.

I hear a distant chuckle. "Polo!"

I walk around a corner to where the living area is. "Marco?"

"Polo!" he calls back. I'm getting closer. I walk up the curved set of stairs that leads to the second floor. I chose the bedroom downstairs and told Fallon he had to sleep upstairs.

I open a set of double doors and enter his room. Fallon is bent over the bed going through bags filled with the clothes he bought for himself. Fallon is also shirtless. I'm a girl who can appreciate good-looking guys, so of course I ogle his muscled back and the tattoos he's sporting—that is until I see the crisscrossing of several faint scars that span the width of his torso. They're barely noticeable, but I know knife wounds when I see them because I have several.

"Jesus, Fallon." I rush over to him and lay my hands against his skin. His body goes rigid and taut.

"Elizabeth, I would strongly advise that you remove your hands."

I ignore him. "What happened to you?"

He turns suddenly and grabs both of my wrists in a crushing grip. "Life," he growls out.

My heart goes out to him because I understand. He really is just as broken as I am. I wrench my wrists out of his hold and step away from his furious gaze. I pull my shirt up and off and throw it on his bed. As he looks at my bra-covered upper torso, his angry gaze changes to shock then quickly morphs into desire.

I point to my butterfly tattoos that cover my scars. The scars *He* gave me when *He* plunged a knife into my side and chest. "You should never be ashamed of your wounds, Fallon. They're proof of how strong you are. That you're a fighter. I should know."

Fallon comes closer and falls to his knees in front of me. I hold my arms over my head so he can examine my scars better. He gently glides a finger up and down each raised ridge. I notice that his hands are shaking but his face is full of fury and his mouth is pressed into a tight line.

"Where'd you get your ink?"

"A non-profit in Seattle that helps trauma victims."

His fingers gracefully glide over every part of each broken butterfly. I watch as his eyes travel south to my stomach. He touches my C-section scar above the waistband of my jeans, and I suck in a breath.

"What about this one?"

"That's a secret for another day," I reply and grab my shirt, pulling it back on. Fallon remains kneeling on the plush hotel carpet looking up at me. "Maybe one day you'll tell me about yours," I softly say down to him.

He nods and stands up. Clearing his throat, he tells me, "There's a club I'd like to take you to. We can get wasted and dance until we pass out."

Sounds perfect. "Oh, before I forget, I'm adding another condition to our deal."

Fallon groans and throws himself back on the bed like he's cliff diving into a pile of clothes.

"I promise it's a good thing. I want to visit a

women's shelter while we're here."

"Can I ask why?"

"Nope."

"You wanting to do some volunteer work there or something?"

"Or something," I tease.

"Can't I just donate some money to whoever so we can spend our day doing something more fun?"

"That's not the point, Nutter Butter. You're surrounded by all this wealth. I know I sound a bit hypocritical since I'm currently the one spending and enjoying the fruits of your money, but I think it will be good for both of us if we go. As for why the women's shelter, specifically? I feel like it's something I need to do, because of what happened to Hailey. Is that alright with you?"

"Where you go, I follow, remember?"

"Can we also go to Times Square tomorrow?"

"Yes, kitten. Now go get dressed. I suggest you wear the red mini dress."

I roll my eyes, something I seem to be doing a lot of recently. "You don't tell me what to do Fallon Montgomery," I sing out and walk downstairs. I put on the red dress anyway and pair it with some black knee-high dress boots that Fallon also picked out for me today.

It's the first day of November, which in New York City means it's cold, and the boots will be better than strappy heels. Besides, I'm also not dumb enough to wear high heels when I'm expected to dance all night. I leave my hair down in its usual mess of haphazard waves. The pink tips and streaks in my hair have faded and are barely visible. I'm not a makeup wearing type of girl, but I do put on some mascara and lipstick which I stole from Tatiána's stash in her bathroom.

"I'm ready!" I yell out when I exit my room. Fallon's waiting for me. "Looking good," I say when I see him. He's dressed in snug-fitting jeans and a long-sleeved dark blue button-up. He doesn't return the compliment, but I notice his eyes keep straying to my ass as we take the elevator down to the private parking garage.

Fallon leads me to an awaiting dark sedan, and I must have a mirthful expression on my face because he asks, "What?"

"Nothing, really. I'm just surprised it's not a limo or a Lamborghini. I mean, it's *you* we're talking about. Sedans aren't your typical style."

He smiles and slaps the top of the car with

his open palm. "Get in the fucking car, kitten."

As soon as we're buckled, I ask him, "Where are you taking me?"

"New club that opened up about six months ago. They know we're coming."

Of course, being with Fallon means we don't have to wait in line or go through the front door bouncers. Instead, Fallon drives down a side street to the back of the building and we're met by two nicely dressed men. They usher us through a nondescript door that leads directly upstairs to the VIP section. There's no escaping the pounding of crappy techno music, so I grab Fallon's arm and drag him back downstairs to the main dance floor.

Turns out, Fallon is actually a great dancer. I close my eyes, raise my hands in the air, and let my mind go numb, trying hard to put the past few days behind me and just exist in this moment. Flashes of colored lights dance in front of my closed eyelids and I'm taken back to the night of the bonfire in eleventh grade when Jayson got drunk and we stumbled upon Jacinda giving Ryder a blow job against the dilapidated warehouse. It switches to Fallon's party when I found Jacinda wrapped around Jayson in an upstairs bedroom, and then later that night when Ryder climbed through my window. Too many emotions flash outward, overwhelming me like wildfire on dry kindle.

I hear Fallon say, “Fuck off,” as he pulls me against him. My eyes open and I notice a girl scowling up at him then me before she slinks away and disappears into the crowd.

“What was that about?” I have to raise my voice for him to hear me.

Fallon adjusts his grip on my hips and turns me around, so my back is to his front. “Some chick who doesn’t understand the words ‘not interested.’”

“You promised me a night of alcohol,” I shout at him over the music. I need something to help me forget, even if just for a few hours. I can’t handle the memories and the sadness of thinking about Ryder and Jayson right now. Fallon takes my hand and leads me off the dance floor and up a flight of stairs to a sectional leather sofa against the wall of the VIP lounge. I fan my face with a cocktail menu, hoping to cool off a bit.

“What’s your poison, kitten?”

The VIP section is located on the second floor, and each section has its own balcony that overlooks the dance floor. It’s also quieter so I don’t have to shout at Fallon when I talk.

“Tequila okay with you?” I answer.

Fallon holds up four fingers to the awaiting server. No one asks to see my ID or his. The server comes back within a minute carrying four shot glasses and a bottle of tequila.

I grab two of the glasses, and after the server fills them halfway. I hastily tip them back, one after the other. “Holy shit, that stuff’s strong,” I gasp.

“Keep that up and I’ll have to carry you out of here.”

I grab the shot Fallon’s holding and tip that one back as well. “That’s the goal,” I say with a wince as the tequila burns a path down my throat to my stomach. “Total oblivion.”

“Elizabeth, what’s going on in your head right now?”

I’m feeling an instant mellow as the alcohol quickly filters into my bloodstream. “Too much is going on in my head. I need a few more of those and I’ll be good to go.” I wave our server back over and order two more shots. Fallon doesn’t say anything; he just sits back and watches.

After downing my fifth shot, I announce out of the blue, “I hate Jacinda.”

“Why the fuck are you thinking about that

bitch?"

My tongue feels a bit thick and I slur, "Did you know I caught her going down on Ryder when we were in high school? And then of course, there was your party where I saw her climbing all over Jayson, who was half-naked by the way." I wave my hands in the air and giggle, then frown. "She was always trying to touch my men."

"I think it's water for you from now on."

I ignore him. "Jayson tried to fuck me against a tree the night of the bonfire party. He was so drunk. Maria was flirting with Ryder. That night sucked," I pout. "God, I hate having my memories back. I just want them to go away. Can you do that, Fallon? Can you make them go away?" I plead, tears springing up in my glassy eyes.

Fallon leans forward and wipes away my drunken tears with his thumb. "I promised you that I would help you, Elizabeth. It won't happen overnight. Come on. Let's go dance," he says, and I stumble beside him back downstairs onto the dance floor.

The music changes tempo to a slower beat and I feel someone's hand cup my ass and squeeze. At first, I think it's Fallon. The tequila has slowed my reaction time, and before I'm even able to confirm whose hand it is, Fallon is punching some guy in the face.

"You don't fucking touch what doesn't belong to you, asshole!"

For a second, the guy Fallon just knocked to the floor looks up at me, and I swear he's Jayson. I startle back and ram into Fallon. The guy picks himself off the floor, his hands held up in supplication, and backs away. I shake my head to rid it of Jayson's image.

"I think I agree with you on no more alcohol," I tell Fallon. "I'm going to grab a bottle of water from the bar."

I take my time making my way off the dance floor, still feeling a little wobbly on my legs. I notice a tall guy standing at the bar. I get a brief glimpse of his shirt, which has a Randy's Custom Auto logo on it. Ryder's here? How did he find us? I am so unbelievably happy in that moment. I shove my way through the crowd desperate to get to him.

"Ryder!" I shout. Someone knocks into me, and I slam into a guy to my left. I push him away. He's not the man I want. I look back to the bar and Ryder is walking off. "Ryder! Wait! Don't leave!" Fallon calls my name before he grabs my arms. "Stop it, Fallon. Ryder's here. Let me go." I try to wiggle out of his grasp.

"That's not him, kitten."

"He's right there." I point to the guy walking away from the bar. Wait. I'm confused. The guy wearing the logo shirt has red hair and a nose ring.

"But, I thought..." More tears form behind my eyes and a deep melancholy settles inside my heart.

"I think you're done for the night," Fallen tells me, placing his hand on my lower back, and pushing me off the main floor.

I blindly go where he leads me, not caring anymore. As soon as we're out on the secluded side street, the valet pulls up with Fallon's car. Fallon buckles me in and drives us back to the hotel as I cry silent tears that don't want to stop. I let him carry me into our suite, my head as heavy as my heart as it drops onto his shoulder, but instead of taking me to my room, he sits me down on one of the sofas and pulls off my boots.

"I miss them," I whisper, like I'm telling a secret that I don't want anyone else to hear.

"Who?"

My parents. My sister. Ryder. Jayson. Julien. I miss them all.

"It's too much," I tell him, breaking down into wracking sobs. The loss of my parents and my sister. The loss of a child I never knew. The loss of what Old Elizabeth had with Jayson. The loss of what New Elizabeth had been building with Ryder. I feel it all, and it's just too much. Pain. Sorrow. Heartbreak. Loss. Grief.

"I want my mom," I finally choke out.

"I know you do," he says softly. Fallon holds me and lets me cry. It's something I hadn't allowed myself to do until now.

"I want to go home. Take me home, Fallon."

"Close your eyes and tell me who you see."

I give him a surly look.

"Close your eyes, kitten."

I do.

"Who do you see?"

"Ryder and Jayson."

"Then you're not ready." Fallon shifts on the sofa beside me. "Come here," he says, and pulls me into his arms.

I'm tipsy and sad, and my eyes burn from crying. I snuggle into Fallon's warm body and listen to his heartbeat. Old Elizabeth imagines it's Jayson and remembers all the times she would fall asleep with her head resting on his chest.

"I hate you," I tell her in a slurred murmur.

Right before I succumb to my drunken exhaustion, I think I hear Fallon say, "One day, kitten, you will truly hate me."

Fallon

I place a blanket over Elizabeth who is out cold on the sofa. I stand over her and watch her sleep for a moment. She was having fun tonight and I was right there with her. She didn't even blink an eye when I punched that guy. When I saw him grab her ass, I wanted to do more than punch him. Elizabeth just watched as I clocked him, then she laughed and kept on dancing like nothing happened. Whoever this new, screwed-up, damaged version of Elizabeth is, I like her. She also looked hot as hell in that little red dress. I've always been attracted to Elizabeth and having her around me twenty-four seven has taken everything in me not to drag her to my bed. The non-stop urge to fuck her tight little body has me jerking off several times a day. *Fuck*. I allow myself one more minute to gaze down at her slumbering form, then pop a stick of gum in my mouth and walk upstairs.

I've been sending Ry text updates like I promised Elizabeth I would. It's like he has the phone plastered to his hand or something because no matter what time I text him, whether it's the morning or the middle of the night, he responds immediately.

Me: Your girl misses u.

Ry: I miss her so damn much.

Ry: Got into another fight with Jay. He's going apeshit that she hasn't come back. Jules isn't much better. I'm getting a lot of heat here bc I agreed to let you take her away. We already missed over a year with her when she was in Seattle. This is killing me. It's killing us. Tell me it's worth it.

Me: First, hope u kicked his ass.

Me: Second, I can't promise anything. She thought she saw u at the club tonight. She's been a mess ever since she realized it wasn't u.

Ry: I can be on the next plane to wherever u r.

Me: Like I told her 2nite, she's not ready yet. Stay put.

Ry: Dammit, Fal!

Me: Talk to u 2morrow.

When I reach the top of the stairs, my phone vibrates since I have my ringer turned off. It's an unknown number. Shit. What does he want now? But when I answer, it's not who I think it is.

"What?"

"Where is she?" Jayson's irate voice demands.

"How the fuck did you get my number?" I'll make sure to change it tomorrow.

"Where is she, Fallon?"

"With me, but you already knew that." I know I'm stirring the hornet's nest and I take great pleasure in doing so because I can't stand the guy.

"Put Liz on the phone right this damn minute, Fallon!"

"She's sleeping. We had a long night and she's exhausted," I reply vaguely, feeling joy at riling him up and stirring the pot.

"You motherfucker! If you've done anything to her—"

"Shut the fuck up, Jay, and back the hell off. She's upset and confused and needs time to figure things out. I don't know why I'm even telling you this because I couldn't give two shits about you. If you truly love her like you say you do, you'll give her the time she needs. She'll come back when she's ready."

I hang up and turn my phone off. It wouldn't surprise me if Jay hired that shitty PI again to get my number. Well, I can guarantee tonight's unexpected phone call won't happen again.

I strip my shirt off and walk over to the bed. My back is stiff and a little sore. It's the result of muscle scar tissue. Elizabeth is a very perceptive girl, and she knew exactly what she was seeing when she noticed the faded marks on my back. We are alike in so many ways, she and I. Alike in more ways than she could possibly imagine.

Chapter 6

Day 4: Finding Myself

New York City

Elizabeth

I'm dreaming and I hope I never wake up because when I do, I know I'll be alone again without my boys. Without Ryder, Jayson, and Julien. So I remain in my dream of Ryder, needing to feel his presence close to me, even if it's only a figment of my subconscious mind. In my dream, Ryder's hard body is beneath me, his golden gaze heated and locked onto my face, his strong hands roaming freely across my flushed skin. I feel our emotions swirling in the air. The lust, desire, and love that permeates every atom of every state of matter surrounding us.

"You're too damn sexy for your own good, Ryder, and I'm going to show you how much I want you." I gently bite his pectoral and lick it, the salt from his skin delicious. "How much I love you." I

kiss his clavicle. "How much I am yours and only belong to you." I pop the button on his jeans and slide my hands around to palm his backside.

Another shadowy form materializes in front of me, reminding me of memories lost. Old Elizabeth touches Ryder's face and I warn her to stay away from him. He's mine.

She just smiles vacantly at me and leans down to whisper in Ryder's ear. "I chose Jayson."

I startle awake, feeling like I've been sucked into a dark nothingness as I struggle for breath. Then I realize where I am. The blackout curtains in the hotel suite block out all outside light, making it impossible to know if it's day or night. Looking around for my phone, I grumble when I remember that Fallon has it. He unplugged and threw out all the phones in the suite. I also don't know how he managed it, but my key card only activates the elevator to our floor and unlocks the hotel suite door. It doesn't work on the business room downstairs where the guests can use computers for free. I know because I tried. Fallon also has been watching me like a hawk. And if he can't, one of the five employees assigned to our suite does. It's fucking annoying.

Bastard.

Sitting up on the sofa, I wrap the blanket

around my shoulders. I modify his title of bastard a little when I realize Fallon must have covered me with the blanket sometime during the night. He's a sweet bastard for taking care of me, but a bastard none the less. I get up to go to my bedroom and notice the hotel clock on the bedside table telling me it's five in the morning. No wonder I woke up. It's the time I usually run with Julien. I wonder if he's running this morning with Elijah. I wonder if he misses me like I miss him.

I quickly change into a workout bra and yoga pants, put on the new running shoes I bought with Fallon's money, and slip out of the room to take our suite's private elevator down to the fitness center, hoping my key card works there. When the elevator doors open on the tenth floor, I'm greeted by one of the hotel staff members. It's a little freaky to me when they pop up like they somehow know exactly where I am or where I'm going.

"Good morning, Miss Fairchild. Visiting the fitness facility?" the young woman politely inquires. She's dressed in a black skirt suit with a cream-colored blouse. Her chestnut hair is rolled into a tight knot at the nape of her neck. I step out of the elevator and smile broadly at her when I see the phone case clipped at her waist. *Don't do it, Elizabeth,* I tell myself. Of course, I ignore my own advice.

“Good morning” —I look at her nametag— “Veronica.” I increase the wattage of my smile. “I forgot my phone in my room. Would you mind if I borrowed yours? I promise it will only take a second. I’d hate to have to go all the way back to my room for mine.”

“Please, be my guest.” She slides her phone out of the case, unlocks it, and hands it to me. I send up a silent hallelujah.

“Thank you so much, Veronica. You are a life saver.” I step away and dial Ryder’s number.

“Hello?” his sleep-husked voice answers. God, he sounds so good. My heart both melts and breaks at the same time at the sound of his deep, baritone voice.

“Ryder?”

His sleepy tone quickly evaporates. “Elizabeth? Fuck, baby, it’s good to hear your voice. Wait. Where’s Fallon?”

“Asleep. This isn’t my phone.” I peer over my shoulder to make sure Veronica isn’t eavesdropping. “I’m sorry, Ryder. I’m so sorry. You must hate me right now.”

“I could never hate you, sweetheart.” *Sweetheart.* It gets me every damn time.

“I remembered, Ryder. It all came back. I

don't know what to do."

Ryder's silent on the other end and I feel my world start to unravel. I've lost him. He doesn't want me anymore. I've ruined everything.

I hear his deep inhale at the same time I hear a dinging noise behind me.

"I love you so much, Ryder. If you doubt anything about us, please never doubt that. I love —" The phone is snatched out of my hand and I yelp out in shock and spin around. "Hey!"

An angry Fallon is standing before me, eyes iced with frigid blue indignation. I try to take the phone back, but he holds it out of my reach and brings it to his ear. "Hey, man. Sorry about that. I'll talk to you later."

"Fallon, give that back!"

He menacingly steps toward Veronica, who shrinks back a little, and shoves the phone at her. "Let her use your phone again and you'll be out of a job."

He grabs my wrist and pulls me toward the open elevator doors. I don't struggle. Instead, I glower and pout. Very mature, I know.

"Fallon, what the hell?"

He pulls me the rest of the way inside the elevator and places our room key up to the electronic scanner. Once the box starts going up, Fallon whirls on me and shoves me against the wood-paneled elevator wall.

"I should be asking you that, kitten. You wanted my help and I'm giving it to you. Stop acting like a brat, sneaking around, and making secret phone calls."

I glare up at him. "You can't tell me what to do. I can call Ryder or Jayson or even Julien whenever the hell I want."

Fallon presses in until our faces are so close, we're breathing the same microcosm of air. "You gave me the right to tell you what the fuck to do when you came to me and asked for my help. Either accept my rules or go the fuck home. I don't need this shit."

My lower lip quivers but I suck it up and raise my head high, eyes flashing.

"There she is," Fallon says with approval. "Now close your eyes." I do with a huff. "Who do you see?"

"Why do you keep asking me that?"

"Tell me, kitten. Who do you see?" He grabs my chin with his fingers.

I open my eyes. "I see Ryder and Jayson."

He nods once and steps away. "Then there's

your answer."

Damn him, he's right. Again. I can't go back until I know who I am, who I want to be, and who I want to be with.

"What if it's too much for them? What if by finding who I am, I lose both of them?"

"What if Starbucks gets rid of my favorite chocolate caramel latte? Who the fuck cares, Elizabeth? Grow a goddamn spine and woman the fuck up. Make a choice. Make a decision. Let me help you. Otherwise, pack your shit up and leave. I'm not your damn babysitter."

Fallon's words are like a sledgehammer hitting a thumb tack. The elevator doors open to our suite and he stalks off leaving me standing there. Alone. The doors begin to close. I throw my hand out to stop them.

"Fallon, wait!" I run after him. He slows and turns around, his facial expression unreadable. I'm used to cocky Fallon, asshole Fallon, crazy Fallon, and weird Fallon. I'm not used to this Fallon.

"I'm womaning the fuck up," I say breathlessly.

He cocks his head, and it reminds me of those times before when he would look at me and do just that. Those times when Old Elizabeth was wary and unsure of him. But I'm not.

"No more bullshit?" he says.

"No more bullshit," I agree.

"You'll follow my rules and stop being a sneaky bitch?"

"Yes. I promise."

"Good girl. Let's order some breakfast."

"I hope they have your favorite chocolate caramel latte," I tease.

"Shut the fuck up," he replies with a crooked grin, and I laugh.

I officially both love and hate New York City. I love that there are endless things to do. I love the hustle and bustle of the culture. I love how when you turn a corner, there's something interesting to see. What I do not love is all of the people. I'm a small-town girl and this huge city is just crazy-packed full of people. You walk down the street and you're surrounded by people. You go into a restaurant—same thing. Go into a store—more people. I wanted to see the infamous New York City subway system, but as soon as we got underground, I turned

Fallon around and walked us right back the way we came. Crowds of bodies packed like sardines in small, confined spaces is a huge no for me. I decided New York City is like an ant colony. Thousands upon thousands of little ants all bumping into each other but still getting their jobs done.

This morning, Fallon took me sightseeing. In Times Square, I got to jam with a street band and learned how to play the steel drum. He kept his promise about our second deal and found a local women's shelter that we visited for a few hours. They allowed me to sit and talk with some of the women who were staying there, many of them with small children. The women told me their stories. Stories filled with abuse and pain. I felt every word they spoke to me. They humbled me and strengthened my resolve to do more for women like them. Women like me. Women like my sister, Hailey. Women who lived through incredible trauma but fought back and survived, not just for themselves but for their children. I wish I could have fought harder for Elizabeth Ann. I wish I could have fought harder for Hailey.

Once I'm finished talking with the women in the center, I go in search of Fallon. I find him out in the center's courtyard shooting hoops with a few of the younger boys. I stay hidden in the shadows along the wall and watch. Fallon doesn't smile much, but when he does, it's breathtaking. I watch him joke and smile with the younger boys, and every single one of them absorbs his attention like sunshine. Fallon will make a great father one day. If I told him so, he'd more than likely vehemently disagree with me and tell me to fuck off with that typical Fallon smirk, but I see him. I know there is more to the man than the façade he carries. Deep down he feels more than most people. He cares.

The day is overcast and cold enough that you can see the cloud of your breath when you exhale. I love the feel of the cold, crisp air as it tingles a slight burn when it fills my lungs. It's not uncommon to get snow in New York in November. I wonder if we'll see it snow before we leave for Iceland tomorrow. I know we'll definitely see snow in Reykjavik.

"You've got a very nice young man there," the director of the women's center, Janice Berkeley, says beside me.

"Oh, we're just friends," I reply. "But yes, he is. He doesn't allow many people to see it though."

"His generous donation to the center will help fund so many programs."

I turn my head to gawk at her. "He made a

donation?"

Janice smiles and nods, not saying anything more. She pats my hand and thanks me for talking with the residents. She tells me they enjoyed spending time with me, then walks back inside leaving me alone to watch Fallon and the younger boys.

"There she is," Fallon calls out. "Get over here, kitten."

I hear one of the boys ask, "Her name is kitten? What a stupid name."

"Hey, little dude. No disrespecting my woman. Got it?" My approaching steps falter when I hear him say that.

The young boy looks down at the ground. "Sorry. I didn't mean anything by it. I swear."

"I know you didn't. Always remember though, words can hurt as much as punches." Fallon claps the boy on the shoulder with gentle encouragement.

I make my way over to their group. There are five of them including Fallon, and the boys look to be around the ages of ten to fifteen.

"Hey guys," I cheerfully say.

"Kitten here can be our sixth man. What do you say? A little three on three?"

"But she's a girl," the boy with the gap teeth and curly black hair says. "They don't know how to play basketball."

"Oh, we don't, do we?" I grin and take the ball from Fallon. Old Elizabeth was never athletic, but New Elizabeth sure as hell is. I shot a lot of hoops at the rehab facility I was at in Seattle, mostly when I was bored, but it helped with my strength training and flexibility.

I take off my winter coat and gloves and lay them on the ground. I dribble the ball a few times, then pivot and shoot it in a high arc. It swishes through the net with ease. The boys start whooping and cheering. Fallon just does his little head cock at me.

"Nice," he says.

"She's on my team," the gap-toothed boy tells everyone. I learn his name is Devon. He adds Trevaughn to round out our team of three. Fallon's team includes a cute blond boy named Butch with thick, round black glasses, and Seamus, an older, taller mocha-skinned boy with green eyes like mine. We decide the first team that gets to ten points wins.

My team wins the coin toss and has possession of the ball. Fallon towers over all of us at slightly over six feet tall. He steals the ball from Devon and passes it to Seamus who does a lay-up for an easy two points.

My team scores the next four points thanks to some awesome footwork and ball passing between Devon and Trevaughn. Fallon then shoots a three-pointer. His team is up five-to-four. Devon fouls Butch allowing him two free throws. He misses one but gets the other. My team is now down six-to-four.

Devon runs in front of Seamus to steal the pass from Fallon. Devon passes it to me, but Fallon blocks my way. I fake and pivot and land a three-pointer off the backboard. That gets me high fives from my teammates because we're up seven-to-six. I wipe my brow with the sleeve of my sweater because I'm sweaty and hot, despite the cold outdoor temperature. I glance over to Fallon who's huddled with his team. He looks up, sees me looking at him, and gives me a wink.

"Okay, boys. It's time to show them who's the best," he says.

"I'm sorry. Are you talking about us? Thanks for the compliment!" I yell back.

Fallon bounce-passes the ball to Butch who performs a perfect jump shot for two more points.

"Dammit," Trevaughn says.

"Hey, teamie, we've got this," I reply, and we fist bump.

I hand the ball to Trevaughn. He does a between-the-legs dribble then passes it backward to me. I'm at the three-point line. If I make this shot, my team wins. I grip the ball and plant my feet ready to let the ball fly when I feel hands come down on my hips, pulling me backward. I stumble and begin to fall over to the side, but Fallon moves one of his hands from my hips to my back, so we end up in a dancer's closed position.

"I call foul." I laugh up at him.

"I call fair play," he says, hovering above me. I grip his shoulders. He pulls me in.

"Fallon."

"Yes, kitten."

"Kiss her already so we can finish the game," Devon shouts. My cheeks blush scarlet.

I swear, if Fallon wasn't holding me, I would have melted straight into the tarmac when his lips get mere inches from mine. I'm looking up at him with big, wide eyes and he's looking down at me with a shit-eating grin. Coming to my senses, I smack his shoulder and he pulls me back up to stand, leaving me more breathless than I already was from running up and down the basketball court. Fallon hands me the basketball, pushing me toward the free throw line.

"You called foul, right?"

Fallon is messing with you like he always does.

I dribble the ball to the end of the court. "Hey, Fallon. If I make the shot from here, we win."

"What do you say, boys? Think she can do it?"

"No way!" Seamus, Devon, and Butch call out. Trevaughn only gives me a nod of encouragement.

"Watch and learn, Nutter Butter." I bounce the ball twice, side grip it, and throw it as hard as I can. We watch in trepidation as it hits the top of the backboard and drops in.

Devon exclaims, "Holy shit!" while Seamus says, "She actually did it!"

My teammates run over to me and we hop around and chant in celebration.

"That's my girl," I hear Fallon tell the others. Ryder and Jayson used to call me their girl. Fallon must notice the sadness that suddenly appears on my face because he walks over, putting one arm around my shoulders.

"Thanks, guys, for the game." Fallon fist bumps all four boys and picks up our coats and gloves from the ground.

"Will you come back again and play hoops with us?" Butch asks, childlike hopefulness sparkling in his eyes.

"I'm taking Elizabeth on a long vacation, but you know what? I promise we'll stop back by on our way home. How does that sound?" That seems to appease the boys. They wave bye then go back to playing. Fallon helps me with my coat, and I put my gloves back on.

"You are such a big softy, Mr. Montgomery."

"Don't tell *anyone*."

"I heard you donated money to the center. You work fast."

"They need new equipment, beds, and books for the library. A few million should cover it."

I pull Fallon to a stop. "You gave them three million dollars?"

He shrugs and shoves his hands in his coat pockets.

"Holy shit!"

"It's nothing, Elizabeth."

It is something. It's a big something.

"Thank you for agreeing to come here today," I go on when he remains quiet. "It opened my eyes to so many things. Being able to talk to women like Hailey and myself, women who have been hurt and scared but found a way to fight and survive. It means a lot that you came with me."

Fallon still doesn't respond. Instead, he offers me his arm and I loop mine through his as we stroll down the sidewalk.

"Can we go ice skating at Bryant Park later?" I ask.

"You're shitting me, right? Me on ice skates?"

"Have you ever done it before?"

"No. Can't say I ever wanted to try."

"I remember going a few times with Hailey when we were younger. I still can't believe she's gone; that they're all gone. I can't believe that I forgot them. She was like them—the women at the center," I tell him. "They reminded me of Hailey. The guy that killed my family, he abused her for a long time before that night. There were signs. I was so stupid because I saw the warning signs. I saw the bruises. I allowed her to convince me they were nothing important. Casual bumps into doors or falls during PE class. What kind of sister was I to not see what was right in front of my face?"

"You were a great sister, Elizabeth. You and Hailey were close and you both loved each other. I wish I could say the same about me and my siblings. Things are good between me and Tatiána, but Trevor? I wish I had with him what you had with Hailey. Remember the good times with her."

"Trevor is a good guy, Fallon. You should sit down and talk to him. Get to know him better. Do you mind if I talk to you about Hailey?"

"Whenever you want to talk about her or your family, I will always listen."

"Other than Tatiána, you haven't said anything about yours. Are they going to be mad at you for skipping out of town with me and missing class? Or giving away millions of dollars to a women's shelter?"

The sharp curse that erupts from Fallon causes several nearby pigeons to scatter and take flight. "My parents could give a flying fuck what happens to me. Right before he passed away, my grandfather set up a trust fund for me that my parents cannot touch. I have my own money and they can't do shit about it. Pisses the old man off that he can't control me anymore."

Fallon's mood grows ominous, and I regret bringing up the subject.

"I'm sorry, Fallon."

"Nothing to be sorry about, kitten. As long as I carry on the family name and take over the business when I graduate, that's all my grandfather asked of me. I'm left to my own devices the rest of the time, just the way I like it."

"That sounds very lonely."

Fallon just shrugs and unhooks our arms, sliding his gloved hand down to my hand. His fingers tangle with mine and hold tight. He takes me for a carriage ride through Central Park and listens to me talk about my memories of my sister. Being able to talk about her, laugh about the times when we were silly, reminisce about her beautiful poetry, helps mend a part of my heart that was cracked and fractured. And I have Fallon to thank for that.

After our carriage ride, Fallon takes me ice skating at Bryant Park under the cloak of darkness. When we return to our hotel suite, we order room service for dinner and watch a movie. At midnight, we sit out on the balcony and enjoy a beer as we survey the city around us. We're flying out to Reykjavik in the morning.

Fallon walks back inside the suite and returns a minute later holding a passport out to me. I choose not to ask how the heck he was able to get a passport for me in such a short amount of time. Mom had gotten passports for me and Hailey in preparation for our summer vacation trip to England after my high school graduation. The photo inside the passport Fallon just handed me is the same one I took senior year for that passport. Fallon must have some very good contacts if he was able to get a new one delivered in twenty-four hours. So instead of asking questions, I simply tell Fallon thank you.

“Secret for a secret?” he asks me before finishing his beer.

“Hmmm,” I hum, feeling pleasantly relaxed after a long but fulfilling day. “I had a great time with you today.”

Fallon rolls his head to the side to look at me. “I did, too.” He reaches out with his hand and I place mine in it. “Close your eyes, Elizabeth, and tell me who you see.”

I allow my eyelids to flutter close. “I see Ryder and Jayson.” I open my eyes. Fallon is still looking at me. “But when I open my eyes, I see you, Fallon.”

He breathes deeply and stands up, lifting my

hand to his mouth and pressing a soft kiss to my knuckles. "Good night, kitten. Be ready to go by six." He turns my hand over and kisses the center of my palm, then walks inside.

"Good night, Fallon," I whisper.

Fallon

Me: Jay called me last night.

Ry: WTF!

Ry: That's why he asked to borrow my phone.

Me: I thought he used the PI. Change your damn passcode asshole. If he starts blowing up my phone again, I won't give u my new number.

Ry: <middle finger emoji> What did he say?

Me: Same Jay bullshit he always says.

Me: We're off to our next destination tomorrow.

Ry: Are u ever going to tell me where you guys are going? Are u even still in the country?

Me: Currently, yes. Tomorrow, no. And no, I'm not going to tell u. She picked out all the

places we're going though.

Ry: Is she doing any better?

Me: Actually, yeah.

Ry: That's so good to hear. Her friend Meredith is frantic to speak with her. Think Elizabeth can call her or something sometime?

Me: No.

Ry: Trevor asked how she was. He and Elizabeth have gotten close.

Thinking about Trevor anywhere near Elizabeth just pisses me off. Goddamn Trevor.

Ry: Tell Elizabeth I love her. I didn't tell her that today.

Chapter 7

Day 5: Finding Elizabeth

Nordurljosavegur

Fallon

I have never seen anyone more excited to see snow and hot water than Elizabeth. I thought she would get a kick out of seeing the blue lagoon, so I arranged for us to stay at a retreat in Nordurljosavegur instead of Reykjavik. When she saw the blue waters of the hot thermal springs for the first time, she told me, "The blue is almost like the color of your eyes." She took off her gloves and touched the heated water, surprised pleasure exploding across her face. I'm going to make it my priority to put that wonderous look on her face every damn day she's with me. Because I know there's an end date to our little adventure. I'm not the man who will get the girl at the end of the story. I'm actually the villain. I'm the man who is destined to destroy her. But not yet. Today, I get to enjoy her giddy smiles and I'm devouring every one of them like they are the last supper before my execution.

"Kitten, what's taking you so long?" I call to her from the living area while looking out of the floor-to-ceiling windows. I watch the steam rise from the thermal river that runs right next to our room. The snow-covered rocky terrain adjacent to the blue waters creates a majestic contrast between ice and heat. It reminds me of the dichotomy between Elizabeth and me. Ice and heat. Light and dark. Good and evil. Virtue and impurity.

"I'm not sure I'm ready to do this," she says from the other room. I told her to put on a bathing suit so we could take a dip in the lagoon before dinner.

"Get your ass out here or I'm coming in to get you."

"Not fair! There are no doors in this place," she grumbles, and I chuckle.

Elizabeth tentatively walks out of the bedroom, and my mind goes blank for a second. She's wearing a two-piece bikini set we found in New York City. My gaze lingers on the swell of her breasts then travels down. *Fuck me.* She has her hair piled up on top of her head. Her skin is pale and luminous. Her long legs are lean and toned. I follow the path of her butterfly tattoos before my eyes land on the vertical scar that starts at her navel.

"Stop it, Fallon." She covers her abdomen using her arms and hands. "The way you're looking at me is exactly why I'm not ready to expose myself like this."

"How am I looking at you?" I cock my head at her.

"You're scowling like my scars either disgust you or you pity me." I didn't realize I was scowling.

"Disgust was the furthest thing from my mind," I assure her.

"You pity me, then."

I walk up to her, moving her hands to dangle by her sides and trail my fingers up the soft skin of her arms. She shivers. The devil in me comes out to play. My fingers glide down the sides of her torso and she pulls in a shaky breath. I tempt fate by splaying my hands across her abdomen, gliding them up, so they stop just below the curve of her breasts. Elizabeth closes her eyes and her lips part slightly, little puffs of air escaping like the fluttering of tiny wings.

"Does this feel like pity to you?" I exhale

against the shell of her ear. "Now, let's go and enjoy ourselves, shall we? Don't forget to put on your robe and slippers."

I walk out of the suite, leaving a dazed and glassy-eyed Elizabeth standing in the middle of the room. I adjust the painful hard-on I'm sporting as I hit the elevator button.

Elizabeth is floating on a thin mat beside me, and every so often she'll wiggle her fingers and toes in the warm water and sigh. "This feels so fucking unbelievably good."

"Told you."

"Can I ask you a question?"

"Depends on the question," I tell her, and she starts to giggle. "Did I say something funny?"

"Don't you remember?" she asks me. I turn my head on my mat to look at her. "You said basically the same thing to me at Curtis's party."

"Did I?" I don't remember much from those days. I made sure to live every hour wasted, high, or with my dick shoved up some random girl's pussy.

She stops giggling. "Yeah, you did. Why did you stop?"

I know exactly what she's talking about. My propensity for using drugs, mostly weed, to numb my pain was strong back then. "Something happened that made me open my eyes for the first time and see how I had wasted most of my life."

"I'm proud of you."

Why does hearing her say that inject me with an enormous surge of joy that shoots straight to my blackened heart?

"You shouldn't be. I'm still damaged. I'm still dangerous."

"Not to me."

She couldn't be more wrong.

Elizabeth floats closer to me. "Have you ever been in love, Fallon?"

I don't answer.

"Julien always tells me that my capacity for love is infinite. I guess, maybe, that's how I can love him, Jayson, and Ryder at the same time. But I think there's a difference between loving someone and falling in love with someone. Love changes and evolves over time, don't you think?"

I remain silent and watch the misty vapor rise from the water while listening to her melodic voice.

"Love is constant like the sunrise and sunset. You know they will always happen, just like your love for someone will always be in your heart, even if you aren't *in love* with them. I'm not making much sense, am I?"

"You're naïve, kitten. Love is just an illusion. It's a word used to justify possession and jealousy. If love was real, it would last. Couples say they love one another then break up a year later. A husband will tell his wife he loves her every day, then fucks anything in a skirt behind her back. Parents say they love their children then ignore them or abuse them. Love is complete bullshit."

"You're wrong, Fallon."

"Am I? You can't even decide who you love, Elizabeth. Your entire life, you've been manipulating three men who say they love you and who you say you love in return. You're a coward. That's not love. That's you being scared and selfish."

"Fuck you, Fallon. How dare you presume to know anything about me or how I feel? I have loved more deeply than your cold heart could ever comprehend. I ran because I'm broken and no good to anyone right now, including myself. I had a life that was taken from me. I survived what *He* did to me and was building a new life, one that I cherished and wanted more than anything. Then that was taken from me too, just like my daughter. So fuck you!"

Elizabeth jumps off her floating mat and swims away from me, heading back in the direction of the hotel. Daughter? What the hell is she talking about?

"Elizabeth!" I yell at her. She doesn't stop but does toss back her middle finger at me as she gets out of the water and puts on a robe. *Shit*! I go after her.

I catch up to her in our room. "You said daughter. What the hell did you mean by that?"

"And I said fuck off." She glares at me. If I were a smart man, I would back off and leave her alone.

"What did you mean, Elizabeth?"

She grabs her suitcase from the closet and begins throwing items haphazardly into it. If she thinks I'll let her walk out of this room or allow her to leave me, she is out of her goddamn mind. I yank the case from the bed and throw it across the floor.

"You are such an immature asshat."

"Tell me something I don't already know. What daughter?" I'm like a pit bull unwilling to let go. She tries to move past me, but I push her back. I'll get physical with her if I need to.

"What daughter?" I ask again. She rips her robe off exposing her bikini-clad body to me and points to the scar that slices right down the middle of her abdomen.

"The daughter that was taken from me. The daughter I lost because of *Him*. The daughter I never knew existed because I was in a coma when I lost her."

What the fuck? She was pregnant when she was attacked?

"Now you know all my dirty little secrets, Fallon."

"Elizabeth," I solemnly say because there is nothing else that I can say at this moment.

Tears leak down her cheeks and I about fall to my knees wanting to beg forgiveness for being the cause of her current pain. She clenches her hands into tight fists as if she is preparing to punch her way out of the room to get away from me.

"You're so wrong, Fallon. Love is real. It's not

selfish or possessive. I love my daughter more than anything in this world. Jayson and I created her from our love. If I could have given my life in exchange for hers, I would have done so without a second thought."

"I'm so sorry, Elizabeth."

Her face heats and her eyes blaze like an emerald inferno. "You can take your apology and shove it straight up your ass. I don't want it."

"You want to fight, kitten? I'm more than ready to take your punches and verbal blows. If that's what you need right now, then bring it on."

"I hate you," she seethes.

"No, you don't."

She stomps over to me and pushes at my chest with all her might. I have to admit, it hurts. She may look delicate, but she is strong. She's a fighter.

"Get out of my way, Fallon."

"Make me," I taunt her, and she growls in frustration.

She gets up in my face, pure fury overtaking her common sense. Most men know not to challenge me, but this slip of a girl shows her true grit by standing up to me. I have never wanted anyone else like I do her right in this moment. I want her anger and hate. I crave her passion and fire. And even though I told her that love was not real, I would sell my soul to Lucifer himself for her to share her love with me. Even knowing it would be taken away the moment she learned of my secret, it would be worth it.

"I want to fuck you so bad right now," I spit the words at her.

Elizabeth doesn't even blink. "Then do it." She may not have blinked at my threat, but I do at her challenge. "Do it, Fallon. I dare you."

I stand there like an idiot, not able to make a sound or a move.

"I didn't think so," she says and pushes past me. "You're also a coward, Fallon, and a liar."

The beast within me snaps and snarls, wanting to be set free. Wanting her to see how lethal I can be. I wrench her arms up over her head and shove her face-first against the wall, causing her to yelp in surprise. I pin her with my body and reach around to slide my hand up to her neck, pulling her head back to me. Squeezing my fingers around her throat, I apply just enough pressure to make it difficult for her to take a deep breath.

"You say I don't know you, kitten, but you

don't know me." My fingers grip her flesh tighter.

"You won't hurt me, Fallon," she rasps out. I release my hold around her neck, and she slumps forward on the wall.

"Yes, I will."

She turns around and cups my face in her hands. The contact makes me jerk. No one has ever touched me like this.

"No, you won't. Ask me to close my eyes and tell you who I see."

I narrow my frigid blue gaze at her, searching her face. For what? I have no idea. "No," I grit out and push her back against the wall once again, causing a picture frame to fall off and smash to the floor. I can't hear her say Ryder's or Jayson's name right now.

"I see you, Fallon," she continues.

"Stop it, Elizabeth."

"Fallon—" she says, and I steal from her what I've been coveting since the day I first saw her at the Fields.

"Goddamn you," I say right before I kiss her.

It's not a pretty kiss or a nice kiss. It's not a playful kiss. It's a kiss filled with anger and hurt. I stop myself from touching her the way my hands are craving for me to, because I know if I do, I'll fuck her against this wall and there will be nothing she can do to stop me. I may have allowed the beast to come out, but I strap a short leash on him.

I plunder her sweet mouth, taking what I want and not giving a damn. I can regret it later. Each swipe of my tongue against hers tames the beast inside me until he rolls over and supplicates. She continues to cup my face, applying enough pressure to push me away from her. I don't comply and instead press fully into her body, feeling every part of her fitting with me like we're two puzzle pieces locking into place. I force her lips to part wider and kiss her deeper. I'm instantly addicted to the way her soft lips feel against mine, to her taste. Elizabeth is finally able to break the kiss. I can feel the pounding of her heartbeat as it matches the beat of mine.

She looks up at me, lips swollen and red. "You shouldn't have done that."

"You make me so goddamn crazy, Elizabeth."

"You still shouldn't have done that."

"You wouldn't shut up."

We both start laughing.

"We're so messed up," she half-heartedly says, shaking her head.

My arms go around her waist and I hold on to her for dear life. I take full responsibility for what just happened. I'd hate to think what *would* happen to me if Ryder ever finds out I kissed her.

"Completely damaged and unrepairable," I agree.

"But perfect in a non-perfect way."

"I don't even know what that means," I reply. "I'm sorry about your daughter."

"Her name is Elizabeth Ann Jameson. The men who cared for me while I was in Seattle —Daniel and Drew—named her. She's buried there."

Elizabeth pulls back and lifts the heart pendant up for me to see. I finger it and turn it over to see an inscription. "I noticed that you wore this every day but didn't think anything of it."

"Jayson gave it to me. We're supposed to go visit her grave next month during Christmas break."

"I can take you there now if you want to go," I offer.

"I appreciate that, but it's something I need to do with Jayson."

A flash of light catches my eye outside.

"Look, kitten." I point at the glow coming through the floor-to-ceiling windows. She turns her face, following where I'm pointing and gasps.

"Oh, my God!" she gushes, seeing the auroras for the first time. "Oh, Fallon. It looks like the sky is painted like a Claude Monet watercolor. It's the most beautiful thing I've ever seen."

I want to tell her she's wrong. She's the most beautiful thing.

"Go put on some dry clothes and we can sit out on the terrace and watch."

I need to change as well, but instead go out on the terrace and move the two seats next to one another to form a makeshift love seat. I recall something Elizabeth said today. She told me she had a feeling this journey with me was going to irrevocably change her life in more ways than just deciding which Elizabeth she was going to be. "Perhaps another Elizabeth will emerge along the way," she said. Would that Elizabeth belong to me? I think about our kiss. I won't kiss her again. I won't allow my darkness to consume her light.

When I hear her step out onto the terrace, I motion for her to come over and sit down. "I'll be right back," I tell her and go inside to put on some warm clothes and make us a drink. Whiskey would be good right about now.

Even though it's in the lower thirties, we stay outside for hours, unwilling to take our eyes off the night sky's iridescent light show. She snuggles up to me and rests her head against my shoulder as we sip our whiskey in silence. When she finally drifts off to sleep, I pick her up and take her to her bed. I have my own room and my own bed, but I slip under the covers with her, needing to feel her warmth for just a little bit longer. I play with the ends of her long hair and bring a lock of it up to my nose and sniff. She smells like goodness. After an hour, I slip out from under the covers and tuck her in, an unfamiliar and unwelcome emotion flowing through me that I don't recognize.

"Sweet dreams, kitten," I say and walk into my room. I never get around to texting Ryder.

Chapter 8

Day 14: Finding Elizabeth

Paris

Elizabeth

We spent four days in London where we walked around the historic city looking at everything. I wanted to go there because it was where our families were planning to take us for summer vacation after we graduated high school. As Fallon and I strolled along looking at the Thames, I imagined all of them were there with me: Mom, Dad, and Hailey, Ryder, Brea, Jamie, Faith, and Randy, Jayson, Julien, Freda, and Mitch. I could perfectly picture Hailey and Brea walking arm in arm, their heads together while they whispered and giggled. I could feel my hand in Jayson's as we casually walked along enjoying the sights of London like any other couple in love. I could hear Ryder and Julien cracking jokes and their deep booming laughter. I could see Dad with his arm around

Mom and hear him hum one of his songs to her as they walked side by side. Being in London with Fallon was both bittersweet and heartbreaking. It was a promise fulfilled. It was also where Fallon gave me real memories to cherish alongside my imaginary ones.

Wonderful memories like him taking me to watch a Shakespeare play at the Globe or us strolling across the Jubilee Bridge. We rode in a double-decker bus and on the London Underground, where I giggled every time I heard "mind the gap" before the doors closed. Fallon held my hand when we were high above the city riding in the London Eye. He took me to St. Paul's Cathedral, Buckingham Palace, Big Ben, Hyde Park, and Trafalgar Square.

We stopped at pubs, drank some pints, and ate fish and chips—without the vinegar because that's just absolutely disgusting. I learned how to play snooker. An Irish band was playing at a beer garden we found, and I joined them on stage. Fallon had never seen me play a guitar before. We danced and drank. A lot.

Fallon took me to Goodwood where, somehow, he arranged for me to drive a McLaren Senna, a Porsche 911 Turbo S, and a Ferrari SF90 Stradale. We went for a picnic lunch at the Fishbourne Roman ruins and drove to Bath, stopping by Avebury along the way. We also helped out at a volunteer center passing out prepared meals to those in need. Our days were packed from morning until late at night. I'm surprised I'm still standing after the whirlwind trip through the southern parts of England.

When our time in England was up, we rode the Chunnel to Paris, France. Fallon took me to the Eiffel Tower where we ate lunch. We visited a perfumery and a chocolatier where I got to sample the most delicious dark chocolate; it had no dairy in it. We visited the Louvre and the Palace of Versailles. We volunteered to help pick up trash along the banks of the Seine. Tonight, Fallon is taking me for a helicopter ride over the city.

Each day, little by little, without me noticing, I'm changing. I'm becoming the woman I need to be. When I close my eyes now, I see me. I see the real Elizabeth Penelope Fairchild. Not the old version of me, and not the newer version either. I'm something different and unique.

I'm hesitant to tell Fallon this because I don't want our adventure to end just yet. I want to enjoy life by his side a little bit longer before I have to give it up, give him up, and return home to fix the damage I know is waiting for me there. The damage I created. Fallon hasn't tried to kiss me again since that day in the hotel in Nordurljosavegur. He's actually been quite mellow, which is not a normal state of being for him. It's different, but nice in its own way. However, I'll always prefer cocky asshole Fallon; the version of him that lights me up and challenges me.

"You ready?" he asks me as we step off the elevators.

The helicopter's rotor blade is already spinning creating swirls of whipping wind that blow my hair all around my head in a blond whirl. I grab hold of Fallon's hand and we duck and run under the rotating blade. A man helps me up into the cabin, and Fallon gets in after me and buckles me in. He hands me a set of sound-dampening headphones with a microphone and I put them on as he does the same.

"We talk to each other through these," he tells me, and I give him a thumb's up. I listen to Fallon and the pilot chat for a minute, and then the helicopter lifts off its pad and we're off. My stomach tightens at the brief feeling of heaviness as we ascend, and I grab Fallon's hand, squeezing it tight.

"We're good, kitten. Just enjoy."

It was cloudy all day today, but it doesn't hamper our views of the city tonight. As we fly over a dazzling Paris, Fallon points out various landmarks and monuments. I get to see the Eiffel Tower lit up like a Christmas tree and it reminds me of the Valentine's Day when Jayson did the same thing to the old oak tree between our two houses.

"I'm going to have a lot of bridges to repair when I get home," I say into my microphone. Fallon switched our sets over to another channel so that the pilot can't hear our conversation.

"Why the fuck are you thinking about that now?"

"I don't know. Just something that popped in my head, I guess."

"Well, stop. That time will come soon enough, kitten."

"Fallon, I have to start planning for what comes next. I can't travel the world with you forever."

"We can do whatever the hell we want."

"I have school to finish. I want to become a doctor. Regardless of the screwed-up states of my relationships with everyone, if nothing else, Ryder, Jayson, and Julien are my best friends. Meredith and Trevor are my friends, too. And I just up and disappeared on everyone...again. I've put all the people I say I care about through hell and they deserve much better than they've gotten from me."

"Screw them. You don't owe anyone a damn thing," Fallon argues.

"Yes, I do. I also need to talk to Daniel and Drew. I haven't spoken to either of them for a while. And I need to see my daughter."

I hear Fallon's exasperated sigh.

"I'm looking forward to meeting Tatiána tomorrow," I say, hoping to ease the tension I now feel rising up in him. Fallon had mentioned that Tatiána would meet up with us while we're in Barcelona. I'm actually quite excited to meet her.

Fallon leans over to my side and points to the Arc de Triomphe below us. "The feeling is mutual. I'm going to have to keep a close eye on the two of you. I have a feeling that you and her together will spell nothing but trouble for me."

He rests his chin on my shoulder as we both look out the window. We circle the city before heading back. Once we land, I step down from the cabin and my legs feel like jelly. Being up there, hovering over Paris, was like the tower drop at an amusement park—fortunately without the sudden drop back to the ground.

"That was awesome!" I shout at Fallon so he

can hear me over the noise generated by the helicopter's motors and blades.

Fallon doesn't say anything until we get into the elevator and the doors close. He presses the button for the ground floor where a car is waiting to drive us to dinner and then a club after.

"Things will change once you go back, and I'm not ready to let you go yet," he solemnly states.

I lean back against the elevator wall and look at him. "Of course things are going to be different, because I'm different. But I've gotten to know the elusive, secretive Fallon Montgomery and I like him, a lot. You're a good man, Fallon. You're my hero."

Fallon stands up straighter and tilts his head at me. I love it when he does that. "I'm not the hero, Elizabeth. I'll never be your hero. I'm your worst fucking nightmare."

The elevator doors open and Fallon escorts me to our town car. We eat our dinner in silence because he's in a mood, and instead of going dancing like we planned, Fallon takes me back to our hotel suite. I leave him alone and go out onto the terrace to enjoy my last night sky in Paris.

I've learned to allow Fallon his mood swings and know he'll soon seek me out when he's ready. Sure enough, I hear his footsteps walking over to where I'm standing and the hairs on my arms raise when he gets nearer.

"I'm sorry about tonight. I wasn't very good company."

Now it's my turn to be silent. I can hear the lilting notes of a violin coming from the street level down below. I recognize the tune and hum along with it. Fallon moves behind me and extends his arms on either side of me against the terrace railing. I start to sway to the music of the violin. Fallon's arms move from the banister to wrap around my front. I lean my head back against his chest, and we rock lightly from side to side.

I don't know when it happened, but I've come to care about Fallon. I enjoy his company and his friendship. Most importantly for me is that I trust him. He's broken and scarred and gets under my skin like no one else can, but he's caring and dependable and bluntly honest in an 'I-don't-give-a-shit' kind of way. He's doesn't treat me as fragile. I've become stronger being with him on this trip.

"Did you know Paris is called the city of love?" he says next to my ear, his tone somber and a bit sad.

"La ville de l'amour et la ville de la romance,"

I reply and feel him smile against my cheek.

"Tu parles français?"

"Un peu."

"What if I told you that I was in love with you and I wanted you to choose me? That I wanted you to stay here with me?"

I stop swaying and turn in his arms so I can see him. "First, I would remind you that you told me recently that love was a selfish lie used to manipulate people."

"What if I've changed my mind?" he says curtly.

"Then I would tell you that my heart belongs to someone else."

"You've decided?" A look of panic crosses his face.

I have. It's taken two weeks, but I've made my decision. However, right now, I want to be with Fallon. I want a few more days, a few more adventures, before I go back.

"You said you're not ready to let me go, and I'm telling you that I'm not ready to leave yet. I want to finish our journey. We can wait a few more days to decide what happens next."

Fallon grips my waist and pulls me with him

to the terrace doors. "If I only have a few days left with you, I want you next to me. I want to fall asleep holding you. Even if it is just an illusion, I want to pretend that you're mine."

"It's not an illusion, Fallon."

A part of me will be forever his now, just like a part of me belongs to Jayson, Ryder, and Julien. Life is not about giving your love to only one person. It's about giving your whole self in every way possible to those who deserve it. It's like I told Fallon—it's possible to love more than one person. You can love your friends and your family and still have love to share with someone new who you're lucky enough to have stumble into your life along the way.

"I swear I won't do anything more than hold you. Can you give me that for tonight?" His vibrant blue eyes sparkle as they look at me. He really is a gorgeous man. He's just not the man I'm in love with.

"Yes, I can do that," I reply, and he exhales the breath he had been holding.

"Thank you."

When we get inside, I go to my room and grab a large shirt and sleep shorts, then walk into the bathroom to change. When I come out, Fallon is waiting for me. We climb under the covers and he pulls me to him, his arms band-ing around my middle. And that's how we stay for the rest of the night.

Fallon needs me just as much I've come to depend on him. There's a darkness inside of him that needs me to help bring it toward the light. I may be crossing some lines with what I'm doing. I'm pretty sure that Ryder or Jayson wouldn't be happy to see me and Fallon in bed together even though nothing will happen between the two of us. For me, it's platonic; just two friends giving each other comfort. I can't even count how many times me and the guys slept at each other's houses, most often all piled together on the same bed.

"Why do you think I'm going to hate you?" I ask him because I'm curious to hear what he says, but also because I want him to tell me his fears so I can help fight them with him. One day he'll tell me about his scars, both the physical and the mental ones.

"Because you will hate me once you find out the truth."

I rest my palm on top of his heart and I can feel how heavy it's pounding. Whatever his secret is, it terrifies him.

"I want to be there for you, if you'll let me."

"The devil took my soul a long time ago, kitten. I'm beyond saving." He readjusts our positions so that his head is resting on my shoulder. "You always smell so goddamn good."

"Thank you," I chuckle and continue to rub his neck and up into the hair on the back of his head. Fallon soon falls asleep, and I hold him close to me throughout the night wondering what could be so bad that the thought of me finding out scares the shit out of him.

Fallon

I woke up a couple of hours ago with Elizabeth curled around me. She's wrapped in my arms, her sweet scent infusing the air around us with the aroma of jasmine. I've been watching her sleep. I have a habit of doing that, and I really need to stop. I just can't seem to help myself. She's so beautiful. An ethereal goddess among monsters. She refuses to believe that I am one of those monsters.

Elizabeth told me yesterday that she's made a decision. I know I only have a few more days left before I lose her. I don't want to hurt her, but I'll be the one to destroy her eventually, nonetheless.

I reach over to grab my phone with my free hand. Elizabeth stirs in the arm I keep wrapped around her. I shush her and kiss her temple until she sighs and settles back down.

Me: Going off the grid for a few days.

Ry: Why? What's going on? Where's Elizabeth?

Me: Right next to me asleep.

Let him assume what he wants from that. I know I'm being an asshole and that Ryder is the only true friend I have, but I'm so goddamn angry. I want the one thing I can't have. I'm going to hurt her and when I do, I'll burn to blackened cinders one of the only truly good things I've ever known.

Me: Talk to you soon.

I pull Elizabeth closer to me and she mumbles something in her sleep. The sound of it stabs a hot dagger into my icy heart.

Chapter 9

Day 15: Finding Fallon

Barcelona

Elizabeth

Fallon had his jet meet us this morning at the Paris-Charles de Gaulle Airport where we boarded and flew to Barcelona. Once we landed, a limousine was waiting for us. After what seemed like a long drive from the airport through gorgeous, scenic countryside, we finally came to our final destination—a grand and majestic countryside estate. Fallon told me on the plane that we were staying at his sister and her husband's home, just one of several homes they owned throughout Spain and Europe.

"I have to warn you," Fallon says as he gentlemanly helps me out of the limousine, "my sister married very young. She's eighteen now and her husband is twenty years her senior. But he treats her like a queen, so I have no problem with him. Yet," he adds.

I pull my sunglasses down to shield my eyes from the bright sunlight and look around. The temperature is mild, around the mid-sixties, and feels wonderful. The beauty of my surroundings is breathtaking. You can clearly see the attention to detail in the design of the property's landscaping and the colorful design of the home with its stained-glass windows and mosaic tiles. Ivy tendrils climb up along the sides of the house giving it an old-world feel. The roof is made of red and brown terracotta tiles and the outside stucco is a muted tan color.

"What style of architecture is this? I don't recognize it?"

"Catalan Modernism," a woman's accented voice replies. This must be Tatiána. She is absolutely stunning. Her hair is jet black and straight, but I can see the purple and gold-foil strands interspersed throughout her shiny locks. I'll have to ask her what she used in her hair because it looks cool. Her eyes are as crystal blue as Fallon's, and the contrast between her dark hair and her light eyes is mesmerizing. She smiles sweetly at me and I instantly like her.

Fallon breaks away from me and moves toward his sister; the grin that lights up her face is one of pure joy. Before he can get to her, she runs over to him and throws her arms around his neck, kissing him very enthusiastically on both cheeks. Fallon lifts her up, causing her yellow dress to blossom out and flow around them as he twirls her around in a circle. They speak to each other in what I think is Spanish, but many of the words I don't recognize. Once he lets Tatiána go, she looks over at me and pokes Fallon in the ribs.

"You are right, brother. She is very pretty."

I blush at her compliment. "It is so nice to meet you," I greet her, walking over to hold out my hand. I know it's an American custom, but it's one I'm used to. "Thank you for allowing me to stay in your home."

Tatiána ignores my hand and embraces me in a hug instead. She leans back and kisses me on each cheek, then takes my arm and starts walking me toward the house. "Fallon, be a good boy and make sure her bags are taken to the Rosa room."

We hear him respond with a few choice words, which makes us both laugh. I look back over my shoulder and wiggle my fingers at him, then I blow him a kiss.

"He seems happy," Tatiána comments as two

grand twelve-foot doors gracefully swing open for us like magic. I get my first glimpse at the interior of her home and it's as gorgeous on the inside as it is on the outside. A woman carrying a tray of drinks approaches us and gives a small curtsy. Tatiána takes two flutes of bubbling liquid off the tray and hands one to me.

"Are these real flowers?" I ask when I notice the purple and white blossoms floating in my glass. I sniff the drink and it smells divine.

"Yes. I use fresh, edible flowers in most things. The flowers come from a world-renowned grower in Barcelona."

I take a sip of the drink and the bubbles pop on my tongue. I was expecting champagne, but this is more like a floral-infused sparkling water. It's light and delicious.

"Your home is lovely."

"Once you settle in, I will give you a tour. My Eduardo is out of town on business until tomorrow so it will be just the three of us tonight." Her accent is so charming and lyrical. I was raised in the South, so I have a slight Southern twang when I talk. Spending over a year in Seattle muted it down a lot and I barely hear it anymore except when I get angry or passionate about something.

"I would very much like that. Thank you," I

tell her.

"You are very pretty, Elizabeth. I can see why Fallon is so taken with you."

I blush again. "We're just good friends. He's helping me with something."

"Ahh," she says, the look she's giving me tells me she's not convinced. "Regardless, I'm happy he has a friend. It's not often I get to see him, so your visit is a nice surprise."

As she walks me through different rooms, a Steinway grand piano catches my eye. Tatiána notices me staring. "Do you play, Elizabeth?"

"I do, yes." My fingers start to twitch, and I think I drool a little over the Steinway.

"Please, be my guest. I play a little, but I am not good."

I walk over to the grand piano and lovingly glide my fingers across the black and white keys. "Are you sure?" I ask her.

Tatiána is already sitting down across from the piano waiting for me to start playing. "Music is the sound of the soul. It would be my honor to listen to your soul, Elizabeth."

"Would you like for me to play something classical, Baroque, romantic, contemporary?" I take my seat on the piano bench and place my feet on top of the pedals, my fingers hovering over the keys.

"I would like to hear you play something from the heart," she replies.

I warm up my fingers by playing a few scales.

"There you both are. This house is a fucking maze to navigate," Fallon complains as he walks into the room.

"Come, brother. Elizabeth is about to play for us." Fallon takes a seat beside his sister and she takes his hand in hers. It's clear how much she loves him and how much he adores her. I wish he could have this type of sibling relationship with Trevor. When we go back home, I'm going to try my best to make that happen, or at least open Fallon up to the possibility of letting Trevor in.

"Something from the heart?" I ask her and she nods.

I look at Fallon who hasn't taken his eyes off me since he entered the room. I decide on something modern. Something that reminds me of Fallon. I close my eyes and begin to play "Wonderlust" by Will Post. As my fingers move over the keys and the melody flows, I sing the lyrics. I love the words of the song. It's a perfect theme for the journey I'm on with Fallon.

When I finish, Tatiána leans over to Fallon and tells him, "She's very good, brother," then stands up. "You are welcome to play any time you wish, Elizabeth. You both must be tired from your journey today, so I will give you some time to rest before dinner." She kisses Fallon on both cheeks again and walks over to do the same to me before taking her leave.

"Why haven't you done more with your music?" Fallon asks me, his tone almost sounding accusatory.

"My dad taught me. It was always something we did together. Something that connected me to him. I had no desire to pursue a music career even though he was in a band. I play the drums, too." I smile at him.

"Of course you fucking do. I don't think there's anything you can't do."

"Thank you, I think. Are you upset with me about something?"

Fallon walks over to the piano and hugs me. I jolt a little at his unexpected show of affection. I hug him back.

"This is nice," I say. He sits down next to me on the bench and punches a few keys with one finger.

"Can you play?" I ask him.

"If you count chopsticks as playing, then yes."

I get an idea. "Here, help me turn the bench." We maneuver the bench so that it's vertical to the piano. I push Fallon down to sit in a straddle and then sit in front of him.

"What are you up to?"

"You'll see," I reply and move his arms around me to position his hands on the keys. Then, I place my hands on top of his. "Now, relax and let me do all the work," I tell him. "All you have to do is feel the music and let me lead."

I press down on his thumb, middle finger, and pinky to play a C-major chord. Fallon peers over my shoulder to see what I'm doing. He moves closer behind me and rests his chin on my shoulder.

I tap his fingers. "Relax, Fallon. This won't work if your fingers are stiff as a board."

I try again until his fingers loosen up and allow me to guide them. I am the puppet master and he is my puppet. I go slowly at first until he gets the hang of what I'm trying to do. With my hands over his, I start playing a simple version of Pachelbel's *Canon in D major*. When I need to shift to a different key position, I gently lift his hands up with mine and move them where I need them to go. After a few tries, Fallon gets the hang of what I'm doing and allows me to manipulate his hands and fingers with ease.

"This is how my dad first taught me to play," I tell him. "I always loved those days when it was just him and me in the music room. He converted one of the back rooms in our house to a music room, soundproofed it and everything. That's where he kept all his instruments. I would sit in that room for hours as a little girl and just mess with all the cool instruments he had in there. One day he caught me and that was the first day he sat me in his lap and showed me how to strum a guitar. I was instantly hooked."

I can feel Fallon's breath against my cheek as he watches our hands move in synchronicity across the keys.

"I'm sorry about your parents, kitten."

I shrug off the tears that want to form because what more can I say at this point? I've already screamed and cried and thrown things. All that does is give me a headache. It doesn't bring them back.

"I'm supposed to go back home with the guys for Thanksgiving." Then it hits me. "Wow, I just realized that Thanksgiving is only two weeks away." My fingers stop playing. "I haven't been home since that night. I told Jayson I wasn't ready to see it, but I agreed to go back with them for Thanksgiving. With my memories back, I don't know if I'll ever be ready to face that part of my life. After what happened there, how can I look at my childhood home and not see a goddamn house of horrors?"

As I divulge my fears, Fallon turns his hands over to grip mine. "*He* will never hurt you again, Elizabeth," he says with certainty. "You already lost your memory once. Don't allow *Him* to steal all of your good memories of your family as well. Those are the ones you should dream about."

I move our joined hands to my chest and hold tight. "Will you come with me when I go back?"

"Wherever you go, I follow, remember?" Fallon lets go of me and stands up from the bench. "Let me show you to your room. It's pink. You should love it," he says, smirking and tugging on my hair.

I laugh, glad that some of the tension that suddenly popped up between us eases. I pat the

Steinway one last time in reverence and follow Fallon out of the room.

"Tatiána is so nice. How can the two of you be related?" I tease.

"She was lucky in the fact that her mother is a loving woman who cherished her daughter. That, and Tatiána never had to live in the same house as my father. I envy my half-siblings for that alone."

"Trevor mentioned that he speaks with your father on occasion."

Fallon mumbles something under his breath that I don't catch.

"Will you tell me someday, about your childhood. About your scars?"

"Someday," he replies. "If there was anyone I would trust enough to tell, it would be you."

"Fallon, did you just say something sweet to me?"

"I take it back."

"Oh, no. No takebacks. I heard it and you can't make me unhear it. See, Nutter Butter, you are a big softy."

We walk down a long hall. "Jesus, not that shit again. Don't you dare tell my sister that stupid-ass nickname. I won't hear the end of it."

"What do I get in return for keeping my mouth shut?"

I release a gasp when he shoves me against a wall and spreads his hands flat on either side of me. "What do you want, kitten?"

I've ventured into dangerous territory. I lick my suddenly dry lips and his aquamarine eyes zero in on them. "Right this moment, I want to see where I'll be sleeping."

"Liar," he retorts, but backs away, allowing me to release the breath I didn't know I was holding.

I spend the next hour in my rose-pink room, unpacking and thinking about the choices I have made and the choices that are yet to come. What do I want? At this very minute, I think my answer would shock the hell out of Fallon.

Tatiána has her culinary staff prepare us a lovely meal for dinner. Earlier, she gave me the grand tour of her palatial home while Fallon disappeared to who knows where. I quickly learn that I will have to make sure to eat something mid-day as dinner is regularly served late at night. Dinner consists of small plates of various local foods and dishes that my unrefined Southern self would call sampler platters back home. I am introduced to another Spanish favorite, the after-dinner drink carajillo, which is a hot coffee with a shot of liquor; in this case, anisette. Honestly, I don't care for it, but I enjoy the experience of trying something new. As the night is still mild for the time of year, we eat dinner outside in the central courtyard gardens.

"I fucking knew that getting you two together was a bad idea," Fallon complains good-humoredly. It's almost midnight and while we enjoy our carajillos, Tatiána has been telling me stories about her summers with Fallon that have me snorting with laughter.

"I can't wait to tell Ryder that one," I hiccup, trying to catch my breath. My stomach is sore from laughing so hard and eating so much.

"Try it and be prepared to suffer the consequences," Fallon threatens, but he's not able to hide the partial smile tugging at the corners of his mouth.

I stick my tongue out at him and he leans over to tickle my sides. I squeal and wiggle off my chair, landing unceremoniously on my ass. Thankfully, I'm wearing jeans and not a dress.

Tatiána giggles at my predicament and I glare up at her. "How much alcohol did you put in my coffee?"

"Not enough," she concludes and pours more anisette into my almost empty cup. I notice she isn't drinking any coffee and has stuck to water the entire evening.

Fallon comes over to help me up, that smug smirk of his making an appearance. When he offers me his hand, I tug hard and pull him down with me. Instead of landing on his derriere as I had hoped, he lands in a push-up position hovering over me as I fall backward, my hair fanning out all around my head.

"Hi." I giggle up at him and flick his nose with my finger.

"So goddamn gorgeous," he says back.

"I'm sitting right here," Tatiána loudly announces. My eyes widen and I push Fallon off of me. This time he does fall over on his ass with an *umph*. "Are you sure the two of you are not together? You act like una pareja enamorada."

I start mentally choking when my brain finally translates what she just said. "No, no, no. Fallon and I are just friends. I'm in love with—" I blurt before I realize my almost word vomit and shut my mouth tight.

"What is the phrase your countrymen use? Friends with benefits? Um, fuck buddies? That's what I am trying to think of." Tatiána snaps her fingers when the words come to her.

"Just friends," I repeat, poking Fallon in the side with my elbow because he's being quiet on the subject. He pulls me between his legs—much like we were earlier at the piano bench—and wordlessly grins up at his sister with a wink.

"Hmm," Tatiána hums. "It is late, and I want to be fresh and beautiful for my husband's return tomorrow. I will leave you two to wrestle like piglets on the floor and bid you a good evening. Fallon, breakfast is at seven. Elizabeth, it has been lovely spending time with you." She bends down, "You are good for my brother," she whispers to me then walks through the open archway back inside the house.

"You are such a little shit," I declare and pinch Fallon's forearm. "She totally thinks we're sleeping together."

"Technically, we are." *Hello, cocky asshole. Welcome back.* "Speaking of which," he announces and lifts me up from the floor. "Time for bed."

"You are not sleeping in my bed again tonight, Fallon Montgomery."

"Wanna bet?" He lifts me off my feet and over his shoulder and walks into the house.

"What is it with you guys carrying me caveman-style?" Jayson and Ryder used to do this to me all the time.

"I get a nice side view of your ass."

"You stare at my ass all day long."

"True. You have a great ass, so it's really not my fault," he rejoins. At least he hasn't smacked my butt, so I give him props for that alone.

Once we reach the Rosa room where I'm staying, he throws me bodily onto the high, large four-poster bed. I bounce a few times on the soft mattress and decide that was fun, so I stand up and start springing up and down a few times on it like a trampoline before I remember this is not my house and I am being an irresponsible guest.

"What the hell are you doing?" Fallon's looking at me like I've lost my mind.

I plop down on the bed, legs outstretched. "You've never jumped on your bed before?" He shakes his head no. "Pillow fights?" Again, he answers no. Did he have any fun as a kid growing up doing stupid kid stuff? "Come here," I motion to him to get on the bed with me.

"Kitten, the only bed acrobatics I do are with my dick inside a pussy." That startles a belly laugh out of me.

"Think that's funny?"

"Yep!" I reply, popping that 'p' with emphasis and collapse back on the bedspread.

Fallon reaches over and tugs at my ankles until my body slides across the bed to where he's standing at the foot. My arms are splayed above my head, my cheeks are red from jumping around, and I have a silly grin plastered across my face.

"I want to fuck you," he snarls at me like he's angry at me for the desire he feels.

My grin evaporates. He said almost the exact same thing to me in Nordurljosavegur. God, it would be so easy to go there. To let him take me and use my body, to feel him on me, over me, and inside me, and not care about the consequences. Over the past two weeks, Fallon has infused himself into my heart in a way that will remain lodged there forever. He has been my savior, my friend, my comfort, my confidant, and my lifeline when I was drowning. I have fallen in love with Fallon, just like I did with Jayson, Ryder, and Julien when I was a kid. But Fallon is not what I would call my heart's love. Only one man owns me in that way, and that's the man I'm *in* love with. It's like I said: you can love many people but there will only be that one special person you will give your whole heart to with all of your love. Fallon isn't that person for me.

He studies my face and releases his hold on my legs. "I'm sorry," he exhales, scrunching his brow.

I sit up and grab his arm. "Fallon, I wish I could tell you that things were different. I really do. It would be so easy to let go with you. Forget everything, forget my life, forget my responsibilities, and be with you. But I can't, and I won't. I'm in love with someone else. I've made my choice."

He strips off his shirt and jeans until he's wearing only his black boxers. Even though I already told him we wouldn't be sleeping in the same bed together again tonight, he climbs on top of the bed covers to sit beside me. I should tell him to go, but the lost and lonely expression on his face has me reconsidering.

"Come on," I say, pulling him off the bed so we can brush our teeth and I can wash my face.

We've become very comfortable around one another's personal routines. A few mornings during the past couple of weeks, I have sat on the lip of the tub and watched Fallon shave. It's something I did often with Ryder. Fallon finishes brushing his teeth and leans a shoulder against the door frame, watching me dry and rub lotion on my face.

"Why are you staring?" I can feel the intensity of his eyes boring holes into me.

"What do you remember about the man from that night?" Well, that came out of left field.

"*His* eyes. One blue, one brown. I remember *His* voice. If I ever hear *His* voice again, I'll be able to recognize it instantly."

"What else?"

I push him out of the way so I can close the bathroom door and change. Once done, I open it again and walk past him to get under the bed covers. He turns off the lights and joins me. Just like last night, we face each other and snuggle in. To me, at least, it feels like we're two friends having a sleepover.

"*His* smell. I remember the way *He* smelled like cigarettes and nutmeg. There is one thing that I still don't understand though."

Fallon smooths my hair back off my face, his hand stopping to cradle the nape of my neck. "What's that?"

"*He* wanted me to see something. *He* kept repeating that over and over. *He* was screaming at Hailey saying she was stupid to think she could ever be me. It doesn't make sense. What did *He* mean? I'm certain this was the older man Hailey had been sneaking around with. The man who abused her and hurt her. Why would she stay with him if *He* hurt her? Why didn't she come to me for help? Why didn't I see what was happening to her and save her?"

"I don't think you'll ever understand the why. He could have been obsessed with you, and Hailey was his way to get access to you. He could have been using Hailey as a substitute because he couldn't have you."

"Like a stalker? Don't you think I would have noticed some man creeping around? Jayson, Julien, and Ryder sure as hell would. The four of us were always together."

"You'd be surprised by how many monsters surround you without you ever realizing that they're there."

"If you're placing yourself in that group, you can cut that shit out right now, Fallon."

His fingers clench in my hair at the base of my head to the point of pain and I wince. "I am a monster, kitten. I hurt people, and I couldn't give a shit. I cause pain because I like it. I do what I want, and I will steamroll over anyone in my way. My reputation is what it is for good reason."

I decide to take the plunge and dive off the deep end into dangerous waters. "Who hurt you, Fallon?"

"You don't want to go there, Elizabeth," he bites out, jaw rigid and teeth clenched.

"Yes, I do. Who hurt you?" He pulls at my hair again, but I refuse to react. He wants to scare me, to deter me from pushing for more. Joke's on him. I've seen the real Fallon and I know he would never really hurt me. "Who hurt you, Fallon?"

This time he curses and shoves up from the bed as if he's preparing to walk out of the room. I watch his chest heave with strangled breaths. I wait him out, allowing him the time he needs to decide whether he trusts me enough to let me in.

I hear him rasp out, venom coating every word, "My father. My mother. My brother. Everyone in my life who was supposed to love me." He thumps a closed fist on the mattress and the bed shakes.

With his bare back to me, I can see the scars on his lower torso. "Tell me," I whisper, crawling up behind him and placing my hands over his scars. Every muscle in his body goes taut and his breath hitches violently like he's forcing back tears but refuses to let them fall. I want to help ease his pain. I want him to know that he is loved. By me, by Tatiána, by Ryder. Fallon deserves to be loved.

I don't know how much time passes, but eventually he starts talking.

"My father is a cruel son of a bitch. He only cares about money and getting his dick wet in any available pussy. I hated living in his fucking house. I escaped every chance I got. I don't remember the first time he hit me or locked me in the closet. I do remember the last time his did because that was the day I fought back. I was no longer the small, timid boy he could bully. I grew up and learned how to hold my own." He crooks his head slightly to the side as if he needs to make sure that I'm still there.

"That last time, he tried to burn me with a lit cigar. I broke his goddamn right hand," he recalls and holds his hand up in front of him as if remembering. "Took a hammer and cracked every bone." Fallon chuckles mirthlessly. "It ruined his golf game. He hasn't been able to properly hold a club since."

Tears run freely down my face as I listen to Fallon's childhood horror. If I ever come face-to-face with his father, that man better run in the opposite direction because I think I might actually kill him.

"Then there's good ol' mom. The grand dame, Patricia Montgomery. The queen of the fucking castle. I bet her elitist friends would shit a brick if they found out she liked to fuck little boys."

I gasp against his back. After hearing about his father, I don't know if I'll be able to hear what I think he's about to tell me. *Please, no,* I pray with everything in me. What the hell kind of deranged parents were they? I add his mother to my list of people I will likely kill given half a chance.

"I came home one night and found my brother and Patricia in my bed. I never slept in my room again after that night. I found out later that she had been molesting him for a while."

I'm openly sobbing now, and I wrap every part of me around Fallon, needing to shield him from his memories. Then something he said penetrates my sadness. "Wait. What brother? I thought Trevor was your half-sibling?"

"Not Trevor. I didn't even know about him back then. I had an older brother, Peter. He was ten years older than me, so by the time I was born, Peter was already messed up. After he turned fourteen, he was in and out of drug rehab and mental facilities for the rest of his life. Pretty sure what Phillip and Patricia did to him made him that way. My parents made sure that no one outside the family knew about Peter. Most people thought he was part of the hired help. I didn't think anything of it because that's how it was growing up.

"About a month after I found him and Patricia in bed together, I woke up to Peter straddling me. That night I had bunked down in one of the guest rooms. He was doped up on meth and had a knife in his hand. He said it should have been me and not him. I woke up in the hospital days later. Alone. Ry was the only person who came to visit me the entire two weeks I was stuck there recovering."

That's how he got his scars, I conclude, reading between the lines. I don't ask about Ryder, even though I'm so desperately want to. I don't ask Fallon anything more. I can't hear another word. It's too painful. His parents *are* monsters. He was a child, and no one protected him. The only thing he ever felt growing up was pain. He has been hurt by every person who should have loved him.

"I'm so sorry, Fallon. I'm so fucking sorry." I don't know what else to say. No, that's not true.

I know exactly what I *need* to say.

"I love you, Fallon."

"What?"

"I love you," I repeat.

He turns around and stares at me, confusion and need warring within his blue eyes.

"No, you don't. You can't. I'm unclean. Every piece of me is filthy and tainted. You don't want my darkness touching you," he angrily tells me, but I feel his hands tremble like he's fighting himself not to reach out to me. Fallon saved me. I want to save him. So I make the first move and reach out to him.

I band my arms around his neck and hold him. I squeeze him to me as hard as I can. "I love you, Fallon Montgomery. I love your strength. You had your childhood stolen from you by people who should have loved you. You survived their cruelty and didn't let them break you. I love your heart. You care so deeply. I've seen it. Playing basketball with the boys at the women's center. The way you take care of me. The way you are with Tatiána. The way you have always looked out for Ryder without him even knowing. You took me in without a second's thought when I showed up on your front doorstep. I love how you treat your sister with respect and kindness. I love how you fight for not only what you want, but also for your friends. You jumped in and protected me from Marshall that night at the Fields. You protected me at the party last month when Maria and Jacinda showed up. Even though no one would tell me the whole story, I can assume it was you who got the video of the fight taken down so Jayson, Ryder, and Julien wouldn't get into trouble. And it was you who got Marshall kicked off his soccer team. And it was you who threatened Jacinda to leave me alone. You shielded me then and you continue to protect me now. You are a wonderful, beautiful man, and I love every filthy, tainted piece of you."

That's the moment when I feel Fallon break, and a part of me breaks with him. He buries his face against my chest, clutching me to him. And cries. His tears are not gentle. They are ugly and hard and filled with desolation. They soak my shirt and run down my skin like I am being bathed in his grief. Through it all, I tell him I love him over and over again until his body stops trembling and his eyes run dry. I give him every possible comfort I can. I kiss his wet cheeks. I rub my fingers across his scalp and up and down his back. I sing to him and cradle his body like a mother does a child—like his mother should have done when he was a little boy. I can tell by the smooth, easy rhythm of his breathing when he finally falls asleep, the emotional exhaustion having drained him completely.

"Thank you for trusting me," I whisper so not to disturb him. Right before my own exhaustion pulls me under, a question pops into my mind. What happened to Peter and where is he now? I also wonder how quickly I can choke the life out of his parents to make them suffer for what they did to him and his brother.

Chapter 10

Day 16: Finding Fallon

Barcelona

Fallon

God, my bones ache like I've been pummeled by boulders. It feels worse than the mornings I would wake up in an alcoholic haze after a bender or when I would crash down from a high. Thank fuck I don't do that shit anymore. I stretch my arms up to relieve some of the stiffness and instantly feel a soft warmth beside me. Elizabeth. My eyes feel swollen and gritty and it's hard to open them, so I reach over to her. I need to feel her. I need to hold her goodness.

My hands touch the skin of her bare legs and she jumps; pieces of paper fly off the bed and onto the floor. "Shit, Fallon, you scared the mess out of me."

I squint to see what she's doing. "What time

is it?"

"Past nine, last I checked."

"We missed breakfast," I say and scrub my hands over my face.

Fuck, Tatiána is going to be pissed we missed breakfast. I roll over to get out of bed when the rich aroma of coffee tickles my nose.

"Tatiána had it brought up. She really thinks we're fuck buddies now after seeing you in my bed when she came up earlier. We have thoroughly confused your sister."

"I thought I smelled coffee." I rub my face and eyes again, then open them fully.

Elizabeth is sitting up against the headboard, one pen in her hand, another behind her ear. She's concentrating on a piece of paper in her lap but reaches over with her free hand and rubs her fingers through my hair. My eyes almost roll to the back of my head at her touch. Jesus, this girl will be my undoing.

I sit up and rest my back against the headboard in an imitation of how she's sitting. Our shoulders touch and I give her a slight nudge. "What are you doing?"

Elizabeth bites the end of the pen she's holding then scribbles something down. "I got inspired," she tells me, then scratches out what she wrote. She's writing music: a song. I'm instantly intrigued. But coffee comes first.

I get up, not caring that my morning wood is on display, and walk over to where a rolling cart and tray have been parked next to the bed. I pour myself a cup of steaming, dark liquid and grab a pastry. There are several sheets of paper on the floor, all of them filled with hand-written musical notes along five-lined staffs.

Elizabeth puts down her pen and looks up at me with concern. "How are you feeling this morning?"

"Exhausted."

"I'm not surprised."

"But I also feel good," I confess. The smile she gives me almost causes my knees to give out.

I don't know what I expected when I woke up this morning. Part of me thought Elizabeth would have packed her bags and fled into the night, wanting to get as far away from me as she possibly could; escape my dark secrets. I have plenty more to share, but not yet. She said she loved me last night. I'm not stupid enough to presume she meant it in the way where we run off into the sunset and live happily ever after. But hearing those words from her beautiful lips felt so fucking good. Will she still say it once I break her?

She pats the bed next to her. “Come here, Nutter Butter.”

“Fuck,” I grunt but I do as she says and take my place beside her on the bed. Elizabeth grabs the coffee cup from my hand, taking a sip, then passes it back.

“Listen and let me know what you think.” She picks up one sheet of her music and begins to hum while tapping her fingers on my thigh like it’s a piano. Starving, I scarf down my pastry, sip my coffee, and listen. The way her voice hums the melody is haunting, yet peaceful. It’s a beautiful piece of music.

“What do you think?” she asks me when she finishes.

“It’s really wonderful, kitten.” She fucking beams that smile at me again and I’m thankful I’m already sitting down because this time my legs really do go to jelly.

“I wrote it for you.” She bites her bottom lip, causing me to zero in on its pink, pouty fullness.

And this is when my obsessive fascination with Elizabeth turns into an all-consuming love. I told her the truth when I said I didn’t believe in love. This blond-haired, green-eyed girl just made me a liar. What the fuck am I supposed to do now? I choke down the rest of my coffee, not caring that it's still scalding hot.

Elizabeth gathers and rearranges her sheets of music and stacks them together. She places them on the bedside table next to her. "I'll play it for you properly on the piano later."

I wrap my arm around her shoulders and pull her to my side. She rests her head on my upper arm and we sit there in silence as an internal battle quietly rages inside me over the new and intense emotions I'm feeling for her.

"Knock, knock," a quiet voice calls from outside the bedroom door as it cracks open. Tatiána pokes her head in. "I thought I heard voices. May I come in?"

Elizabeth waves her inside and scoots me over to make room on the bed for my sister.

"Good morning, dear brother," Tatiána chirps and kisses me on the cheek. "I see you finally woke up. Eduardo will be here within the hour. I thought perhaps you both would like to enjoy the pool for a while before lunch. I'm not sure if you are aware of our customs here, Elizabeth, but lunch is our big meal of the day, then we settle down for a siesta. Later, Eduardo and I would like to treat you both to an afternoon in town."

"That sounds lovely, Tatiána. Thank you," Elizabeth tells her.

"Fallon knows where everything is. My husband and I will meet you down at the pool later." Tatiána kisses me once more and gets up. Elizabeth gets up as well and they walk together to the door, whispering in each other's ears like schoolgirls. I see Elizabeth blush, and Tatiána giggles as she leaves and closes the door behind her.

"What was that all about?"

"Girl stuff." Elizabeth does a belly flop onto the bed and props her chin in her hands to look at me. "Are we good, Fallon?" She's referring to everything that was said last night.

"We're good."

"Good," she says.

"Yep."

"Glad that's settled."

"Yep," I repeat.

"I meant every word," she says.

"What was it you told me? No take-backs."

"No take-backs." She grins. "Now, let's put on our swimsuits and go down to the pool. Have you ever played 'Blind Man's Bluff' before?"

"Can't say that I have."

"Well, then, Mr. Montgomery, let's go have some childish fun."

Elizabeth

"I've decided that you have to convince your sister to adopt me. How long does it take to get Spanish citizenship?"

"What are you going on about?" Fallon mumbles, eyes closed behind his sunglasses as he floats beside me.

"Tatiána has a *lazy river*, Fallon," I emphasize like it's the most important thing in the world.

We've been enjoying the pool while waiting for Tatiána and Eduardo to come out. Once I saw there was a lazy river, I was done for. I mean, who actually has a lazy river as part of their backyard pool? Filthy rich people, apparently. And it's heated, otherwise it would be too cold to go swimming this morning.

"Yeah?" He still sounds perplexed.

I'm lying stomach-down on a float. Not the round ones that you usually see at water parks, but a proper one that I can stretch out on. Fallon is floating beside me on his back, one hand holding on to the side of my float, his toes poking up out of the water.

"She has a lazy river. That's a good enough reason for me to move to another country and beg her to let me live in her house."

Fallon chuckles and sinks below the surface of the water. I don't have time to ask where he's going before my float is flipped over from below and I tumble into the water. When I resurface, Fallon is swimming away from me at a fast clip, laughing his ass off.

"Coward!" I yell.

I notice Tatiána waving at me from the patio. A tall, dark-haired man is at her side. He looks every bit the distinguished older businessman, except he's not wearing a suit. Eduardo is tall and lean, dressed casually in a crisp blue dress shirt and fitted black dress pants. His hair is ebony black, where it almost looks deep purple when the sun hits it at just the right angle. He leans over and places a kiss to Tatiána's temple, and she melts against him like ice cream on a hot summer's day. I wave back to acknowledge that I see them and swim over to where some steps lead out of the pool. Just when my foot hits the bottom step to climb out, Fallon grabs me from behind and lifts me up high above his head. A tiny squeal escapes and I have to brace on his forearms so I don't slide right out of his hold, our bodies still wet and slick from the water.

I hear Tatiána tell Eduardo, "See what I mean," and his deep, masculine chuckle follows in answer.

I give up my futile attempts to wriggle out of Fallon's grasp and just go with it. If he wants to carry me around like a sack of potatoes, so be it. As we get closer to his sister and brother-in-law, I see the age difference between Tatiána and Eduardo that Fallon was talking about yesterday. He had told me she married very young and that Eduardo was about two decades older than she was. I regard the silver gracing his temples and the crinkles around the corners of his eyes. But I also notice the warmth of his smile when he looks down at Tatiána, the love shining in his deep, brown chocolate eyes, and the way his hand possessively wraps around the curve of her waist. This is a man completely in love with his wife and it shows.

Eduardo is first to greet Fallon when we stop in front of the happy couple. Of course, Fallon doesn't put me down, and my cheeks heat with embarrassment.

"Fallon, so good to see you again. Tatiána has been most happy that you are here. And you as well, my dear," he says to me with a genteel bow of his head. "My Tati has had nothing but wonderful things to say about you, Elizabeth. It's a pleasure to meet you. I regret that I wasn't here to welcome the both of you when you arrived as I had some business to attend to. But let me offer you a formal welcome to our home."

"Fallon," I hiss out between gritted teeth, trying to get him to put me down. He finally gets the message after I pull his arm hair.

"So sorry about him," I apologize and hold my hand out to Eduardo. He takes it and brings it up to his lips. "It's nice to meet you. You have such a lovely home," I tell him.

Fallon kisses Tatiána's cheek, then mine, and excuses himself. "Sorry, I need to make a phone call. I'll be right back." I hadn't thought too much about the fact that he hasn't called anyone or received any calls that I know of the entire time we've been on our trip.

"You make him happy, Elizabeth," Tatiána says, bringing my attention back to her.

"Just friends," I remind her.

Eduardo suggests I go get changed as an early lunch will be ready soon. I go to my room and take a quick five-minute shower to wash away the chemical smell of the pool from my skin. For clothes, I choose a long-sleeved floral day dress that falls just below my knees. As I'm walking out of my room, I hear Fallon's voice coming from the bedroom across from mine. I know I shouldn't eavesdrop, but I quietly tiptoe over to the closed door anyway. I can't make out much, but I do hear snippets of phrases like "It's time" and "See you soon." When I don't hear anything more, I slip down the hallway and make it to the stairs right before I hear footsteps coming up from behind me.

"Nice dress," Fallon comments and takes my arm as we descend the stairs. He must have changed before I came in because he's wearing jeans and a fresh shirt. The urge to ask who he was talking with is dancing on the tip of my tongue, but I let it go and instead say, "Eduardo is nice. He clearly is head over heels for your sister. The age difference is a bit weird, though. I mean, if she's eighteen now, when did they meet?"

"It was actually an arranged marriage between Tatiána's mother's family and Eduardo's father. Tatiána has known Eduardo her whole life. They got married when she was sixteen."

I stutter in surprise at both the arranged marriage and her age. "At sixteen?"

I couldn't imagine getting married that young, but then I remember that Jayson began talking about marriage and children not too long after we started dating. I also remember how I hated that he had planned out our entire lives without giving me much of a choice about it. So much has changed since then and life did not unravel the way I thought it would.

"Where'd you go?" Fallon's voice intrudes into my heavy thoughts.

"Pardon?"

"You spaced out for a second."

"Just thinking," I give him a timid smile.

We walk back out to the pool area. Somehow within the short amount of time of me going inside to change, a dining table and chairs have appeared. They've been placed out on the terracotta paver stone patio underneath a very large portable patio gazebo with tied-back curtains. Baskets of fresh flowers in a varied array of oranges and yellows adorn the table and surround the gazebo.

"Looks like we're right on time." Fallon places his hand on my lower back and guides me over to where we will be eating lunch. Like a gentleman, he pulls a chair out for me and a perplexed look must be on my face because Tatiána starts laughing.

"Oh, brother, you must not be that romantic if doing the simple courtesy of helping a lady into her chair makes her look, how do you say?

Flabbergasted."

"I make up for my lack of chivalry in other ways." He winks at her. Now I give a snort of derisive laughter as Fallon takes his seat beside me.

"What? You don't agree?" He leans forward, grabbing a crystal pitcher, and fills my wine glass, then his. "Should I remind you of New York City, Nordurljosavegur, London, and Paris?"

I concede the truth to Tatiána, "He's right. Fallon has filled every day of our adventure with more fun and excitement than I could possibly hope for. I've had a great trip."

Servers appear holding tray after tray of platters filled with food that smells delicious and makes my mouth water. I thank my server as he places a plate of herbed crusted chicken and julienned vegetables before me. I nibble on one of the edible flowers Tatiána said she likes to use in the food, and I decide it's not bad.

"How did you and my brother meet?" Tatiána inquires. She and I haven't had much of an opportunity to talk one-on-one yet.

"We've known each other for quite a while but never really talked much until recently. Fallon and I went to different schools. He actually kind of scared me back in high school," I admonish, remembering how uneasy I used to be around him.

I wish I could go back and smack Old Elizabeth for being so clueless and timid. She never fully opened her eyes to see what was truly around her. How much living she missed out on because she was afraid and let others make choices for her. Fallon was never the scary, crazy guy she built him up to be in her mind. If she would have taken the time to look closer, she would have seen a lost boy trying his best to survive in a world where his family hurt him on a daily basis and life continuously screwed him over.

"Eduardo scared me as well. I had been aware of him my whole life since our families were close, but I remember the exact day when I really saw him for the first time through the eyes of the young woman I became. It both thrilled me and scared me at how fast I fell in love."

Tatiána upturns her face and Eduardo presses a kiss to her lips. "Our age difference must be confusing to you," he adds.

I go with honesty. "Fallon filled me in when we got here, and I did ask him questions. But what I notice most is how in love the two of you are. How Tatiána glows standing next to you, and how you look at her like she's the most precious thing in the world. When it comes down to it, that's all that really matters."

"Tell us more about you, Elizabeth," Tatiána invites as she offers a roasted grape tomato to Eduardo with her fork. He bites into it and she eats the rest. The way they act with one another reminds of Julien and Elijah. A pang of longing cracks through, causing me to miss my best friend. Julien and Elijah are two more relationships I'll need to salvage when I get home. It's just another reminder on how I have fucked everything up so horrendously.

"There's not much to tell," I reply with evasion because my life has been a shitty soap opera up to this point. Fallon is silent next to me, but I feel his hand reach over to my leg under the table to let me know he's there to support me.

"Everyone has a story, Elizabeth. What is yours?"

"Why are you being so fucking nosy?" Fallon snaps at Tatiána.

I see Eduardo tighten up ready to say something. In order to avoid an argument, I blurt out, "I had amnesia." Both Tatiána and Eduardo's mouths fall open then shut. "I lost my memory a year and half ago, but everything came back two weeks ago. My life is a bit messed up at the moment. I created a new life for myself, one that I loved, but then my old life came crashing back. Fallon is helping me work through some things. He's been great. Exactly what I've needed." Fallon's hand squeezes my thigh.

"I'm sorry that I pried. I meant no offense, Elizabeth."

"It's okay. It's just hard for me to talk about."

Thankfully, she changes the subject to something I'm more than happy to talk about. "Elizabeth is a very talented pianist," she tells Eduardo. "Perhaps you wouldn't mind playing for us again after we eat?" she asks me.

"It would be my pleasure. I composed a new song last night. I love your Steinway, by the way," I tell Eduardo.

"Before I forget," Tatiána says, looking to Fallon, "I had to make a last-minute decision. Eduardo and I will be leaving tonight to go back to Madrid. We would still like to show you around town before we leave. You are both more than welcome to stay and enjoy the house for as long as you would like."

I'm a little disappointed because I was hoping to spend more time with her, getting to know Fallon's sister better. "Is everything okay?"

"Everything couldn't be more wonderful." She beams, grabbing hold of Eduardo's hand on the table. "I didn't want to say anything until I was able to tell Eduardo first, but…I'm pregnant."

Fallon is up and rounding the table to hug his sister before I can tell her congratulations. Dual emotions swirl around my mind; happiness for Tatiána and a sad sense of loss for Elizabeth Ann. I choke down the melancholy and join Fallon in celebrating their good news.

"How far along are you?" I ask her.

"Twelve weeks."

"I'm so happy for you," I tell her and kiss each cheek.

"Thank you, Elizabeth. Now, let's finish lunch, listen to you play the piano one last time, and enjoy the remaining hours we have together."

Tatiána wasn't exaggerating when she said lunch was their big meal of the day. We eat and talk under the gazebo for about two hours before Tatiána asks if I'm ready to play something on the piano. After hearing me play the song I wrote for Fallon and a few other classical pieces, Eduardo writes a name and contact number on the back of one of his business cards and hands it to me. He tells me if I ever decide to pursue a career as a concert pianist, I should give the number on the back of the card a call. It's for someone who works with the Spanish Symphonic Orchestra in Madrid. I'm a bit dumbstruck by his offer, so I say thank you and tuck the card away in my dress pocket, knowing it's a path in life I will never want to follow professionally. I'm determined to become a doctor, but Eduardo's compliment is still flattering.

Afterwards, we're driven into Barcelona and spend the rest of the day walking around the city. It's a phenomenal city with incredible architecture; Gothic-style being my favorite. Tatiána and I exchange contact information and she invites me to come back to visit her in the future, with or without Fallon. We do a little window shopping and a little real shopping. I add to my collection of souvenirs I've bought from every place Fallon and I have visited. I think it's going to take a suitcase of its own to carry back all the things I have purchased for Ryder, Jayson, Julien, Elijah, Meredith, and Trevor. I also sneak in a few surprise items that I will give to Fallon later, and pick up a few baby items that I give to Tatiána as a thank you for hosting me in her home. Knowing all the different foreign transaction fees I'm accruing, I don't want to see my credit card bill next month.

Tatiána and Eduardo make their departure around seven in the evening, leaving me and Fallon to while away the rest of the night together. Fallon takes me to the Gothic Quarter, and we party until two in the morning. Once we return to the estate, it's almost three and I'm utterly exhausted from my long day. I flop down on the slate-blue and pale yellow striped sofa that sits in the family room. Fallon makes himself comfortable next to me and picks up my legs to drape across his thighs. I'm about to ask him what he's doing when he starts massaging my feet, and I emit a very unladylike moan.

"You sound like a fucking porn star," he muses with a chuckle and I slap his leg.

"Don't ruin my Zen, asshole. Oh my God, that feels incredible," I enthuse, falling back on the arm of the sofa and closing my eyes in pure pleasure at what his hands are doing to my feet. I purr like a cat getting its ears stroked. "What do you think about becoming an uncle?"

The rhythm of his hands slows. "Shit, it never occurred to me. I'm going to be an uncle. Christ, that kid is so screwed."

I peek over at him. "Fallon, you are great with kids. Don't sell yourself short. You'll spoil that kid rotten."

"At least I know he or she will have two great parents and a loving home," he replies.

And just like last night, my heart breaks for the boy he once was. "What are you doing for Thanksgiving?"

That catches his attention. "What I usually do. Enjoy a tumbler of good scotch and find a hot girl or two to fuck." I kick him in the ribs with my left foot, making him grunt.

"Why don't you spend it with me?" I throw it out there hoping it'll stick. I've got a plan in mind. Something I've been thinking about the past few days. I don't know if the boys will still want me coming home with them like we planned, so if that falls through, I will create my own Thanksgiving with Fallon, and somehow convince Trevor to come as well. I'll invite Meredith, too. And if I do go home with the twins and Ryder, Fallon can still join us. I'm going to make sure that Fallon's Thanksgiving and Christmas this year are good ones filled with laughter and love.

Fallon says incredulously, "You want me to spend the holiday with you?"

"Did I stutter?"

He pulls my legs and slides me down the sofa

in punishment for my sass, then braces himself over me. "Why?"

I slide back to sit up and tuck my legs underneath me, my dress spreading out and draping down the front of the sofa. "Why not? Do you already have plans, or anything better on your turkey day to-do list other than a 'good scotch and a hot fuck'?" I say with air quotes.

He turns over and lays his head on my lap. His beautiful blue eyes fix up on mine. "No, but —"

I stroke his sandy-blond hair the way I know he likes it. "Then it's settled. With you around, it'll be the best fucking Thanksgiving ever," I exclaim, trying to sound like him.

Fallon doesn't respond for a minute and I wait anxiously as he processes through his thoughts. I hear his phone ding and he holds it out to the side where I can't see it. He takes a quick look then puts it back in his pocket. "Are you sure, Elizabeth?"

Without hesitation, I answer, "Absolutely." And then I aim my arrow true to its target when I tell him, "You're my friend and I love you. I couldn't imagine you not being there to share the holidays with me. That includes Christmas as well, by the way. What do you say about getting a ten-foot tree? I've always wanted a huge tree."

I expect Fallon to give me one of his cocksure grins or one of his mirth-filled laughs. I wouldn't have been surprised if he flat out said no, or better yet, fuck no. What I never would have predicted was for him to flip back around, get up in my face, and plant a whopping big kiss to my mouth. It's not a sexy kiss filled with tangling tongues or a sweet kiss filled with airy caresses and barely-there touches. It's a kiss where he smashes his lips against mine in a way that feels like desperation. I'm too stunned to react at first because it came out of the blue. I'm about to push him off of me when Fallon pulls back and places something small and metal in my hand.

As I look down to see what it is, he gets up from the sofa. "Password is kitten," he says and leaves the room.

I stare at the phone he just laid in my hand and my breath hitches. "Fallon, what?" I look up but he's already gone. He gave me his phone. What does this mean?

I turn it on and type in 'kitten' to unlock the screen. Holy shit. Am I ready for this? Deep breath in, exhale out. I dial Ryder's number. My heart is beating so fast, I feel it might beat a hole right through my chest. Ryder's phone rings once, then twice. On the third ring, I hear his baritone voice answer and I about pass out from how much it affects me.

"Ryder?"

I hear shuffling noises and something like the low hum of a car engine in the background. "Elizabeth?"

I swallow a few times not knowing what to say next.

"Elizabeth, are you still there?"

I answer with a breathy, "Yeah."

Just like the last time, Ryder goes silent and my stomach clenches with nausea. Every self-doubt I've been carrying with me comes flooding back like a tsunami, breaking my resolve and decimating my hopes that everything will be okay.

"Open the door, baby."

"What?" My ears pick up a faint noise coming from the front of the house.

"Open the door, Elizabeth."

I hear the noise again. I jump off the sofa and run as fast as I can to the front door. I fling it open like the house is on fire. And standing before me, looking handsome as sin, is Ryder Cutton. The man I love more than anything. The man I want to spend the rest of my life with.

My body starts shaking uncontrollably and I drop Fallon's phone. He can afford another one.

"How?" I can't seem to speak anything other than monosyllabic words.

Ryder gives me that heart-stopping grin, his amber eyes liquid with unshed tears. "There's my girl."

I burst into tears.

Chapter 11

Day 17: He Found Me

Barcelona

Elizabeth

Before my legs have a chance to buckle, Ryder swoops me up in his arms and I swear to God, I have never felt anything more wonderful in my entire life.

"I love you so much. I'm so sorry," I weep uncontrollably, the floodgates to my heartbreak opening, dumping everything out.

"Sweetheart, everything is going to be alright." Ryder kisses the side of my hair, my face, and my lips several times then buries his face deep into my shoulder, inhaling deeply. I clutch him to me tightly, afraid that if I let go, he'll disappear, and I'll be lost again.

"How did you find me?"

"I called him," Fallon says from behind me.

My head swivels to where he's standing at the bottom of the stairs, hands shoved in his pockets, wearing an inscrutable expression.

"Fallon?" I say his name in question.

"Private jets, kitten," he says with that infamous Fallon smirk. I think it takes about nine hours to fly from North Carolina to Spain. Ryder must have left immediately after Fallon's mysterious phone call this morning to be here now.

Ryder puts me down and I rush over to Fallon and hurl my arms around his neck, hugging him fiercely. "Thank you. How did you know I chose Ryder?"

"Kitten, there isn't much I don't know when it comes to you."

"You are a wonderful man, Fallon Parker Montgomery," I whisper against his cheek.

"Go be with your man. It's time, kitten." He kisses my nose, then releases me, walking upstairs and leaving me and Ryder alone. I turn back around to look at the man whom I have loved for most of my life, so starved for the sight of him. He's watching with curiosity as Fallon ascends the stairs.

As Ryder tracks Fallon, my eyes devour every inch of the man standing before me. I still can't believe he's really here. He came for me. I have missed him so goddamn much. His hair is a little longer on the sides and on top, like he hasn't had a haircut in a few weeks. His eyes have bags under them like he hasn't been sleeping well, and his face is slightly gaunt with worry lines etched at the corners of his eyes. He's wearing his usual faded jeans and T-shirt, and the black work boots I like because they make him look badass. Haggard-looking or not, he's still the most amazingly handsome man I have ever laid eyes on.

Ryder drags his gaze from the top of the stairs and slides those mesmerizing copper eyes my way. "You look good, but also different somehow," he says.

Why does everything between us suddenly feel uncertain?

"I love you, Ryder," I loudly exclaim, not able to help myself. I have so much to make up for. I will crawl buck-naked across broken glass for this man if he can find it in his heart to forgive me.

"Thank fuck," he exhales, the tension in his shoulders dissolving right before my eyes. Neither of us makes a move toward the other, even though my body is screaming at me to catapult myself back into his arms.

"Please forgive me."

"We have a lot to talk about, Elizabeth. A lot that needs to be said."

"I know." He's too far away. I need him in my arms. I need my mouth on his. I just need him so much.

"You remember? Everything came back?"

I nod. "Yes."

Tense silence ensues.

"I love you so much. It's you, Ryder. I only want you. I will beg and plead and do whatever I have to if you can give me another chance. No more running. No more confusion. I know what I want. I know who I am."

"And who's that?"

"*Yours*, Ryder. I'm yours if you still want me."

A joyous smile spreads across his face like an exploding supernova. I sprint across the entryway and into his ready arms once again, peppering kisses all over his face, neck, and jaw until our lips collide in a desperate open-mouthed claiming. His mouth goes deep over mine and I'm flying apart from the scorching heat being generated between us. I press myself into him, so hungry for his taste. It will take a lifetime for my craving of him to slake, yet I know I'll never be satisfied; my need for this man is too great.

"I love you, Elizabeth," he professes against my lips, languidly flicking their bottom fullness with his tongue like he's reacquainting himself to the feel of me. It's been weeks since we last saw each other; since I kissed him or touched him. There is no known hyperbole that can describe my state of concupiscence at this moment.

"Make love to me," I beg in a half pant, half plea, as I push the hem of my dress up and hook my legs around his waist. His large, capable hands cup the round cheeks of my ass to hold me in place as he licks the sensitive patch of skin under my ear. I chase Ryder's mouth because I have to taste him again. He is the sustenance to my starvation.

"Where?" he grunts against my mouth, the sound of it so sexy my entire body trembles with anticipated excitement.

"Stairs. Fourth room on the right. Hurry," I pant harder, my desire to have him inside of me obliterating every coherent thought in my brain.

Ryder deftly carries me up the curved staircase with ease and once he gets to the correct room, he shifts me so that he's holding me up with one arm. Using his free hand, he turns the knob and pushes the door open with a foot. Once inside, he quickly shuts and locks the bedroom door.

My mouth moves to his neck and I nibble every part of it while whispering dirty words that graphically tell him every little thing that I plan to do to him tonight and want him to do to me in return. We will not leave the bed until I have made good on each and every single one of my filthy promises. By my words alone, Ryder groans out a sexy moan and hurls us both bodily onto the bed, neither one of us letting go of the other.

"Rip it off. All of it," I plead, wanting us skin to skin as soon as possible, the fabric of my dress too much of a barrier between us.

He obeys. With a couple of hard tugs, the fabric splits in half and falls away. Next to go are my bra and panties, leaving me splayed out completely naked and vulnerable under him. I attack his jeans while he pulls off his shirt. He stands up briefly to remove the rest of his clothes and shoes, and I whimper at the absence of his body against mine. My greedy hands pull him back before he's finished. I use my feet and legs to help push his boxers all the way down and off. I pull him savagely against me, wanting to feel his full weight pressing down on me, smothering me until all I can see and breathe is him.

"We have a lot to discuss, baby," Ryder says with shallow, rocking thrusts of his hips that wipe away any other thought other than how good it feels. He slides his hard cock against my folds and up to my clit, lubing himself with my wetness, and I'm about to lose my goddamn mind.

"But tonight, I'm going to love you. Everything else can wait." I nod my head in agreement and grab his neck, pulling him down so I can kiss his delectable mouth. Even the sound of his deep, raspy voice turns me on like nothing else.

With one hard thrust of his hips, he seats himself fully inside me, the girth of him stretching me and filling me up. Our twin hisses of pleasure echo throughout the cavernous bedroom. I was so incredibly wet beforehand that there was no need for foreplay. My hips rock upward of their own accord wanting him even deeper. I feel his cock pulse inside me like a heartbeat, and my core clenches around him in response. It's the most delicious feeling. I'm finally complete. I'm home. Ryder is my home.

He bends his arms to rest on his elbows and

grabs my face with both his hands. We don't move. We stare at each other for a very long time. It has felt like ages since I last saw him, and my eyes can't seem to take in enough of his stunning face. I trace the scruff of his stubble with my fingertips, and sparks surge through my nerve endings. I touch his mouth, pulling his bottom lip down and rubbing it with my thumb. My other hand glides across his eyebrows and into his hairline, feeling the soft hair that falls forward. Ryder is mirroring every caress on my own face. When he pulls at my bottom lip, I gently bite down on the pad of his thumb and flick my tongue out to taste its saltiness. His pupils dilate and he gradually leans in, butterflying his mouth across mine with feather-light kisses.

I'm so full and happy and in love. Ryder pulls his hips back slightly and slides in once more, lighting me up like one of those sparklers you buy for the Fourth of July. I squeeze my thighs against his sides and use my muscles to leverage him closer. I suck his tongue into my mouth as he moves in and out of my slick channel in a bold assault of pulsing, thrumming thrusts. It feels so damn good, my toes curl. Our bodies are already slick with sweat, and our skin glides over each other's like silk against satin.

Ryder swivels his hips and a bolt of something powerfully electric travels up my spine. I shudder from the intensity of it. "I think you found my G-spot," I tell him, my hands moving in a frenzied exploration of his smooth, hot skin.

"Yeah?" He sends a wicked gleam my way and repeats the motion. I cry out a strangled gasp and almost climax from the sensation.

"Holy shit," I pant, my eyes watering.

"Let's see how many times I can get you to come. I'm aiming for five within the next hour."

Hell, yes.

I'm about to reply with a sassy retort but my skeptical laughter dies as Ryder pistons in once more and I explode in a torrent a million glittery pieces, coming unexpectantly with a long, convulsive moan that seems to echo around the room.

"That was sexy as fuck," he says, kissing me.

As I quiver beneath him, Ryder gentles his pace, riding me through my orgasm, the glide of his cock inside of me slow and determined. As my second orgasm builds on top of the remnants of the first, I reach between us and slide my hands down his abs to where we're connected. His whole body jerks.

"Fuck, I'm going to come," he grunts and rolls us so that I'm now on top. I grab the headboard as he cradles my breasts, pinching and pulling each nipple between his thumbs and middle fingers. My head arches back in exultation, my pale blond hair whipping out all around. I eagerly move up and down his shaft, using my leg muscles to jackhammer myself on him, chasing yet another orgasm which is hurtling at me at light speed.

Ryder sits up and takes one tight pink bud into his mouth, sucking hard, and I'm done; the flick of his tongue on my aroused nipple sending me over the edge for a second time. I death-grip the headboard and sing out his name. Ryder soon follows. After he thrusts up into me a few more times, I feel the warmth of his release penetrating deep, the sound he makes while coming inside me better than any music I could ever write. I'm drunk off of the cascade of sensations I'm feeling. After the last tingle fades, I collapse on top of Ryder, my body draping over his left shoulder like a limp rag doll. He bands his arms around my middle and nuzzles my chest with soft licks and tender kisses.

"God, I've missed making love with you," I say, my voice breathy and sated. Ryder rolls us once more so he's on top of me again, our bodies still intimately connected. He relaxes and compresses my body down into the mattress, knowing exactly how I like it. I love feeling his weight on top of me after we make love. We spend several minutes giving each other languorous kisses. I rub my hands up and down his back, steeping in the sensual feel of his tight, defined muscles. The world is right again. I have my perfection back. But I also need to start working for his forgiveness.

Dragging my fingertips down the side of his face, I begin. "That night you went to see Fallon, I decided it was time to go through some old boxes that Daniel and Drew had packed for me. Stuff from my old room, my old life."

I panic when Ryder tries to move off me, so I pull him back down, lifting my head to meet him with a kiss. "Please just listen. Let me finish," I implore him, and he stills.

"There wasn't a lot in the boxes. Mostly pictures and scrapbooks. There was a scrapbook full of Hailey's poems. I read every one of them. They were so beautiful, and I became sad because I couldn't remember her."

"The two of you loved each other very much. You and Hailey were as much best friends as you were sisters."

"I know that now because I remember. I couldn't have asked for a better sister. I miss

Hailey so much. I miss Mom and Dad," I say, choking back the tsunami of tears that are threatening to escape. "I found some pictures of you and me as kids and thought it would be cool to make a memory board to hang up in the bedroom. As I went through the boxes' contents, I kept pulling pictures of us out and placing them in a separate pile. I found another scrapbook. It was of me and Jayson. When I picked it up, something caught my eye. There was a ring. I didn't know what it was at the time, but when I picked it up, it was like something clicked. Like the final puzzle piece snapped into place and I was able to see the full picture. All of my memories came pouring back. Every single one. *Everything*. The first thing that I remembered was that night. I remembered what happened, Ryder. I felt it all. I felt everything *He* did to me. I saw Mom and Dad and Hailey. It was like dying all over again."

I begin to cry, the dam giving way and bursting forth. I feel wet droplets dripping down on my shoulder and realize that Ryder is crying with me. I wrap my arms around his neck and hold on to him for dear life.

"Why was I the only one to survive, Ryder? Why me? It's not fair. I would give anything to go back and take their places. I would give anything to sacrifice myself so that Hailey could live."

Ryder tightens his hold around me. "Please, baby, don't ever say that. Don't ever think that. I never want to exist in a world where you aren't in it."

"Even though I didn't die, losing myself with the amnesia felt like death. The last thing I remember was you lifting me in your arms and telling me you loved me. I needed you to know that I loved you too. I remember saying it. I hope you heard me."

"I heard you, sweetheart. I heard you."

Ryder covers my face in wet kisses, the saline from our combined tears is like the first spring rain washing away the desolation of winter and bringing renewal for new life to grow.

"When my memories returned, it was like I was possessed by two people. My mind split between Old Elizabeth and New Elizabeth. Old Elizabeth took over. I don't remember how I got to Jayson's. It was raining and I somehow made it to the condo in the rain. When I woke up the next morning, I rolled over to reach for you, but it wasn't you next to me. I didn't understand why I was in Jayson's bed. Like the night before, when my memories returned, everything that happened hit me all at once. I'm so sorry, Ryder. I slept with him. I wish so desperately that I could go back and not open those damned boxes. I didn't want to remember. I was happy with my new life. All I wanted was you. I'm so fucking sorry. I've hated myself since. I hate what I did. I never meant to hurt you or Jayson, and I wound up hurting everyone."

Ryder pulls back slightly, grabbing my face with both his hands. "Why didn't you come to me? Why did you run to Fallon and not me?"

It takes me a minute to calm myself enough to continue. I meet his eyes, finding enough strength to go on. "I felt like I was losing my mind. I didn't know what was real anymore. A part of me wanted to give up and curl into a ball on the floor, to disappear. I was so ashamed. I didn't know who I was. I didn't want to hurt anyone else. I couldn't face you or Jayson or Julien. I managed to walk to Fallon's. It was the only place I could think to go."

"Home," he says gruffly. "You should have come home, Elizabeth. To me. You turned off your tracking software. I went to the condo to see if you were there or if Jay or Jules had heard from you. I had looked everywhere trying to find you."

A small, sad chuckle comes out when I say, "I forgot my shoes. I walked barefoot for over a mile to Fallon's."

Ryder kisses me once, ever so softly. "Baby."

I shake my head at his tenderness. I don't deserve it. "I couldn't face you after what I'd done."

"I saw the note."

I shatter when he tells me that. He's known this entire time that I betrayed him in the worst possible way and slept with Jayson? I feel like I'm going to be sick. My body shakes as I gasp for breath trying to pull heavy oxygen into my lungs. Ryder has known this entire time and he still came for me? He still loves me? How will I ever be worthy of this man? He should hate me for what I did. Thick repulsion at myself slithers its way up my esophagus and I push Ryder off, running to the bathroom to vomit up nothing but dry heaves.

Ryder sits down beside me on the cold tile floor, pulling my hair back even though nothing more than strangled gags come out. He rubs a hand in soothing circles around my back, and I rest my head on my forearm that's propped on top of the toilet seat. I should be grossed out by the fact I'm leaning on a toilet, but I'm too distraught to give a shit.

"Baby, please," he begs. "Please don't do this to yourself. I love you. Everything will be alright."

"How can you say that? How can you stand

to look at me? I don't deserve your forgiveness, Ryder."

He slides himself behind me, his warmth enveloping my back. He brushes my long hair to the side so he can rest his chin next to my ear, making sure I hear everything he next tells me.

"I have loved you for an eternity. I was given a second chance, one brought on by tragedy, but one I will never regret taking. You are everything to me, Elizabeth. I know you didn't mean to hurt me. I'm not going to lie and say you didn't, because it was one of the worst pains I have ever experienced—knowing you had regained your memories and the first thing you did was run back to him. All my fears came true, and it was like everything you had said to me was a lie."

I don't think anything could have prepared me for the agony his words bring me. I hurt the man I love. I broke his trust. I don't deserve him or his love, but if given another chance, I will spend the rest of my life making it up to him.

"You've been through so much already, Elizabeth, but I promise we'll work through it. There's something Fallon said when he called to let me know you were with him. I told him that you went back to Jay, and his exact words were, 'No, she didn't.' It took me a minute to understand, but I do. If it's Old Elizabeth that needs my forgiveness, she has it. But she's not the woman in front of me now. She's not the woman I hope to spend the rest of my life with. When you came back to us after being gone for over a year, you were different. You had changed, whether you meant to or not. That's the woman you are. The feisty fighter with pink-streaked hair who loves new adventures. The one who drives a Hellcat. The one who curses and drinks and gave me her whole heart. The first woman I ever made love to. And I love you with every fiber of my being."

His words slay me. Ryder Cutton is the most amazing man, and I am so damn grateful for his love. I'm about to tell him how much I love him in return when he rises up from his place behind me and I hear the shower turn on. He lifts me up and carries me under the spray where he holds me as the warm water sluices down my cold body. Too emotionally exhausted to do anything, I give myself over to Ryder as he tenderly washes me, holding me upright with one strong arm wrapped around my waist. As he rinses the shampoo from my hair, I look up at him with huge, green eyes filled with love and desperation.

"Fallon has helped me so much these past couple of weeks. I wouldn't have made it without him. I owe him so much. I know who I am now. I will spend the rest of my life loving you with everything in me. I only want you, Ryder. I don't want Jayson or anyone else. You're it for me. My heart will always belong to you. It already did. Ever since I was nine years old."

Ryder's dark hair is plastered to his head, rivulets of water dripping down his face and chest and stomach. But my eyes never waver from his. "My love for you is and will never be a lie, Ryder. I have always loved you. That night after I left your garage, I had already decided. I was going to choose you. I will always choose you. You're my forever."

"And I choose you, Elizabeth. I don't want to spend another day without you by my side. I know we'll have a lot of things to work through, and then there's Jayson and Julien to deal with. But if it's absolution you need, Elizabeth, then you have it. I forgive you."

How many times can I shatter tonight? Hearing him say he forgives me both rips me apart and glues me back together.

"I forgive you, Elizabeth," he repeats, adding steel to his words. "I know you didn't mean to hurt me. You must have been so scared. I'm sorry I wasn't there with you to help you through it."

God, this man, his soul so pure and good. I may have to reconsider my hatred of the Fates. I would endure any trial, any struggle, any fight, to have this man love me.

Ryder bends down and takes my mouth in a gorgeous passion-filled kiss that leaves me breathless. I haven't lost him. He still wants me. I wasn't expecting his forgiveness even though I was desperately hoping for it. Julien talks about my capacity for love, but this beautiful man standing before me puts it all to shame. His love humbles me, and I will cherish it and protect it for the rest of my life. My heart expands and my skin warms as if the sun is breaking through the dark clouds of a thunderstorm, creating a rainbow in its wake. We kiss and caress one another in the close confines of the shower until the water runs cold and our skin is wrinkled and pruned. Ryder finds two large towels rolled up in a cabinet in the corner of the bathroom and wraps me in one of them when we exit the shower. The past hour of great sex and heart-felt confessions has been cathartic, leaving me feeling lighter and unburdened.

I smile. "There's one good thing about my memory returning. I have every memory of you back, and I wouldn't trade those for the world."

"Even the one of me doing a backflip on the motorcycle?"

"Especially that one. You were so sexy that night. I wanted to rip your clothes off."

"I think you succeeded in that objective quite well earlier," he chuckles, looking at the clothes littering the bedroom floor. His laughter makes my stomach cartwheel in that special way only he can make it do.

I tug his towel away from his waist and throw it across the room. "Let's see if I can work on some more of those promises I whispered to you earlier."

"I think I also remember guaranteeing you more orgasms," he adds.

He tosses me back onto the bed, and my laughter fills the room until it turns into moans of delight as he crawls between my legs.

Chapter 12

Day 18: He Found Me

Barcelona

Elizabeth

After our marathon of make-up sex, and with the effects of jetlag catching up to him, Ryder falls into a very deep sleep. Even though I've been up well over twenty-four hours, my brain doesn't want to shut down. I've spent the last several hours wrapped in Ryder's arms, staring at the man I love more than life itself, and tracing the lines of the tattoo above his heart. I'm still in disbelief that he's here; that he forgives me. It's so much more than I deserve, but I will grab hold of it and never let go again.

Knowing Ryder should be asleep for a while to come, I disentangle myself from his arms and legs and go in search of Fallon and coffee. I slip on a pair of leggings and a hoodie and make my way downstairs. Through the window, I see

Fallon sitting out on the patio. I make two cups of coffee and take them outside, placing one in front of him on the table, then sit down in the chair beside him.

"Thank you, Fallon."

"I take it things went well?" he casually inquires, but I see the smirk he's trying hard to hide.

I blush hard because there is no possible way that he didn't hear my very vocal orgasmic screams coming from the bedroom all night long.

"Where's our boy?"

"Still asleep," I reply and take a sip of coffee. I reach over and take Fallon's hand in mine. "Fallon, seriously, thank you for everything. I will never be able to repay you for what you've done for me and what you've given to me."

Fallon chews on the side of his lip and I don't think I've ever seen him look so lost. "I guess this is it then."

"What do you mean?"

"Ry's here now. You'll be leaving to go back home with him."

"Are you trying to get rid of me?" I tease, causing Fallon's icy blue gaze to harden. "Fallon, I'm not going back yet."

"What?" he says in disbelief.

"If I recall, we still have Venice, Amsterdam, and Sydney left on our adventure."

He stares at me in confusion. "You still want to go? What about Ry?"

"He can come with us if he wants to. I really hope he wants to. But if he doesn't, I'll understand. However, I'm still going to go with you. I've got money I can access from the trust that Daniel and Drew set up for me. I can pay my and Ryder's way for the rest of the trip."

"What the fuck are you talking about? I'm not taking your damn money, or Ryder's." Fallon turns to face me in his chair so that our knees touch. "Are you serious? About the rest of the trip?"

"Totally and completely," I say, and lean over to hug him. "These weeks on our adventure together have meant the world to me, Fallon. You mean the world to me, and I want to finish what we started. That is, if you want to."

"Fuck, kitten," he relents. "If you're sure and Ry can handle it, then hell yeah. Let's finish this thing."

I squeal and bounce in my seat while still

hugging him. Fallon lets out a laugh that warms my heart. "You're still coming for Thanksgiving and Christmas," I remind him.

"What's going on?" Ryder says from the portico that leads to the patio, his gaze fixed on me and Fallon hugging.

I stand up and quickly make my way over to him. "You're up," I comment happily, eye-fucking the hell out of him because every inch of Ryder Cutton is gorgeous, even though at this moment his hair is sticking up all over the place and he looks exhausted.

Ryder's light brown eyes soften as he watches me approach until we're standing toe to toe. "Good morning," I happily sing as my hands explore his expansive, bare chest and my thighs clench with a desire to have him inside of me again. Ryder reaches down to grab the back of my thighs, pulling me up to straddle his waist and proceeds to kiss the daylights out of me.

"Good morning," he says when we finally pull apart. He nips me tenderly on the tip of my nose and looks over my shoulder.

"Hey, man," he says to Fallon who has been watching us. Ryder carries us over and sits down with me in his lap. I adjust slightly so I can see Fallon. Ryder reaches for my coffee and drinks it down in two gulps. Fallon slides his cup over and Ryder thanks him, then guzzles that one down as well.

"I think I'm going to need about a gallon's worth today. Jetlag sucks ass," Ryder complains. "Thanks for the lift over."

Fallon barks out a laugh and shakes his head. "My personal jet is not an Uber, fuckwad."

"I'm so happy you're here," I tell Ryder, and because I can't help myself, I start kissing a path up his neck to his ear.

His hand that's cradling my thigh gives it a squeeze, and I'm about to pull Ryder back inside and up to the bedroom when he says, "Babe, I need to talk to Fallon. Do you mind giving us a moment?"

I'm about to ask what and why but decide to trust him, just like he's putting his trust in me. I kiss him lightly on the lips and tell him that I love him. I ruffle the top of Fallon's hair and call him Nutter Butter when I pass by him. He throws up his hand, giving me the middle finger.

Once I get to the doors that lead back into the house, I hesitate for a second. With my heart hammering thunderously beneath my ribcage, I shove aside the worry that's creeping up my spine and make my way inside the house. I guess I can keep myself busy making us something to eat while the two of them talk.

Ryder

I watch Elizabeth go and I know she's worried about why I would need to speak with Fallon in private.

"I don't know if it's the weeks we've been separated, but she is even more beautiful than I remember."

Fallon makes a humming sound and rubs his thumb across his bottom lip. He reaches into his pocket and takes out a stick of gum, something he's done a lot since he stopped smoking.

"She's been through a lot. She's in a good place right now. Settled and happy. You being here makes it perfect for her. I told you she just needed time and distance."

"Thank you for being there for her. It seems you were exactly what she needed. But things are about to become very hard for her. She left a lot of angry people back home."

"Then we'll both be there to protect her," he says.

I narrow my eyes at him and ask the question that's been rattling around my brain since I saw how they acted together at the bottom of the stairs last night.

"Is something going on between the two of you?"

I love Elizabeth and I told her I forgive her, but part of me is still hurt about the whole thing with Jayson. Add the fact that she ran to Fallon for help and not me, and my uncertainty about where I stand with her skyrockets. Watching the easy and intimate way Fallon and Elizabeth interact with one another also has my jealousy flaring. With everything that has happened, my insecurities are running high.

The brief widening of his eyes makes my stomach drop, but I need him to tell me everything. I may have to beat the shit out of him afterward.

"If you're asking if I fucked her, the answer is no." *Oh, thank God*, I think, then he says, "But that doesn't mean I didn't want to or didn't try."

"What the hell, man?"

"You wanted honesty. Shut the fuck up and let me finish."

I sit back, crossing my arms so I don't punch him in the face, and listen to what he needs to tell me.

"She was broken, Ry, when she appeared on my doorstep. The girl we knew didn't exist anymore. She was in jagged, damaged pieces and she needed someone to help her put herself back together. She couldn't face you, and she hated herself for it. She kept talking about Old Elizabeth and New Elizabeth. She destroyed my room, by the way. Even broken, she's still a fighter. But I watched as she shut down and started to disappear. I knew if I didn't get her away from you and Jay and Julien, she might never have recovered. She had been through too much, and the weight of it was crushing her. Elizabeth was at a point where one more thing would tip her over that cliff of no return, and if that happened, she would never come back to us. I couldn't live with myself if I allowed that to happen. So I took her, and we got the hell out of town. I told you that you wouldn't like my methods."

The resentment I feel over the fact that she went to Fallon for help dissipates somewhat. "But it worked," I tell him. "Whatever you did, it worked. I was pissed as hell about it, but I owe you for what you did for her."

"I'm not finished. You said you wanted everything," he warns me. "I may not have had her in my bed, but I did kiss her… twice. Those are on me. I was the instigator. And I won't apologize for it. We may have also shared the same bed a time or two, but I swear, nothing happened," he finishes, staring at me, unblinking so I see that he's telling the truth.

I groan out a frustrated sigh, looking up to the sky for guidance. "You really want me to beat the ever-loving shit out of you, don't you?"

Then Fallon hits me with something totally unexpected. Something that I don't think I could have ever prepared myself for.

"I love her, Ry. I love her in every fucked-up way imaginable. I've never loved anyone before. I even told her that love was a lie. I don't like feeling this way, but I can't help it, and it pisses me the hell off. None of it matters because you are it for her. I know that I'll never have a shot at a future with Elizabeth because she is completely in love with you. However, if you screw this up with her, I can promise you that I will be standing right there, ready to take her away again—for good this time."

"You try it, and I will bury you," I growl. "We've been through a lot together, Fallon, and I've always had your back, but Elizabeth is mine. I love her too damn much. I'm not letting her go again. You try and mess with that and you'll regret it."

The threatening scowl that was on Fallon's

face falls away into a huge grin. "That's exactly what I wanted to hear. You continue to fight for her. She loves you, Ry. You're the man she wants." He sits back and gives me a pointed look. "But like it or not, she and I have gotten close. She understands my darkness, and I trust her with my secrets. I'm not asking for your approval and couldn't give a shit if you don't like it. It is what it is. I hope you can accept that."

Some people may think the entire situation is screwed up and so way out there, it's unbelievable. Me, Jay, and now Fallon all in love with the same girl. Hell, throw Julien in there too because he also loves her; he just loves Elijah more. All I can say to those people is: Go fuck yourselves. You can't help who you fall in love with.

I'm mulling over what Fallon has told me when he adds, "And just to warn you, she's invited me for Thanksgiving and Christmas." He grins at me like a snarky asshole, and I punch him on the arm. "She also wants you to come with us on the rest of our journey," he finishes.

That takes me by surprise. I had assumed she and I would be going back home after today. "What are you talking about?"

"She wants to finish our adventure and she wants you to join us."

"She never said anything about that."

"When could she? You had your dick shoved up her pussy all night long. The walls are not soundproofed."

"Shit, Fallon. Warn a guy next time," I cough, then grin like the Devil because I'm the man who had his girl screaming in ecstasy all night long. Hell, I hope the whole of Spain heard her yell out my name.

"So, what are the plans then?" I ask.

"The last cities on her bucket list are Venice, Amsterdam, and Sydney. We were planning on arriving in Venice tomorrow. What do you say? You coming with?"

If Elizabeth and I are going to be together, I have to accept her new friendship with Fallon. Fallon has never cared for a girl before. He always used them and threw them away. The fact that he says he loves Elizabeth doesn't sit well with me, but I'm also happy that he has allowed himself to open his heart to the possibility of love. After everything he's endured, that alone is huge. I guess it comes down to whether I trust my friend and my girlfriend, and the answer is, I do. Fallon can be a dangerous son of a bitch, but he's also loyal to a fault and extremely protective of those he lets in. He'll protect Elizabeth with his life, and I couldn't think of anyone better for her to have on her side.

"I want us home for Thanksgiving," I tell him.

"Fine. Now let me catch you up on what's been going on and tell you how your girl knows how to hustle me at pool, drink me under the table, and dance like a pole stripper."

Elizabeth

I spend a very long time making all of us a huge breakfast. Finding some Italian sausage and Danish bacon, I whip up a crustless quiche and squeeze a bag of oranges to make fresh orange juice. I add pieces of toast, bowls of fruit, and a fresh carafe of coffee to complete the meal. I find a rolling tray cart to pile everything on and push it outside. Once out on the patio, I listen for the sounds of yelling or fists hitting flesh, but all is quiet, thank goodness. Breathing a sigh of relief, I plaster on a brilliant smile and make my way out.

"Breakfast!" I call out. Ryder and Fallon are where I left them, mirror images of each other as they sit back, legs splayed out in front of them, grins on their faces. Fallon turns his head my way and winks at me. Ryder stands up and smacks him on top of the head as he walks over to me. My breath goes all wispy watching him come nearer, and my hands shake, causing the cart to rattle. "Is everything okay?"

"Couldn't be better." He smiles. He places his hands on mine to still my jittery nerves. "Baby, everything is good. Stop worrying." He kisses me lightly and peels my fingers from around the cart's handle. "I heard we're going to Venice."

I shriek with happiness. "You're coming?"

"Couldn't keep me away."

I spin around doing a happy dance, and Ryder shakes his head with laughter. "I love you! I love you! Thank you, Ryder!"

"Hop on," he tells me, and I eagerly jump on his back. "I'm starving and this breakfast looks fantastic."

I ride piggyback on him to the table and then jump off and hug Fallon. "You're the best," I enthuse.

"Damn straight, kitten."

Ryder goes back for the cart, and we all dig into our food but leave the entirety of the coffee to Ryder. He needs it much more than we do.

"Since it's just the three of us here, I want to know the story behind the two of you," I tell them. Then I say to Ryder, "I thought I knew everything about you, but apparently I don't. You visited Fallon in the hospital?"

"You told her about that?" Ryder looks at Fallon, bewildered.

"Like I said, she knows more of my secrets than you do now. I trust her."

"Well, hell. Um, okay. You may not like what we tell you."

"I love you, and if we're going to be together, there can be no more secrets. I will tell you anything and everything you want to know, and I'll answer any question you ask of me. I expect the same in return."

"She's a feisty thing, isn't she?" Fallon quips, slinging his arm across the back of my chair.

"She's perfect," Ryder replies and leans over to kiss me while also pushing Fallon's arm away. "She's also *my* woman. Hands off."

Fallon smiles his approval and I roll my eyes. "Stop delaying. Spill. I want to know. What is the deal between you and Fallon?"

"No one knows about this, not even Jay or Julien." Ryder takes his time pouring himself another cup of coffee as I wait patiently for him to begin. "Fal and I worked for this guy stealing and stripping cars."

Mind blown. "What? How the hell did I not know about this?"

"Ry and I first met at the Fields when I was like, what, eleven and you were ten?" Fallon asks Ryder. "I saw Ryder racing his dirt bike and I thought he was one cool motherfucker."

"Ah, the beginning of the secret bromance," I say.

Fallon laughs. "Call it what you will. As you know, I hated being home and loved getting in trouble. My family name caught a lot of attention, even when I was young. One day, this guy approached me while I'm watching Ryder race his bike and asked me if I'd be interested in doing a job for him. I guess he saw something in me that he liked. Rebelliousness. Recklessness. A young boy who didn't give a fuck. Hell, I don't know. Anyway, he explained how he needed someone on the inside to get access to certain luxury cars and told me I was perfect for the job because no one would suspect a kid my age. He asked me if I knew how to drive, which, of course, I did—but that's a story for another time. The guy told me all I had to do was keep my eye out for certain cars and let him know which ones I found. He would then tell me which car he wanted me to jack. Once I did, I would drive it to his garage where it would be stripped for parts or sold, illegally, of course. I was bored, so I said yes."

"But you were eleven!"

Fallon gives me his famous head tilt as if to say, "remember who you're talking to."

"Fal and I had already become friends by that time. We'd hang out at the Fields or he'd come to Dad's garage when I was there."

"You also let me bunk in your room a time or two by then as well," Fallon reminds him.

"Fal told me about the guy and said his first job was to swipe a Mercedes SLR. I didn't want him going by himself, so I told him I was coming along to make sure someone had his back."

Again, I scoff at how young they were. "But you were ten! How did Faith and Randy not notice? Or Brea or Jamie?"

"It was easy sneaking out of the house in the middle of the night when everyone was asleep. Earlier in the day, I would hide my bike in some bushes down the street and then once I was able to sneak out of the house, I would meet up with Fallon."

"Needless to say, I'm glad Ry had my back because we got into a lot of fights, even as kids. I never knew people were so damn possessive over their cars. Do you remember what happened that first job with the Mercedes when I set the car alarm off?" Fallon looks at Ryder, a mischievous grin splitting his cheeks.

"That wasn't half as bad as stealing the McClaren. I thought for sure those guys were going to shoot our asses."

They both laugh at the memories and I decide not to ask for clarification. Perhaps ignorance truly is bliss.

"We worked for this guy until high school," Ryder continues.

"By that time, the fun of it had worn off, so I gave him enough money to disappear and live the rest of his life comfortably in a non-extradition country. Just in case."

"The both of you are shitting me, right?" Fallon merely smiles and Ryder ducks his head, not meeting my gaze. "Again, how did I not know any of this?"

"People see what they want to," Fallon blithely states.

"Damn." I really was clueless back then. Ryder had been helping Fallon steal cars for years. I should be upset about it, but for some reason, I'm not. Old Elizabeth would have been outraged. Good thing I'm not her anymore.

Ryder hasn't smiled once, and I can tell he's ashamed of his part in it all. In contrast, I'm strangely and oddly excited. "Did you guys ever have to hotwire a car?"

"A few times," Fallon says.

"Why do you ask?" Ryder says.

"Think you could teach me?"

Ryder's mouth drops open as Fallon laughs maniacally.

"Hot damn! I really like this New Elizabeth," Fallon shouts and stands up. "Enough secrets for now, kitten. I'm going to leave you two to enjoy the rest of your day. Don't break the bedsprings. Make as much noise as you want, though. Eduardo sent all the staff home yesterday."

I choke on my orange juice. "Where are you going?" I manage to ask.

Fallon picks up his plate. "There's a Tramontana I want to take a look at in town. I'll bring something back for dinner." He kisses the top of my head and leaves.

I put my fingertip to my mouth, biting the tip as I grin at Ryder. "I can't believe you were a little hoodlum. You've always been this knight in shining armor to me."

He counters with, "I can't believe you want me to teach you how to hotwire a car."

"I can't believe I never noticed what you were up to."

"I'm sorry if you're disappointed in me." Ryder leans back in his chair, chest and arm muscles stretching his shirt taut, which apparently is a cue for my hormones to go haywire as my greedy eyes devour his innate masculinity. I know I'm totally screwed if the simple act of him sitting in a chair turns me on this much.

"No, it's not that. Honestly, if I had known what you were doing, I would have helped. Just like you had Fallon's back, I would have had yours." Old Elizabeth wouldn't have condoned what they were doing, but if she couldn't have stopped them, she would have joined them and been their lookout. At least that's one positive quality of my old self that I can agree with.

"Like Bonnie and Clyde?"

"Without the machine guns."

"I love you, Elizabeth."

"I love you, too. I know I've said this about a million times, but I'm so happy you're here."

Ryder slides his chair over to mine and nibbles on my neck. "Want to get naked?"

"Hell, yes. But aren't you tired?"

"Between sleep and my sex with my girlfriend, my girlfriend always wins."

I melt when he says I'm his girlfriend.

"I've never had pool sex before. It's heated and there's a lazy river attached to the back," I tell him, stripping off my hoodie and leggings and rushing off to leap in the pool before the cold outside air penetrates my naked body. Ryder makes a vocal whoop and soon follows.

I'm so incredibly happy. I get to spend another ten days traveling with the man who saved me and became a friend, and the man who was my childhood best friend and became the love of my life.

Chapter 13

Back to New York City

Elizabeth

"Hoops! Mr. Fallon! Y'all came back!" Devon yells across the basketball court and rushes over to me and Fallon, the gap between his front teeth on full display with his wide grin.

We had to stop twice to refuel on our way back from Sydney, and if the jet didn't have a private bedroom with a large bed, I think I would be comatose right now. Ryder and I slept most of the way back to the States. Well, that's not entirely true. We joined the mile-high club too. With the gap-stops for fuel, it took us over a day and a half to get to New York. Seeing Devon's happy face makes the long journey worth it.

"Told you we would be back," Fallon says as Devon plasters himself to my side and Fallon high-fives Trevaughn and Seamus. I look around for Butch but he's not out here.

"Who's that?" Devon asks, eyeing up Ryder who is standing next to me.

I wrap my arm around Ryder's waist. "This is my boyfriend, Ryder. Ryder, this is Devon, Trevaughn, and Seamus—the best unsigned basketball players in New York." I wink.

"Hey, man," Ryder fist bumps each boy. "Nice to meet you guys."

Devon scans Ryder skeptically. He crooks his hand at Fallon, motioning for him to bend down so he can whisper, "You okay with him being with your girl?"

I bite my lip to hold in my laughter.

Fallon mock-whispers back, "Yeah. She was his girl first. He's cool."

Devon nods his head as if what Fallon said made perfect sense. "Cool."

"Want to shoot some hoops with us?" Seamus asks.

Fallon looks around. "Where's my other teammate?"

Trevaughn is bouncing the ball in front of him between his hands while looking around and not at the ball—a skill I have yet to master.

"He and his mom split a few days ago. Said his aunt in Illinois was taking them in for a while."

When we arrived at the women's center, Mrs. Berkeley was surprised to see us again. She proceeded to gush all over Fallon. I would too if he had given my organization three million dollars. I saw a couple of the women I had spoken to before and introduced Ryder to them. Mrs. Berkeley showed us some of the things they had gotten for the center using Fallon's donation. I was happy to see the new books they purchased for the reading nook and the re-modeled family art room. They took the open space they were already using for arts and crafts and added more tables, chairs, and a huge wall-length bookcase filled with art supplies. Mrs. Berkeley also said that new beds and mattresses had been ordered and would come in after the holidays. Wanting to see the boys before we left, Fallon and I knew exactly where they would be, so we made our way out to the center courtyard.

"Ryder can take Butch's place on Fallon's team," I tell the boys. I place a quick kiss on Ryder's lips and break off with Devon and Trevaughn. "Alright, what's the game plan?"

Devon spins the ball on his finger in thought. "Is your guy any good?"

"Ryder? Yes, he is."

"As good as you?" he asks.

I peer over and consider my boyfriend. I've seen Ryder play basketball before with Jayson and Julien. He's so athletically inclined, he can pick up almost any sport with ease. Ryder's also an adrenaline junkie, so I know he'll try for the fancy shots and power plays during the game.

"I think I can handle him."

"If Hoops can make a couple of three-point shots like she did last time, we're golden," Trevaughn says. He grabs the spinning ball from Devon's finger and bounces it to me. I like that they call me Hoops; it's much better than being called princess. Hoops is a show of respect, whereas princess makes me feel like I should be a damsel in distress—powerless, instead of powerful. Fallon calls me kitten, but at least kittens have claws and can bite. Why in the hell am I thinking about this now?

Seamus calls over, "Hey! Are we going to stand around all day or are we going to play?"

"Since you're so eager, you can have possession of the ball first," Trevaughn announces with a chest pass to Seamus. "It's not like we need it since we'll be whooping your asses anyway."

"Hey baby!" I call to Ryder. "You may need

to check your teammate. He likes to foul." That earns me a cocky side-smirk from Fallon.

We get in position and Seamus is able to pass the ball to Ryder even though I'm covering him like flypaper. Sneaky man does a fake to the right and spins around me. Luckily, I'm able to recover quickly and block his shot.

"My girl has game," Ryder says, slipping in a quick kiss as he jogs by.

Watching Ryder play basketball is a total turn-on, and I'm completely distracted. My attention has been glued to his ass and the flex of his biceps for most of the game. Currently my team is down eight-to-six because I haven't been able to focus. One more basket from them and we lose. Devon passes me the ball, but Ryder is in my way. I dribble a few times checking to make sure no one else is near us. I turn so my back is against his front as he blocks me and I grind my derriere into his crotch as I dribble the ball.

Turning my head to the side so only Ryder can hear me, I tell him, "Virgin territory," and give my backside a little wiggle.

Ryder stands up abruptly from his slightly bent position. "What?" he croaks, his face turning a nice shade of pink.

His hesitation is enough for me to pivot

around him and set up for a three-pointer. It swishes in with ease, and Devon and Trevaughn shout in celebration.

"Thanks, babe," I say, patting him on the chest.

"Oh, no you don't, sweetheart. You can't say shit like that to me and not expect a reaction."

"All's fair in love and basketball."

Ryder stalks forward and I retreat back a step, a giggle escaping.

"Come here, Elizabeth."

I love seeing that heated look in his eyes that I know is all for me.

"We have a game to finish." I giggle again and sprint over to where I can seek protection behind my teammates. I blow Ryder a kiss over Travaughn's shoulder.

The game is down to which team can make the final basket. Odds are not in our favor since Fallon has possession of the ball. He pretends to do an overhead pass to Ryder but instead sprints away from Trevaughn. Devon blocks Fallon, arms wide, then snatches the ball in a lightning-quick move when the ball is mid-bounce. As I turn, I smack into Ryder's hard chest, grabbing hold of his fleece jacket to steady myself.

"I should call foul." His warm breath fans over my face, his hands trailing over my winter coat to my dip above my hips.

"In that case, you owe me about a half dozen free throw shots," I tell him.

"Were you serious about earlier?" Ryder asks, his voice dropping to a husky murmur. I'm already hot and sweaty from running around the court, and Ryder's question has my body temperature ratcheting up several more degrees.

"I trust my body with you."

Ryder and I have had a lot of sex the past ten days, both of us rabidly insatiable for one another. We had a lot of sex before. Each time with him feels like the first time. Ryder could twist me in a pretzel and hang me from the ceiling, and I would trust him to take care of me, knowing the end result would be nothing but endless pleasure.

Someone calls my name, but I can't seem to break my gaze from Ryder's serious, amber one. Every part of him is drop-dead gorgeous. His heart is pure and kind. He's supportive and protective without being overbearing about it. He always puts me first. How did I get so lucky? Too many emotions are flying around inside of me. Tears prick behind my eyes making them shimmer and glassy. Ryder notices and caresses my cheek in his cold hand.

"I love you so much, Ryder."

I watch the movement of his Adam's apple as he swallows. He folds his arms around me and lifts me in his arms. It's like we're hugging a goose-down pillow between us because of all the winter gear we're wearing. He holds me like that for several minutes until it dawns on me that we're in the middle of a basketball game. I look over and see Fallon and the boys messing around with the ball at the other end of the court.

"Who won?"

Devon answers me. "They did. Mr. Fallon got in a lay-up."

"We didn't want to ruin your moment," Fallon quips, and shoots the ball one-handed into the basket.

Ryder sets me down. "It means a lot that you wanted to share this with me, Elizabeth. Coming here. Wanting me to join you and Fallon for the remainder of your trip. Thank you for letting me in."

"You were already in, Ryder. You've had a permanent place in my heart ever since you sat down beside me on the third-grade reading rug."

"It's not just that. I've spent the last week with you and Fal, and I've gotten to see why it was so important for you to have this time away from me, and from the guys. Fallon was right. If you had stayed, we would have made things worse for you. Put too much pressure on you. Jay and I would have more than likely been in daily fistfights with one another. So, thank you for letting me share in your journey. I love you, sweetheart." He bends down and graces me with a kiss so soft and pure, my bones turn to liquid.

We'll return home tomorrow and this magical, carefree bubble I've been living in will come to an end. It will be back to the real world and all the problems that await me. Am I ready? With Ryder by my side, I will be.

Chapter 14

Elizabeth

"I'm scared."

"We've got you. We will not once leave your side," Ryder ensures me, linking our hands together. I rise up on my tiptoes and kiss his soft lips, needing that connection to help settle my quaking nerves. I look over at Fallon on my left and he takes my other hand in his.

Ryder, Fallon, and I spent the past ten days flying from Barcelona to Venice to Amsterdam, then finally to Sydney, Australia with a return stopover in New York. Venice was gorgeous, truly a city meant for lovers. Ryder and I spent a day, just the two of us, walking the floating city, riding a gondola, and sightseeing. We visited a glass-making shop and tried our hand at blowing glass. It didn't go so well. The number of pigeons in St. Mark's Square was astonishing. I got pooped on by one while I was waiting to climb the Basilica's tower. Someone in line told me that it was a sign of good luck. Yeah, but no. Being shit on by anything, even a bird, is not good luck.

While in Amsterdam we walked the Red Light District because I was honestly curious to see this most infamous place. Despite having Ryder and Fallon by my side, I was propositioned by not one but three different men asking me how much for my services. Ryder and Fallon were not amused. Fallon took us to see one of the 'naughty' shows and laughed the entire time at my reaction, which was mostly me with my eyes closed and my hands covering my face. Luckily, I also had Ryder's shoulder to hide my scandalized, red face in. After the show, poor Fallon went through packs of gum as he avoided all of the coffee shops that sold weed.

After leaving Amsterdam, we didn't stay long in Sydney, only two short days. A bit exhausting because of the jet lag, but Fallon promised Ryder he would have us back home by Thanksgiving, and we were quickly running out of time. The spring weather in Sydney was hot and sunny while we were there, so we took advantage of it and spent most of our time at the beach. I was terrified of going into the water. I've watched shark week on television, so I know what lurks off the Australian coast. Not to mention that program I saw about Irukandji jellyfish. The waves there were also much bigger than what we get back home in North Carolina. I kept to the shoreline and enjoyed watching Ryder and Fallon battle it out on surfboards that they rented.

Every day with the two of them was filled with new and wondrous experiences, and every night, Ryder made love to me until our bodies were sweaty and our hearts sated. I'm only nineteen years old, yet my life has undergone so many drastic changes. I'm glad that Fallon metaphorically kidnapped me and made me face myself, but I can't live under his protection any longer. It's time for me to fight for the life I want and the people I love. That being said, I'm terrified of facing Jayson and Julien for the first time since I ran off four weeks ago.

That thought snaps me back to the present. I can't believe I'm here on Fallen Brook Drive. My childhood home is right down the street, as are Jayson and Julien's. I'm overwhelmed with so many memories, ones that were lost to me for over a year but are now back with full force. If I didn't have both Ryder and Fallon holding on to me, I think I would crumble under the sheer intensity of it all.

It's the day before Thanksgiving and we're standing on the front porch of Ryder's family's home. I can perfectly picture Faith inside preparing the turkey to cook for tomorrow while

Randy watches football on TV from his recliner. Brea should be in her room watching the Hallmark movie marathon she and Hailey used to love, and Jamie is more than likely knitting something to give away as a Christmas present. I know Ryder's family almost as well as I know my own, but mine are no longer here.

"I think you should have warned them I was coming," I say to Ryder. "I don't want to freak anyone out."

"They're going to be overjoyed, baby."

"What if they want to ask questions about that night?"

"They won't."

"How do you know?"

"Kitten." Fallon bumps my shoulder. "Relax."

"Easy for you to say," I grouse.

Okay, I can do this. I lift my hand and press the doorbell with a tentative finger. Then I wait. My heart is thudding, and I feel like all the blood has drained out of my body and is leaking out through the soles of my low-heeled pumps. I'm not used to the cold North Carolina weather after spending a couple of days in Sydney where the weather was hot and humid. I'm wearing the long coat, scarf, and gloves Fallon bought for me in New York, but the shaking that's vibrating through my limbs is not from the cold. My posture straightens as the front door opens.

"It's about time you showed up," Faith greets Ryder cheerily before her smile drops to astonishment when she sees me. "Oh my God! Randy!" she screams, reaching forward and grabbing me in a crushing hold. "Oh, sweet girl. Oh, my precious girl," she cries. She smells the same as I remember, like cinnamon and sugar.

Ryder's dad rushes to the door to see why his wife is yelling. "Holy shit!" Randy booms and joins Faith in crushing the life out of me. I couldn't care less. I've missed them so much. Brea and Jamie come running when they hear their dad bellow.

"Lizzie?" Brea screeches, and Jamie shouts, "Holy shit!" just like her dad did. The girls sandwich me between them and their parents as we all cry and hug. Other than being in Ryder's arms, this is the best feeling in the world. I'm finally home.

"Mom, Dad, can we take this inside?" Ryder asks them. "It's freezing out here." None of his family is willing to let me go, so Ryder winds up pushing all of us through the open doorway.

My body is being tugged in different directions by eight hands, and four different voices are talking on top of one another. The cacophony of it echoes like a marching band in the small foyer. Ryder pulls me out of his family's stranglehold and wraps his arms around my front.

"I know everyone has a lot of questions, but we've had a long trip and Elizabeth is tired and a bit overloaded right now, so can we all just calm down and give her a minute."

The sudden silence that follows is startling in its contrast. Four pairs of wet eyes zero in on me and I squirm, feeling like a bug under a magnifying glass.

"Hi," I lamely say, and they all start talking excitedly again. *Oh, boy*.

"Fallon, take her upstairs so I can deal with this."

"Come on, kitten. This shit is giving me a headache."

Thankful for the small reprieve, knowing it's not going to last long, Fallon puts his hands on my waist and pushes me up the stairs and into Ryder's bedroom. Once inside, I fall back on the bed with a whoosh of expelled air from my lungs. Fallon looks down at me, a gleam in his wicked blue eyes.

"If the words 'I want to fuck you' come out of your mouth, I think I might knee you in the balls," I warn him.

"I didn't say a thing," he muses.

"I can see the smirk in your eyes."

"You're no fun, kitten," Fallon rejoins and flops down next to me.

I turn my head on the bedspread and look around Ryder's room. It's exactly the same as I remember. Walls painted a dark blue color. Posters of motorcycles and exotic cars plastered to the walls. Various trophies and photos adorning the dresser and desk. So many childhood days were spent up here with us playing board games, doing homework, or just chilling and talking. I hope they still have the firepit out back. That was one of my favorite places. I shift to turn on my side, but my long coat catches under my hip. I shed my outerwear and toss everything on the chair next to Ryder's desk.

"You seem to know your way around the house. Did you come over often?" I ask Fallon. You would think I would have noticed Fallon hanging around, but I remind myself that old me was apparently so oblivious, she couldn't see the forest through the trees.

"On occasion, Ry would sneak me in late at

night when I needed a place to crash or escape my dad's fists."

"Fallon," I begin when Ryder opens the bedroom door.

"Ready to come back downstairs?"

"I guess so," I reply, but feel unsure.

"I'm starving," Fallon announces. "Going to go raid your fridge." He pats Ryder on the shoulder as he squeezes past.

Ryder closes and locks the door behind him, his gorgeous lips curling in a naughty curve.

"What are you up to?"

"You look fine as hell splayed across my bed. You don't know many nights I laid awake as a teenager thinking of you like this," he says as he stalks forward. And just like that, I am soaking wet for him.

"Ryder, your family is waiting for us downstairs," I half-heartedly argue as my legs fall open to accommodate his muscular width, my body addicted to him and so needy for his touch. He bends over me, dark hair tousled on top, a black long-sleeved Henley stretched tight across his chest and ripped jeans that ride low on his waist. So incredibly sexy.

"They can wait a little longer."

Gripping my wool leggings, Ryder pulls them down, sliding me down the bed at the same time. His mouth is on me before I can blink, his tongue on my clit skyrocketing me into a quick haze of shuddering tingles. Ryder's mouth should be considered one of the seven wonders of the world. My man definitely is a master at oral. I let go and succumb to the pleasure he's giving me with nips of his teeth and glides of his silky tongue. Gripping his head with both of my hands and my thighs, I purse my lips tight to hold in the moan that wants to escape, but I can't prevent the loud gasp from making its way in.

He furls his lips and pulls hard on my tight bundle of nerves as he slips two fingers inside my wetness and plunges them deep. My hips violently arch up off the bed and the vibrations of Ryder's murmur of approval add gasoline to my impending orgasm. One more thrust and flick of his fingers is all it takes, and I come hard, grabbing his pillow to smother the sound of my long vocal release. If his objective was to get me to relax, he can pat himself on the back for a job well done. My muscles are nothing but jelly at this point. Ryder crawls up my body and I meet his mouth hungrily, tasting myself on his lips.

"You know, that's not really fair because

you're not going to let me return the favor."

Ryder shoves his callused fingers under my sweater to fondle my breasts, playing with my hardened nipples until I'm panting.

"With everyone else and Fallon in the house, I foresee us having to get very inventive with finding places to be together."

I scratch my nails along the sides of his head and through his soft, dark hair, tilting his head up to expose his neck. I take advantage and lick up the masculine column, then bite gently down on his chin. "We're two educated people in college. I'm sure we can figure things out. There's always your dad's garage," I suggest. That's where Ryder and I kissed that first time.

"Smart girl." Through my sweater, he administers a love bite above my breast and then lifts himself off me. "Let's get downstairs before the fam decides they can't wait any longer."

I tug my leggings back on and smooth my hair down. Before I unlock the door, I spin around and shove my hand down Ryder's jeans, finding him hot and hard for me. "One more thing before we go downstairs," I say and seductively go down on my knees in front of him, pulling his zipper along the way.

"Hell yes," he moans and lets me have my way with him.

Ryder

Fal, Dad, and I are sitting outside around the fire pit while Elizabeth, Mom, and my sisters are inside the house talking. I'm completely antsy which makes my right leg jiggle up and down. I want to be with my girl right now. She, Mom, Brea, and Jamie have been inside way too long for my liking. After I had Fallon take Elizabeth upstairs, I chewed everyone out for making her uncomfortable. I felt guilty as hell when Mom started crying. Then she kept insisting she call Freda, Jay and Jules' mom, and I had to put a stop to that idea real fucking fast. The guys don't know we're here yet, and I don't want to spend my first day back home in a fist-fight with my two best friends.

"So, Fallon, how have you been?" my dad asks him. Fallon may look relaxed and laid back in his chair, but I notice how his eyes keep sliding to the back door of the house.

"Doing good, Mr. Cutton," he replies, again with the eye slide. My leg bounces faster.

"Are you boys going to make me pull teeth or are you going to tell me what the hell is going on?"

Dad—always straight to the point. "What do

you want to know?" I offer, knowing any question he throws at us will have to be navigated like a minefield.

"Is Elizabeth okay?"

That's an easy one. "Yeah, Dad. She's good. Her memory came back."

"I heard about that. But I mean, is she *okay*? How is she handling things? Does she remember everything?"

He's asking about that night. I can't go there with him right now. I promised Elizabeth. Fallon and I both look over at the house. If she's not out here in five more minutes, I'm going in after her. She doesn't need Mom, Brea, or Jamie pestering her with questions like Dad is doing now with me and Fallon.

Fallon steps in. "She's better now. Not so much before. She's been with me the past several weeks." Fallon leaves out the part where I joined them in Barcelona.

"What did Jayson have to say about that?"

"What the hell does that mean?" I snap.

My dad narrows his eyes at me trying to figure things out. "Jayson told Freda and Mitch that he and Lizzie were back together, but something came up and she wouldn't be coming for Thanksgiving."

Fallon starts laughing. "God, I hate that jackass. Of course, that's what he would say."

"Dad, Elizabeth isn't with Jayson. She's with me." I guess now's a good a time as any to fill him in on all the stuff I've been keeping to myself. "She and I started dating and we kind of moved in together."

Dad looks totally taken aback. "You're not living at the condo with the boys anymore?"

I shake my head no. "I moved in after—" Fuck, I can't tell him about the baby or all the other shit that went down. "Yeah, I moved in with her and have been staying at her place. About four weeks ago, her memories came back."

"That's where I come in," Fallon explains. "She needed time to get her head on straight, so I whisked her out of town, and we got the hell out of Dodge. Once I felt she was ready to come back, I called my boy up and flew him out to Barcelona to meet up with us."

Dad sits forward. "Hold up. You've been in Spain and you didn't tell us?"

I cringe slightly at his tone just as I used to when I was a boy if he was upset at me. One thing I never want to do is lie to or disappoint my dad.

"It was a very last-minute thing and I had to leave immediately. But yeah, Spain, Netherlands, Italy, and Australia," I inform him, thankful for the passport they made me get when our families had planned for us to go to London together the summer after we graduated high school.

"Huh," he mumbles and sits back. "So, you and Elizabeth?"

"Yeah, Dad. Me and Elizabeth. I love her and she loves me."

"About damn time. I've watched the two of you dance around each other almost your entire lives. I'm happy for you, Son. How is Jayson handling it?"

"Jay can go fuck himself," Fallon casually says. My dad scowls at Fallon's language but remains silent. He knows how Fallon is and lets it slide, just like I do. "Jay thinks that because she has her memory back, she'll run back to him."

"You know he and Julien are home, right?"

"I know, Dad. We're going to drop by tomorrow, but they can't know we're here yet."

"It's going to be a shit-show is what Ry isn't saying. Myself? I can't wait," Fallon gleefully grins, the light from the fire casting a devilish glow on his face. Fallon thrives on chaos.

We hear female voices and Elizabeth's laughter as she, Mom, Brea, and Jamie come outside. Dad and I table the rest of our conversation for later.

My mom has her arm wrapped around Elizabeth's shoulders and their heads are together. I scan Elizabeth's face to make sure I see no worry or tension, but all I see is her beatific smile and bright green eyes. As soon as she gets close enough, I snag her wrist and pull her down into my lap.

"Everything go okay?" I whisper in her ear.

"Yeah," she whispers back, and because she smells so damn good and I missed her, I tilt her chin up and kiss her soundly.

"I knew it!" Brea shouts. "Every time your name came up, Lizzie would blush," she announces, looking pleased with herself.

My mom says, "Oh, my sweet babies, finally together," and starts crying again. Dad pulls her to him and pats her back.

"Mom, that's just gross," Jamie complains and fake gags a little to make her point. "You make it sound like incest."

"Lizzie knows what I mean. She's always been like a daughter to me," she sniffles.

I feel Elizabeth tense up in my arms.

"Fallon and our son were just telling me about their trip," Dad cuts in.

"What trip?" Brea asks.

"Why does it feel like we're in trouble?" Elizabeth asks me. I settle her back against me and shrug.

"Girls, apparently we missed something while we were inside," Mom says.

"Did you drop out of college?" Jamie exclaims bluntly.

"Our son forgot to mention that he was in Europe with Fallon and Lizzie. And they've been living together."

"You're living with Fallon at the frat house?" Mom's voice rises.

Fallon holds his hands up, "Hey, don't drag me into this."

"Not with Fal, Mom."

"Then... *Oh my*!"

"What 'oh?'" Brea wants to know.

"The 'oh' where he's shacking up with a girl," Jamie leans over to Brea and clarifies.

"You're cheating on Lizzie?" Brea shrieks.

Holy hell. My family. "No!"

"Um, he lives with me. Or at least, I hope he still wants to," Elizabeth timidly says, raising those emerald beauties up to look at me, questions and hope swirling in their depths.

"He definitely wants to," I tell her, and then, "I never left." I bring her lips to mine again and kiss her, slipping my tongue in, completely forgetting we're not alone. Every time my mouth or hands are on her, nothing else exists in my reality. Well, nothing except for what I hear Mom say next.

"Randy, we're going to have such beautiful grandbabies."

I break our kiss. "Oh my God, Mom!"

"Lizzie's pregnant?" Brea and Jamie both shout.

Elizabeth's face turns bright red, and she hops off my lap like she's sitting on a mound of fire ants. "Fallon, can I get your help with something. *Inside.*" She pulls him out of his chair and practically runs inside the house.

Needing to nip the current train of conversation in the bud, I say, "No, she's not pregnant. Can you guys chill the hell out."

Dad and Mom start snickering while Brea and Jamie talk animatedly to each other about who is going to be the better aunt.

"Remind me not to come home for Christmas," I grumble and stomp off after Elizabeth and Fallon to the sounds of my parents' laughter behind me.

Chapter 15

Elizabeth

"Kitten, I don't like this one bit."

"Babe, we're coming with you whether you like it or not. I'm not letting you do this alone."

Faith made us an early Thanksgiving supper because I wanted to go see Jayson and Julien this afternoon. I can't avoid them any longer. I also know the two men in front of me are not going to budge on their demands. I need to start repairing those broken bridges. However, the trepidation I feel over the possibility of seeing my childhood home makes me more than a little nauseous. The twins' house is right next door. How can I expect to go there and not come face-to-face with what happened *that night*?

"I don't want any fights. I mean it. Let me handle things my way. Please."

"Can't make any promises," Fallon says, folding his hands behind his head as he watches me from Ryder's bed.

"Then you can sit your ass on the driveway and wait," I warn him.

"We won't come inside. We'll wait outside on the curb," Ryder suggests. I agree to his compromise.

"Thank you. Both of you. I know you're just trying to protect me, but I'm a big girl. I can do this. New Elizabeth, remember?"

Ryder catches me in a reassuring embrace. "I know you can take care of yourself, baby. You're the strongest person I know. I trust you."

I trust you. I won't give Ryder any doubt about my love for him. I've made my choice. Now I have to find a way to tell Jayson. I also need to face Julien.

"I'm ready."

We don't have a car because we came straight here from the airport in one of Fallon's corporate sedans. I'm assuming Fallon's car is still at the marina, and who knows where Ryder's is as I haven't asked how he got to the airport to meet up with Fallon's jet. So, we walk. I have my gloved pinky finger wrapped around Ryder's. Several families are out, enjoying the crisp Thanksgiving Day weather. A few do double-takes and give me odd looks. I recognize Mrs. Weatherby and her husband. I tip my head down and keep walking, not wanting to be recognized.

It's cold but the sky is clear, and a sliver of a crescent moon is showing in the late afternoon sky. I love it when both the moon and the sun share the sky together. When I was little, I used to tell Hailey how the sun must be lonely being up there all by itself. The moon had stars to keep it company, but the sun lived alone in solitary existence. The first time I saw the moon out on a sunny day, I was so incredibly happy that the sun had a friend and wouldn't be alone anymore. It was the same day I met Ryder for the first time.

The closer we get to the end of the street, the more nervous I become. I train my eyes on Jayson and Julien's house and I try my best to ignore the dark house right next to it. I stumble to a halt when I see the old oak tree. It's lit up, like a beacon calling to me. Did Jayson turn the lights on? Does he know I'm here? I turn to Ryder.

"They promised they wouldn't say anything," he says, reading my thoughts.

I let go of Ryder and take a tentative step forward along the walkway that leads from the street to the front steps of the Jameson's house.

A torrent of memories assails me. This is going to be so much harder than I could possibly have imagined. I loved Jayson. I still do, just not in the way he wants me to. Twelve years of my life were so deeply entangled with his. He's the father of our daughter. He was my first kiss, my first date, my first everything. We lost our virginity to one another. Jayson gave me so much. I don't want to hurt him, but that is exactly what I'm about to do.

I wipe away the tears which are dripping like melting icicles down my cheeks and ring the doorbell. I take a quick look behind me but allow myself only a millisecond to glimpse back at Ryder and Fallon standing like sentinels at the end of the driveway.

A male voice filters through the closed door and I know exactly who it is before it swings opens.

"Hey you," is all I get out before Jayson slams into me and buries his face in the scarf tied around my neck.

"Holy fuck, princess. You're here!"

My hands convulse around him. I don't think I can do this. Why does it hurt so much? I can't breathe. Black spots start to swirl in my vision, so I clutch Jayson tighter trying my best not to pass out.

He lifts his head and I know the moment he spots Ryder and Fallon because I feel his entire body go rigid with tension.

"What the hell is going on? Why the fuck is he here?" I don't know whether he's talking about Ryder or Fallon. Probably Fallon.

"Jayson, can we go inside and talk?"

"Have you been with him the entire time? What the hell, Liz?" Yep, definitely about Fallon. "Why is Ry here?"

"Jay, Mom said the turkey is ready. Time to eat. Who's at the door?"

I spot Julien coming out of the living room into the front foyer. He turns white as a ghost when he sees my face poking over Jayson's shoulder.

"Liz?" I watch as Julien goes from sheet white to flush with anger, his silver eyes flashing with scorn. He aims an almost sneer at me, turns around and walks off. Holy crap. Julien has never been angry with me before.

Jayson tries to pull away and charge down the steps to confront Fallon and Ryder. I yank at his arm to stop him. "Jayson."

He suddenly spins around and lifts me up, smashing his mouth onto mine. Is he trying to prove a point? Rub this kiss in Ryder's and Fallon's faces? A tiny part of me that is still clinging to Old Elizabeth rejoices, wanting a repeat of the night she returned and ran to Jayson then screwed his brains out. But I'm not her anymore.

I wrench my head to the side. "Jayson, stop. We need to talk. Please."

Fallon is holding a fuming Ryder back and I know if I don't get the situation under control—and fast—things are going to detonate. Thankfully, Freda comes to the rescue.

"Jay, Julien said Liz was here?" she says in a question, then rushes forward when she sees me, just like Faith did yesterday.

"Oh my goodness. Look at you! So grown up and so beautiful," she exclaims. "Jay said you weren't going to be able to make it. Come inside. We're about to eat." She notices Ryder struggling against Fallon's hold and her smile falls.

"Jay, go tell Ryder and his friend to come on inside. Your father is carving the turkey."

"No, Mom. Liz and I need to talk. Alone. Start without us," he tells her and grips my hand so hard I wince. He pulls me around the side of the house and toward the forest where our fort is. Ryder and Freda both shout my name, but Jayson doesn't slow down.

"Jayson, you're hurting me," I speak softly because I can tell how angry he is right now. He eases his grip but doesn't let go.

It's easy to see the remains of the fort up ahead since all the trees are barren and have lost their leaves. It's a bit run down, a few pieces of plyboard are broken and faded. Hailey and I would spend hours out here when we were younger—raking the pine needles to create pathways through the forest, collecting things from the creek bed to store in jars, nailing sticks into tree trunks to create ladders to climb. It was also the place where Jayson and I made love for the first time, and those memories are still potent in my mind, like the recollections of first loves usually are.

Jayson goes into the front of the fort and hauls two stumps out, offering one to me. I place a gloved hand to the wood. My dad made these for me and Hailey. Jayson and I sit down at the same time and he hesitantly touches my face with his cold hands. He's wearing a thin shirt and jeans and nothing else, not even shoes.

"Aren't you cold?"

"Where have you been? Why did you run off?"

I swallow. Here we go.

"I've been with Fallon."

"Where, Liz?"

I gnaw on my thumbnail, a nervous habit of mine. "Um, we took his yacht to New York City, and then flew to Iceland, then England, France, Spain, and a few other places."

"Why did you leave me? Why did you leave my bed and disappear? Why did your note say it was a mistake?" Jayson's voice breaks along with my heart. Those icicle tears come back.

"I'm so sorry, Jayson. I shouldn't have done that to you. But I didn't know what to do. I was so scared and lost."

Jayson tries to reach for me, but I resist. "Why won't you let me hold you?"

"Jayson, we can't go back to the way things were between us."

"You came back to me. You remembered and you came back to *me*."

"But I didn't," I cry. "That wasn't me. I wish I could explain it better, but the girl that night wasn't me. That was Old Elizabeth, and she doesn't exist anymore."

"Liz, you're not making any sense. What the

hell has Fallon done to you?" he accuses.

Hearing him blame Fallon raises my hackles and I bite out, "Fallon is a good man. I won't stand by and allow anyone, even you, Jayson, to bad-mouth him."

"What the hell is wrong with you?"

"Jayson, please listen to me. I was messed up after my memories came back. It was like I was two different people. I didn't know what to do. The morning after we were together, I somehow managed to walk to Fallon's frat house. He took me in. He helped me. I owe him so much. Without him, I think I would have crawled into a hole and died. I hated myself for what I did."

I take a deep, calming breath because getting into an argument with Jayson about Fallon will only derail the conversation we need to have. Jayson hates Fallon and vice versa. No amount of expounding on Fallon's good points will change that in Jayson's eyes.

"You hated being with me?" he asks in a pained voice.

I take his hand from my face and grip it between both of mine. I stare into his silver eyes, eyes that used to look at me with love but are now filled with hurt.

"I'm not explaining myself well. There will

never be a time I will ever regret being with you. You were my first love, Jayson. I will always love you. But I'm not *in* love with you."

"You're in love with *Fallon*?"

"It's not what you think. I do love Fallon. Just like I love you and Julien. But the person I'm in love with is Ryder. I want to be with Ryder. I choose Ryder." I'm sweating like mad and my words are coming out choppy, but I said them.

"That shit again? Is this why Ry went off the grid the past week?"

"Yes. He's been with me and Fallon."

"I don't understand," Jayson exclaims and stands up to pace in front of me. "You love me and then, *poof*! No memory, so you don't love me anymore; you say you love Ryder. Not to mention I found out you kissed Julien—twice. Then when you get your memories back, you come running to me. You fuck me," —I cringe at his crass words— "you tell me you love me after we screw each other for hours, then you run away and go straight to Fallon, who by the way, you now say you love too. Am I missing anything, because Jesus Christ, Liz, that all sounds like crazy bullshit and makes you nothing but a whore."

I jerk back in horrified shock at him calling me a whore. Without thinking, my hand snakes out and slaps Jayson across the face, the sound echoing between the trees. We both freeze in shock, staring wide-eyed at each other.

"I guess I deserve that," he says, rubbing his cheek where I slapped him. It's already showing the red imprint of my hand.

I'm still livid. "You bet your ass you do!"

"Well, can you blame me?" he yells back. "This is confusing as fuck. You came back *to me*, Liz. You fucked me like the world would end. I had bite marks and scratches to prove that night was real. You fell asleep in my arms and told me that you loved me. I woke up to a note. A fucking note saying that everything that happened between us that night was a mistake!"

A single tear slithers down his red cheek like a raindrop falling down a windowpane. I grab his icy hands to pull myself up from the log seat. We're both breathing hard, our dual breaths creating mist that floats away in the cold winter air.

"I'm so sorry about everything. I've fucked things up so badly. You deserve better. I don't know how else to explain myself or justify what happened. I will always love you. We created Elizabeth Ann from our love. But I'm not coming back to you. I'm in love with Ryder. *I choose Ryder*," I repeat, hoping he finally understands.

Jayson grabs my wrists so hard I know I'll have bruises tomorrow. "No, princess, you came back to me."

"Jayson, will you please listen to me? I don't want to hurt you, but you need to understand that I'm not coming back to you."

He continues on like I hadn't spoken. "And I told you that night in the hospital that I would never stop fighting for you. We belong together. You. Are. *Mine*."

Jayson backs me up against the tree next to the opening of the fort; the same tree he and Julien hung upside down on when I saw them for the first time thirteen years ago. Two snaggle-toothed brown-haired boys that I called my princes. My breath gets knocked out of me from the force of my back hitting the trunk and it takes me a second to get my lungs working again.

"Jayson, please stop," I wheeze out.

He pulls down my bottom lip with his thumb, the pupils of his metallic eyes narrowing to a pinprick.

"These lips belong to me, just like your body

and your love belong to me. There isn't a single part of you that hasn't felt my touch. You remembered and you came back."

"I'm not that girl anymore, Jayson. And you haven't listened to a word I've said. I love Ryder!"

"We'll see about that," he replies angrily, pressing into me harder and making it difficult to move.

Before me is the boy I grew up and who I know better than most anyone, other than Ryder and Julien. Jayson panics and reacts by acting out in the heat of the moment without thinking. It's just like when Ryder told Jayson and Julien his feelings for me. Jayson panicked and came straight to me, declaring his love. He felt like he had to be the first one to stake a claim on me. Or the night at the bonfire in eleventh grade when I was jealous over Ryder's attention toward Maria, and Jayson tried to drunkenly take me against a tree next to the abandoned warehouse because he felt insecure. Or every time he tried to push me into accepting that I was his girlfriend even though my amnesia left me with no memories of us being together that way.

"Elizabeth!" Ryder's voice calls from the edge of the forest as he, Fallon, and Julien quickly approach. Jayson steps away from me and the suddenness of it has me falling to the ground. Within seconds Ryder is sliding across the leaf-littered ground, catching me in his arms.

"Don't you touch her again," he snaps at Jayson just as Jayson is crouching down to help lift me up.

"Liz, baby, I'm sorry," Jayson garbles out like he's coming out of a trance.

"Liz, you alright?" Julien asks me, coming into my line of sight as he shoves Jayson back.

Fallon lunges forward but I'm able to grab the bottom of the leg of his jeans to stop him from charging Julien to attack Jayson.

"I'm fine. I just lost my balance."

"The fuck you did," Fallon snarls.

Ryder helps me to stand back up. The four boys square off. Jayson and Julien on one side, Ryder and Fallon on the other, with me in the middle.

I've had enough. Nothing more will get resolved today between the five of us.

"Please apologize to Freda. I didn't mean to ruin your Thanksgiving dinner. We all need to sit down and talk soon. I have a lot of explaining to do and apologies to give. I owe both of you apologies," I tell Jayson and Julien.

"I don't want your damn apologies, Liz," Julien angrily hurls at me. "You lied to me. You promised you wouldn't leave again, and you lied."

"You don't know what you're talking about," Ryder tells him.

I open my mouth to speak but Julien shuts me down. "I'm not interested in anything you have to say right now. Come on, Jay. Mom and Dad are waiting for us and dinner is getting cold. Fallon, I don't know how you factor into everything, but if it wasn't for this shit-show, I would say it's good to see you."

Fallon acknowledges Julien with a chin jerk, his focus never leaving Jayson.

Jayson shoulders past Ryder and Fallon and cups my face with his cold hands. He bends down to my ear and whispers, "It will never be over between us, princess."

A cold shiver makes its way down my back as I remember my nightmare from that first night I was on Fallon's yacht. I recall Old Elizabeth telling me, *"You will never find true happiness with Ryder. You're deluding yourself if you think you can. Jayson will never let me go."*

Jayson turns back around and shifts his attention from me to Ryder. He takes a deep breath and I watch as Jayson's entire body language changes. "Heard you had a good trip. Can't wait to hear about it. Welcome back." He holds his fist out to Ryder for a bump.

What the hell? The whiplash caused by Jayson's sudden change of demeanor has me off-balance.

Ryder knocks his fist to Jayson's like they weren't about to come to blows five minutes ago. "Good to be back."

"Why don't we all meet up at Ruby's tomorrow for lunch?" Jayson suggests. "You can come too, fuckwad," he tells Fallon.

"Wouldn't miss it, dickhole," Fallon replies.

And then, like nothing ever happened, the boys start chatting away, leaving me very much perplexed on what the hell is going on. The only exception is Fallon. He sticks close by me watching Jayson. Ryder wraps his arm around my waist and pulls me to his side as we walk with the rest of the group back toward the house.

"Jules, where's Elijah?" Ryder asks him.

"We broke up."

What? Then I remember. Elijah was going to propose today.

"What happened, Julien?" I reach for his hand, concerned for my best friend.

Julien jerks away from my touch as if I threw acid on his skin and ignores me. Instead, he continues talking to Ryder and Fallon. "You guys want to come in for a bit?"

"Nah, man. Thanks though, but we need to head back."

Jayson's eyes laser back to me. "Liz staying at your house, then?"

"Yeah. Fal, too. We'll head back to campus on Saturday."

Fallon leans over to whisper in my ear, "Have you had enough of this kumbaya bullshit yet?" I nod yes. "Come on, kitten. Let's get out of here. You guys can continue to shoot the shit. I'm taking kitten with me," he tells Ryder.

Ryder squeezes me tighter to his side as Jayson stares holes into me. "Hold up, man. We're coming," Ryder tells Fallon.

And then I see it. The thing I have adamantly avoided. I made sure to fix my gaze away from it when I walked up to Jayson's front door. I made sure to look away from it when Jayson dragged me into the forest. But I can't avoid it anymore. My childhood home stands before me like a haunted house of horrors. It's dark inside, curtains closed. It looks old and decrepit, a twisted shell of the warm, welcoming home of my memories.

"Baby, look at me," Ryder begs, but I can't. I can't tear my eyes away from it.

"Fuck," I hear someone say.

"Get Liz out of here."

I forcibly remove Ryder's hold on my waist. "No." I walk up to the back patio steps. I feel so small standing there, like a lost soul staring up at the gates of Hell.

"Mom said no one has lived here. It's been locked up and empty for a while," Jayson informs me.

I trail my fingers along the deck railing. Hailey and I would come out here and lie in the sun during the summers. I never was able to get a proper tan no matter how long we stayed out here. Jayson and I would recline together on one of the loungers and watch the night sky or we would come out here when it rained. I always loved the sound of the rain hitting the deck flooring, or the earthy scent of the air after a storm.

I press my palms flat against the back door. *He* ran out through this door that night. This is the door *He* used to escape after killing my family and stabbing me. *He* destroyed my life then fled. *He* took my family from me. How is any of that fair? I pound my closed fists against the door and the glass panes rattle. I turn around to see wide-eyed faces standing at the bottom of the steps not knowing what to do. Except for Fallon. The tips of his lips curve up. He understands what I need.

"Look down and to the right, kitten."

I do as he says. There's an old, weathered baseball bat lying on the deck. I remember it. It belonged to this little boy, Danny, that lived down the street. Hailey would sometimes babysit him at our house on the weekend. He must have left it here. I strip my gloves off and bend over and pick it up. The metal of the handle is cold to the touch. It's covered in dirt and the painted letters of the brand name are mostly worn off. I test its weight then fist the handle with both hands and swing with all my might. Two glass panels on the back door explode and shatter into diamonds.

"Jesus Christ, Liz! What are you doing?" Julien yelps.

"Elizabeth, stop," Ryder says next.

Fallon tells them, "She needs to do this. Let her."

I swing the bat again. More glass breaks, tiny shards collecting on my shoes and leggings like snowflakes.

I tune out the male arguments behind me knowing Fallon will keep Ryder, Jayson, and Julien away. I swing again at the back door. And again. And again. The doorknob flies off and I kick the door in, holding the bat like a broadsword. I step inside and almost vomit at the musty smell that accosts me.

I yell over my shoulder, "Stay out!" and then I disappear inside the darkness.

Chapter 16

Elizabeth

It takes a minute for my eyes to adjust but when they do, I scan my surroundings. Everything looks the same as I remember. It's as if the house has turned into a museum where each room is a diorama or an exact replica of itself from two years ago. I'm in the kitchen. Instead of the putrid, stale smell of the interior air, my senses smell the aroma of the apple crumb muffins Mom used to bake. I see the kitchen island where Hailey and I would sit and laugh while Mom puttered away cooking. I notice that there are only three chairs instead of four at the kitchen table. I was tied to the fourth chair. I broke it trying to escape from *Him*. I scan the floor expecting to see pieces of broken wood scattered across the tile, but there's nothing. It's like the events of that night never took place right where I'm now standing.

My gaze tracks to the pantry door, which is open and empty. My unfocused eyes watch in a trance as *He* pulls Hailey out of it by her hair and drags her limp body across the floor. I squeeze my eyes tightly shut trying not to see what comes next. If I don't open my eyes, then I won't see what *He* does to Hailey. But I still see it. I still hear it. I hear her dying gasps as he plunges his knife into her. I hear his grunts as he savagely assaults her in front of me. I hear him screaming at me to look, to see. I still don't understand what he meant, and not knowing is driving me mad. What did he want me to see so badly? Why did he keep saying those words to me?

My eyes fly open. I'm at the living room entrance. There's no more carpet on the floor. As if removing the carpet would prevent me from seeing the large pool of blood spreading out around the prone bodies of my parents. Their dead eyes locked on me while I was tied to that chair.

I slowly make my way down the short hallway to the music room. It's empty. Where did all my dad's instruments go? I walk up the stairs to my old room. The door is already open. The glow of the lights from the tree outside my bedroom window casts shadows along the walls. I almost expect to see Jayson climbing through my window and I imagine him doing just that. Despite our recent fight, I smile at the memory.

I walk through the jack-and-jill bathroom that connects my room to Hailey's. I can feel Hailey's hands finger-comb through my hair as she uses the heated straightener to smooth out my messy blond mane for prom. How she was able to transform my unruly hair into a sleek waterfall of platinum tresses is a miracle. It took her over an hour to fix my hair that night. I don't recall how many times she burned her fingers. I just remember us laughing while she placed red flower clips that matched the color of my prom dress throughout my hair.

I look at my reflection in the bathroom mirror and remember seeing Hailey's bruises for the first time as she got out of the shower. There is no shower curtain in here anymore, but I can still picture that morning as if was yesterday. I should have pushed her harder to talk to me. I shouldn't have accepted her easy excuses about how she got the bruises and the burn mark. If I just would have opened my eyes, my sister would still be here with me now. *Open your eyes, Elizabeth.* I failed Hailey in so many ways. I failed so many people, not just my little sister but also my parents, my daughter, my three best friends. Christ almighty, being back in this house is devastating.

I leave the bathroom and walk into Hailey's adjoining bedroom. Her bed is still here, the mattress stripped and bare. I climb on top of it and lay down. I close my eyes and I hear Hailey's soft, sweet voice as she reads me one of her poems.

"I miss you so much, Hales. I'm so sorry. Please forgive me," I weep into the mattress. I don't fight it anymore. I give in and allow myself to feel everything, to remember everything. It hurts so goddamn much. The pain and the loss. I cry for my family and for myself. I cry for all the things I have lost. And as I expunge all of the desolation and loss in the form of wracking tears, something new weaves its way inside of me. It's a feeling of calm and of hope. It's a feeling of a new beginning in which my past is a part of me but is no longer an insurmountable burden.

Because, for the first time since that night or the night that my memories came back, the pain is no match for all of the love and laughter this house still holds. My life has been blessed with love. I had two wonderful parents who showed me every day how much they loved me. I had a kickass sister who I adored and who always had my back. Mom, Dad, and Hailey are still with me. I can feel them every day. I can feel their love. I have Jayson, Julien, and Ryder. My three best friends. My three princes. I have Ryder's love and Fallon's friendship. I will fight to fix my friendships with Jayson, Julien, Elijah, Meredith, and Trevor. I have Freda, Mitch, Faith, Randy, Brea, and Jamie. And even though I haven't spoken to them in over a month, I know I have Daniel and Drew as well. And now, I have myself too. My journey with Fallon helped to heal most of what was broken inside of me. Being back in this house, I realize that love will always conquer hate. And my life is filled with so much love.

I take a deep breath and wipe my eyes with the sleeve of my coat. I startle a little when I notice Fallon standing in the doorway.

"I told them to stay out for a second while I came in to see how you were doing. I'm amazed they didn't put up much of a fight. I figure we only have about a minute before they all barge inside."

I half-heartedly chuckle. "I'm sure you're right."

Fallon eases himself down beside me on the bed and presses his forehead to mine.

"You okay, kitten?"

"I think so. Actually, yes. I am okay," I sniffle, then make a decision. "Fallon, I want to buy the house. I want to fix it up. Make it a good place for another family to live in. This was a great house to grow up in. It needs to be filled with children and laughter again."

"I'll make a call."

"I'm paying for it with my trust money."

"We can discuss that later." Of course he would say that.

"I'm serious, Fallon."

"I know, kitten," he says softly.

A random thought pops into my head. I'm emotionally exhausted from this whole day; first, dealing with Jayson, and then being back in this house. I'm no longer upset with Jayson for how he reacted when we talked. It's my fault things are so confusing and messed up between us. He has every right to be angry with what I did. But right now, I want to tune everything out for a few hours. I need some time to regroup my thoughts.

"They used to have midnight bowling open on Thanksgiving night at Bowl-O-Rama. Want to get out of here and enjoy the rest of Thanksgiving?"

"Whatever you want."

I give a tentative smile and Fallon smiles back. "Let's get your back door boarded up first."

"Sorry about that. I went a little Terminator

on it."

"That was pretty fucking righteous watching you bust it down. If I said it turned me on and I got a huge boner, would you threaten to knee me in the balls again?"

For the first time today, I laugh out loud. "No, your balls are safe from my knee. I would say you need therapy."

"You and me both, kitten."

"I'm already in therapy. Want to join me?"

Fallon doesn't answer. Instead, he hugs me.

I feel the bed dip and two more strong arms come around me. I don't have to see who it is to know that it's Ryder. His gorgeous masculine scent envelops me as much as his arms do. Ryder kisses the top of my right shoulder then rests his chin on it.

Jayson comes through the bedroom door next and squats down on his haunches in front of me. He takes my hands in his and holds on. Julien doesn't come inside to join us. He's standing in the hallway looking unsure.

I scan Hailey's room one last time. I've done what I needed to do. I slowly stand and walk downstairs, the guys trailing behind me. When I reach the kitchen, I turn around one last time and say goodbye. As I walk away, I leave Old Elizabeth behind for good.

Chapter 17

Jayson

"Jules, stop being a pussy and come to lunch."

Julien pokes his head out of the open fridge and glowers at me. "I'm not being a pussy. I'm pissed. There's a difference. And why do you want to go so damn bad? You hate Fallon."

"Not going for Fallon."

Jules crosses his arms and pouts like a petulant five-year-old. "She left us. She promised me she would never leave again, and she left. I'm not ready to forgive her."

I stayed up all night thinking about what Liz said. She thought I wasn't paying attention, but I heard every damn word that came out of her gorgeous mouth. I still think it's bullshit. I don't know what voodoo Fallon has over her, but clearly his claws have dug deep into my girl. I'm the one who'll have to clip them. She can try and convince herself that night was a mistake, that she wants to be with Ryder, but I know it's all a lie. Liz is just scared. I need to prove to her that she can trust me, that I am the man who will protect her heart and love her for the rest of her life. My plan had been working too—like that night in the hospital when she thought I was going to kiss her, or when I gave her the heart pendant of our daughter. She kissed me as we sat on the kitchen floor. When her memories came back, I was the one she ran to, the one she couldn't get enough of. My Liz was back.

"Fine, Jules, have it your way. If you change your mind, you know where we'll be."

I grab my keys and wallet and head out to my truck. I look over at her house. It took us an hour to board up the back door yesterday. When we were done, Liz left with Ryder and Fallon. Julien and I went back home where we got questioned by our parents about Liz for the rest of the evening. It wasn't fun. This Thanksgiving sucked ass. To top it all off, I was woken up this morning by a work crew who came and installed a new back door and frame at Liz's house. I had only gotten a couple hours of sleep because I couldn't stop thinking about her. It kind of freaked me out seeing her so out of control, wielding the bat like a sledgehammer and then kicking the door in. Liz never acted like that before. She also never used to hit people, but I've been the recipient of her punches and slaps twice now; once when I barged into her apartment, and then yesterday.

When I park my truck in front of Ruby's, I see Liz through the front glass window. She has her hair up in one of her favorite messy buns. I used to take great pleasure in pulling out her hair band, mesmerized by how her pale blond locks fell around her shoulders. I could spend hours threading my fingers through her silken hair. The older she gets, the more beautiful she becomes. Sometimes it hurts to look at her, she is that stunning. I watch as Ryder leans over and kisses Liz, and my teeth clench. Those should be my lips on hers, not his. Then Fallon says something that has Liz throwing her head back and laughing. It's impossible not to notice the special dynamic between the three of them. It's like what she, Julien, and I used to have. That special bond, the closeness, the familiarity. I miss it. I miss her. She was my sunshine and I've been stuck in the darkness for far too long. It's time I open the curtains to let the light back in. It's time I got my girl back.

I open the diner door and head to their booth. Liz is the first to see me and her smile does wonders to brighten my mood. It's as if our fight yesterday never happened. She taps Ryder on his arm, and he stands up so she can slide out of the booth.

She smiles at me. "I'm so glad you're here."

"Wouldn't miss seeing you for the world. Besides, it was my idea," I reply and press a lingering kiss to her cheek, causing her to blush. Fallon coughs out an "asshole" under his breath beside me.

"Is Julien coming?" I shake my head no and her smile falls. "Oh."

"Don't worry, princess. He'll come around. Have you ordered yet?"

"We were waiting for you."

Liz slides back in the booth and I quickly follow, leaving Ryder standing there, then having to sit across from us with Fallon, where he belongs.

"What's up, Ry?" I casually throw his way. I catch the muscle twitch in his cheek.

"Hey, man."

"What's up, fucker," Fallon quips and opens a menu. I feel Liz's leg move past mine under the table as she kicks Fallon in the shin and gives him a look that says to behave.

"This is almost like old times," I comment and throw my arm behind Liz on the back of the seat.

"I was thinking the same thing," she replies. "Do you remember that waitress who used to work here? The one who hated us because we were always throwing food or shooting spit-balls at each other?"

Ryder and I both chuckle at the memory. Fallon, however, just stares at Liz with a smirk across his face. He has always been obsessed with her. It's creepy.

My fingers graze the back of her neck and they touch something delicate and metallic. She's wearing the locket necklace I gave her in remembrance of our daughter. And just like that, my mood sours.

"Jayson, what's wrong?" Liz whispers near my ear. She could always sense my moods.

I slip my finger under the chain and lift her locket out from beneath her sweater, folding my fingers around it.

"I miss her too," Liz says.

"I passed by Kinlay Park the other day. The one we used to play at as kids. I found myself sitting in my truck watching the parents and their kids run around. I could perfectly picture me pushing Elizabeth Ann in the tiny swing. You know the one that has those leg holes in it? I could hear her giggles as she begged me to push her higher."

Liz gives me her sweet smile. "You paint a beautiful picture, Jayson. Perhaps we can tell her that story when we visit her grave next month. I've already bought a couple of books I want to read to her."

I bring the locket up to my lips and press a kiss to it. Liz's breath hitches and tears pile up around her green irises. Our moment is broken when the waiter comes over—some high school kid—and takes our order. Fallon is glowering at me as he clips off his order to the kid. Ryder's expression is inscrutable. I tuck Liz's necklace back under her sweater, my gaze never faltering from the stare-down with the two men across from me.

The waiter asks Liz what she wants. She asks for a large basket of fries and a side bowl of mustard.

"You know that stuff ain't gluten-free, kitten," Fallon remarks about the fries.

"I'm not allergic to gluten like I am dairy. I just prefer to eat GF. And nothing beats Ruby's steak fries."

I lean closer to Liz so that only she can hear me. "Mom and Dad would really like to see you. Do you think you have time to stop by today? I also think it's time to tell them about Elizabeth Ann."

"It's okay to talk about it in front of Fallon. He knows." Why the fuck does that not surprise me?

"I know what?"

"About our daughter," she replies, then asks Ryder, "Do you mind if I take a couple of hours after lunch and go back with Jayson? It's time we tell his parents about their granddaughter."

"Why don't we come with you?" Fallon interjects.

"Why don't you not," I tell him. "This is a personal matter between me and Liz."

"I have to agree, Fallon. Would you mind?" she asks Ryder again.

"Of course not, sweetheart," Ryder tells her.

Fallon wiggles his phone. "Got a text from a friend. They're doing a race tonight at the Fields. We're going."

Liz bounces in her seat. "That would be awesome! How about we all go? Except it won't be the same without you racing," Liz says to Ry, reaching across the table and linking her hand with his. Luck is on my side; the waiter comes back with our food meaning Liz has to let go of

Ryder's hand.

"Is that good?" Fallon asks her as Liz eagerly dips a fry in her spicy mustard.

"Here," she offers, holding a fry across the table and dripping mustard all over the Formica. Fallon leans over and bites it from her fingertips.

"Not too bad," he munches. "Now mayo, that's the thing."

That surprises me. "You like mayo on your fries?"

"Yeah. Why?"

"Jayson does too," Liz answers.

"Huh," is all Fallon says and digs into his burger.

"Do you think Julien would be willing to come with us tonight to the Fields?"

"I don't know, Liz. We can ask him when we get home. He should be there."

"He's really upset at me."

"You know he loves you, Liz."

"I know. It's just that this is the first time Julien has ever been this angry with me. It makes my universe feel off-kilter."

"Once you talk to him, babe, everything will work out." This time Ryder reaches over and takes Liz's hand. Lunch can't be over soon enough for me. At least afterward, I'll have Liz for a few hours without Ry and Fallon hovering.

Chapter 18

Julien

Liz's voice filters upstairs to where I'm resting on my bed reading a magazine on my tablet. I want so badly to go downstairs and see her, to be in her presence. But I'm still too goddamn mad.

"Jules, get your ass down here. Family meeting," Jay calls up to me. If it turns out he's trying to do an intervention to make me talk to her, I'll turn around and leave.

"Jules!"

"Coming!" Shithead, I mentally add. I toss my tablet on the bed and stomp downstairs. Liz is standing at the bottom and she looks up at me. Christ, why does she have to look so fucking innocent? And beautiful?

"Hi," she says, verdant eyes imploring me for a hint of compassion or forgiveness. I slow at the bottom step, my hesitation ticking me off, then I walk on by. I feel more than hear her dejected sigh.

"What's up?" I ask when I see Mom and Dad waiting with curiosity on the couch.

"Liz and I are going to tell them," Jay says to me.

Oh. *Oh*! Oh shit. Those eight little words have my anger at Liz evaporating faster than a raindrop in the Sahara Desert. With Jay being my twin, and with my very close relationship with Liz, I always thought of Elizabeth Ann as mine almost as much as she was Jay's. I felt the loss of her nearly as much as he did. I'm as invested in this conversation as they both are.

"Tell us what?" Dad asks.

Liz walks over next to Jay, and they clasp hands, united.

"Are you getting married?" Mom shrieks, looking happier than I have ever seen her. I go over and sit by Mom, knowing that the news she's about to receive is going to break her heart.

"No, Mom. We're not getting married. There's something we need to talk to you about and it's going to be hard for you to hear. I know you both have so many questions for Liz and you want to spend time with her, but this can't wait. Just bear with us, alright?"

Jay grabs one of the armchairs and moves it directly in front of our parents. He sits and pulls Liz down to sit on his lap. She's stiff as a board and looks uncomfortable, but she doesn't get up.

"We've already told you most of what happened to Liz. How she was in Seattle with a distant cousin; how she was in a coma for two months, and then how she had no memory when she woke up. You also know that her memory recently did come back."

Mom nods her head. "Yes. You told us about that. Lizzie, we are so sorry sweetheart. We wanted to come see you as soon as we heard you were back, but..." She trails off, not wanting to blatantly throw her two sons under the bus.

"Jules and I wouldn't let you," Jay finishes. "A lot of stuff has happened since August. Liz ended up in the hospital, and—"

Mom cuts him off. "Why didn't you tell us? Were you hurt or sick, honey?"

"No, ma'am. When my memory was trying to return, I was having these blackout spells. One was really bad and that's how I wound up in the hospital." She angles her face back to look at Jay. "Jay found me in the library. He was there when it happened."

Jay kisses her temple, and she finally relaxes and leans back into him.

"We found out something while she was in the hospital," Jay says.

"A nurse came into my room and saw one of my scars. It's on my stomach. I always thought it was from that night. But it wasn't."

Mom gasps loudly and covers her mouth. Dad puts his hand on her knee, but I can see his eyes hardening. Has he figured it out? Liz and Jay start talking quickly now, their sentences running into each other's, as they rush to get it all out.

"I didn't know what the nurse was going on about. She kept talking about C-sections and asking me about my baby."

"Daniel, the cousin who had been caring for Liz in Seattle, confirmed everything. Liz had a baby."

"*We* had a baby. A girl. She was Jayson's and mine."

Mom is openly sobbing now and tries to stand up, but Dad pulls her back down. "You said *had*," he states.

"Did you give her up for adoption? Where is

she? Where's our grandbaby?"

"Mom, she's gone. She didn't make it." Jay's voice breaks when he says it. Liz has tears silently falling down her cheeks. God, even I'm about to lose it.

Dad's lower lip quivers and it about breaks me. I have never seen him cry, not once. Dad and I are trying hard to console Mom who has collapsed against Dad's side and is weeping uncontrollably. Dad struggles to speak. "What happened to her?"

"Daniel said that I was already pregnant when I was attacked. The trauma was too much, and she died in utero weeks later. I developed an infection and they had to do an emergency C-section to get her out. I was still in a coma when all of this happened. I never got to see her. I never got to hold her. They named her Elizabeth Ann and buried her in Seattle."

"Ann, like your mom," Freda whispers.

"I need a minute," Dad says gruffly and walks out the front door.

Liz pulls Jay out of the chair so they can sit on the other side of Mom in the space where Dad had been sitting.

Liz takes Mom's hands, trying to provide her some comfort. "Freda, we're going to go visit her grave in Seattle over Christmas break. You and Mitch are more than welcome to come with us. Jayson and I would like to have you both there."

Mom sniffles and nods her head emphatically. "Yes. Yes, I would like that very much. Oh, Lizzie. I'm so incredibly sorry. You have been through so much. You're such a strong girl. Ann and John would be so very proud of you, honey." Mom crushes Liz in a motherly embrace and rocks her back and forth.

"Do you want me to go find Dad?" I ask.

"No, baby. Let him have his time." She wipes her face dry. "I think we all need a cup of hot tea. If you'll excuse me." Mom kisses me, Liz, and Jay, on the tops of our heads and quickly exits into the kitchen.

Liz puffs up her cheeks and blows out a huff of air. "That was really rough."

Jay wraps his arm around Liz and looks over at me. "At least now they know."

"I hate just springing it on them like that. The loss of our daughter still hits me hard every single day. I can only imagine what they must be feeling right now."

Jay brings Liz's head to cradle in his shoulder and rub circles on the back of her neck. "Me, too, babe."

Wanting to give them some privacy, I shuffle off the couch. "I'll go check on Mom."

"Julien. I'm sorry I hurt you by leaving. I was always going to come back. I know I promised I would never leave you. I was in a messed-up place and I needed to get myself straightened out."

I hunch my shoulders. "You did hurt me, Liz."

"I know and I'm sorry. The night my memory came back—it was all so fucked up."

"I'm not going to ask what that means. We can talk more once we get back to CU."

"We will?" she asks, her face full of hope. "I've missed you. Both of you."

"We've missed you too, princess," Jay tells her while lifting her face up to his. He leans in like he's about to kiss her, but she pulls back slightly and turns her face so that his lips meet her cheek.

I don't know what is going on with everyone, but I guess I'll have to wait until we get back to CU to find out. Jay told me and our parents that he and Liz were back together. He said that as soon as Liz regained her memories, she came back to him, just like he and Elijah predicted. That surely didn't look the case yesterday when Ryder and Fallon were here. It looked to me like she was with Ryder, and then I got even more confused when I saw how she acted with Fallon.

Jay thumps me on the shoulder. "We're going to the Fields later. Want to come?"

"Might as well," I answer. I have nothing better to do and hanging out with Ry is always fun. Add Fallon to the mix, and tonight should be hellraising.

Before I'm able to go check on Mom, she comes out holding a tray with several steaming cups of tea. At the same moment, Dad walks back inside. His eyes are red and his face blotchy, but we pretend not to see it. We all spend the next hour huddled together on the couch listening to Mom talk Liz's ear off. And during that hour, if my knee somehow finds its way to press against Liz's and my fingers brush up against her wrist, we never acknowledge it.

Elizabeth

"Holy moly! This place is packed!" I exclaim as Jayson parks his truck along a field furrow.

Jayson offered to drive us to the Fields. Julien is sitting shotgun in the passenger seat up front while I'm in the middle of a Ryder-Fallon burrito in the back. I've been thumb-wrestling the both of them and have beaten Ryder four times with my left hand and Fallon seven times with my right hand. Julien remained silent the entire time, but Jayson was uncharacteristically chatty. He's spent the entire drive asking me questions about my trip with Fallon and Ryder. As soon as we turned onto the dirt road that led up to the Fields, I was astonished at how many people were here. When we would come out to watch Ryder, there would be maybe a hundred people. Tonight, it was more than double that amount.

Julien says something to Jayson and then hops out of the truck and walks off.

Jayson notices my crestfallen face. "He's getting there."

I hope so. Having Julien not only mad at me, but also not talking to me is torture.

Someone shouts Fallon's name. "Looks like a lot of us are here tonight," he says, tilting his head at several guys we used to know from school. I guess that's why it's so busy tonight. All the college kids are back home on break on top of the high school kids who come out here anyway. "I'll catch up with you guys in a minute," Fallon tells us and saunters off toward a group of guys.

The revving of car engines coming up the dirt road has me looking around. Two identical Mustang GT500s, both blue with white stripes down the middle, and a cherry red Camaro, make their way toward the track. The Camaro slows down to a crawl next to us, but the dark-tinted windows aren't enough to hide Marshall's scowling face as he sneers at me. He guns the engine, causing me to jump, and spins his back wheels so that they pepper my legs with dirt and small rocks. Thankfully, I'm wearing jeans, boots, and a long winter coat.

"What the fuck, asshole!" Jayson yells at the Camaro's taillights as it drives away.

"Babe, are you okay?" Ryder asks as I wipe the dirt off my boots with my gloves.

Seeing Marshall has me wanting to get amnesia again. I hate him with the passion of a thousand suns. Marshall went to Highland High with Fallon and Elijah, but caused a lot of problems for me, Jayson, Julien, and Ryder. When Marshall played on the Highland High soccer team, he purposely tripped Julien and rammed his cleats into Julien's calf, shredding it to pieces. Julien was in PT for months afterward and still has scars. Marshall also tried to pick a fight with Julien at one of Fallon's high school parties by saying some very nasty things about me. That night ended with everyone getting into a knockdown fistfight. Jayson beat Marshall so badly that he was in the hospital for a couple of days. Then, Marshall tried to run Ryder off the track here at the Fields during a race. That night, it was me who punched Marshall in the face and broke his nose. If it weren't for Fallon jumping in, Marshall would have punched me back. Seeing him here, tonight, does not bode well for our evening. However, I'm not the timid, meek Elizabeth anymore. I can hold my own against that douchetwat.

"It was Marshall," I say with a small growl.

Jayson huffs out a breath of disbelief. "You've got to be fucking kidding me? Out of all the nights."

"Just ignore him. He's not going to ruin our evening."

"Once he finds out that Fallon is here, he won't try anything," Ryder surmises, tucking his hand in mine.

I reach for Jayson to get his attention. "Do you think we should find Julien and warn him?"

"Yeah. Yeah, you're right. I'll go find him."

"Elizabeth, we can leave. We don't have to stay. I know Marshall is a sore spot for you."

I love how Ryder always tries to protect me. I crook my finger at him to get him to bend down. "I love you," I whisper then tiptoe up and kiss his lips. Our skin is cold, but our breaths are warm and the contrast between the two causes tingles to erupt across my cheeks. I swipe my tongue against his one last time and drop down.

Ryder's eyes are glassy and hooded. "You better be glad we are in an open, public place right now."

I wink at him and giggle, giving him a silent promise of more to come later tonight. A familiar profile catches my eye. "Is that Elijah?"

Ryder turns to look where I'm pointing. "Crap, it is. Jules is going to shit a brick."

"Do you know why they broke up?"

Ryder won't directly look at me. "Yes, I do, but it's something you need to talk with Jules about."

Well, that's cryptic and worrying. And impossible at the moment since Julien refuses to talk to me. I take out my phone and type.

Me: On your left.

I watch as Elijah takes his phone out, looks at the screen, then looks to his left. He finally spots me after a few seconds.

Elijah: Ha, ha. I guess that means I have America's ass.

Me: The man next to me owns that title <wink emoji> Thought you'd like the Avengers reference. Coming over.

"You're back!" Elijah's grin splits his face as Ryder and I walk over.

I run the rest of the way into his open arms and am lifted in a huge bear hug. "I am back. I'm sorry I left. I have a lot to tell you. But it looks like you have a lot to tell me too."

"Is he here?"

Ryder cuffs his shoulder in greeting. "Yeah, man."

Elijah sets me back down and kisses my cheek. "I knew we'd run into each other eventually. We do go to the same college and live in the same county. So, when did you get back?"

"We arrived the day before Thanksgiving."

"We?"

"Fallon flew Ryder out to meet us in Barcelona. He stayed for the rest of the trip," I happily reply, hugging myself to Ryder's side.

"Wait. I thought Jay said—" Elijah shuts up when his gaze flicks to Ryder.

"We so need to talk," I tell Elijah. "Ryder, do you mind?"

"I'll go hang with Fal while you guys catch up." He gives me a quick peck and I swat his butt as he walks away. Yep, my man definitely has a world-class ass.

"Are you back with Ryder or still with Ryder? Your life is very confusing sometimes, Liz."

"Don't I know it. I'll give you the condensed version. Yes, my memory came back. Yes, I did something with Jayson that I'm not proud of, but something that is not up for discussion at any time now or in the future. I was in a messed-up place. Yes, I went off with Fallon. He helped me figure things out. No, I'm not back with Jayson. I love Ryder. I'm with Ryder. Hopefully, one day, I will drop down on my knee and ask that man to marry me." I can do unconventional.

Elijah startles out a cough and I realize what I just said. "Shit, Elijah. I'm sorry. I wasn't thinking." Yesterday, Elijah had planned on proposing to Julien.

"It's fine. I wish things were different."

A few people walk by us, one guy in particular gives me a long look. "Hey, isn't that—" I hear him say to the girl next to him. I won't be made to feel like a sideshow freak. Our town is not that big, and what happened to me and my family wasn't that long ago. There are bound to be people here tonight that will recognize me.

"How can so much change in four weeks? What happened between you and Julien?"

Elijah pulls me to a more secluded spot between two cars. "Please don't take this the wrong way, but things between Jules and me started going downhill after you came back."

"I don't understand," I say, shocked. I'm the reason they broke up?

"Liz, I'm not laying blame on you. Julien had been in a bad place for a while. After you disappeared at the end of senior year, it took everything I had to keep him from sinking into the same dark place Jay went to. Then when you came back, all Julien wanted to do was spend time with you. I got shoved to the side. Our relationship hasn't been a priority to him for a while now."

"Elijah, I don't know what to say. Julien loves you so much, you know that."

"He lost it when you went off with Fallon.

Nothing I did helped and all we did was fight. You of all people know how much I love Jules, but I feel like I've given up my life and my dreams just to take care of him these past two years. I can't do that anymore. He has to want to be with me, not just need me because I'm convenient and there to help pick up the pieces for him."

I throw my arms around his neck. "I will fix this. I promise I will."

"Liz, you can't always fix what's broken. He needs to show me that I matter. That he loves me enough to put me first. It's up to him, not you."

I know I hurt Julien, but right now, I want to kick him for being such a stupid jackass.

"Son, the races are about to start," a man's deep voice booms behind us. I lift my face from Elijah's shoulder. It's Elijah's dad.

"Hey, Dad. You remember Liz?"

His dad gives me a visual perusal and I notice his lips thin into a hard line of worry. Elijah's dad used to be a deputy for our county. He would come out to help supervise the races at the Fields, and make sure that things didn't get out of control or too rowdy. From the sheriff's badge clipped to his front, it seems Mr. Barnes is no longer a deputy.

"Yes, I remember Liz. How are you, sweetheart?" By the tone of his voice, I know he's referring to more than just how I feel.

"I'm good. It's nice to see you again, sir."

"Please call me Rick, or at least Mr. Barnes. I assume the boys are with you since you're here?"

"If you mean Ryder, Jayson, Julien, and Fallon, then yes. They're around here somewhere."

"Fallon is with you?" Elijah asks.

"Oh! I forgot to tell you. Marshall is here too."

"Oh, shit."

Rick asks, "Do I need to be worried?"

"No, Dad. Unless he starts something. Marshall was the guy who messed up Jules's leg, and the guy Liz punched that night after he and Ryder raced."

Rick gives me an amused look of approval. "Well, come on over and watch the races. I will say that there hasn't been anyone nearly as good as Ryder, but we do have some young up-and-comers. I'm sure having Ryder Cutton here tonight will cause a stir among the crowd. It's like having a celebrity visit."

Sure enough, I hear a roar of applause and commotion and see Ryder surrounded by a couple of dozen people. A few girls sidle up to him vying for his attention. A brunette puts her hand on his arm and I'm about to go rip her fingers off when Ryder beats me to it by removing her grasp. I also notice Marshall leaning against his car and staring at Ryder. Maybe Rick does have a reason to be worried about tonight.

The three of us start making our way over to Ryder and Fallon, but Rick stops me before we get there.

"Liz, I want you to know how sorry I am about your parents and sister."

"Thanks. It's been hard being back here, especially since I got my memories back."

"I heard about your injuries and memory loss. I'm familiar with your case. Detective Harnett is a friend of mine and I know he's been trying to get in touch with you. Is there a reason why you've been avoiding him?"

"Look, Mr. Barnes, I don't want to be rude. Too much has happened recently and I'm finally settling into a good place, mentally. Once I'm ready, I promise I'll call him."

"Alright, sweetheart. If you need anything, no matter what it is, call me." Rick hands me one of his business cards. "My personal cell phone number is on the back."

"Thank you, Mr. Barnes," I tell him and slide his card into my back pocket. He walks off to join a deputy standing near the track.

The place is lit up like Las Vegas. They've added a few more pole lamps to go with the ones that were installed years ago, and the track appears to have been widened a bit. I chuckle a little at the memory of Mr. Jacoby's cows getting out and running across the track in the middle of a race.

Strong arms swoop around my middle and swiftly lift me up before setting me back down. "What's up, Elijah?" Jayson greets him.

"Heard J is with you tonight."

"You heard right," Julien responds, appearing from behind his brother. "How are you, E?"

The air surrounding us turns thick and heavy from all the tension radiating between Julien and Elijah.

"Good. You?"

"Same," Elijah exhales a frosty breath, his head hanging down so he doesn't have to look directly at Julien.

I can't take this anymore.

"This is ridiculous. You both love each other."

The angry Julien who has presented himself to me the past two days comes rampaging back. "It's none of your damn business, Liz."

"You blaming me makes it my damn business," I counter, pulling him farther back between the cars for some privacy. I don't want to air out our dirty laundry to everyone milling about. "I'll keep apologizing to you for as long you need me to, but me leaving had nothing to do with you, Julien. I'm sorry it hurt you, but *I* was hurting too. I was no good to anyone, not even myself. If you can't understand that—" I stop and take a second to calm down before I say something that I'll more than likely regret. "You're being petty and stupid. That's not you, Julien. You are kind and loving and supportive. What happened to that man? What happened to my best friend?"

"You destroyed him the day you broke your promise to me. The day you left. *Again*," Julien whisper-shouts in my face.

"Fine!" I hiss. "Then be mad at me. Why take it out on Elijah? He's been there for you and you've treated him like he's disposable and unwanted. He loves you. I know for a fact that you love him back just as deeply. Stop being an ass and talk to him."

Julien's face contorts. "When did you get so bossy?"

"How about we blame it on Fallon," I answer.

"Blame what on me?" I never noticed when Ryder and Fallon joined our little circle.

"For me being bossy. And what did you say to me before, Jayson? That I had a sassy mouth?"

"I also remember saying you were a fighter," he replies.

"Damn straight." I poke Julien in the chest with my finger, "And I will keep fighting you with my sassy mouth and bossy attitude until you give in. Give in already so I can have my best friend back."

I watch as Julien deflates, all the anger and fight leaving his body. "What if I want to stay mad at you?"

"I'll give you until tomorrow."

"*Ugh*," Julien groans out and raises his eyes to the night sky as if asking a higher power for help.

"I love you, Julien. I truly am sorry I hurt you. Now, stop being a dick and go get your man back."

"I don't know if he wants me back."

"Oh, he definitely wants you back," Elijah says, walking up behind me. "But he also expects you to grovel and crawl a little first."

Julien shoves his hands in his pockets, but the glint in his eye is straight-up happiness. "I can do that."

My spirits soar when I hear Julien say that. Unfortunately, it doesn't last long. My jubilant mood sours when I hear Marshall, "Isn't this a sweet reunion. Come to reminisce about your high school glory days?"

Without missing a beat, Fallon counters, "Still living my glory days," and strolls over to where Marshall has been leaning against the hood of his car watching us the entire time. That guy is such an asshole.

Fallon glides his hand over the side and across the door of Marshall's Camaro as he slowly walks around it. A crowd has gathered to watch what's going down between Fallon and Marshall.

"Nice car," Fallon says.

"What the fuck is it to you?" Marshall straightens, watching Fallon carefully like a gazelle would a lion.

This is the side of Fallon I love most. Dangerous, cocky, with a side of egotistical bastard thrown into the mix. I take great pleasure in watching Fallon make Marshall squirm.

"Hey, kitten! Feel up to a little race?"

"Against Marshall? Hell, yes!" I shout back.

"What the hell are you doing?" Ryder seethes, tugging me behind him in a protective move like he used to do. His act of chivalry actually turns me on, and I glide my hand up his jacket-covered back in appreciation. Ryder angles his head to look over his shoulder at me, his eyebrow cocked, and I give him my sexiest smile hoping my mental telepathy of "just wait until later tonight" comes out loud and clear. The higher arching of his brow tells me it does.

"Liz, you can't race him. You've never raced here before. It's too dangerous," Jayson says.

Marshall bends over at the waist and laughs. "Oh, this should be good."

I turn around and walk backward, pointing fingers at Ryder and Jayson. "Trust me. I've got this." I spin round to face Marshall. "You're right, Marshall. This should be good."

"Where's your car, *princess*?" I want so badly to punch Marshall in the nose again.

Fallon aims his blue gaze at the guy standing next to one of the Mustang GT500s. "You know who I am?"

The guy swallows a few times, nods, and squeaks out a yes. "Good. Give me your keys, fucker."

Like magic, car keys suddenly appear in Fallon's open palm. He throws them at me. "She has a ride. Let's race." I will never understand how the heck he does that. It's like Fallon has Jedi mind trick powers over people.

Marshall scoffs. "I don't race for fun. Make it worth my while."

"Fine. She loses, I'll give you the Equus Bass that's stored in my family's garage. You lose and I get your Camaro. Fair enough?"

A smarmy grin makes an appearance on Marshall's mouth. "Deal."

Fallon yells out, "Get the track cleared!" and people scramble to do his bidding. "You got this, kitten. Smoke his ass."

"Thanks for letting me drive your car. I promise not to wreck it," I tell the poor guy as he stands idly by, looking helpless and a little green in the face. I get into the driver's seat of his car and the guy staggers back out of the way. I should feel guilty about taking some stranger's car without asking, but I don't. My hatred for Marshall supersedes reason at the point. And I think I may have a little bit of Fallon in me. I did beat down the back door of my house yesterday, and today I'm one step away from being a car thief.

The passenger door opens and Fallon hops in the back, all grins. Ryder sits down in the passenger seat and buckles in.

"You know you guys are just adding weight to the car that'll slow it down."

Fallon leans between the front seats. "Shouldn't hinder you from winning. Stop bitching and let's do this."

There's a knock on my window and Jayson, Julien, and Elijah are standing there. I roll it down.

"You remember everything Ryder taught you?" Jayson asks me.

"Yep."

"Ry, keep an eye out for anything dirty. I don't have to remind you what Marshall did to your car last time."

Fallon thrums his fingers on the back of Ryder's seat. "My head will be on a three-sixty.

We've got her covered."

Julien tries to nudge Jayson out of the way but Jayson shoulder-checks him and bends down so we're at eye level. "I know you won't listen to me if I tell you to not do this. So, instead I'll say, go be badass, princess, and show that ass-wipe what you're made of."

Wow. Coming from Jayson, that means a lot. He always tries to shield me from everything. If I get a splinter, he acts like it is the end of the world.

"You really mean that?"

He flashes a grin at me and moves so Julien can see me.

"You let him beat you and I'll never speak with you again."

"Then I'll make sure not to. Besides, aren't you still mad at me and not talking to me anyway?" I smile to let him know I'm teasing, even though a part of me isn't. I'm pretty sure after tonight, Julien will go back to being angry at me again.

Julien gives me a quick peck on the forehead and taps the side of the car with his knuckles.

I roll the window up and hand Ryder my phone. "You know what to play."

Ryder leans over the console and grabs the back of my neck, bringing me in for a hot, wet kiss. "I love you so fucking much."

Fallon sits back. "Stop with the front seat porn unless I'm invited."

Ryder kisses me deeply one more time while giving Fallon the bird. Seconds later "Alive" by P.O.D. starts blasting from my phone. It's the song we listened to when Ryder came and got me from the library to be the first person to ride in his Hellcat.

As I make my way up to the starting line, I look over at Marshall. I kiss my middle finger and blow it at him.

"Hey, Fallon. Does that mean if I win, I get your Equus?"

"Shit, kitten, when you beat that fucker, I'll give you my yacht."

"Alrighty then."

Chapter 19

Elizabeth

The door crashes inwards and Ryder and I stumble around in the dark, mouths fused, hands groping. He reaches back and bolts the lock.

"Lights?" I gasp.

"Don't need them. Know where I'm going," he grunts out, lifting me up and latching onto my neck with a hard suck that makes my nipples pucker and my core clench. He's marking me and I plan on doing the same to him.

Another door goes wide as Ryder kicks it hard with his foot. I scrape my nails along the back of his head, loving the feel of his soft hair against my fingertips. Then I'm being spun and dropped on the hood of a car.

After I thoroughly kicked Marshall's ass in the race, we celebrated my victory at a local sports bar. Ryder and Jayson didn't drink for obvious reasons since they were driving, but Fallon and I enjoyed a couple of beers together—thank you, fake IDs. At the bar, we sat around, talking and laughing, mostly about the pissed-off look on Marshall's face after the race. Marshall was forced to hand over the keys to his Camaro to Fallon after he lost. Fallon gave them to the guy whose Mustang I drove. I'm pretty sure that the guy will give the keys back to Marshall, but it was still a hell of a lot of fun to watch Marshall squirm.

About thirty minutes after we arrived at the bar, Julien and Elijah escaped to a dark, secluded corner to talk, and by the end of our evening, they were getting very cozy. Julien left with Elijah sometime before we did. I'm pretty sure I'm not the only one who was going to get laid tonight. As soon as we got back to Ryder's house, and after Fallon conked out for the night, Ryder and I snuck out and drove to his dad's auto garage. It was the only place we could think of where we could have some privacy and make as much noise as we wanted to.

"Shirt," Ryder commands. We already ditched our coats in the car. I rip my top off and shiver, the cold of the garage bay teasing my skin with prickles.

"You too." And he does. Even in the darkness, my eyes make out the ridges and dips of Ryder's muscular chest and lower torso. My hands are on him instantly, followed by my mouth. We fight each other for dominance. I'm trying to eat him alive while he's trying to get my pants off. I lift my hips up from the hood of the car and he yanks my jeans and panties down in one go. I kick them fully off with my feet.

"What car is this?"

Ryder briefly looks down and to the side. "Hellcat." He zeroes in on my breasts and cradles them, his thumbs moving back and forth over my tight nipples.

I gasp at the sensations his fingers are causing, then start to giggle when what he said registers in my lust-laden brain. "Seriously? A Hellcat? It's perfect."

Bending down, he licks up the middle of my chest between my breasts. "No, these are perfect. God, I want you so bad. You were incredible tonight. Watching you drive that car made me so damn hard." He circles his lips around the circumference of each round globe, then fondles my right nipple with his tongue and flicks my left with his thumb.

"That feels good. Don't stop." He doesn't.

Feeling with my hands, I find the button and zipper of his jeans and undo them. Using the heels of my feet, I jerk the material down to expose that which I have been craving. He has gone commando again and I send up a thrilled yet silent thank you. I grab hold of his shaft and squeeze. He moans. I love it.

"I'm not done with you yet," Ryder sexily threatens and jerks my hips down the hood of the car. As he does so, he takes both my hands in his and pins them above my head on the hood of the car. The shock of the cold metal is like being hit with static electricity all down my spine. The sensation is wonderful. I squirm under him and hook my feet around his upper thighs just below his butt, arching my body up for him to take.

Stretching me out along the hood, Ryder's mouth goes on a frenzy of exploration across my skin, my breasts, my stomach, up my clavicle and neck, to my ear, then finally my mouth. I have always loved kissing. There is something very sensual in the way lips move together. Kisses can be soft or hard, dry or wet, tongue or no tongue. The moment when my full lips meet Ryder's soft ones is such an exhilarating feeling. We open to one another, that first tentative touch of the tips of our tongues, then the soul-wrenching clash and tangles of the dance and glide of our mouths with one another. No one has ever kissed me the way Ryder does.

And kiss me he does. Over and over until I'm

panting hard and so aroused, I may go up in flames right here on the hood of the car.

"In me now," I tell him.

"Not yet."

"Yes, yet," I argue, and he chuckles, his warm breath cascading down my quivering torso. "I'll make you," I tell him.

"I'd like to see you try."

Challenge accepted, my sexy man. I slip right down off the hood and take him in my mouth before he can react.

"*Fuuuck*, Elizabeth," he moans, and grabs my hair as I grab the backs of his thighs, his jeans pooled at his feet. He's not going anywhere. I tease the tip, licking the saltiness, then take him deep until I almost gag and my eyes water. Ryder tightens his grasp in my hair but allows me to remain in control of his pleasure.

"I love your mouth on me," he rumbles, head tilted back, eyes closed. When I feel him thicken and shudder, I know he's close. The sound that softly rumbles up from deep in his chest is enough to tease out my own orgasm.

Suddenly, I'm pulled up and flipped around. Ryder bends me over the hood of the car, my breasts pressed flat against the hard metal, my arms draped up toward the windshield. Ryder slides his hand up my spine and bends over me, his chest molding over my back. He turns my head to the side and kisses the top of my shoulder, giving me another soft bite above my scapula.

"You ready, baby?"

Oh, hell, yes. "Ryder," I beg. I need him to fill me. I need that connection. I just need him.

I'm so wet, it only takes him one effortless, hard thrust, until he's seated fully inside of me. We both let out loud joyous moans. Slow and unhurried, Ryder pumps in and out of me before gradually increasing the rhythm of his thrusts. As his hips increase their tempo, he moves one hand to my hip to hold me in place while the other sneaks around to stroke and strum my throbbing womanhood with determined care. My hands have no purchase as I claw at the hood of the Hellcat. I hope I don't leave scratches in the paint. How would we ever explain that to his dad? Oh, shit. What if we dented the hood already? Too late now.

Ryder's next hard thrust hits that spot inside of me that lights me up and cry out his name.

"Say you're mine," he demands, thrusting into me.

I am. "I'm yours, Ryder." Only yours.

"Say you're mine forever." Another deep thrust.

For eternity. "Forever, Ryder."

"I love you, Elizabeth."

I'm teetering on the edge, so close.

"I love you too. Come with me. Together."

"Together," he replies, swiveling his hips. His thumb and forefinger giving my clit a tender pinch and my body hums in pleasure, clamping tight all around him inside of me. We both explode at the same time. His name falls from my lips, mine groans out of his, as we fall into bliss. Shudder with our combined releases. So in love. Together.

Ryder

I feel a pinprick on my hip, almost like the scratch of a tattoo needle but not nearly as painful. Then a gentle blowing. My abs seize and my cock hardens.

"Looks like someone is finally awake." I love her voice, especially when it's husky and smooth like it is now. I go to roll over. "No, don't move. I'm almost done."

I turn my head on the pillow. “What are you doing?”

Elizabeth has a black Sharpie marker clenched between her teeth, her thumbs and fingers swiping across my hip. “You’ll see,” she says around the marker.

The bedsheet is pooled around our upper legs, exposing her luscious pale breasts to my line of sight. My morning erection stiffens even more until it’s almost painful with the need to be inside her again. I drink in her pink nipples and they pucker right before my eyes, turning a dusky rose color with arousal.

“Stop that,” she mumbles. “I can feel your eyes.”

“You’re so beautiful,” I tell her. I hope she never gets tired of hearing me say it, because I’ll never stop telling her. “‘*She walks in beauty, like the night, of cloudless climes and starry skies; and all that’s best of dark and bright meet in her aspect and her eyes.*’”

Those ethereal sage green orbs dart up, capturing my light brown ones. “Byron?”

“Yeah.”

“You amaze me every single day, Mr. Cutton.”

Somedays, I amaze myself. I don’t know

where that came from. It just popped out. Elizabeth leans over my side, her nipples grazing my upper arm. I can feel her heart thudding like a bass drum and its beat, along with the emotional look in her eyes, stirs something deep inside of me. Elizabeth presses her lips to the side of my mouth then leans back.

I watch as she brings the tip of the black marker to the skin above my hip, a mischievous grin slowly inching across her gorgeous face, then I feel the subtle scratching sensation again. She's drawing on me. My interest is piqued, but I relax into the pillow and let her finish, my mind drifting. Mere hours before, I had her naked body draped across the hood of a Challenger in my dad's garage bay. After coming so hard I almost blacked out, I'm amazed that I was able to drive us both back home. We took a quick shower and immediately fell asleep. I don't think I'll ever get over the amazement of holding Elizabeth in my arms as we fall asleep. How am I the lucky guy she chose? I know it has been a hard, painful journey to get here, but fuck, it was so worth it. I know without a shadow of a doubt, this magnificent woman is going to be my wife and the mother of my children.

Elizabeth scrunches her nose in concentration. The way she does it is adorably cute. Popping the top back on, she flings the marker over her shoulder. "There. Done. Want to see?"

I sit up. Looking at her handiwork, I see that she's drawn a staff of music along my hip. It takes me a second to figure out the melody since I'm looking at it upside down. I wasn't the greatest at reading sheet music, no matter how much her dad practiced with me. Eventually, I'm able to decipher the notes. Liz wrote a section of our song, "Helium" by Sia.

"You marked me last night," she says, pointing at her neck to the love bite I gave her. "So, I'm marking you. I'm claiming you. You're mine, Ryder, just as I am yours."

"I have always been yours, Elizabeth," I tell her and pull her on top of me. She nestles her wet heat on top of my hard length. I cradle her gorgeous tits and she gives me a smile of delicious awareness. Just as she lifts up to take me inside of her, a loud, thudding knock jolts us and we both scowl at the door.

"It's noon and I'm bored!" Fallon shouts from the other side.

"Hold on!" I yell back, sitting up, and kissing Elizabeth's laughing mouth. "Get some clothes on, baby."

We quickly dress and I unlock the door. Fallon struts in, looks between the two of us, and grabs Elizabeth by the waist, flinging her over his shoulder.

"Fallon!" she shrieks.

"Sexy time is over folks. I have a car coming in an hour to pick us up. Your parentals want to spend some time with us before we leave. Chop, chop! Before I forget, hoss, I had someone pick up your car. It's parked at Elizabeth's." He disappears downstairs with my girl. I listen to her sweet giggles.

I'm not going to ask how he got my car seeing as I have the keys. Fallon has his ways and I rarely question them. We're heading back to CU today. Back to our regular life. I'm looking forward to having Elizabeth under the same roof with me again. Just the two of us. And hopefully no more cockblocking distractions.

Chapter 20

Elizabeth

It's Sunday afternoon and classes resume tomorrow. Fallon, Ryder, and I got back yesterday evening. We ordered takeout and watched movies while piled together on my living room sofa. Fallon left around midnight to go back to his frat house. Ryder and I took advantage of our first night back. I woke up this morning totally blissed out, a little sore, and so much in love with Ryder. It wouldn't surprise me if I'm surrounded by a cloud of sparkly rainbow glitter as I walk across campus to the freshman dorms. I see a few people I know from class and wave. Chelsea, a girl in my organic chem class who sits next to me and Julien, stops when she sees me entering McKlellan Dorm, Meredith's dorm.

"Where have you been?"

"Hey, Chels. I was out of town."

"Oh. I thought you'd dropped out or something. You've been gone for like a month and that really hot guy, Julien, that you hang out with wouldn't tell me what happened to you."

She and I walk together to the elevators. "Anything new going on in class?"

"Only the test that was on the syllabus. Oh! You missed Heath's firebomb in the lab."

The elevator doors open, and we step inside. I press the button for the third floor.

"What happened?"

Chelsea has long, straight black hair that she's always twirling around her finger when she talks. I don't think she realizes that she does it.

"He dropped a ball of potassium in a beaker of water and it exploded."

"Was everybody okay?" Heath is the class clown. I guess every college has them, just like high school.

"Let's just say, Heath won't be returning to lab. The professor kicked him out. He's also under academic probation because he snuck into the storage lab to get the potassium without permission. Did you go on a trip or something?"

The elevator stops and we get off. I lean back against the wall. “Fallon took me to London, Paris, Barcelona, Amsterdam, some town in Iceland that I can hardly pronounce correctly, Venice, and Sydney...” I trail off when I see her eyes go Jupiter-wide. “What?”

“Fallon? As in Fallon Montgomery?” she practically shouts, her voice getting higher and higher as she says his name. Several girls walking down the hall cut-off in mid-conversation and look at us.

Oh boy. “Um, yes. He’s a friend. My boyfriend, Ryder, came with us for the last half.”

“Ryder Cutton?” Again with the shocked yelling, and more girls staring at me. I nod slowly. “You’re friends with Fallon Montgomery and you’re dating Ryder Cutton? Fuck my life!” She throws up her hands in the air. “You lucky bitch.” Then she grins sheepishly when she sees all the other girls eavesdropping in the hallway.

I’ve now become the campus prized pony. Perhaps an accident on the side of the road based on all the rubbernecking going on in the hallway right now. I narrow my eyes at each of the eavesdropping girls. They break away, whispering excitedly, as they walk down the hall with an occasional head swivel back our way.

"Thanks for that," I tell her.

Chelsea has the presence of mind to look sincerely apologetic. "Sorry. But holy mother of all that's hot and sexy. You are in the inner circle of two of the hottest guys on campus." Her phone dings. "Oh, crap! I was supposed to meet my boyfriend like ten minutes ago. See you in class?"

"You bet."

"And we're definitely having lunch together soon. Maybe a double date," she calls as she rushes back to the elevators.

I walk down the long hall. Finding the room number that I'm looking for, I tentatively rap on the door. Several other dorm room doors are open and the sounds of talking and music filter into the hallway. I knock a little louder. Seconds later, it opens.

"I'm so freaking mad at you." Meredith stands with her hands fisted against her hips like a pissed-off fairy. In the month since I last saw her, her hair has gotten longer.

"I know. I came to apologize. I brought you presents," I add, holding out the bag of wrapped items I bought for her while in Europe and Australia.

She taps her foot, waiting.

"My memory returned."

"Well, shit. Come in," she huffs and backs up to allow me to enter. Before the door closes, she throws her arms around me. I'm seven inches taller than she is so it's like hugging a little sister.

"I've missed you, Mer."

"Apology accepted."

My body trembles with laughter. "Just like that?"

Meredith shoves me over to her bed and pushes me down to sit. "Just like that. That's what friends do. But you still owe me an explanation. And give me that bag."

I hand it over. "That I do."

"Did your memory really come back?" she asks while tearing into the wrapping paper of the first present.

"All of it. I have a lot to tell you."

"Elizabeth, this is gorgeous!" she exclaims when she opens the box and sees the silver charm bracelet I got her.

"I picked out a charm for you at every place

we stopped." I show her. "An NYC for New York City, a snowflake for Iceland, a Union Jack for London, the Eiffel Tower for Paris, a windmill for Amsterdam, a flower for Barcelona, a gondola boat for Venice, and a kangaroo for Sydney."

"I definitely forgive you now," she says and clasps the bracelet on her wrist.

"But you said you already forgave me."

"That was my metaphorical forgiveness. This is my literal forgiveness."

"I missed you, Mer," I tell her again. She leans over and hugs me again, and we both giggle.

"Selfie!" she says, taking out her phone. We press cheek-to-cheek for the picture, sticking our tongues out, and making devil horns with our hands. She shares the picture with my phone, then types out something I can't see before putting her phone down.

Meredith walks over and grabs her hairbrush and some hair clips from her desk. "You know I'm not a keep-still-kind-of girl with my ADHD. Have to stay busy. So while you spill, I'm going to play with your hair. What happened to the pink?"

"It faded out. I'm thinking of maybe doing blue streaks next, or possibly green to match my eyes."

She glides the brush down my hair. "I really liked the pink."

"Pink it is."

While Meredith twists and messes with my hair, I tell her everything. I don't leave anything out. By the time my voice is tired from talking, Meredith has given me a hairstyle fit for a debutante ball.

"Holy shit, Elizabeth. That's a lot to take in. Like, a lot, a lot. I think I need a drink." She goes over to a minifridge and pulls out a wine cooler and offers me one. I decline since I drove here, but that doesn't stop her from guzzling hers down.

"Enough about me. What's been going on with you? How's Trevor?" There's a knock at the door and then it opens.

"Speaking of Trevor."

"Heard my wildcat is back."

"Trevor!" I squeal and jump into his hug. He squeezes me tight and lifts me up. "How did you know I was here?"

"I texted him," Meredith says.

"Heard my brother kidnapped you."

"Other way around. I kidnapped Fallon. Do I need to apologize to you too?"

"For what? Taking a trip?" He sets me back down and grabs the beer Meredith holds out to him. She's younger than I am. How does she have a secret stash of booze in her dorm room?

"That trip pissed a lot of people off."

"Well, that's just stupid as fuck," he says.

"I hurt a lot of people with my sudden disappearance, but I appreciate your comment."

He tilts his head to the side taking me in, and it reminds me so much of Fallon that I can't help but smile. "I like your hair," he says in amusement.

"I did it," Meredith chirps happily.

I sit back down on Meredith's bed and Trevor takes the spot next to me. Meredith sits in her desk chair.

"Look what Elizabeth gave me." She shows off her charm bracelet to him.

"I have something for you too," I tell him, "but I wasn't expecting to see you today. I'll bring it to class tomorrow."

"Tell him about Iceland. Actually, tell him everything. I want to hear it again."

"A lot of it involves Fallon," I tell Trevor.

"Yeah. Lay it on me."

And I do. In the middle of my retelling, Meredith's roommate, Sara, joins us. She was going to do my Halloween makeup before I left with Fallon. I apologize profusely to her for bailing at the last minute, but she waves me off like it's no big deal. The four of us sit and chat for a while, catching up on things. As I get to know Sara better, Meredith goes through another wine cooler or three. Sara's from Iowa and is an art history major. We're laughing hysterically at a cow-tipping story from her high school days, when my phone pings as a text comes in.

MyBoyfriend: Hey, babe. When u coming home?

I changed Ryder's tag from Hellcat to MyBoyfriend yesterday. Fallon gave me back my phone the morning after Ryder arrived in Venice. I've been overly protective of it ever since.

Me: Didn't realize the time. Have been here with Meredith, Trevor, and Sara. Leaving soon. Want me to pick up anything?

MyBoyfriend: Made dinner. Just waiting for u.

That wonderful man. I decide that he'll get

treated to a blowjob in the shower when I get home. Dinner can wait.

Me: Give me 15. Put food on to warm. U get dessert first. <kiss emoji>

MyBoyfriend: Dammit Elizabeth. You can't say stuff like that to me when ur not here for me to get my hands on u. Hurry home.

I hit video call. Ryder's handsome, unshaven face pops on screen. I don't think I'll ever want him to grow a full beard, but the stubble I like very much. I have stubble scratches between my legs and all over my torso from last night.

"Hey, baby!"

"Now you're just being a tease. I said I wanted to get my hands on you, not look at you on a video screen."

"Is that Ryder Cutton?" Sara loudly whispers to Meredith.

"You're quite the infamous man on campus today. I had about a half a dozen girls swoon in the hallway at the mention of your and Fallon's names."

"And just think, you get me all to yourself."

"Damn straight! Ryder, this is Sara, Meredith's roomie." Sara turns every shade of red and pink imaginable when I turn my phone's screen her way then back to me.

"Your hair looks very nice," Ryder says to me.

Meredith yells out, "I did that!"

"How are you doing, man?" Trevor asks him offscreen.

"Better now I have my woman back. Thanks for everything, by the way."

"Wait. What did you do?" I poke Trevor's leg.

"For me to know and for you to find out."

"Now I'm curious." Meredith sticks her head in the camera view. "Hi, Ryder."

"Hey, Meredith."

"Elizabeth and I kissed and made up. Well, not really kissed, but you get what I mean. I promise not to blow up your phone anymore."

"Leave the poor guy alone," Trevor tells her.

"Geesh, just because you sleep with a guy once or twice, he thinks he can boss you around."

I splutter and Trevor's face heats. "She really needs a filter," Trevor says.

"She may be a little tipsy from the three wine coolers she guzzled," I point out.

Meredith falls over on top of me, hugging me fiercely. "I'm glad you're back. We need a girl's night."

Ryder gives up trying to have a conversation with us. "Hey babe. I'm hanging up. Hurry home. Love you."

Trevor takes my phone and points it down at me and Meredith. Meredith presses her cheek to mine and we both grin up at Ryder. "Be home soon. Love you back."

Meredith and I purse our lips in twin kissy puckers at Ryder.

"You guys are so fucking cute," he chuckles again and hangs up.

"Trevor, a little help here," I plead when Meredith starts kissing my cheek enthusiastically.

Trevor lifts her up and off me. "Coffee for you, my friend," he tells her and hands her off to Sara.

Meredith hugs Sara like she was hugging me. "I have the bestest roomie and the bestest friend and the bestest fuck buddy."

"Don't even ask me how she is at parties," Trevor deadpans.

"Walk me out?" I ask him. I know Trevor is big on that kind of thing as he usually walks Meredith to her dorm after our study sessions. "It was so nice to finally meet you, Sara," I say, flashing a friendly smile as she struggles to push a very affectionate Meredith off her.

"You too, Elizabeth. Hope to see you around."

"Why don't we all go to Belly's this Friday night?"

"I love their karaoke nights," Sara replies. "I'm in."

"Me, too!" Meredith excitedly agrees, leaping off Sara and engulfing me in another hug.

Trevor, once again, has to pry me free of Meredith and pushes me out into the hallway. As we walk to the elevators, two of the eavesdropping girls I recognize from earlier are walking toward us. They stop and gawk as Trevor and I get on the elevator.

"That's one of the guys, Trevor Montgomery. What a slut. Can you believe five guys at once?"

Hearing what the girl says, Trevor throws his hand out to stop the elevator doors from closing. "You bitches need to watch your mouths."

The Trevor before me is the one from Fallon's party. The one who said he would hit Maria and Jacinda if they didn't apologize to me. This Trevor is a bit scary. And since when did I become the hot topic of campus gossip? I feel like I'm missing something.

"Now fuck off," Trevor angrily tells them, and the two girls scamper quickly down the hall. "Sorry about that," he says to me as the elevator doors close. "Do you know what in the hell they were talking about?"

"Not a clue," I answer. "I appreciate you standing up for me, Trevor, but you can't go around threatening girls all the time."

"They disrespected you. Besides, I would never lift a finger against a woman. But I'm not going to filter my words when a girl is being a straight-up bitch. Come on. Let me walk you to your car."

"How did you know I drove here?"

"Wildcat, you always drive to campus."

True.

"Hey Trevor? If I asked you to do something for me with no questions asked, would you?" I want to start working on my plan to build a bridge between Fallon and Trevor.

"Let me turn that around on you. Do you trust me, Elizabeth?"

I give him a hard, considering appraisal. "Yes-ish?" I laugh at his facial expression, and he shoves my shoulder in jest. "Yes, Trevor. I trust you."

"Then, the answer is yes to your question."

We reach where my car is parked in the student lot. Trevor leans on the hood as I fish my keys out of my pocket. "You look good, wildcat. Happier."

"Fallon is a big part of that. Ryder too. You know Meredith likes you, right? Why haven't you asked her out?"

He shifts from one foot to the other. "I've got some stuff I need to finish. Things to deal with before I graduate. Besides, I'll be out of here in a few months. Why start a relationship that I would just have to break off in May, you know?"

"If you really like someone, you could find a way to make it work. But what you're saying makes sense."

"Besides, the best girl on campus is already taken." He winks at me and I punch his arm. "See you in class, wildcat."

"Bye, Trevor."

I text Ryder to let him know I'm on my way. I get in my car and lock the door, then I flip through a few texts that I haven't read yet.

Tatiána: Eduardo won't let me do anything. He thinks pregnancy means I'm helpless.

Tatiána and I have been texting each other almost daily since she and Eduardo left Barcelona and went back to Madrid.

Me: They say pregnancy hormones make you horny. Go screw his brains out. Men will agree to anything after sex.

I hit send knowing it's the middle of the night in Spain, so she won't see my text until the morning.

I read Fallon's text next. He's checking up on me. I send him a response and tell him I'll drop by his frat tomorrow after my chem class. I read Jayson's text. He wants to do breakfast tomorrow morning. I send him a thumbs up, but I don't tell him that I'll be there early to catch Julien as he leaves for his morning run. I may be ambushing Julien, but enough is enough. This ignoring each other crap is getting old.

Then I read the last text.

Unknown: I'm coming for you.

Well, that one is weird. I delete it.

Chapter 21

Julien

"Good morning, running buddy!"

I think I jump about five feet. Liz is leaning back against the railing across from my front door. "Christ, you scared the shit out of me."

Biding my time, I bend down to re-tie and double knot my shoelaces, secretly happy that she's here. I do a few stretches and Liz does the same. She has her hair pulled up in a high ponytail and is wearing long exercise pants, a Randy's Custom Auto hoodie, and gloves since it's cold out this morning. Her cheeks and nose are already rosy from the chilled air. God, I've missed her.

I take off at a slow jog, my feet finding a steady rhythm. Liz keeps pace, staying at my side.

"I think I may drop out of CU and become a tattoo artist."

She's trying to cut through the tension between us by making light banter. I give her side-eye but say nothing.

"Apparently, I'm very good at drawing on people. I think I scored an entire opera of musical notes on Ryder's body with permanent marker. Oh, and I wrote a song for you last night. It's called 'I'm sorry and I love you and please don't be mad at me anymore because I miss you and need you in my life.'"

The snort of laughter escapes before I can stop it.

"I can sing it for you." And she does. She uses the beat of our feet pounding the ground to keep time with the words as she chants like an army drill sergeant. A few other joggers give us bemused looks as they pass by. I know she's making up the lines as she goes, but it's funny as hell and very endearing—and I give in. I love this girl too much to stay upset with her.

I come to an abrupt halt, causing her to trip over her feet and slam sideways into me. We fall on the frost-covered ground in a heap of tangled limbs.

"You're relentless, you know that?" I playfully admonish from my supine position.

"Do you forgive me, Julien?" The hopeful

puppy dog expression on her face would have done me in if I hadn't already surrendered.

"You knew full well that I couldn't stay mad at you forever."

"One day of you being mad at me feels like forever, and it's been days which means longer than eternity."

I stand up and her pull her with me. "That's not even mathematically possible."

Strands of her ponytail are sticking to her face. I take each piece and gently push them back into place. And because I've missed her so damn much, I plant a smacking kiss on her frosty pink lips.

"Don't leave me again. I'm serious. If you need to escape or need room to breathe, let me know. Send pigeon carrier mail for all I care. Just let me know."

"It may have to be pigeon mail. Fallon confiscated my phone while we were away, but he texted Ryder almost every day. Didn't Ryder tell you and Jayson?"

"He told us, but it's not the same as hearing from you. And I was envious that Ry was the one Fallon was communicating with and not me." I reach for her hand and loop it through my arm at the elbow. Liz snuggles into my side and we start walking.

"You going to tell me what the hell is going on between you, Jay, Ry, and Fallon? Jay said that the two of you were back together. That's clearly not the case, is it?"

A cloud of vapor rises up like smoke as Liz exhales hard. "I feel like I've been on repeat the past few days explaining the same things to everyone."

"Let me make it simple. Are you and Jay back together?"

"No. But I did make a very, very big mistake the night my memories came back. That's why I ran away. I had to sort things out in my head. You know how much I loved Jayson."

I can only interpret that very big mistake to mean they had sex. I also catch the last sentence – *loved Jayson*, not love in the present tense. A slip of the tongue?

"I will always love Jayson. But I don't love him the way I love Ryder."

"And Fallon?"

"As much as you, Ryder, and Jayson care about me, you couldn't help me in that moment. Us being around each other would have only made things worse for everyone. Fallon was dead on when he told me that. That's why I went with him. He understands me in a way that the three of you couldn't. I know how that must sound, especially since we've been inseparable for most of our lives, but Fallon was the only person who could help me. I don't regret going with him. He literally saved me, Julien, and I will be grateful to him for the rest of my life."

I chew on that for a minute, wanting to ask more about what's going on between her and Fallon. There's clearly something deeper there.

"Where does Ry fit into all of this?" I ask her.

"Ryder is my everything, Julien. That night with Jayson should not have happened, but I'm the only one to blame. I didn't mean to make things worse, and now Jayson won't listen to me. He refuses to accept that I'm with Ryder."

"You know how stubborn my brother is when it comes to you. You know he'll never give up." Knowing my brother, Jay will scorch the earth to get her back, especially now that her memories have returned.

She winces. "Julien, I don't even remember how I got to your condo that night. That's how messed up I was. I only realized what had happened after I woke up the next morning."

"Have you spoken to your doctors? What do

they say?"

She winces again. "No. I'm going to see Dr. Clairemont later this week."

I give her a hard stare. "And your neurologist."

"Why? I'm feeling great. I've had no other issues this past month."

"Liz, I mean it. Full check-up from every doctor. I'm not budging on this. I'm surprised Ryder hasn't strong-armed you into every one of their offices yet."

She laughs. "Oh, trust me. He has been on me like ants on honey."

I snicker at her double entendre, "I bet."

"Okay, you've got me there." She grins.

If Liz remembers everything now, then she remembers that night. The only good thing to be said about this mess is that she may be able to recall details about her attacker to help the police finally catch the depraved murderer who hurt her and killed her family.

I switch subjects. "How are you doing after all the Thanksgiving drama?"

Liz kicks a pinecone down the path. "It was a lot. The house, telling your parents about Elizabeth Ann, talking to Jayson. Elijah's dad wants me to call the detective in charge of the case. Speaking of Elijah…"

"E and I are taking things slow. I guess it was kind of hypocritical of me to be mad at you when I was hurting him in almost the same way."

"Don't think I didn't notice the two of you sneaking off together the other night. I'm glad you guys are working things out."

"Me too. I'm trying to do by better by him." I look at my watch and see the time. Jay had told me last night Liz was coming over for breakfast. I was going to stay away after she would have left for class. Looks like my plans have changed. "You ready to head back?"

"Wow, has it been an hour already?"

"I don't know how you've been keeping up with your coursework while away, but I made sure to take really good notes for you in chem."

"You were angry with me and still took notes for me? Aww," she gushes and squeezes my arm. "Fallon said he had it covered, whatever that means. I guess I'll find out today. I can't believe the semester is almost over and then it'll be Christmas break and off to Seattle."

"Have you spoken to Daniel or Drew at all?"

Liz's face falls and she rests her head against my shoulder as we walk. "No, I haven't. Not since the hospital. That's something else I'm going to rectify soon. I just don't know how yet. Drew has been texting me. With everything he's going through with his chemo, I feel so damn guilty about not reaching out to him. It's just I'm still so angry at them. How could they keep secret the fact that I was pregnant and lost my baby?"

I don't reply because I'm also still mad as hell that Daniel kept what happened to Liz and Elizabeth Ann a secret. "You and I still have so much we need to talk about, Liz."

"I know."

But at least this morning was a start. Hopefully, it will be smoother sailing from here on in.

Elizabeth

"There's a fight tonight," Jayson says as he walks me down to my car. I couldn't stay long for breakfast since I have to rush back to my apartment and shower before my nine o'clock class.

I settle back against my cherry red car. "Are

you asking me to come?"

"Well, you mentioned before that you wanted to."

After I disappeared, Jayson started fighting in what I can only describe as underground college fight clubs. It seems to be a thing these days. Instead of drinking himself unconscious, he turned to using his fists as a way to deal with his emotions. I asked him to stop fighting when I saw him with bruises and scabbed-over cuts on his face, but Jayson confessed to me that he couldn't; he said he needed it. I felt so damn culpable at the time, knowing what happened to me was the reason he was fighting.

Jayson reaches out and takes my hand, his thumb tracing slowly back and forth across my knuckles. "Will you come?" he softly asks, and that's when I see it. Hope. He has so much damn hope in his eyes.

Jayson is opening the door for me, begging me to come inside, needing me to see *him*. The dynamic between the two of us over the past several months has been complex and often strained. With my amnesia, I didn't remember him. I didn't remember us. And then I fell in love with Ryder. And a month ago, the worst thing happened. My memories came back and the first thing I did was sleep with Jayson. It took Fallon, one month, and a trip around the world for me to come to grips with everything. Only then was I ready to choose who I wanted to be and who I wanted to be with. In the end, my heart chose Ryder.

And there lies the guilt. Jayson wants to fight to get me back.

I should tell him no, that I won't come watch him tonight. But I can't. Jayson was always my best friend before we became more, and I miss that part of us. I miss him. I miss the silver-eyed boy who would play knights and dragons with me. The boy who would stomp in the creek while holding my hand as we drenched our shoes and clothes. The same boy who would monkey across the oak tree between our houses and climb through my window. If there is even the slightest chance that boy still exists in the fierce man in front of me, I need to try and connect with that part of him. In a perfect world, Jayson and I could remain friends even though I would be with Ryder. But as life has shown me over and over again, perfect is never an option.

No one should blame Jayson for his anger. I sure as hell don't. I would be fucking angry too if I lost the person that I loved only to have them come back and not remember me, then fall in love with someone else. I get it, I really do, but I can't help the way I feel. I may be

Ryder's girlfriend, but I'm still Jayson's friend. Part of being a friend is being there for the other person, and I want to be there for Jayson.

"Yes, I'll come." His silver eyes flash at my acceptance. "How safe is it? Should I be worried about the cops showing up?" I pull my hand back from his intimate hold, needing to re-establish boundaries.

"We've never had problems before. Do you remember how we would get GPS coordinates the day of the bonfire parties that told us where to go?" I nod. "That's basically what happens with the fights. We get texted a location a few hours before. It's usually some abandoned field or warehouse out in the middle of nowhere. Your friend, Trevor, said he used to fight. He should know how things are done if you want to ask him."

"Maybe he'll want to come." I'm a little trepidatious about being around a group of testosterone-filled college guys who want to beat the shit out of each other for fun. It's a given that Ryder will come with me, possibly Fallon too. Might as well go all in and ask Meredith if she wants to come as well. Watching sweaty, muscled men punch each other should be right up her alley. Julien is going out with Elijah tonight and I am not going to get in the way of their reconciliation by asking them to join us.

As I'm unlocking my car door to get in, Jayson cups the back of my neck and pulls me in to press a kiss to my forehead. "See you after chem?"

I hastily get in my car and plaster on a smile. "Absolutely."

Jayson hesitates like he wants to say something else, then shakes his head slightly and raps his knuckles on the hood of the car.

I roll my window down. "Jayson?"

"Yeah?"

"Would you like to come over this weekend? To hang out or talk?"

"Yeah, Liz. I'd like that," he replies. In my rearview mirror, I see him standing in the parking lot, watching me as I drive away.

Rushing home to get ready for school, I barge into the apartment, throwing my bag on the floor and hurrying to the bedroom. I hear the shower running. Perfect timing. It takes me less than ten seconds to strip and step inside the humid air of the bathroom.

I'm filled with optimism this morning. Julien forgave me, I'm working on rebuilding my foundational friendship with Jayson, Fallon is...well, Fallon, and I adore him, black soul and all. I'm back in Meredith's good graces. Trevor and I picked up our friendship right we left off. I spent Thanksgiving with Ryder and his family. We visited with Freda and Mitch. And most importantly, Ryder loves me.

"Any room for one more?" I ask, stepping behind Ryder in the hot spray. He turns around and wraps me in a warm, sudsy hug. I walk my fingers up the hard plain of his chest and rise on tiptoe to welcome his kiss. Perfect.

"I was going to text you but decided not to since you said you wanted to talk with Julien this morning. I didn't want to intrude. How did it go?"

He hands me my bottle of jasmine soap and I lather it in my washcloth. "We talked and made up, so all is right with the world again."

Ryder takes the washcloth from me and begins to rub it over my body. I can't help the illicit moan that escapes. I slap my hand over my mouth and giggle up at him with wide eyes. "You always bring out the wanton hussy in me."

Ryder smiles devilishly and turns me around in the spray to rinse off the soap. "Do we have time?" he asks in that low, husky voice that makes my thighs clench together.

"I so very much really wish we did, but I only

have like twenty-five minutes to get to class," I tell him as my sneaky hand reaches back and curls itself around his thick, smooth cock and strokes him from base to tip.

"Elizabeth," he moans, and I flip us around so he's directly in the shower spray.

I rise up and murmur in his ear while continuing my leisurely stroking of him. "You missed a spot here with the soap. I'm just helping clean it off." I rub my thumb in circles around the tip and use the lubrication of the water to start pumping up and down in long, hard, smooth motions.

Ryder glides his hand down my stomach, and I open my legs wider for him. I have no doubt we can get each other off within five minutes. Plenty of time for me to grab a trail bar, throw on some clothes, and get to class.

Fifteen minutes later, Ryder drives us to campus in my car. On the ride over, I tell him about going to watch Jayson fight tonight, and of course he says he'll come. We park in the student lot, and as we walk hand in hand across the quad to Mason Hall, my skin starts to prickle and feel uncomfortable, erasing the effervescent feeling I'd been enjoying since the orgasm Ryder gave me in the shower. An eerie foreboding of someone watching me slithers its way down my spine. I look around and notice several groups of students blatantly staring at me and Ryder, some with hands cupped around their mouths like they're passing secrets. After the comments from those girls yesterday at Meredith's dorm, having more people stare at me today puts me on edge.

Ryder drops me off at Mason Hall with a sweet kiss and a reminder that he'll meet me after class. I, in turn, remind him that I'll be dropping by Fallon's after chem class and that he should meet up with me there when he gets out of his afternoon class. Once in the auditorium, I take my usual seat with Meredith and Trevor, but I still feel several eyes on me and it's starting to really freak me out. I dart my gaze around the room.

"Is it me, or are a lot of people staring over our way?"

Meredith is overt in her perusal of the auditorium. Several heads turn away from her glare.

"Nope, not just you. What's up with that?" she says. She checks her clothes, smooths her hair, and lifts up her shoes.

"What are you doing?"

"Making sure there's no toilet paper stuck to the bottom of my shoes or a bird in my hair." See roams her gaze over Trevor, then me.

"Nothing embarrassing sticking on or out of us. So those bitches better stop staring!" she announces loudly, sticking her middle finger up at a group of girls who won't stop giggling and pointing our way. I notice Trevor tense up and scowl at the girls, so I try and distract him before he flies off the handle like he did yesterday.

"If you guys aren't busy tonight, Jayson is fighting, and I told him that I would come."

Like I knew she would be, Meredith is instantly distracted from her sneer-war with the rude, giggling girls.

"Hell, yes. A bunch of aggressive alpha males. Count me in," she replies.

Trevor leans back so he can talk past Meredith to me. "It can get pretty gruesome. Are you sure you want to see that?"

Because I'm curious, I ask him, "What was it like? You said you fought for a couple of years and then stopped."

"I needed an outlet for my anger after my mom died. What was it like? A bunch of dickheads with very loud mouths, bigger egos, and little to show for it. Most of the time, a couple of well-placed punches to the face would take them down. A lot of guys think they know how to fight. It was easy money."

Meredith and I both express surprise. "You got paid? To fight?"

"What? Did you not expect anyone to place bets on which fighter would win his round, or for the winner to get a cut of the pot?"

No, I honestly didn't. "Why did you stop?"

"Told you before. I had other things to worry about," he answers vaguely.

I reach into my bag and pull out the gift that I bought Trevor in Barcelona. "Before I forget, this is for you. You can open it later."

Trevor accepts the wrapped item from my hand. "Elizabeth, you really didn't have to get me anything, but thank you."

"I got a bracelet." Meredith shakes her wrist at him completely forgetting that she already showed him yesterday when we were all hanging out in her dorm room.

"Firecracker, how much did you drink yesterday?"

"Not enough." Meredith taps me with her pencil. "When and where should we meet you?"

"It'll be someplace outside of town. Jayson will let me know once he gets a text later today."

"Very clandestine." She giggles. "I love it!"

"I can't let the two of you go by yourselves. Count me in."

"Ryder is coming, possibly Fallon. Will you be alright with that?"

Trevor rolls his eyes at the mention of his half-brother but says he'll behave as long as Fallon does. Our conversation is cut off when Professor Hallenger and his TAs walk in.

"Alright class. The semester is almost over which means your final exam is imminent. It counts for the majority of your grade. While Terry and Francine pass out study guides for it, could Elizabeth Fairchild please come up if she is present today."

Why does he want to speak with me?

"I'm here," I call out and make my way up to the front. I pass the girls that Meredith flicked off earlier and they start giggling again.

"You wanted to speak with me, Professor?"

He motions me to the side and addresses me quietly so that other students can't hear our conversation. "Good morning, Miss Fairchild. I apologize that I haven't gotten much of an opportunity to meet one-on-one. There's just too many of you." He chuckles. "The dean has personally spoken to me about your extension, and I wanted to make sure that you understand what that entails and ask if you have any questions."

I look at him blankly. "Extension?"

"For your leave of absence."

Oh shit. And the dean is involved? That means that Daniel probably knows that I've been absent from class for a month. I play along, wanting to strangle Fallon for not giving me a proper head's up when he told me "everything was taken care of" when it came to my classes.

"Oh, that. Right. Could you explain again what I need to do?"

"You'll have until January twenty-first to finish up your assignments and the two quizzes you missed. You will take your final exam sometime in the last week of January in my office. We will schedule the exact date and time later. Since the next semester will have already begun, I hope you will be able to handle a couple of extra weeks of work to make up for the month you were gone."

"Yes, absolutely. Not a problem. Thank you so much."

"I hope I'm not being too forward, but may I ask if everything is alright? I was told by the dean that you were on medical leave. I hope it was nothing serious."

"I'm good now. That's all that matters, right?" I brightly evade with a smile on my face. I thank Professor Hallenger and return to my seat. Several eyes follow me as I go.

"What was that all about?" Meredith asks.

"He just wanted to go over my missed work. I have until the end of January to get everything completed."

"You know we've got you covered," Trevor says.

"Thanks, guys."

For the rest of the class, we go over what the final exam will entail and are given our last novel assignment. When we're all dismissed, Trevor, Meredith, and I leave together so I can wait for Ryder at the bottom of the steps outside.

A male voice catches me when we near the glass doors at the exit. "Elizabeth Fairchild, right?"

Three guys are blocking our way. I think two of them are probably on the football team based on their build and the jersey shirts they're wearing. The third guy is more preppy-looking than his friends with his baby blue V-neck sweater and brown loafers.

"Damn, she's prettier than in those pictures," one of the bigger guys says.

What pictures?

The tall preppy blond steps forward. "Heard you liked to fuck multiple guys at the same time. Me and my friends are interested. Want to meet up later?"

He reaches out to slide a finger down my cheek and I'm about to smack his hand away and tell him to fuck off when Trevor steps in front of me and shoves the guy hard, slamming him into the doorway. Meredith jumps in ready to join the fight, even though she's more than a foot smaller than all of the guys. I grab her hand to stop her.

"What the fuck did you say to her?" Trevor growls threateningly.

Before preppy can respond, the door opens behind him and two campus security guards walk inside. They slow down when they notice Trevor and preppy guy facing off.

"Everything good here?" one of the officers asks.

Preppy guy wipes his hands down his jeans and gives a nod. "All's good," he says and thumps his two friends to signal they should leave. Trevor watches the guys until they are out of sight, while I stand there completely confused.

What the hell was that all about? How did those guys know my name, and what pictures were they talking about?

Ryder

Fallon: Get to my frat asap.

Me: On my way.

Fallon sent me the text right after I kissed Elizabeth goodbye at Mason Hall. His frat is about a ten-minute walk, so I should be back in time to pick Elizabeth up after her class. When I turn up the walkway to the house, Fallon is sitting outside on the steps. He doesn't look happy.

"I'm here, so what's up?"

Fallon's indignant eyes flick toward the front door. "Come inside. I need to show you something."

Several of his fraternity brothers are hanging out in the living room. One is passed out face-down on the couch, snoring loudly. The lucid ones cautiously watch Fallon stalk up the stairs to his room, with me trailing behind. He goes to his laptop and hits the space bar then jerks his head at me to come over.

"I found out about this shit last night. It took a while for me to get it taken down, but I screenshotted everything so you could see. By the time I was told about this, it already had over three hundred views."

My ass falls into his desk chair, my brain disbelieving what I'm seeing. "What the hell is this?"

"Someone is trying to mess with our girl."

On his laptop, I flick through screenshot after screenshot of images of Elizabeth posted on some random campus social site. The more I see, the angrier I get. Someone uploaded pictures of me and her kissing in the quad; Jayson and her in high school when he carried her into the school after her big fight with Maria; her with Julien out jogging; me, Fallon, and her at the bowling alley we went to on Thanksgiving; and Trevor and her in the student parking lot. In every picture, Elizabeth is either kissing me, Jayson, or Julien, or she's hugging Fallon or Trevor. Included on each picture is a commentary about Elizabeth—how she likes a good dicking, how she likes to fuck more than one guy at a time—preferably twins. How we all pass her around like a fuck-toy.

Then I get to the last picture. It's clearly a fake, but someone took the time to photoshop all of our faces on a gang-bang picture where a woman with Elizabeth's face is on all fours with a group of guys having sex with her at the same time. The entire thing is vile and disgusting. Fury like none I've ever felt overtakes me. I swear to God, if I find out who did this, I'm going to break every bone in their worthless body.

"Who?" I seethe, so angry my teeth clench.

"I have someone looking into it. Hopefully by tonight, we'll have a name and address."

"I can't keep this from Elizabeth." I scrape my hands over my face a few times. "God, I want to."

But I know only relationships based on trust are the ones that survive. I kept my past with Fallon from her, thinking I was protecting her. Daniel kept her daughter a secret from her. Jayson kept things from her all the time in high school. She's had too many people in her life hide things from her, justifying it was the right thing to do because they were protecting her. And still, the bad stuff happened. I'm breaking that cycle.

Fallon closes his laptop. "My bet is on Marshall. Kitten has humiliated him twice now."

"Marshall is too afraid to go up against you."

"I never said that dickhead was smart. Maybe I need to send him a reminder."

Marshall was livid when Elizabeth beat him at the Fields a few days ago. He was in town for Thanksgiving break then so he could have seen us at the bowling alley and taken pictures of Elizabeth and Fallon. But how did he get a hold of the high school one of her with Jayson? Or the ones here on campus? It's like someone has been following her around, stalking her. It's damn creepy. Every protective instinct in me flares to life.

"I need to get back. Elizabeth's class will be ending soon, but she said she would be dropping by here later. Do not say anything to her. I need to be the one to tell her. Send me those screenshots."

Fallon claps me on the back. "You got it, hoss. I promise, whoever this asshole is, we'll make him pay."

Someone is targeting my girl and I need to find out who and stop them. I decide to loop in the twins.

Me: We need to talk. It's about Elizabeth.

Jayson: Do I need to ask?

Julien: Just saw her this morning. Is she ok?

Me: I'll explain everything later. It's important. Meet me and Elizabeth at the main library in thirty.

It takes me longer to walk back to Mason Hall than I expected. As I cross the center quad, I see Elizabeth, Trevor, and Meredith walking out of the building but even from a distance, I can tell something is wrong. I jog the rest of the way and the relief that explodes across my girl's face has me taking her in my arms as soon as I get within reach of her. Trevor is cursing under his breath and searching the quad for something or someone. Meredith is hovering at Elizabeth's back giving me worried looks.

"Someone going to tell me what's going on?" I ask them.

Elizabeth talks into my jacket. "Just some jerks mouthing off."

Trevor makes a scoff of disgust. "Not just some jerks. Three guys came up to Elizabeth as we were leaving and straight-out asked her to fuck them; said they'd heard she liked taking on multiple guys at the same time."

"It's straight-up bullshit is what it is," Meredith spits out.

"Where?" I follow Trevor's line of sight as he continues his search of the quad.

"Campus police came in and they bolted. But I'll recognize them again if I see them."

Fallon said the post had over three hundred views before he was able to get it taken down.

Elizabeth tilts her head up to me. "I thought something odd was going on yesterday when I went to see Meredith. A couple of girls called me a slut. Trevor was there. He went off on them. Then today, people kept staring."

I thought I was angry before, but now I'm fuming. Elizabeth never said anything to me about that last night or this morning.

"Elizabeth, why didn't you tell me?" I ask her at the same time Trevor says, "You didn't tell him?"

"That's what I would like to know as well. You should have told me too," Meredith tells her. "If those girls live in my dorm, I want to know who they are."

"Why is everyone getting mad at me?" Elizabeth asks us.

I bend down and kiss her. “I’m not mad at you, baby. I’m mad about what happened.”

“I need to go grab something to eat before my next class, so you, girl, are going to tell me everything tonight,” Meredith threatens while pointing at Elizabeth. Elizabeth turns around in my arms to look at her, but I don’t let her go. “And you and Trevor better text me what those two girls look like. I know almost everyone in that dorm. I mean it! Text me! You also need to text me where we’re meeting up tonight,” she yells over her shoulder as she walks off toward the cafeteria.

“You really do need to ask her out on a proper date,” Elizabeth tells Trevor.

Trevor shrugs. “Already told you why that’s not such a good idea.”

I interrupt. “Babe, I need to talk to you about something and it’s kind of important. It can’t wait.”

Elizabeth is distracted as she watches people walk past, so I look at Trevor. “I’m meeting the guys at the library. You’re more than welcome to come.”

“Why do I have the feeling that it’s not good?”

That catches Elizabeth's attention. "What's not good?"

She's still wrapped in my arms, so I tip her chin back and kiss the side of her mouth, happy when she shifts her sole focus to me and not the assholes I notice who are watching. She's had to endure this for the past two days?

"I love you," I tell her.

Elizabeth sighs and melts into me. "I really needed to hear that."

"Come on. We're heading to the library."

"Why?"

Trevor chuckles. "You really weren't paying any attention, were you?"

Chapter 22

Jayson

When Julien and I get to the library and I see Fallon and Trevor standing next to Liz and Ry, my good morning disintegrates. Why the hell are those two douche canoes here? My main concern is Liz. Her face is pinched with what could be worry or irritation. I can't tell which.

"We're here. What's going on?"

"That's what I want to know," Liz says.

Ry ushers us inside the building. Once we find a floor that is empty, we walk to the back of the stacks. We find a lone table and four chairs there. Julien and Trevor take a seat. Fallon stares bullets into Trevor who stares right back. Liz bites her thumbnail, and Ry takes out his phone. Well, if this isn't awkward as hell.

Liz looks over at me, silently asking if I know what's going on. My shrug communicates back to her that I have no fucking clue.

Without taking his glare off Trevor, Fallon barks out, "Kitten, stop biting your nails." She drops her hand.

I'm tired of waiting. "Ry, come on, man," I start, but he interrupts with, "Give me a sec."

Finally, he places his phone on the center of the small table so we all can see. What the fuck?

"Fallon found out about this last night and told me about it this morning. We don't know who posted it yet, but before he could get it taken down, a lot of people had already seen it."

Liz snatches up the phone, her eyes wide with shock. "Oh my God!"

Julien and Trevor hunch over Liz's shoulders to see and both release a few choice expletives including a very loud, "goddammit," from Trevor. I've seen enough. I reach over and take the phone from Liz's hands, ignoring her protests, and I stab it back at Ryder. "She doesn't need to see that. What's wrong with you? And people think I'm the insensitive prick," I say heatedly.

"She needs to know," is his response. "We all need to know so we can figure out what to do about it."

"Then use your words next time. Liz has

been through enough already without having those visuals seared in her brain."

"Jayson, it's alright. It's sick and disgusting, but at least now I know why I've been getting all these creepy stares for the past couple of days."

"You're getting verbally assaulted and harassed is more like it," Trevor scowls.

"What the fuck are you talking about?" Fallon asks his brother.

Meanwhile, Julien remains silent, but I can see his anger. Hearing Trevor's choice of words hits too close to home for us.

Liz bristles, "Do you know how freaking tired I'm getting with having to explain stuff over and over to everyone?" She slams her hands flat against the wall in frustration. "Can I not catch just one fucking break?"

"Elizabeth." Ryder reaches for her.

"Just give me a minute."

"Yeah, screw that," Ry says and hauls her into his arms. "I promise, baby, we will find out who did this."

"You bet your ass we will," Fallon says.

"Why? Why me? I don't understand. What

did I do to deserve that?" She points at the phone on the table, its screen now blank.

I look into the eyes of each man standing there and reflected back at me is the same emotion: rage.

Liz dries her tears and kisses Ry on the shoulder. "I just need a minute, okay?" she brokenly says and walks off toward the exit to the stairs. The five of us watch her go like a bunch of stupid, helpless assholes.

"You're not going after her?" I aim at Ry.

"She said she needed a minute. Respect what she wants and give her space," he responds.

"How did you find out about this?" Julien asks Fallon.

"Preston."

Ry looks shocked. "Preston?"

"Who the fuck is Preston?" Trevor asks, and for a split second the similarity between him and Fallon is so striking that no one would doubt they were related.

"Doesn't matter who he is. He saw it and called me. I'd told him to let me know if he ever saw kitten again. I'm just pissed that I hadn't learned about it sooner. Whoever posted that trash is going to fucking pay."

Julien spears his metallic eyes at Trevor, his anger visibly growing. "What did you mean when you said she was getting assaulted and harassed?"

"Some girls said a bunch of shit to her yesterday, and then some guys today. I handled it."

Fallon looks like he's about to blow a fuse. Ry says, "I'm hoping this will die down, but just in case it doesn't, I wanted you all to know what was going on so we can keep our eyes open and protect Elizabeth. Besides, when I find out who did this, I'm going to need your help."

"You don't even have to ask," Julien says. "Christ, it feels like high school all over again."

I explain for Trevor and Fallon. "We had to walk Liz to every class in our senior year after *his* ex-girlfriend, Maria" —I gesture to Ry — "and two other girls, Jacinda and Samantha, kept messing with her."

"You can cut that shit out right now, Jay. And let's not forget that Jacinda was *your* problem," Ry rounds on me.

"I handled Jacinda," Fallon says, and my brow cocks up in disbelief.

"You may think you did," I return.

Trevor speaks up. "I know I don't have the

whole 'growing up together' relationship with Elizabeth that you guys do, but I care about her. She's been a good friend to me since we met. Trust me when I tell you that those girls yesterday, and the guys today, did not get away lightly with the shit they said to her."

"Well, *that shit* has been going on for days, hasn't it? And unless you beat the ever-living fuck out of all of them, then I say they got away too lightly," Julien seethes. My brother is usually the calm and controlled one. The peacekeeper. You know things are really fucking bad if he loses his cool.

Ry circles back around. "A lot of those pictures are recent on campus, but the one of her and Jay is from high school. It's like I told Fallon, it's stalkerish."

"You think Liz has a stalker?" Julien asks with concern and motions for Ryder's phone so he can take a look at the images again. He taps something out and I hear his phone ding. He must have sent the images to himself.

"Honestly, I don't know what to think," Ry tells him.

I get Jules' attention. "Forward those to my phone."

"How likely is the possibility that the guy who attacked her is behind this?" Shit, it never occurred to me. Julien and I look at each other.

Fallon leans back in his chair. "Not likely. This online shit is juvenile and petty. My bet's still on Marshall."

Liz hasn't come back yet, and for the life of me, I don't know why Ry hasn't gone after her. "I'm going to check on Liz." I don't wait for a response.

As soon as I open the exit door, Liz's jasmine scent hits me. I go down a few flights of stairs, but I stop when I see her sitting on the bottom stair facing a wall that's painted with a small mural of the campus bell tower. She's lost in thought and playing with the locket I gave her. I quietly make my way down the remaining steps and sit beside her, arms resting on my bent knees. She tilts her head and lays it on my shoulder.

"I may join you tonight. I feel like pummeling something."

My arm goes around her, her floral scent surrounding me. "I don't think you'd like getting punched in the face much. It's such a beautiful face too. Wielding a baseball bat like a mafia enforcer is more your style."

Liz snorts. "There is a campus intramural softball team I can probably join. Or maybe work as a money collector so I can bust some kneecaps."

"I'm sorry shit keeps happening to you, princess."

"Yeah, well, life sucks donkey balls sometimes."

"That's really gross." We look at each other and start laughing.

"I wish I could understand why someone would do this. But at least now I know why people have been staring and sniggering at me the past two days."

I nudge her elbow. "First, only you would find something positive about the situation. Secondly, who says 'sniggering' nowadays?"

Liz exhales a quiet laugh, then turns serious again. "But having those guys today come up to me and, well, I'm not going to repeat what they said. I felt violated."

"We're going to handle this. Just like we did before."

"Not without me this time, Jayson. I appreciate what you said to Ryder, but I also made him promise me no more secrets. You guys kept so much from me in high school. I'm not that girl anymore. I can handle it. I need my eyes wide open so I'm never vulnerable to anyone ever again."

I shift to my left so that I can see her better. The pink streaks and tips in her hair are no longer visible, her long mass of pale blond hair is hanging down in messy waves. I smooth a strand behind her ear.

"You're the strongest person I know, Liz. I have and will always do whatever I can to protect you." I lift her locket up and kiss it before tucking it back under the collar of her shirt.

"You've always been my best friend, Jayson. I've missed being able to talk to you."

I don't think I've ever hated two words more. *Best friend.* I have to remind myself not to stray from my game plan in winning Liz back, even though I want nothing more than to sink my lips and my body into hers. Scenes from the night she came to me when her memories returned are still fresh in my mind.

"Come on. Let's go grab the guys and get you to class. Have I told you that I'm happy you're coming tonight?"

"Once or twice." She grins. "You'll actually have a full audience. Everyone's coming."

"I guess I'll need to make sure I win then."

"I'm betting a hundred dollars that you do

just that."

Chapter 23

Elizabeth

"Sweetheart, I wish you'd talk to me about how you're feeling." I roll my head on the headrest and take in Ryder's concerned profile.

Jayson texted me about an hour ago to let me know the fights would be happening at an old junkyard about twenty minutes from campus. Fallon, Trevor, and Meredith are meeting us there. After the library, I finished up my classes for the day and went home with Ryder. All the guys basically stuck to me like glue the entire day, and just like high school, someone escorted me to each of my classes. Hell, I wasn't even allowed to go to the restroom without an escort to the door. By late afternoon, I was fed up with it. I knew they meant well, but it was overbearing. I felt suffocated. After the morning's fiasco, things seemed to have settled down with the staring and the whispered comments. That doesn't mean they stopped altogether, but it was manageable. As soon as

Ryder and I got home, I escaped to the bedroom, telling him I needed some space. I hadn't had time to fully process everything. Someone had painted a target on my back, and I was not going to play the damsel in distress. That was Old Elizabeth's way of handling things; let someone else fix the problem. That wasn't me anymore.

Ryder glances my way and meets my gaze before turning his eyes back to the road. "What did you and Jay talk about at the library?"

Oh, that's a can of worms if I ever saw one. Ryder has been upset about the online photos and stewing ever since Jayson and I emerged from the stairwell. Even after all the times Ryder and I talked and poured our feelings out to one another since the day he showed up in Barcelona, there's a lingering sense that part of him still doesn't trust that I'm completely, totally his. That he's it for me. I'm not going back to Jayson. Ryder is the love of my life. Can I blame him for his insecurities though? It's my fault things got so screwed up to begin with.

I reach my hand over the console and trace the side of his face from temple to jaw with the back of my fingers. I love this man more than life itself. I need to remember that he is as affected by things as I am. We're in this together through the good times and the bad.

"I love you."

Ryder takes my hand and brings it to his lips. "I love you too." He places our joined hands on his thigh, his left hand still firmly grasping the steering wheel as he drives.

"Jayson and I just talked. As friends. Nothing more. My head is still trying to wrap around why someone would post that filth about all of us. It's not just me they hurt with those pictures, but you guys as well. I'm angry. I'm not shutting you out, Ryder. I just needed some time to process."

I see his chest move out then in as he takes a deep breath. "Thank you," he simply states.

"For what?"

"For talking to me."

He pulls into the lot for the junkyard. There are already about a dozen cars parked and people milling about. As soon as he turns off the engine, I unbuckle myself and crawl over to his lap, straddling him the best I can in our close confines.

His gorgeous light brown eyes dilate as I press in to kiss the tender spot at his ear. "I should be thanking you," I voice gently beside his ear. "Thank you for not keeping things from me. Thank you for telling me what was going on. You don't know how much that means to me."

"I promised no more hiding things from you, and I meant it."

"I don't know what I ever did to deserve you." Thoughts of spending the rest of my life with him dance around my mind. What would it be like? What would our children look like? All I know for sure is, I am looking forward to my future. One filled with him and our life together.

I trail light kisses across his cheek as he chases my lips, trying to capture them. One of his large hands slides up to cradle the swell of my breast. Neither of us give thought to the fact that we're in a parking lot where anyone could see us. The driver's side window starts to fog up as our kisses get more heated, our groping becoming more frenetic. A loud knock on the window causes both of us to jump.

"Didn't I say no front seat porno unless I was invited?" Fallon's wide-grinning face laughs at us through the glass.

Ryder holds up his left hand and gives Fallon the middle finger. With his right hand, he grabs the back of my neck and pulls me in for one last heart-pounding kiss.

"Aw, come on, man!" Fallon protests.

"Did you just growl?" I giggle against Ryder's mouth, feeling his low vocal vibrations against my smiling lips.

"Yes."

"My sweet alpha man," I tease, kissing him on the brow. Ryder opens the car door, bending over to get out so I don't hit my head. He carries me along with him and I tuck my chin in his shoulder, still giggling. "Hey, Fallon."

"I swear to God, the two of you are like horny rabbits."

"Have you seen Meredith or Trevor yet?" I ask him.

"Nope. Just got here."

I look around. The place looks straight out of *Nightmare on Elm Street*. Sheet metal walls surround piles of compacted cars, busted cars with no windows, various pieces of scrap metal scattered all over the place. Several spotlights mounted on telephone poles light up the place. A small, dilapidated shack that serves as the main office sits adjacent to the dirt and gravel parking lot.

As soon as I spot Jayson's truck parked across the lot, I hear his voice. "Liz!"

Jayson walks up to our group. "You made it."

"I told you I would. This place is creepy."

Jayson gives Ryder a guy half-hug and ignores Fallon. Fallon couldn't care less. "The guy who owns it is letting us fight here tonight. Come on. I'll introduce you to some of the others."

"You're friends with the guys you fight with?"

Jayson grabs my wrist and pulls me away from Ryder and Fallon. "Everyone knows it's not personal. See that guy over there? I broke his nose and a few ribs last year. He and I go out and shoot pool every once in a while. No hard feelings. That's part of the sport."

"Jayson, I'm not sure about this. It sounds like you can get seriously hurt."

"It almost sounds like you care about me."

I look at him aghast. "Of course I care about you."

"Yeah?" he asks, taking my hand. I deftly remove it from his grasp.

"Jay-man! How are ya doin'?" a pot-bellied older man, with a long dark beard and hair pulled back in a ponytail, greets him. "And who is this fine lady?"

"Ray, this is Liz. Liz, this is the man you give your money to when you want to place a bet."

I don't like how this guy is looking at me and I instinctively step a little closer to Jayson. "Nice to meet you, Ray."

"We've got some girls fighting tonight if you're interested."

"Back off, Ray. She's not fighting."

"Pity," he says, leering at me. "Hey, Staci is here tonight. She's been asking about you," he says to Jayson who quickly diverts his gaze from me.

Because I'm dumb and need to learn when to keep my mouth shut, I ask stupidly, "Who's Staci?"

Ray gives me another slick smile. "Well, catch ya later, J-man. Need to make my rounds."

"Jayson?" Yeah, something's up because he's fidgeting like crazy and won't look me in the eye.

"She's a fight groupie. I never had sex with her if that's what you want to know."

Oh, thank God. I was about to flip out thinking I needed to get myself and Ryder tested.

Jayson and I didn't use protection the night my memories returned.

"That's very specific," I point out because it sounds like he may have done something with Staci even if he didn't stick his dick into her.

"Liz, I'm not talking about this with you."

I wipe my concern away as if I was turning the page in my e-reader. "No need. I'm not upset. You can go at it with whomever you want."

"For fuck's sake, Liz. You were gone for over a year. What did you expect me to do?" Jayson argues.

"Jayson, I'm not being sarcastic. I want you to be happy, and that includes supporting you moving on and finding someone who will love you as much as you deserve to be loved. You're my best friend."

He sighs in disgust. I hear Meredith's talkative voice behind us and look over my shoulder. The gang is all here. I thankfully and quickly excuse myself as Jayson is approached by some guy who wants to talk to him.

"Elizabeth! Oh my God, girl!" Meredith squeals.

"I know, right?" I agree, looking around at

the crowd that keeps getting bigger by the minute. I wrap my arm around Ryder's waist and snuggle close. Jayson's comments have me wanting to ask Ryder if he was with anyone while I was in Seattle. Fallon and Trevor's low, angry voices have me turning my head their way. Fallon notices me watching and says something to Trevor who looks over at me. They both stop talking and slowly make their way over. I'll make sure to ask Fallon about that later.

"Hey, Trevor."

"Hey, Elizabeth," he says back. "What do you think?"

"I think guys who do this are straight-up crazy," I reply honestly.

"And that's why women should rule the world. We're masters at getting shit done without punching anyone. But you have to admit, it's sexy as hell," Meredith says, seemingly forgetting her willingness to jump into any fight.

I groan. "You and I need to have a long talk," I tell her and she smiles.

"What happens now?" she asks.

Trevor looks around and nods to someone. "The guys will size each other up and decide who they want to fight. If their challenge is accepted, they fight." He makes it sound so simple and easy. I still think it's stupid.

"I can't believe you did this shit," Fallon says to his brother.

"Like you're the one to talk, little brother."

"Guys, it's neither the time nor place," I reprimand them both. I will get those two together to sit down and talk if it kills me.

To lighten the mood, I joke, "The guy Jayson is talking to asked me if I wanted to fight."

"Hell no!" Ryder says as Fallon says, "Fuck, yeah!"

"No, Fallon! She's not fighting," Ryder's grip around my waist tightens.

"I have to agree with Ryder," Trevor says.

"And when did you all decide it was okay to make decisions for me?" I glower at both of them.

"I actually agree with Fallon," Meredith adds. "How cool would that be, watching Elizabeth kick some butt? Am I allowed to fight?"

"That's a fuck no to you too, firecracker. Not on my watch," Trevor tells her.

"Remind me again why we slept together?"

"Remind me again why you keep bringing it up?" Trevor counters.

I throw my hands up. "You know what? Everybody needs to shut up."

Jayson finishes speaking with the random guy and jogs over. "What's up, Trevor? You fighting tonight?"

"Nope. Just consider me part of Elizabeth's entourage."

Meredith wraps her small hands around Jayson's upper arm and squeezes. He looks down at her in question. "What? I just want to sample the big guns. You're very big. And hard. I'd put down a solid Benjamin on you to win."

"Is she for real?" Jayson looks to me for help. I un-grip her hands from molesting him further.

"She can be a bit handsy," Trevor replies, and Meredith snorts, "Didn't hear you complaining. Either time."

"Would you please stop bringing that up?" Trevor says in exasperation. Fallon is holding a fist to his mouth to stop his laughter from escaping.

"Behave," I tell her.

"I can't help it. It's testosterone overload out

here and it's making me a bit punch-drunk. And horny," she whisper-shouts at me.

"Jay! You're up, man. You've been challenged."

I instantly go on alert and forget about everything else. I want to beg Jayson not to fight. I want to plead with him to stop. I grab his arm. "Please be careful."

Those silver eyes shine back at me. "Always, princess." He gives my hand a squeeze and breaks through the circle of people who have created a makeshift ring where the guys will fight.

"He'll be okay, Elizabeth. He's been doing this for a year and hasn't come back home with anything more than a black eye and a split lip," Ryder tries to assure me, but it doesn't help.

"If anything happens to him," I reply, choking off my words. I may not be with Jayson anymore, but I still care for him deeply.

"Come on, kitten. This is something I've got to see," Fallon says, dragging me through the throngs of people already cheering and taunting. Everyone else in our group plows through after us.

Meredith sidles up beside me and Ryder. I see Ray and call out to him.

"You called, pretty lady."

I shove five twenties into his hand. "A hundred on Jayson."

"Oh, me too!" Meredith shouts.

Our money disappears into a large roll of cash as he accepts it. A thin man next to Ray jots something down in a ledger. He gives the man Jayson's name. "Enjoy the show." He winks.

"I can't believe you just bet money on a fight, especially an illegal one." Ryder chuckles, brushing the side of my neck with his nose. "My little criminal."

"Watch it, or I'll make you take me to Vegas next."

"Don't let Fal hear you or he'll have one of his jets up and ready within the hour."

Fallon perks up. "Sounds like a fucktastic idea."

Ryder gives him a firm "no" and shifts me to his other side, farther away from Fallon.

The noise levels have jacked up tremendously with growing excitement for the fighting to begin. Jayson catches my attention and smirks at me. He rolls his shoulders and cracks his neck as another guy walks into the circle.

Trevor claps Ryder's shoulder, pointing to the guy Jayson is about to fight. "That's him."

"Are you sure?"

"One hundred percent."

I feel Ryder go rigid as iron next to me.

"Who the fuck are we talking about?" Fallon asks.

Meredith gasps. "Oh, this just got interesting."

It takes me a second to recognize the guy. It's the preppy guy that came up to me this morning with his two meathead friends.

Fallon yells out, "Jay, that's the motherfucker from this morning who talked shit to Elizabeth. If you don't kick his ass, I will!"

Jayson's eyes narrow on his opponent and I swear his arm and neck muscles grow thicker as he balls his hands into two tight fists.

I reach over and slap my hand over Fallon's mouth. "Fallon! Stop it!" He's egging Jayson on and I won't have it.

"I'm with Fallon," Ryder stonily replies.

"His friends are here too," Trevor points out.

One of the big guys Preppy was with this morning locks his eyes on me.

"Even better." Fallon grins, nudging closer to Ryder. They have a conversation without words that I know means nothing good.

I'm about to chastise both of them when all hell breaks loose. Jayson shoves Preppy hard. "You think you can mess with my girl and get away with it?" he spits in the guy's face.

Preppy takes a swing at Jayson's head and misses by a mile. Jayson steps back and aims a kick to the guy's solar plexus, taking him down, then jumps on top of him and wails punch after punch to his face. The crowd goes feral, smelling blood, loving every second of what they're watching.

I see Preppy's friends break through the raucous crowd, and I scream a warning at Jayson.

Ryder, Fallon, and Trevor rush in to intercept, and I swear I hear Fallon cackle with glee. I turn to Meredith in time to see her eyes go huge. "Elizabeth! Behind you!"

Somehow the fight has spread out and it's now a free-for-all. Fists are slinging in all directions and bodies are being tackled to the ground. No one is safe from the chaos. Meredith's warning gives me enough time to spin around to see a guy charging our way. Are you freaking kidding me? It's one of Preppy's football cohorts from this morning; the one who locked eyes with me moments ago. I shove Meredith behind me and drop low; all of the self-defense classes Daniel and Drew made me do coming back to me. I sucker-punch the guy's balls as he reaches for me, and he falls to his knees with a guttural wail, cupping his crotch. From my crouched position, I kick up with my right foot. I hear the guy's teeth clack loudly as my boot connects under his jaw. I'd be surprised if he didn't lose any teeth after that hit. Meredith rushes forward and kicks the poor guy in the nuts again. I cringe at his long, high-pitched howl.

"Think you can mess with a couple of girls, asshole! Think again!"

Ryder's arms circle around me and lift me up and away. Trevor grabs Meredith.

"We can't leave you two alone for five seconds, can we?" Trevor says to Meredith, hauling her off as she continues to scream obscenities at the guy. His scolding tone does little to hide the approval on his face.

"Where are Jayson and Fallon?" I ask Ryder, yelling above the fray.

Holding tightly to me, Ryder pushes through the crowd, not stopping until we are back at his car. He jerks his head at Trevor who is shoving Meredith in his car. "They're coming, but I'm getting you out of here now." Ryder plants me in the passenger seat of his car and rounds the hood.

Someone yells something but I only hear Ryder reply, "I've got her." He gets in and starts the car. "Buckle up, Cobra Kai." He smirks and for some reason I burst out laughing.

I hiss, "Ow! That stings."

Ryder and I are back at home, sitting on the bed with a first aid kit open next to us. He gently blows on my hand and throws the antiseptic wipe on the bedside table. Everyone, including Julien and Elijah who weren't even there, have blown up my phone with text messages checking up on me. Jayson feels awful that the one night I came to watch him fight, all hell broke loose.

"I would say that should be expected for punching that guy in the nuts, but I'll take a page from Fallon's book and instead say," Ryder leans in and kisses the side of my mouth, "that it was pretty fucking awesome."

My cheeks warm at his praise. I didn't know what to expect from him when we got home.

Anger? Worry? A stern lecture, perhaps. But never would have I guessed admiration and respect. It just solidifies for me how much Ryder loves and supports me and will always have my back.

I smile and begin to inspect his face and hands for any cuts or bruises. Satisfied that he's alright, I admit, "I almost feel sorry for the guy after what Meredith did to him."

Ryder groans and adjusts himself slightly at the thought of getting kicked in the balls. "Yeah, let's not talk about that anymore."

"What if I promise not to mess with another guy's balls again."

Ryder barks out a laugh, and I swear I think he snorts as well. So cute. I shove the first aid kit away so I can straddle him where he's sitting on the bed. His large hands cup my ass and bring me closer as I scrape my fingers up his temples, around his ears, and into his hair, before settling my hands at the back of his head. I massage his scalp, making his eyes flutter close in pleasure.

"Babe, that feels so good."

He drops his forehead to my chest, and I continue to rub his neck and upper shoulders. I can literally feel his muscles relax as my hands release the tension that had taken up residence in his body from the events of tonight.

"Jayson's not too happy about what went down."

Ryder makes a dismissive grunting sound and tilts us sideways, so we are lying on the bed facing each other. I love these quiet times with him. I wish we had more of them. The past several months—hell the past few years—have been filled with the turbulence of one monumental revelation after another. I crave the day when I can live a normal life with the man I love. No more awaiting disasters or tumultuous discoveries. Just the two of us together, building our life and sharing our dreams. The dreams that include me going to medical school and Ryder getting his MBA and taking over his dad's garage. Getting married and building our dream home, the one we will fill with our love and our children. Hopefully, we'll travel and see more of the world. We'll race cars, play music, and dance under the moonlight.

While I'm lost in my thoughts, Ryder shifts me closer to him on the bed and we stare into each other's eyes, using our fingers to trace the outline of one another's facial features. Ryder is so handsome, so uniquely masculine, and just plain perfect. His dark, almost black hair that is cut shorter on the sides than on top. His long eyelashes that I've been envious of my whole life. His dark brown eyebrows that cock up in such a sexy way when he looks at me. His high cheekbones and rounded square jaw that are both manly yet beautiful. And of course, his light brown, amber-colored eyes. I have always loved his eyes.

"What's going on in that head of yours?" he asks, rubbing his thumb across my brow.

I scooch closer to him and wrap my leg over the top of his thigh, sliding my foot up and down the hairs on his leg, enjoying the dichotomy between my softness and his unyielding muscles. "I was just thinking how nice this was, being with you like this. No drama, no chaos. I want more times like this with you. I just want to be with you, Ryder."

Ryder rolls over on top of me and I stare up at his golden eyes, transfixed at the emotion I see in them. "We can have whatever we want, Elizabeth. I want to give you the life and the future of your dreams. All you have to do is tell me. I don't care where we go or what we do. We could travel the world and sleep in a tent. You are my home, and wherever you are is where I am happiest. All I've ever wanted is you."

I lift my head and taste his sweet lips, his beautiful words causing a delicate tear to escape. I pull back and hold his face with my hands, wanting so badly for the dreams of our future to come true. The words I have kept to myself escape my mouth before I can stop them. I realize that I don't want to stop them.

"Marry me."

The raw emotions that had filled his eyes just seconds ago morph into something so powerful and visceral that it leaves me breathless. I drink in the unrestrained love I feel emanating from him, knowing it's all for me. I want to return that love a thousand-fold and let him know, without a doubt, that I want a forever with only him, and that I hope that he is ready to take that unknown leap with me into a future together. One I know will be more wonderful than anything I could ever have imagined or wished for.

"I know this is unconventional and maybe a little unexpected, but I have known in my heart since I was nine years old that I love you with everything I have in me. You have been my friend, my protector, the man who has always stood by me no matter what. You were patient and waited for me. And not even near-death and the loss of my memory could keep me from finding my way back to you. Ryder Randall Cutton, will you give me the honor of spending the rest of your life with me as my husband?"

Ryder crushes his mouth to mine as warm

tears flow from his eyes. "Yes," he says with conviction as our kisses become deeper. "God, yes, I want to marry you. More than anything. Yes, Elizabeth. Yes to everything," he promises, and sears his promise with a kiss so earth-shattering and possessive, my body implodes on itself as I climax out of nowhere. *Holy fucking shit*!

Ryder kisses me ravenously as he captures my orgasmic cry. As I shudder uncontrollably, he gives me a few minutes to come back down from my endorphin high, grinning widely above me.

"Did that really just happen?" He looks very smug and pleased with himself. He should.

"Uh, yeah." I smile stupidly, so freaking happy and still so very turned on, wanting more. I never knew my body could do that. I should have known anything is possible when it comes to Ryder. My body is still buzzing and tingling, so it takes me a second to realize he said yes. "Did you really say yes?"

Ryder kisses a path down my neck and reaches over into the bedside table on his side of the bed. I'm about to ask him what he's doing when I see the small black box he lifts out of the drawer.

"Ryder?"

He adjusts our positions so I'm sitting up on the bed, my legs dangling while he kneels down on the floor in front of me. My hand involuntarily goes to my mouth, my own tears falling, as he lifts the lid of the box. Nestled inside is the most gorgeous princess-cut yellow diamond ring.

"Ryder?" I ask again, unbelieving.

"I was going to plan this big elaborate proposal, but I don't think anything I could have come up with would have been better than hearing you ask me to marry you. But I am man enough not to deprive you of an old-school bended-on-one-knee proposal. So" —he grins up at me— "Elizabeth Penelope Fairchild, soon to be Mrs. Elizabeth Fairchild Cutton, will *you* do *me* the honor of marrying me and being my wife? Because I want nothing more than to be your husband, to be a father to our children, and to be able to hold your hand as we grow old together."

"Yes!" I exclaim and he takes my shaking hand, pushing the stunning ring onto my finger. Once it's in place, he kisses me passionately.

"Do you like it? I've been saving away as much as I can from working at the garage and from the winnings I get from racing. I wanted to be able to afford something you would be proud to wear. I chose a yellow diamond because it reminded me of the way your beauty is like the brightness of the sun."

God, this man and his words. They get me. Every. Fucking. Time. "It's the most gorgeous ring I have ever seen. I love you, you wonderful, perfect man."

Ryder stands up and pulls me into his arms. "I love you more," he grins.

"We're getting married," I gush, switching my gaze between Ryder and my ring.

"We're so absolutely getting married," Ryder replies as we sway back and forth to music that only our hearts can hear.

"Grab your coat and gloves. I want to take you somewhere," he tells me.

I was wanting to consummate our engagement with the filthiest, loudest sex possible. Ryder sees my pout and laughs. "Most definitely later," he promises with another kiss and then reaches for my hand to pull me out of the bedroom.

Even though it's the middle of the night, I don't ask why or where we're going. I would follow my man to the ends of the earth if he asked.

About a half hour later, we park up on the hill he took me to after our first date. His quiet place, he once told me. The place where we danced under the stars. The midnight air is cold and crisp and smells damp. The trees that once sheltered buzzing cicadas are barren, but the view below of the town, campus, and roads is still breathtaking in its lit-up beauty. I can see many houses and businesses that already have their Christmas lights up and turned on.

Ryder pulls a thick blanket out of the back seat and wraps it around us as we sit on the warm hood of the car. The sky is completely clouded over so there are no stars to view tonight, but that's okay. My eyes are already filled with thousands of them as I tip my head back to look at Ryder who has his arms and the blanket bundled around me from behind.

"It just hit me," I say.

"What did, baby?"

"I get to spend my first Christmas with my fiancé," I reply, but then I turn pensive. "I wish Mom and Dad and Hailey were here. I won't have Dad to walk me down the aisle. Hailey won't be my maid of honor."

Ryder turns me in his arms and caresses my arms and back. "Oh, sweetheart. They are here. They are watching us right now. Your Dad will be with you every step of the way down the aisle where I will be waiting to pledge my life to you in front of them, because your family will always be with you," he tells me, placing his hand over my heart to show me where they are and where they always will be.

And to make sure that I know they are here with me, Mom, Dad, and Hailey send down a fluttering of delicate snow flurries. Ryder and I look up at the sky and I smile as each tiny snowflake kisses my face letting me know that my family is sharing this monumental moment in my life with me. Dad loved Ryder like his own son. Mom and Dad would be overjoyed that Ryder and I are engaged. They're telling me so right now.

"How are we going to tell Jayson and Julien?" I ask Ryder as the flurries come down faster.

"However you want to tell them. But I know it's Jayson you're more worried about, isn't it?"

"I just want to hold on to this feeling a little while longer. Our announcement is going to hurt him, and I don't know how he's going to react."

I feel the blanket shift as Ryder takes out his phone and pulls up some music. Of course he plays "Helium" by Sia. This night wouldn't be perfect without us dancing to our song. He secures the blanket around us once more as we dance under the falling snow.

"You mind if we at tell my parents?"

I nod yes. "And Fallon," I add. "Can I tell Tatiána too?" I also want to add Julien and Elijah to that list, but I'm afraid word might get back to Jayson.

"Baby, I will shout it from the rooftops if you want me to. I want the whole world to know that the woman of my dreams said 'yes.'"

"Technically, the man of my dreams said yes first."

"Phone call or visit?" Ryder asks me how we should tell his family. A large wet snowflake lands on my face and he kisses it off my cheek. My body heats under that one small touch.

"We can do a video call with a promise to visit after we get back from Seattle. Finals are coming up and then I want to focus on the trip and visiting Elizabeth Ann's grave, which I know is going to be very emotional for everyone, especially Jayson. I also want to see Daniel and Drew. It's past time I stop avoiding them and get an explanation on why they did what they did. Deep down I know it's because they were protecting me, but I still need to hear it from them."

"Sounds fair. We can stop by my parents' on our way back."

"I told Fallon I want to buy my house. I want to fix it up and make it a proper home again. It was a great place to grow up in. I want that for another family."

I nuzzle my cold nose against Ryder's warm chest as we continue our slow dance. "That sounds like a great idea, Elizabeth. I'd like to help if you'd let me."

"I do. And thank you. I need you to make sure that Fallon doesn't buy it for me."

"He said he was going to buy it?"

"Not in exact words, but I have a feeling that he's going to try and sneak it past me."

The snow flurries start to taper off and Ryder lifts me up, blanket and all, to wrap my legs around his middle before he sits back down on the car hood. The way he is able to hold me like I weigh nothing thrills me to no end.

What Ryder says next, catches me off guard. "While we were in Barcelona, Fallon confessed to me that he was in love with you."

Fallon told him *what*?

"That if I screwed things up, he would step

in and take you away again. I wanted to punch the shit out of him when he said it. But a part of me was happy for him. Fallon told me you knew more secrets about him than I did, so I'm pretty sure you know about his crappy childhood with an abusive father."

If Ryder only knew that was half of it. But it's not my secret to tell, just like Julien's secret in high school was not mine to tell Jayson.

"So why were you happy about it?" I ask, perplexed. Soon after we came back home, I had told Ryder everything that happened between me and Fallon on our trip. He knows about the kisses and about Fallon sleeping next to me in bed. I laid every second out for Ryder, leaving nothing out.

Ryder pulls my winter hat down more securely, so my ears are covered. Little things like that show me how much he cares for me. I would take those small, loving, nondescript actions over a bouquet of flowers any day.

"Fallon has never loved anything or anyone." He touches his forehead to mine. "Until you."

"He loves you, Ryder. In a bromance kind of way of course."

"I'm talking about pure, selfless love. I was happy that he could love you like that. I know he won't do anything to get in the way of us or our relationship. I don't know how to explain it better. In a way, it eases my mind that if something ever happened to me, then Fallon would take care of you and protect you because he loves you."

"Yeah, I'm not so magnanimous. If another girl said she loved you, I would rip her hair out. Then I'd set Meredith on her." We both laugh out loud at that.

"I promise I will never give you any reason to send Meredith my way." He chuckles.

Our song ends and the snow finally dissipates. Ryder tips my chin up, hovering his lips a breath's-width apart from mine. "I'd like to take my fiancé home now and make love to her for the rest of the night."

Tingles spread like wildfire across my chilled skin. "Yes, please."

Chapter 24

Elizabeth

Ryder and I video-chatted with his parents, Brea and Jamie, the next evening. After giving them our news, Ryder and I couldn't get a word in for over an hour. Faith brought up grand-babies again and started crying. Again. Jamie and Brea said they want to help me plan the wedding, and Randy teared up and had trouble getting so much as a complete sentence out. Overall, it went much better than we expected.

Now, I'm sitting in a small café near campus waiting for Ryder and Fallon to arrive. We're going to tell Fallon together about our engagement. However, I decided to kill two birds with one stone, and one of those birds just walked in.

"Hey, wildcat."

I stand up to give him a hug. "Hey, Trevor. Thanks for meeting me on short notice."

He removes his long coat and scarf, placing them on the back of one of the small café chairs. He glides a hand through his messy hair making it stand up even more. I chose a table in the back of the café so we could have some privacy.

Another guy propositioned me today as I was walking across the quad. I hope Fallon is able to find out who posted those pictures. The sooner, the better. I'm getting tired of always feeling eyes on me or hearing snide comments whispered behind hands as I walk by. Meredith texted me earlier and said she found where the girls who called me a slut lived, and that she and Sara were going to pay them a visit today. There's no stopping Meredith once she sets her mind to something, so my only reply was to tell her to be careful. Then we planned to have our girls' night out at Belly's this Friday. Finals are quickly approaching, and pretty soon we won't have any time to hang out before I leave for Seattle and she goes back home for the two-week holiday. That means no boys allowed for our girl's night.

Trevor eyes my hot chocolate. I asked for extra marshmallows and have been waiting for them to melt. "Do you mind?" he asks.

"Go right ahead."

He takes my large mug and sips, licking gooey, white marshmallow fluff from his upper lip. “Okay, that’s really, really good. I’m going to order me one. Be right back.”

Trevor walks over to the counter to place his order. Knowing my time is limited before Ryder and Fallon show up, I mentally go through what I want to talk to him about. I’m calling in the favor he owes from his promise to trust me when the time came.

I watch as the girl behind the counter tries her best to flirt with Trevor. Either he ignores her small touches and bright, overenthusiastic smiles, or he’s completely oblivious. I suspect the former.

Sitting back down, he cups his hot chocolate in his hands, blowing on the rising steam. “Alright, out with it. You’ve been fidgeting since I walked in.”

I have? I still my restless hands. “And if this is about me dating Meredith, I am going to politely say no right now and we can enjoy our drinks in peace,” he continues and relaxes back in the chair.

“Actually, this is about the no-questions-asked favor you promised me.”

He looks intrigued.

"But first, I need to preface that with this," I say, taking off my gloves and showing him my engagement ring. Trevor's blue eyes flare and he takes my hand. "We haven't told anyone yet, with the exception of Ryder's family, so I ask that you keep it quiet for now."

Trevor turns the ring back and forth and looks directly at me. "Ryder is one lucky man. Congratulations, Elizabeth. I really mean that. You deserve a happy-ever-after."

"Wow, okay. That was very sweet. Thank you. We're going to tell Fallon later, and then we'll wait until we get back from Seattle to tell the rest of the guys."

"You're worried about how Jayson is going to react?"

"Yes."

"Need backup?"

I lean forward and consider the man in front of me. Trevor and I met by freak coincidence on the beach a few months ago. I would never have imagined how intricately involved he would become with my life in such a short amount of time. He's Fallon's half-brother. He and my best girl friend slept together. He became a good friend to me. He seems to be at the right place at the right time when some bad shit went down, like at Fallon's frat party or at Meredith's dorm. Trevor stands up for me. Why? Did those Fate bitches put him in my path for a reason?

"Hey, Elizabeth? You with me?"

I blink back to him. "Sorry. Random thoughts." I skip over the mentioning of Jayson and plow forward. "The favor I want to ask you concerns Fallon."

And there's the Montgomery scowl, just like his half-brother. "What has the little prick done now?"

"It's nothing that Fallon has done. It's more what I want you to do."

"And what would that be?"

"Talk to him. Really sit down and have a rational conversation with him. I know you don't think it, but the two of you need each other. He needs his older brother as much as you need him in your life. You both have more in common than you realize."

Trevor scoffs at my statement. "Not possible, wildcat. The only thing we have in common is..." He looks up at me suddenly, a glimmer of panic in his eyes before he wipes it away and gulps down his scalding hot chocolate. I wait him out, wondering what he was about to say.

"Like I said, we don't have anything in common," he finishes.

"Do you know what happened to him when he was just a kid. How much he suffered? What he went through?" I tell him, my ire rising at the thought of the abuse Fallon endured at the hands of his parents. "You may have a preconception that your brother is a spoiled, rich kid who got everything while you got nothing, but I promise you, if you knew the truth, you would be ashamed of yourself."

"Elizabeth, what aren't you telling me? Did something bad happen to Fallon?"

"You're the third person in my life who I'm going to tell it's not my secret to share. You need to be the bigger man and reach out to him. Talk to him. Open the door for him to walk through; be a part of his life. He won't come gently, but I swear to you that you won't regret it."

Trevor rubs his hands together then scrubs them down his face. He stares at me for a long time to the point I start to feel uncomfortable under his intense scrutiny. He thickly swallows as he tries to open his mouth to say something. "Alright. I promise I will try. But, Elizabeth, there's something you should know first. Fallon and I—"

"Hey, sweetheart." Ryder kisses the top of my head. "What's up, Trevor?"

A look of panic flits across Trevor's face when he sees Ryder and Fallon at our table, then his look turns hard when Fallon glares at him.

Fallon sits down beside me and stares at his brother. "Why the fuck are you here? It's like you have Elizabeth tracked on your own personal GPS. You keep popping up every-fucking-where."

"Stop being such a dick. Elizabeth invited me. But I'll be leaving now."

Ryder tries to calm things between the two of them. "Stick around."

"I've got a research paper to finish. Elizabeth, always a pleasure. Oh, and congratulations, man," he says to Ryder, shaking his hand.

"I'm assuming she told you," Ryder replies to Trevor which has Fallon looking at me with a raised brow.

"She did. I'm happy for the both of you. I'll catch you tomorrow at class, wildcat."

"What the hell are you talking about?" Fallon frowns at Trevor.

Trevor bumps Fallon's shoulder, and I catch his hushed, "Can you follow me out? I need to talk to you about something." For once Fallon doesn't argue, and he follows Trevor out the door.

"I consider that progress," I tell Ryder. "Hey, your girl needs some lovin'. She missed you today." I point to my lips. He grins into the kiss and I sigh happily.

"Before you say anything, I asked Trevor to meet me here. I'm determined to get those two to talk."

"I don't know if Fallon would appreciate the interference, babe."

"What's the old saying? If it's stupid but it works, then it's not stupid."

Ryder cracks up and throws a straw at me. I throw a half-melted marshmallow back at him and dissolve into a fit of giggles when it sticks to his chin. Naturally, I nibble and lick it off. Ryder dips my finger in my hot chocolate and brings it to his mouth, sucking the chocolatey goodness off.

"Fucking hell. The two of you are going to kill me," Fallon complains when he comes back to the table and makes no disguise of adjusting himself before he sits down. "I need to get laid."

"Thought you were done with the random hookups."

"Says the man who's getting some twenty-four-seven."

"Chocolate is supposed to be almost as good as an orgasm." I push my hot chocolate over to him with a smile and a wink. "But that might be only for us girls."

"You're such a brat, kitten." But he drinks the rest of my hot chocolate.

"Secret for a secret, Fallon."

That gets his attention. "You first, kitten."

"I asked Ryder to marry me, and he said yes."

Fallon goes stock still. He reaches for my hand once he notices the yellow diamond on my finger. "You did a good job, Ry. It's beautiful. It suits her perfectly. Like fucking sunshine."

"Thanks, man. That's what I thought when I saw it."

"Fallon?" I inquire as he continues to hold my hand and manipulate the ring. As if coming out of a trance, he lets go of my hand and kicks back.

"You're going to be a gorgeous bride. Ry, you got your wish man. I'm so fucking happy for you."

"Thanks. We haven't told Jay yet, so mum's the word for now."

"Like I'd talk to that asshat on purpose," he replies, heavy with the sarcasm. "I get dibs on the bachelor party. Bachelorette party too." He grins devilishly.

"Why am I suddenly afraid?"

A phone starts ringing, and we all check to see if it's ours.

It's mine but I don't recognize the number. "Hello?" A man asks for me and identifies himself. As he talks, anger grows and burns red-hot in my veins. "I'll be right there."

This can't be fucking happening.

"Babe?"

"That was campus police. Someone vandalized my car in the student lot."

We've spent the last hour in the public safety building filling out forms and answering questions. Since I had to register my car and license plate for my student parking sticker, the campus police were able to get my contact information, hence the phone call. Whoever vandalized my car did a damn good job of it. All the tires were slashed. The windows were smashed in like someone took a baseball bat to them. The sides of the car were scratched and dented. Whoever did it also left me a message written on the driver's side door in permanent marker: I'M COMING FOR YOU. Just like the text message I deleted because I didn't think anything of it. I thought it was a mistake or a joke meant for someone else. I now know it was meant solely for me. Receiving the message twice is not a coincidence—it's a warning.

I finish signing the last form and slide it across the table to the police officer. He's young, maybe a few years older than I am, with brown hair cropped close to his head and kind hazel eyes. He taps the sheets of paper on the table to straighten them out and excuses himself saying he'll be right back. Not having gotten to eat at the café, I'm tired and hungry, and just plain pissed-off. I love my car. When I had no memory, that car was my invisible link to Ryder, and now I feel like someone is not only attacking me personally but attacking my relationship with him.

"What now?" I ask, slumping in my chair and taking Ryder's hand to lay on my lap.

I take a deep calming breath and start tracing his handprint on my thigh by sliding my finger along the outside of his hand. Ryder has wonderful hands. Long, thick, masculine fingers with neatly trimmed nails. You would expect him to have a lot of grease or oil under his fingernails with the amount of stuff he does with his car every day, but his nails and skin are pristinely clean and smudge-free.

Ryder hasn't said a word since we arrived. He's been stoic, silently here for me if I need him. He has kept his arm on the back of my chair, kneading my neck every so often when I tense too much, or rubbing soothing circles on my back to keep me calm. I love him more for that. For not jumping in and taking over. For letting me deal with this situation without interference. For waiting to see what I need without forcing what he thinks I need.

"I've already texted Dad to let him know what happened. He's sending one of his tow trucks here tomorrow to pick up your car and take it back to his shop. Hopefully he can have it fixed and looking good as new by next weekend."

I think my mouth drops open a little in amazement, not shock. "Ryder, he doesn't have to do that. I can pay for someone to fix it up. I don't want to take advantage of your dad like that."

"Sweetheart, you've been part of the family since the day we met. Mom and Dad would do anything for you."

"But—"

Ryder edges closer. "No buts," he says against the shell of my ear and gives it a small kiss under the lobe. "He wants to do it for you, so let him. Don't be surprised if he kicks up the HP by 300 and adds red rims."

"Actually, that would be awesome." I brighten up thinking of other mods I could get Randy to add. I take my phone out and do a quick web search on compatible NOS nitrous systems.

"I'm sorry I said anything. Your Cheshire grin is making me nervous." He peeks over and guffaws at my screen. "Oh, hell no, Elizabeth."

"Will you at least think about it? Pretty please? Pretty, pretty please with whipped cream and a cherry and chocolate sauce?"

"Sounds like my kind of party," Fallon mirthfully quips, walking in like he owns the place. An older man in a well-pressed dark gray suit follows him in.

"Why am I not surprised?" I give him a small eye roll when he winks at me.

"I apologize for Mr. Montgomery's manners. I'm Charles Worthington. The lawyer," he announces, extending his hand out to me in a greeting that I stand up from my seat to accept. He carries an aura of authority but has a friendly smile. "And you must be Elizabeth Fairchild."

"Yes," I slowly reply, giving a skeptical glance toward Fallon. "Fallon, why would you bring a lawyer?"

"Patience, kitten."

The young police officer comes back in. "Everything is in order, Miss Fairchild." He hands me a piece of paper. "Your case number is at the top with a description of the damage. You will want to give a copy of this to your insurance company so you can file a claim. My number here is listed at the bottom if you need to reach me. If we find out anything, we will call you."

Mr. Worthington hands the officer his business card. "Did you check the campus security and video feeds yet?"

"They are getting that request in right now."

"How long?"

"Shouldn't take much longer, sir."

"Good. We'll wait then. I'm Miss Fairchild's attorney."

"You are?" I stupidly ask.

Fallon sits down across from me and Ryder. "Yep."

"*Fallon.*"

"Kitten," he responds in a voice that lets me know I won't win any arguments. He waits for Charles to sit down and then points those ice blue eyes at Ryder. "My guy came back with some info. You're not going to like it, hoss."

Fallon and Ryder do that silent communication mind-meld thing that drives me crazy.

"Are you freaking kidding me?" Ryder half shouts. "Are you sure?" Ryder asks him, but his tone is as rigid as the hard expression that shrouds his face.

"Positive."

Ryder pivots in the plastic and metal seat to face me. He takes both my hands in his like a parent would when giving a child bad news. "I think we need to make an official police complaint."

"Isn't that what we just did?"

"Elizabeth, you've had people verbally harass

you. You, just an hour ago, told me about the text message which you should have told me about when it first happened. Now this. It's past time we reported this to the police."

"This is where I come in Miss Fairchild," Mr. Worthington explains. "Do you know Maria Santiago?"

"Yes," I answer lamely.

At Fallon's frat party, I didn't remember who Maria was, but with my memory returned, lucky me gets to remember my ex-best friend now. She was the girl who I thought was my best friend but was only using me to get close to Ryder because she was jealous of me and wanted him.

"I had a guy look into the pictures posted on the website and he traced it back to her registered IP. She's not very smart. She should have used a proxy server," Fallon tells me.

Mr. Worthington continues, "Miss Santiago is being questioned by the Charlotte police as we speak. Mr. Montgomery has asked that I represent you if you decide to press charges against Miss Santiago for online stalking and bullying. These are both class 1 misdemeanors in the state of North Carolina."

I absorb what he's telling me. I know Maria lost it at Fallon's frat party over a month ago, but to stoop so low as to post those sick and repulsive photos about me and the guys? To destroy my car? It doesn't make sense.

Just then, the young police officer—I wish I could recall his name—comes back in and tells us they have video pulled up. He leads us into another room where a large flat-screened television is mounted on the wall in front of a long table.

"Suzie, pull it up," the officer calls over to the woman sitting in front of a computer.

The video feed clicks on after a second. The video image is not great, but there's no mistaking my Hellcat parked at the end of the lot. A figure dressed in black, and wearing a black hood that covers his face, carefully walks by my car, holding what looks like a tire iron. It's clearly a man, not a woman. So not Maria. Maria is tiny, only a few inches taller than Meredith. This person is tall and masculine-looking even though we can't see his face. The figure looks around a few times and then jams the more pointed end of the tire iron into each of my car's tires. He looks around again and then starts pummeling my car to shit with small, quick hits.

"How could no one hear that? It was morning for Christ's sake. The campus was full of students by that time," Ryder argues, his voice angrier than I have ever heard it before.

We watch as the man writes his message then runs off screen, but not before he turns his head in the direction of the camera and I see that he's wearing a black face-covering with eye and mouth openings. *A fucking facemask.* I'm transported back in time to the night when I watched my entire family die right in front of me. The night of my attack. *He* wore a black facemask that night. My stomach rolls and I feel light-headed and nauseous like I'm having an out-of-body experience. I think I'm going to be sick.

The young police officer turns around and is about to say something when I bolt upright, race over to the trashcan next to the door, and throw up. Ryder is beside me in an instant, as is Fallon, but I don't hear what they're saying. All I hear is the buzzing as my brain relives that night. *Every single second* of that night. Every scream of pain and anguish. Every slice of his knife. *Hailey*.

I grab desperately for Ryder and throw myself into his arms, my legs strangling his waist, as I squeeze a chokehold on him and don't let go. My mind is going in a million different directions, down a thousand different roads.

"I've asked the Charlotte police to account for Mrs. Santiago's whereabouts today,"

Mr. Worthington calmly states. Maria always wanted to live in Charlotte and go to university there. I hope she enjoyed it because I'm not letting her get away with what she's done.

Ryder sits back down in one of the hard seats at the table, me still safely tucked in his embrace. I find the young police officer standing near the door where he's speaking with two other officers. All three of them are watching me.

I aim my statement at the CU officer. "I've been harassed and bullied on campus and online. I would like to file an official complaint, and I want to speak with Sheriff Barnes in Wake County, and Detective Harnett with the North Carolina Criminal Investigation Division."

Chapter 25

Ryder

Fallon and Mr. Worthington stayed with us the entire time we were stuck talking to one police officer after another. Elizabeth spoke with Elijah's dad and Detective Harnett over the phone. Maria was supposed to be brought in for official questioning tonight in Charlotte and slapped with a restraining order thanks to Mr. Worthington's legal expertise. Hopefully, she'll get criminal charges too once it's verified that she was responsible for posting the online pictures. The police took possession of Elizabeth's car for fingerprinting and whatever else they do. It's been a while since I watched an episode of *C.S.I.* Not only are we dealing with the stuff from Maria, but the unknown vandal as well.

I had to call Dad to let him know not to send the tow for Elizabeth's car just yet. I didn't exactly tell him why. If I did, I would have to admit what Maria did, and I'm too ashamed at the moment to have that conversation with them. So now we wait, but we also have to get on with our lives while we do.

Elizabeth has been dealing with verbal attacks for days. The thought of some guy putting his hands on her thinking she'd be down with it makes me want to punch something. I mean, what the fuck? The guy at fight night went after her because of the lies Maria posted online to hurt Elizabeth. What the hell was I thinking when I caved and got into a relationship with Maria in high school? How can someone be so cruel? I feel so damn guilty. Maria's obsession with me is part of the reason why Elizabeth is suffering now. If anything happens to Elizabeth because of Maria, I will never forgive myself. I'm this close to giving Fallon the go-ahead to take matters into his own hands to deal with her.

As soon as we got home, Elizabeth jumped in the shower so she could have a minute to herself. I texted the twins. I'm not worried about her need to be alone right now like I was at the library when I thought she was shutting me out.

"Baby!" I shout down the hall to her when I hear the shower turn off.

"Yeah?" she calls back.

"Jay and Jules are on their way over. They're

freaking out over what happened to your car, so be prepared. You may want to put your ring away for the next couple of hours while they're here."

Elizabeth saunters into the kitchen where I've just finished re-heating soup for us to eat. It's been a long fucking day, but she looks so fresh and gorgeous with her damp hair braided to fall over one shoulder, wearing a soft cotton long-sleeved sleep shirt and fleece reindeer pajama pants.

She kisses me thank you and takes the bowl I offer. "I put it on my necklace with the locket. I can't bear the thought of it not being on my finger, so being next to my heart with Elizabeth Ann is the next best thing."

I'm leaning against the counter island across from her. "I love you so damn much." Her returning smile warms my heart. "Wanna elope?"

"Is that what you want?" she asks, silently slurping a spoonful of soup, her eyes reflecting intrigue back at me.

"We could always do a quickie marriage in secret, let my family plan whatever they plan, and get married twice," I jokingly suggest. But then, when I think about it, it sounds like a brilliant idea. Marry my girl twice. I can definitely do that.

"And deprive your mom, Jamie, and Brea of their grand plans? They'd hunt us down and burn us at the stake if we had a quickie marriage."

We grin at each other as we consider the merits of eloping.

"All kidding aside, how are you handling what happened today?"

Elizabeth tips her bowl back to drink the rest of her soup, something she has done ever since we were kids.

"Naturally, I'm upset about my car, but I'm relieved that we know who was responsible for the stuff online. I still can't believe it was Maria though."

I walk around the kitchen island and lift her up to sit on top of it, me between her legs. "I'm so sorry, sweetheart. I feel like it's my fault."

"No, Ryder. Just no. Lots and lots of therapy with Dr. Clairemont has helped me see that, as much as I still want to blame myself because of the guilt I feel, what happened to Mom, Dad, and Hailey is not my fault. What Maria did is not your fault. She's filled with jealousy and anger. Let her choke on it and hopefully get the punishment she deserves from a court of law."

"We need a vacation to get away from everything and everyone for a few days. How about after Seattle and Christmas, we go somewhere special to ring in the New Year?"

Elizabeth slips her arms around my neck. I take the opportunity to run my hands across her ribcage, my thumbs slowly trailing back and forth under the swells of her breasts. I wait to hear the hitch in her breath that I crave. I love it when I can feel her skin warm and I can watch the color rise and flush her chest and neck with arousal.

"That sounds absolutely wonderful. Where do you want to go?" She wriggles until her core is flush with my erection that's pushing against the fly of my jeans.

I kiss my way up the center of her chest, then her neck, and settle my lips behind her ear. "Up to you, baby."

She's starting to pant, and I know I've hit the sweet spot.

Breathlessly she says, "Somewhere where there's lots of snow. I want to snuggle up with you next to a fire and make love all night."

How about we start now, I want to say but never do because the doorbell rings. "That'll be Jay and Jules," I groan, and she follows with her own groan of disappointment.

"To be continued," she assures me.

I help Elizabeth down and let her go get the door to give my erection a chance to calm down. I place our bowls in the sink and hear Julien and Jayson's raised voices as they enter the apartment.

"Why didn't you call us? Why are we hearing about this now?" Jay huffs out.

"We just got home. It took forever to give my statement and file the complaint," Elizabeth tells him. Jayson pulls her into a hug and jealousy flares to life inside of me. I'm getting sick and tired of him always putting his hands on her. Julien joins the embrace with his brother and I ease back a bit and lean against the entryway.

"Liz, we would have been there with you if we knew."

"Ryder and Fallon were with me. Fallon's personal lawyer is representing me."

Jayson growls out, "Of course he fucking is." Jay seems to say things like that a lot when it comes to Fallon and Elizabeth's friendship.

"Why would you need a lawyer?" Julien asks. "Are you in trouble?"

"No, I'm not in trouble. My car, however, has seen better days." My heart drops once again because I know how much she loves her car.

"It was Maria," I say aloud.

Jayson turns his steely eyes on me in accusation. "Maria destroyed her car?"

"Maria was behind the pictures and the online posts. We still don't know who beat the shit out of my car," Elizabeth replies.

"So your goddamn psycho ex-girlfriend is causing trouble for Liz yet again?"

"Hey!" Elizabeth smacks Jay on his arm. "It's not Ryder's fault. It's Maria's."

"Stop being a jackass," Jules tells his brother.

Elizabeth sits the two of them down and tells them everything that happened. The little touches Jay keeps giving Elizabeth as she talks don't escape my notice, but she's so engrossed in her retelling that she seems unaware. But I see them. She's my fiancé, and although he doesn't know that yet, he knows she and I are together. He knows she loves me. The day is going to come when Jay will either fully accept that Elizabeth is not going to go back to him, or I am going to have make him understand.

"Fallon's lawyer—well, Elizabeth's lawyer

now—is putting in a request to expedite the restraining order against Maria. The police are involved now and are investigating the vandalism done to Elizabeth's car," I interject.

Elizabeth adds, "So there is nothing more to do about it until we know more. Honestly, I'm relieved. Fallon once said knowledge is power. He's not the first, but you know what I mean. And knowing who's responsible for posting that filth eases my mind a bit, if that makes sense."

"It doesn't," Jay tells her.

Elizabeth gets up and comes over to where I am, wrapping her arm around my waist. "I can't fight back against an unknown. Now I know who to fight, and a fight is what she's going to get. Old me never stood up to her, but she's going to find out real quick that I'm not the same person anymore."

"Why do I feel like spouting some Dylan Thomas poetry right now?" Julien chuckles.

"More like listening to angry chick music."

Elizabeth gives my side a squeeze and walks over to the piano; the upright I bought her that now lives against the wall of the living room.

"I don't want to talk about Maria or my car anymore tonight. Let's talk about the Seattle trip instead." She looks at all of us while fingering the keys lightly.

Jules walks into the kitchen and comes back with two sodas, handing one to Jay. "Mom and Dad are going to fly up the day after we arrive. They're staying at the same hotel we are."

Elizabeth starts playing Pachelbel. "I know we had talked about all going to the gravesite together, but I think it would be good for me and Jayson to have some time alone with her first if that's alright with everyone."

"I like that idea," Jay tells her.

Jules and I share a look and acquiesce to her request. We know that Elizabeth and Jay will be dealing with a lot of emotional issues when they meet their daughter for the first time. I wish I could spare my girl the heartbreak she will face that day.

"You said you wanted to see Daniel and Drew as well? Do they know we're coming?" Jules asks her.

"I sent them an email last night."

"That's kind of cold, don't you think?"

"Forgive me Julien if I'm still a bit ticked off at them. An email should be enough."

Jay sits down beside her on the piano bench

and hits a few base keys, disrupting the melody of her song and causing her to dissolve in a fit of giggles when he purposefully knocks her hand with his. They change to playing chopsticks. I grab the guitar that's sitting on the stand next to the piano and join in. I wish I could say we sounded great, but honestly, it sounds like a bag of cats.

Jules, not one to be left out, sits on the other side of Elizabeth at the piano and shoulder bumps her. "Heart and Soul?"

"Let's do it."

It's like old times when the four of us would sit around my backyard firepit and Elizabeth and her dad would play their guitars and sing.

"I've been meaning to ask about Christmas."

"We're stopping by my parents' on the way back from Seattle and then heading off for New Year's," I answer.

"I'd like it if you would come to our house for Christmas supper," Jay tells Elizabeth like I'm not sitting right here.

Elizabeth glances over at me from the piano, her eyebrows quirked in question on what to say. I make a suggestion that both of our families could get together that day. I'm sure our parents can hash out the details. More than likely, Mom will have everyone over to our house since it was the go-to place for all of our families for backyard cookouts when we were growing up.

"Don't forget Fallon is spending Christmas with us," Elizabeth reminds me. Jay stops playing and she shushes him when he opens his mouth to comment. "If you can't say anything nice, Jayson Jameson, keep it to yourself, please. Fallon is coming. End of story." He grumps and gets up, flopping back down on the sofa.

"Not to change the subject, but *you* guys should hang out on Friday when Meredith and I have our girl's night out at Belly's. You can have a boy's night."

"Not a bad idea," Jules says. "Elijah has that night off from work."

"There's a sports bar near Belly's. We can meet up for a late dinner after."

"Meredith won't try to remove our balls if we intrude on your girl time, will she?"

Elizabeth sticks her tongue out at Jay. "She's not that bad."

"That girl is a pit bull dressed as a fairy," he states. "I'm glad she's on our side."

"Jay, if you're in, do you mind picking me

up?" I ask. "I'm letting Elizabeth drive my car while hers is in the impound."

"I can drive all of us in my truck."

Elizabeth is smiling widely now. "Have I told you guys how much I love all of you? I love it when we all get to hang out together, and I love it even more when my three best boys get together."

Elizabeth is happy and the stress of the day is gone. Wanting to keep it that way, I suggest, "Why don't you guys stick around. We have enough stuff for tacos, and Netflix added the next season of *Cobra Kai* to their lineup."

Elizabeth pops up from the bench and throws her arms around my neck, giving me a quick kiss. "That's a great idea. I'll start the tacos," she says between a flurry of happy pecks to my face. "Jules, you want to help me?"

"Race you to the kitchen," he calls back, already halfway there, leaving me and Jayson alone in the living room.

"She seems to be taking everything that has happened in stride. How bad was her car?" he asks.

I grab the remote and open Netflix when the television comes on. "Pretty bad. The campus cameras caught it, but the guy was dressed all in black and wearing a hood, so there's no way to identify him."

"Ry, we need to stop this shit from happening again. She's already been through hell and back, and shit just keeps piling on."

I reel in my anger. "You don't have to tell me because I know. Don't you think this is killing me too? Especially knowing it was Maria behind those online posts. Elizabeth had a minor freak-out earlier after viewing the security tapes. The guy's face-covering reminded her of *that* night."

Jay breathes out a "Fuck."

I join him on the sofa. Jay and I may be on opposite sides when it comes to loving Elizabeth, but we will always be on the same side when it comes to protecting her. "We'll all be with her in Seattle and for Christmas, and as much as you despise Fallon, you know he's got the power and resources to protect her better than we can."

"As much as I hate to say it, you're right," he says with a slight chuckle. "Want to fill me in on what the hell happened between the two of them and why they are suddenly best friends? Liz was terrified of that guy in high school. I always felt he was obsessed with her."

Jay would flip his shit if I told him that Fallon confessed to me that he loved her and I'm not ruining the peace of our evening with that story, so I lie. "I only know what you know and that is what Elizabeth has told us. She cares about Fallon and vice versa, so as long as she's happy, that's all that matters."

"Perhaps. I still can't stand that rich, pompous asshole though."

"The feeling, I'm sure you know, is mutual."

Jay snorts.

"I know Seattle is going to be rough for you and Elizabeth. Is there anything I can do to help? Putting all our bullshit aside, we've been friends for a very long time, and I hope you know that I still have your back if you need me."

Jay leans his head back against the sofa and mutters, "Always the better man." He sits back up and looks at me. "Thanks, Ry. I appreciate it."

Chapter 26

Elizabeth

"What can I get you, gorgeous?" the bartender asks me.

I'm at the bar at Belly's waiting for Meredith and Sara to arrive for our Friday girl's night out. Since I'm driving, I'm not going to drink any alcohol tonight. Hence the soda I'm about to order.

"Whatever diet cola you have. I'm not picky."

The bartender winks at me with a "coming right up" and walks to the other end of the bar. I am a bit disappointed Belly's isn't doing karaoke tonight, but they are having a quiz bowl which should be fun. My inner nerd wants to come out and play.

I turn around on the barstool and people-watch while I wait. The place is already packed with college students from campus. There are a couple of groups gathered around the pool tables adjacent to the small stage located at back, and Top 40 music is playing. Where people would be dancing there are now tables to accommodate the crowd that's here for trivia night.

"Here you go, love," the bartender says. I turn around to take my drink and he slides a napkin towards me that has his name and phone number written on it. "Anything else I can get for you?"

The guy is good-looking with dark blond hair and chocolate brown eyes. I look at the napkin and see his name is Bryce.

"Actually, there is," I say. "Is there any way you could summon my fiancé for me? He's at the bar down the street with some friends." I give him a wink of my own and he bursts out laughing.

"You're adorable. Message received." Bryce leans over the bar and says in a low voice, "Although, you're not wearing a ring *and* you're here alone."

Dammit. I didn't want Meredith to see it yet, so it's on my necklace with my locket which are tucked under my long-sleeved shirt. I'm about to whip my necklace out when I hear Sara's voice call out, "Hey Bryce!" A second later, I'm being tackle-hugged by a pixy who turns out to be Meredith.

"Girl's night!" she shrieks. "I've been so looking forward to this all week. Just us pussies! Wait, that sounds wrong."

Sara leans over the bar and hugs the overtly flirtatious bartender. "I see you've met Elizabeth. And this is my loud roommate Meredith. Meredith, this is my brother, Bryce."

"What's up Sara's brother," Meredith greets him.

"Trivia night looks to be popular," Sara comments. She leans over the bar when Bryce taps her on the shoulder. It's too noisy to hear what he tells her, but her raucous laughter comes out loud and clear.

"Bryce, I'm not going to give you her number. Dude, she's with Ryder Cutton."

"No shit?" he says, looking at me again to see if Sara is telling him the truth. I give him an affirmative nod while sipping my soda. "I've seen him race. That guy is badass."

"Yes, he most certainly is," I agree.

"Ryder is uber-protective of her. He would totally hand you your ass for flirting with her," Meredith happily informs him.

Bryce looks at me again. "Damn, girl. Got it.

Don't mess with the hot blond chick."

"Bryce, for fuck's sake. Stop hitting on my friends. Come on." Sara turns to us and pulls us to the back of the room where the pool tables are. "My brother is such a manwhore." Sara sidles up to a pool table and throws a dollar bill down to claim the next game.

Selecting a pool stick off the wall rack, Meredith pokes me in the butt with it. "Where are your boys tonight?"

"At the bar down the street."

"Hey, Sara, did I ever tell you about Elizabeth's unicorn pussy?" Meredith bursts out loudly.

For the second time tonight, I about spew my drink all over the place. "Jesus, Mer, dial it down a notch," I splutter as several male heads turn our way at her outburst. Meredith just bends over laughing. This girl is out of her mind.

Wiping tears from her eyes, she sings, "Or maybe it's the milkshakes that have all the boys running to the yard." Suddenly, the group of guys at the pool table we're waiting next to join her in chorus, singing the song in the style of Maverick wailing, "You've Lost That Lovin' Feeling" from *Top Gun.* Both Sara and I whip out our phones to video the performance, which includes a lot of chest and ass shaking from Meredith. At the end, the room erupts in applause and whistles, and Meredith high-fives all of the guys who played back up to her diva performance. One of them, leanly built with dark auburn hair and blue eyes, whispers something in Mer's ear that has her blushing crimson. She bites her bottom lip up at him and nods yes.

"Keep this warm for me. I'll be back in a minute." She thrusts her pool stick in my hands and walks off with the guy.

"You bitch! It's girl's night! No boys allowed! Hoes over bros!" Sara shouts after her.

"I'll be back in five minutes!" Meredith shouts back and grabs the guy's ass as they make their way down the hall that leads to the restrooms. I cringe at the thought of getting it on in such an unsanitary place, especially with some random guy. There isn't much I would say no to Ryder about, but restroom sex at a bar would be on my hell-no list. Just, yuck.

"I swear, sometimes I worry about that girl," Sara tells me. "And I'm truly sorry about my brother's behavior. In high school, I had to stop bringing my friends home because he would always hit on them."

I wave off her concern, not wanting her to worry about it. "Honestly, it's fine. So, what are your plans for the holidays? Going back home?"

The guys finish their game and give us the table. Sara chooses a stick and I use the one Meredith handed me. Racking up the balls, Sara says, "That's the plan. Bryce and I are driving together. Might as well, ya know."

I help Sara get the rest of the balls from the corner pockets so she can arrange them in the plastic triangle. "Where's home?"

"Myrtle Beach."

"I love Myrtle Beach. I used to call it the Las Vegas of the South."

Sara thinks about it then chuckles. "You're right! What about you? You heading home too?"

Once she's done racking the balls, I chalk my stick, aim, and shoot. Two stripes and one solid go in. "Stripes," I state and move over to the side and eyeball the cue ball to determine the best angle to get the side pocket. "The guys and I are heading to Seattle and then coming back to spend Christmas together. After, Ryder is taking me to Wintergreen for New Year's." I nail my shot and set up for the next one.

"Never been to Wintergreen."

"It's in Virginia."

"Let me know how you like it. I've been wanting to try my hand at skiing. So, you're from Seattle?"

Once my shot falls in the corner pocket, I hold my pool stick at my side and lean on it. "How much has Meredith told you about me?"

"Other than the two of you being friends, she hasn't told me much of anything. Why?" I motion for Sara to take the next shot, even though it's still my turn.

"I know we really don't know each other well, but my life comes with a shit ton of baggage. Stuff I'm not really comfortable talking about. I don't mean to sound like a cagey bitch, but it's hard for me to talk about personal stuff. You're a really nice person, Sara, and I'm glad we are becoming friends. Just know that if I clam up or don't answer a question, it's not because of anything you said."

"Alright, fair enough," she answers and slides the stick between her fingers before hitting the white ball. "I like you too and I think we could become very good friends, so whenever you're ready to let me know more, I'll be there with open ears."

"I appreciate that. I really do," I tell her honestly.

"Appreciate what?" Meredith asks, rejoining us. Her hair is a mess, and her lips are swollen and red.

"Have a good time?" I ask her. "I hope you remembered to use protection."

"We did." Mer smiles broadly, a sparkle in her eyes. "Since Trevor won't let me jump on his train anymore, I had to jump on the next caboose that arrived at the station. My girlie parts were dying for some attention." Meredith and her bizarre references.

"TMI!" Sara wails at her.

"Oh, please. You've done much worse, roomie."

That piques my curiosity. "Really?" Sara's cheeks turn a nice shade of bright red.

"Thank God," Sara says when they announce the trivia competition is about to begin.

The guy Meredith just hooked up with and a few of his friends approach us. "I didn't get your name," he says to Meredith.

"Meredith," she tells him.

"Well, Meredith, I'm Nick. This is Sam, Wes, and Charlie. Do you and your friends want to be on our team?"

Meredith looks at me and Sara and we both shrug.

"That sounds like a plan as long as you're buying. I like anything on tap."

"Deal."

Even though they just had a nameless quickie in the back restroom, Nick places his hand respectfully at Meredith's back and escorts her over to a table where he pulls a chair out for her to sit. Sara and I sit next to Mer, and the other guys pile in around us while Nick goes to the bar to order drinks.

"You girls ever done this before?" Wes asks us.

"Nope," Sara replies.

Nick comes back with drinks, a pad of paper, and some pencils. While drinks are being passed around the table, Wes explains the rules. I slide the beer I was just handed over to Meredith knowing she'll drink it since I'm a teetotaler tonight.

Bryce gets up at the microphone and clears his throat to get everyone's attention. "Alright folks! Strap on your beer-soaked brains and let's do this thing. Winning team gets a one-hundred-dollar gift card and drinks on the house for the rest of the night." A cheer goes up from every table. "Question number one: Who was the very first NFL quarterback to reach forty-thousand yards passing?"

"Aww, come on!" Meredith shouts. "The very first question has to be about flippin' football?"

We let the boys take this one. The next table over holds up their sheet of paper before anyone else. Bryce comes over and reads it. "Give this team a point. They correctly answered Johnny Unitas!" The guys at the winning table all stand up, clink their drinks together, chug them down, and shout, "Whoo-yah! Beta House!"

Bryce waits for the noise to settle down. "Next question. What does haphephobia mean?"

Meredith groans again and bangs her head on the table. "I've got this one," I tell her. I'm the first to hold my paper up and Bryce comes over, reading it.

"Gorgeous and smart," he says to me, which earns him a smack on his arm from Sara. "Point to this table, folks. She got the correct answer. Haphephobia is the fear of being touched."

Sara snorts.

Charlie fist pumps and yells over at the Beta

House table, "Take that, Beta bitches! Gamma house rules!"

"We're not part of Gamma house," Sara replies.

Charlie winks at her. "Honorary members, babe."

Sara snorts for second time.

Over the next thirty minutes, questions and answers fly around the room. I don't care if we're winning; I just enjoy the silliness of the competition and the playful banter that gets thrown. Our table gets five more questions right, but we lose by one point to a table filled with Iota sorority girls. Meredith and Nick started making out ten minutes ago and were oblivious to the last part of the game. Charlie has been flirting with Sara, and I have been texting Ryder under the table.

MyBoyfriend: The video was funny as hell.

I had forwarded him the video of Meredith's earlier performance.

Me: This was actually fun. Not so much of a girl's night but I'm glad I came. We need to get the guys together and to do a trivia night here sometime.

MyBoyfriend: Sounds like a plan. Miss you.

Me: Miss you too. Mer hooked up with a guy in the back bathroom <yuck emoji> What are u guys up 2?

MyBoyfriend: Just hanging at the bar and throwing some darts. Would rather be deep inside you kissing every inch of your soft skin.

My stomach muscles seize when I read his words and of course my mind drifts back to him and me in the kitchen this morning. Eggs and bacon were not the only things Ryder ate for breakfast.

Me: Swoon. Yes, please.

MyBoyfriend: Ready for me to come get you?

Me: So ready.

MyBoyfriend: Let me tell the guys. Be right there.

Me: <kiss emoji> <heart emoji>

I get Meredith and Sara's attention. "Hey, guys. I'm out. Ryder is meeting me outside."

"This was fun. We should do it again," Sara says, hugging me.

"Are we still on for study group with Trevor on Sunday?" Mer tries to ask me with her lips still glued to Nick's. Next week is finals week and she and I planned to meet with Trevor one last time to cram. Julien and I are studying together for our chem exam on Monday. Then it's off to Seattle at the end of the week. I'm both excited and nervous about that. Maybe a little nauseous too. Seeing my daughter's gravesite for the first time. Seeing Daniel and Drew. Being back in the place where I woke up for the first time with no memory of anything from my life.

"That's the plan," I answer Meredith. I kiss the top of her head as I pass by on my way out. "Nick, it was nice to meet you. Please take care of my girl here. I don't want to have to get my very scary boyfriend to come to Gamma house to hunt you down."

Nick has the presence of mind to take my threat seriously. "I promise she will get home safe and sound tonight."

I tell the other guys bye, and I wave bye to Bryce as I pass the bar. He pretends to capture my wave in his hands and place it on his heart. I give him my best eye roll and walk outside to the frigid, winter air. It's much colder tonight than it has been recently. I should have worn a thicker jacket and some gloves. I take a moment to enjoy the holiday lights strung across the street and around the base of the trees that dot the wide sidewalk paralleling the road. I stop for a second to text Ryder that I'm waiting at the corner. My phone pings back with his reply.

MyBoyfriend: Almost there. I can see you from where I am down the street.

I look up and see Ryder, Jayson, Julien, and Elijah a couple of blocks away. My only thought is to get my man, go home, and spend the rest of the night in his arms.

Something hard hits my back and I'm propelled forward into the intersection. "Told you I was coming for you, bitch."

The next things I remember are car lights filling my vision, and my name being shouted in the distance.

Chapter 27

Fallon

I've lived a life full of fear, regret, and anger. My whole childhood was nothing but abuse and neglect from the three people who should have loved me the most. My teenage years were lost mostly to oblivion as I used drugs, sex, and alcohol to numb my pain. The only good in my life was my friendship with Ryder. Whenever the two of us were together, Ry would go on and on about his best friend, Elizabeth. How wonderful she was, how beautiful, how special. How he was in love with her but didn't know what to do because Jayson and Julien were in love with her too. I would razz Ryder about that. I mean, come the fuck on. How could one girl make three guys fall to their knees? Have them panting over her, scrambling for her affection like rabid dogs over a scrap of meat?

And then I saw Elizabeth for the first time. She came to the Fields one day with Ryder and his dad. I mean, sure, I had seen some pictures of her and Ry, or her and the guys, tacked up on the wall in Ry's room. But seeing her in person, seeing her smile. That long, pale blond hair, and those fathomless green eyes—it was as if the sun came out for the very first time, I was so blinded by her. I devolved into a beast that day; one that hid in her shadows, stalking my innocent prey, never directly approaching her but secretly coveting her. Wanting to be closer to her light. Needing to feed off her innocence. Longing to be wanted by her. To be noticed.

Throughout high school, Elizabeth was my obsession. But I could never have her. She belonged to Jay, Ry, and Julien. Jay claimed her first and broke Ry's heart. I hated to see Elizabeth with that egotistical jackass. I hated watching as my friend pined away for her on the sidelines. Ry's love for Elizabeth never faltered. All the while, I loathed that I wasn't the one touching her, kissing her. I filled my loneliness and my bed with nameless girls. Girls that I would fuck while imagining it was Elizabeth I was pounding into. Screwed up, I know. But that's what happens when you're desperate and alone and live under the same roof as Phillip Montgomery. High school was four years of nothing but fucked-up misery drowned out with whatever I could drink, smoke, or stick my dick into.

Elizabeth was also the one thing I wanted

but the one thing my money and power could never buy. After all, why would someone like her want to be with a monster like me? I was messed up. Damaged. Broken. I recently told Ry that Elizbeth knew all of my secrets. That's not entirely true. She doesn't know my worst one. The one that will show her I am truly the monster from her nightmares.

When Elizabeth came to me that morning after her memories returned—after she slept with Jay and ran away from Ry—the beast inside of me roared with triumph. She needed me to help piece her back together. I got to have her to myself for three weeks. I got to live in her fractured light. I fucking fell in love with her despite knowing full well that she loved Ryder. And what damns me the most is that I know she is my ruin. I will never love anyone else the way I love her. I also know my borrowed time with her has to come to an end. Soon, I will lose my sunshine. Soon, she will hate me.

"Fallon?"

I'm sitting beside Elizabeth's hospital bed. I've been clutching on to her hand for the past ten minutes, ever since I arrived. Ry called me after she was admitted, and I think I broke every damn law in the state of North Carolina getting here.

"Hey, kitten."

She squeezes my hand and tremulously tries to give me a weak smile. Her eyes slowly bounce around the room and she lays her head back, exhaling gruffly. "I really fucking hate hospitals."

"I'm going to get you out of here as fast as I can. I promise." I reach over and gently push her hair away from her face. "Please tell me that you remember who I am."

As soon as Ryder saw me out in the waiting room, he pulled me aside and freaked the fuck out. Elizabeth having another concussion or head injury could result in permanent brain damage, or she could lose her memories again.

"Of course I do. *Ohhh,*" she says when she realizes why I asked. I give her a small smile and she tries her best to smile back at me through a wince of pain as she touches two fingers to her head.

"Where's Ryder?" she asks.

"He stepped outside a few minutes ago to deal with your insurance. Julien and Elijah went to grab some burgers to bring back because hospital food sucks." She chuckles and winces, her hand moving to her stomach. "Ry asked if Jay could go grab you some clean clothes from the apartment. Meredith started going rabid with worry, so I called Trevor to come deal with her."

Elizabeth's hand reaches for her chest and gropes around frantically. Her hand bunches around the thin fabric of her hospital gown and a heavy breath escapes her lips, "Oh, thank God. I didn't lose it." I wonder for a few seconds what she's going on about.

She licks her dry lips and repositions herself. "Do you mind?" she asks, motioning to the cup of water with a straw in it. I hold it up for her to sip. "Thanks. So, what's the prognosis."

"Don't you want to wait for Ry?"

"Fallon, just tell me. This isn't my first hospital rodeo."

"Fair enough. Good news is, you only have a slight concussion. The drugs they gave you knocked your ass out. Because of your previous major head trauma and amnesia, the doctors want to play it safe and keep you overnight. You're also going to be black and blue for a little while but nothing is broken, thank fuck."

"I was pushed, Fallon. Someone pushed me in front of that car."

Rage like I've never felt, more powerful than even *that* night, courses through me. It takes everything for me not to jump up right now and burn this fucking town to the ground until

I find out who did this. Son of a bitch tried to kill my sunshine—my best friend's girl—tonight and I will use every resource in my arsenal to make sure the motherfucker pays.

"Fallon." Her voice brings me back from the dark edge I was about to leap from. "Right before I was pushed, he said something. He said, 'Told you I was coming for you, bitch.' He said the same words that someone texted me and the same words that were written on my car. I'm scared, Fallon. All I keep thinking is *He's* back. *He's* coming for me. I can't let *Him* win this time."

Fuck, am I crying? Goddamn it. I swipe angrily at the tears escaping from my eyes.

"Kitten, the man from that night will never hurt you again. It wasn't him."

"How can you be sure? How do you know?"

I look at Elizabeth lying in the hospital bed; her appearance so tired and small; her face, neck, and arms bruised. The green orbs of her eyes gazing back at me with a mixture of fear and trust. She's still the most beautiful woman I have ever laid eyes on.

"I made you a promise." I promised her that *He* would never hurt her again.

At that moment, her hospital door opens.

After stepping inside, Ry comes to a dead stop when he sees Elizabeth is awake.

"Jesus Christ, baby," he chokes, and I have to turn around to compose myself while he barrels over to Elizabeth and breaks down in racking sobs against her neck. "I was so scared, sweetheart. I love you so much. I thought I'd lost you. Please don't ever forget me again," he begs and kisses her face all over, careful not to hurt her.

This strong girl who has more heart than anyone on Earth, comforts Ryder even though she's the one in the hospital bed. She wriggles to make room for him to lie down beside her.

"Shhh. I love you. I'm fine. Just a little bruised. Nothing serious from what Fallon has told me. I'm a tough chick. I've been through much worse, and I'll always find my way back to you. I'm not going anywhere. You and me forever, remember?" Elizabeth tells him, caressing the side of his face.

I step over to the hospital room window to give them a little privacy. I take out my phone and text Charles to direct him to get here as soon as possible. The police have been waiting for Elizabeth to wake up so they can get her statement. I'm also going to get her moved to a private suite upstairs since they're keeping her overnight.

"Need me to text Jay and Jules for you?" I ask over my shoulder.

Elizabeth's hoarse giggle has me turning back around. I cock my head at her to ask what's so funny and she starts to laugh even harder, then groans. "Stop it, Fallon. I hurt too much right now to laugh."

I look at her like she's lost her mind. "What the fuck did I do?"

"The fact you would text Jayson for me, and that you contacted your brother. If I didn't know any better, I think it was you who has a concussion."

"Smart-ass." I smile and flip her off. She returns the gesture with a slight lift of her hand.

"Babe. Think you're up to answer some questions? There are two police officers outside who've been waiting. I've already given them my statement. Jay, Jules, and E gave theirs too."

"She's not saying a damn thing until Charles gets here," I argue.

"Fallon, it's alright. I can speak with them. It's just questions, right?"

"Perhaps Fal is right. Sweetheart, I saw what happened. I'm sorry I was too far away to get to you." Ryder chokes up again. "The bastard got away even with Jay and Jules chasing after him."

"Kitten, you do realize that things have escalated to attempted murder, right?" Her eyes go big when understanding dawns on her. "So, we're waiting for fucking Charles and that's not up for a fucking discussion."

"Okay," she says.

Elizabeth

One brown eye. One blue eye. The devil has come for me again.

"Look at me Elizabeth! I need you to see! Don't you see?"

"No, I don't see. I don't understand. What do you want from me?"

"All I ever wanted was for you to see me.*"*

"I did see you, you bastard! You killed my parents. You abused and destroyed my sister before murdering her right in front of me. I saw the knife you used on my sister before you used it on me! You killed my unborn daughter! I saw everything!"

He *laughs at me. It's such an ugly sound, one I never want to hear again as long as I live. "No, you didn't. You never did."*

A figure dressed in black appears from the mists of my dream and begins to circle me. Round and around until I'm dizzy with trying to track him. I can't turn my back on Him. *I won't run. I'll stand and fight.* He's *taken too much from me. I won't allow him to have anything more.*

"Then tell me."

"I can't. You have to learn the truth on your own."

"You're a fucking coward."

"You would never know. You never allowed yourself to see."

I feel another presence enter and every hair on my body rises. I can feel the hate and anger pulse around me, almost drowning me with its ferocity.

"I'm coming for you, bitch!"

I feel the shove from behind and the force of the impact as a car slams into my side. "No!"

"Elizabeth! Baby, wake up!"

My eyes open to see Ryder above me, his face pinched with concern.

"Fuck," I groan, reaching up to cup his face. "I'm sorry. Did I wake you?"

"How bad this time?" he asks me.

Since being released from the hospital, I've been running on coffee. I basically had to beat all the guys off of me just to be able to go onto campus to complete my final exams. We leave for Seattle tomorrow. Wait, it must be tomorrow now. I glance over and see that it's three in the morning. We have to be at the airport by nine. Fallon was not happy when I refused his offer to take one of his private planes.

I refocus on Ryder. "Same as before," I answer. I've been having these dreams every night this week, and every night Ryder has been there to make the nightmares go away.

He settles down on top of me and kisses me sweetly. I crave his weight pressing down into me and he knows it. He's trying to comfort me, to wrap me in his warmth and protection. My bruises have faded and there are only a few places left are still stiff and sore from where the car impacted my side. The police have been investigating but they still no leads.

I'm distracted from my dark thoughts when I nuzzle my nose in the crook of Ryder's neck. He always smells so goddamn good. My hands run down his defined biceps and slip over his warm, smooth skin to splay across his ribcage before holding on to his waist. His body is such a marvel and I am completely addicted to it; the need to constantly touch him every second of the day is overwhelming. I know Ryder feels the same way because of all the little touches and caresses he gives me too.

I lean up to nip his bottom lip. "I want you," I tell him and feel him harden against my stomach as his heartbeat and breathing increase. We've always been opposite poles of a magnet. Two souls that are only complete when together. Our bodies speak of our love without words. Our hearts beat only in tune with each other's.

Ryder links our pinkies together and raises our hands above my head. His mouth finds mine in a slow, delicious kiss. My breasts tingle against his hard chest. My body blooms and opens for him like a flower. He kisses each breast and each hard nipple, just like he kissed my mouth. Our fingers are still locked together as he slips inside of me and I sigh with pleasure.

"You're my home, Ryder."

"And you're the love of my life," he whispers back.

Chapter 28

Seattle

Elizabeth Ann

Elizabeth

I'm surprised at how sunny it is today. I don't ever recall it being this bright when I lived here for a year. If memory serves me correctly, it was mostly damp and overcast the entire time. It's as if the heavens knew how hard this day was going to be for me and wanted to give me something beautiful to remember it by. The air is clean and fresh with a gentle breeze. Small, puffy dots of clouds sprinkle across the expansive archway of the azure blue sky.

Following the directions Drew emailed me when I contacted him, Jayson and I walk hand in hand across the grass until we get to a large statue. Even in the dead of winter, colorful flowers in pale yellow, vibrant green, and deep burgundy surround the base of a sculpted fairy princess. The gray concrete of the little fairy girl with long flowing hair is so lifelike, I almost reach out and touch her uplifted hand. In her small open palm is a butterfly. I gasp aloud at the emotions assailing me and Jayson pulls me into his side, kissing my temple. I hand Jayson a roll of paper that I brought with us. He takes it and bends down at the placard on the side of the five-foot statue that sits atop our little girl's grave. The thought of her tiny body buried under the earth that I am standing on just about brings me to my knees.

Jayson has been deliberately quiet. I know he's hurting as badly as I am. He unrolls the paper and holds it flat against the placard. I take out the piece of charcoal I brought with me and begin rubbing it over the paper with careful, meticulous strokes. Words appear as I drag the charcoal back and forth. The poem is not one of Hailey's. I would have remembered if it was or would have found it in her binder of poetry that I have stored in the box in my closet. The coincidence of the symbolism of the butterfly is unnerving. How did Daniel and Drew know that the butterfly held a special meaning for me?

ELIZABETH ANN
Born and Died June 13, 2019
Beloved Daughter of Elizabeth Fairchild

Butterfly Angel

In you I see the Butterfly.
For though its appearance seems fragile, truly it is strong.
Its delicate beauty permeates eternal,
The rapid flutter of its wings symbolizes a true strength of heart.
Ceaselessly it will struggle, far distances it will roam;
Its soul forever seeking, searching.
God painted its wings, kissed with colors so bright,
It blinds with weeping honesty.
So beautiful it is, the Butterfly,
That each time and again as I dream of you,
Your small hand in mine, your smile that lights up a room,
The love that was swollen to burst inside of me for you,
I know. I believe.
Even though you've been taken from me—
You go on. You breathe inside me.
For every time I grow desperately lonely and long to hold you in my arms,
My sweet Elizabeth Ann,
I only have to glance up to glimpse the Butterfly.
And I know you are with me,
My ascending angel.

Cascading tears flow down my face as the

sentences take shape and my heart breaks all over again at the hollow feeling of loss in my heart. I think about Hailey's "Broken Butterfly" poem as I touch the place on my side where my own butterfly tattoos live as a beautiful reminder in place of my tragic scars. My hand drifts down to my abdomen. I wonder if I knew she was growing in there when I was in a coma? Did she feel my love for her? Were my mind and body, even though damaged, able to give her love?

Jayson lifts me up in his arms and cradles me against his solid form as we cry together.

"Why, Jayson?" I sob into his chest, hoping to absorb some of his strength.

I can feel him swallowing, trying to find the words to comfort me but not being able to do so. There is no answer as to why. Our baby was a victim of a deranged psychopath. I would have given my life in an instant if it meant saving hers.

Gently lowering me back down, Jayson reaches into his pocket. "Daddy loves you, baby girl," he whispers, kissing a locket just like the one he gave me, then placing it on the ledge of her gravestone. I try my best to dry my eyes but it's futile. I doubt the tears will stop anytime soon.

I kiss my fingers and place them on the mouth of the statue of the little fairy girl. "Mommy loves you too, sweet girl."

Jayson leans over to open the canvas bag we brought with us. He lifts out a large blanket and smooths it flat on the grass for us to sit on. Jayson's parents are with Julien and Ryder back at the hotel. They're going to arrive later to allow me and Jayson some private time alone with our daughter first. He hands me my guitar which I brought with me on the plane. Sitting down on the blanket, Jayson guides me down to settle between his outstretched legs.

"Sing for our little girl, Liz. Let her hear her mommy's beautiful voice," he says, resting his face next to mine over my shoulder. I nod and begin to strum. It takes me several tries before I'm able to find my voice without getting choked up. I sing her the song that meant so much to me and Jayson. The song I sang to him that night in the backyard. The one he played at prom when he dropped to his knee and gave me his promise ring. So many memories and so much loss for such a short amount of time. As I sing, Jayson wraps his hands around my waist and settles them across my stomach like he's trying to imagine Elizabeth Ann growing inside of me.

"Do you remember my wish? The one I wrote

you on the silver star?"

I think of that night. About Jayson, the fairy lights, our tree, and the silver origami stars. How much I loved him. How much I wanted his wish to come true. "Yes, I remember."

"I think she would have looked just like you. Bright green eyes and pale blond hair."

"Silver eyes," I tell him. "She would have had your silver eyes." He hums as he pictures it. "She would have wrapped you around her little finger. Definitely would have been a daddy's girl."

"You think so?" He chuckles and kisses my neck.

"Oh, absolutely."

"We would have spent every summer at the beach so I could teach her to swim. Maybe put in a swimming pool in the back yard."

"I would teach her how to play the guitar and piano."

"And drums," he adds. "Her voice would have sounded like tinkling bells when she laughed. She would be smart like her mom." He smiles, kissing my shoulder, his hands gripping tighter around my waist.

"And brave and strong like her dad."

"No Liz. You are the strong one. So much stronger than I could ever hope to be."

A sharp slice of pain hits me deep inside my chest. Pain caused by a life and dreams I once had that were all wrapped in and belonged to Jayson. Our love, our future, our children, our past. Everything Jayson would tell me he wished for. Jayson was my prince and I was his princess. All of it now gone because of one fatal night over a year ago and the fact that I had loved and will always love Ryder. I want to tell Jayson I'm sorry. I want to beg for his forgiveness. I want him to find a life of happiness and love knowing it will never be with me.

I set my guitar down and turn so I can look Jayson in the eye. "Jayson, promise me that no matter what happens between the two of us, we will always come here on her birthday and spend time with our daughter."

"Liz."

"Promise me, Jayson. No matter what."

"I promise. No matter what," he replies in a hushed voice and crushes me to him in a fierce embrace. We stay that way for a long while, holding each other as we look upon Elizabeth Ann's gravestone.

"Want to read *Goodnight, Moon* to our daughter?"

Jayson and I have been making a list of the things we would have done with Elizabeth Ann this past year if she had been born. On that list are some of the books we would have read to her at night, songs we would have sung to her, places we would have taken her. We both wrote her letters and I purchased a weather-proof lockbox for us to put them in. We're going to bury the box next to her grave and add to it every time we come back.

Jayson reaches inside the canvas bag again and takes out the children's picture books we ordered. We've got about a dozen of them we want to read to her. He hands me *Green Eggs and Ham*. It was one of my favorites when I was little.

Jayson opens the book he's still holding and begins, his deep voice carrying over the wind.

Chapter 29

Seattle

Daniel and Drew

Elizabeth

The long winding drive that leads up to Daniel and Drew's estate is something to behold. The coniferous trees that grow in the Pacific Northwest are nothing like the spindly loblolly pines that grow in Coastal Plains of North Carolina. When I lived here, the landscape reminded me of Christmas even in the summertime.

It's been two days since we first visited Elizabeth Ann's grave. Jayson and I spent hours reading and talking to her before his parents, Ryder, and Julien arrived. They were emotionally exhausting and physically taxing days for everyone. Jayson and I went back again yesterday and planted new flowers amongst the ones that were already growing around the statue. We wanted something from us to grow there with our baby girl. Jayson also helped me make another rubbing as I want both of us to have one. I'm going to get them professionally mounted and framed when we get back home.

"Holy shit," Julien says from the front seat of our rented Tahoe.

I've been snuggled into Ryder's side in the back seat as Jayson drives. Up ahead of us is Daniel and Drew's mansion, or what Drew joking calls their country home. I know exactly how Julien feels as I felt the same way when I first it.

"Jayson, you'll need to stop at the guardhouse up ahead."

"Are you shitting me? How rich are they?"

If he did a little research on them and on D & D Technology, he would already know how much. He slows down at the imposing two-story gate and stone guardhouse and I roll down my window.

"Miss Elizabeth," Hank greets me with a toothy grin. "Welcome back."

"Hey, Hank. You're looking dashing as ever."

"We've missed your smiling face around here. They're expecting you. Don't forget to say goodbye on your way out." The gates open and I wave to Hank as Jayson drives through.

"I thought Fal's place was huge, but it's got nothing on this," Ryder says, leaning forward to peer through the front windshield as Jayson pulls up to the main steps of the house.

There's a place located near Asheville, North Carolina, called the Biltmore Estate. My parents took me and Hailey to visit a few times. The expansive beauty of the Vanderbilt home and its surrounding grounds was awe-inspiring and breathtaking to me, even as a child. The outside of Daniel and Drew's home holds many similar features to that of the Biltmore House but at half the scale. However, where the Biltmore was elegantly crafted in design on the inside, Daniel and Drew's house is homier.

Home. This was my home for a year. It was a place where Daniel, Drew, and I cooked meals together. A safe place where I grew stronger after I left the medical facility. It's a place that sheltered me during my darkest nights. Nights when dreams filled with fractured memories would come and nightmares of *Him* would try to drown me in darkness.

I grab Ryder's hand, but I don't yet open my door to get out.

"Babe, what's wrong?"

Jayson and Julien turn in their seats to look at me.

"Liz, if you're not ready to talk to them yet, we can turn around and go back," Julien offers.

"It's not that, Julien. I'm just nervous, I guess."

Jayson looks back at me. "If at any time you want to leave just say the word."

I look into the eyes of each of these three men. Each of them so integral in my life, playing pivotal roles in the formation of the woman I have become. "I'm ready," I tell them.

Even as we approach the house, I don't know how I should feel or what to expect when I see Daniel or Drew for the first in months. I've been so angry at the both of them. But as soon as the massive double oak doors open and Daniel steps out, my feet take over as I fly into his open arms.

"Oh sweet, sweet girl. Welcome home, Elizabeth," Daniel greets me, lifting me up in his arms to twirl me around. "I'm so sorry, Elizabeth. So very sorry about how I handled everything."

I was sure that I had no more tears left to cry, but I was very wrong. "I'm sorry too. I've missed you."

"Not as much as we've missed you, baby girl."

Daniel puts me down, but he doesn't release me. Since getting my memories back, I'm able to see how much Daniel looks like my dad. I hold his face between my hands and examine every feature. His hair is exactly the same shade as Dad's. His eyes are the same color too, and the shape of his mouth. God, he even smells the same as Dad—clean linen and mint.

"You look just like Daddy," I say.

Shock is the first to come and then realization. "You remember John?"

"Daniel, I remember everything."

"When? How?" he splutters.

"There's so much I need to tell you and Drew."

Ryder, Jayson, and Julien make their way up the stone steps. Ryder takes Daniel's outstretched hand and shakes it, but Jayson and Julien hold back, untrusting and wary.

"Boys, it's nice to see you again. Please come inside."

"Where's Drew?" I ask Daniel as we file into

the open foyer. There are two curved staircases on either side that lead up to the second floor. A Swarovski crystal chandelier hangs above us, catching the light streaming in through the floor-to-ceiling windows.

"He's upstairs resting and waiting for you."

Those words propel me up the closest staircase to seek him out. Video calls aside, I haven't seen Drew since early August when I left to go to North Carolina. I notice the door to the master suite is open and I tiptoe up to it. The noises from a television filter through the open door and it makes me grin as I hear Drew's favorite soap opera playing quietly in the background. I stop at the doorway and knock gently before entering. Inside, I find Drew propped up against the headboard of an enormous ornate bed, a mass of pillows at his back and a cup of tea in his hands. He looks so frail from here. He's lost even more weight since the last time I saw him.

"Hey old man," I say.

The rim of the china teacup arrests halfway to his lips. When he looks over and finds me, a smile so sweet blooms across his face. "It took you long enough."

"Well, you know me. Stubborn to the core."

He places the cup down on the table next

to him and pats the covers. “Get over here and give me a proper hug,” he demands, and I do, squeezing him carefully yet tightly.

Drew is not my blood relation like Daniel is, but it doesn’t make me love him any less. He and Daniel dropped everything when they were called. They took me in, cared for me, fought my battles with me through every step of my recovery. Drew had never met me, and yet he has loved me as if I am his own flesh and blood. How hard it must have been for both of them to have me suddenly thrust into their lives. I was in a coma; my entire family had been murdered. They had to deal with all of that by themselves, making the best decisions they could with what little information and preparation they had at the time. As much as keeping my pregnancy and the loss of my child a secret hurt me, I can understand now why they chose not to tell me at the time, and I believe Daniel when he said they were going to once they felt I was strong enough to handle it.

“You look wonderful, sweetheart. Your hair is much longer. It suits you. I must look a mess,” he says with a shaky hand running over the blue headscarf that covers his hairless head.

“Nonsense,” I tell him, laying my cheek against his shoulder. “You will always be a handsome devil in my eyes. Very sexy, like The Rock or Bruce Willis or Vin Diesel."

He chuckles and turns off the television with the remote. "Have you seen her yet?"

"Yes. The gravesite was beautiful. And the statue and poem. I appreciate the love and care you and Daniel put in to create such a lovely place for her." I peer up into his warm chocolate eyes. "Did you get a chance to hold her before they took her?" I don't know why I'm asking that. I guess I want to know if she felt the touch of someone who loved her before they took her away and buried her.

"Oh yes. She was perfect, Elizabeth. So tiny, about six inches, but absolutely perfect. We had the doctors lay her beside you. We made sure she felt your love. We made sure she was buried with respect."

Goddamn these tears that won't stop. "Thank you," I whisper, my heart breaking then filling with his words.

I don't know how long we sit there, our hands clasped together, lost in silence. Daniel must be keeping the guys downstairs to give me and Drew some alone time together.

"My memory came back two months ago. All of it," I tell him.

"Elizabeth, that's wonderful—"

I gently cut him off, "But so much has happened in those two short months. There's a lot I need to tell you and Daniel. Some of it you aren't going to be happy to hear." He frowns. "I also have some good news, but it has to stay between us for now."

"Alright."

I pull my necklace out from beneath my blouse. "I asked Ryder to marry me. Funny thing is, he had already bought me a ring and was going to ask me. We both said yes. I'm getting married." I laugh softly, ripples of happiness in my voice.

"It's a gorgeous ring, Elizabeth. The last time we spoke over video, I could tell by the smile on your face and the way you spoke about him how deeply you loved him. He must be a wonderful man to have captured your heart."

"Ryder is my best friend. I have loved him most of my life. I have never been happier. He completes every part of me."

Drew shifts slightly and pulls me into a hug, kissing my temple. "Then why the secret?"

Drew doesn't know anything about my past, so I explain, "I haven't told Jayson or Julien yet.

Before the attack, Jayson and I were together. He and his twin brother, Julien, have been my best friends since first grade. They lived next door to me. I started dating Jayson in high school. Elizabeth Ann was his."

Drew blows out a soft whistle. "And you remember all of that? It must be hard for him." That's the struggle and profound guilt I feel when it comes to Jayson. Having me come back, finding out he lost a daughter and then standing helplessly by as he watched me fall in love with another man, a man that was his best friend. I can't begin to imagine how Jayson must feel.

"Yes. Jayson was my first romantic love. But I was also in love with Ryder at the same time. Ryder and I never acted on our feelings toward one another since I was with Jayson, but it was always there. A part of me feels guilty and ashamed about how things turned out for Jayson. He deserved—deserves better from me. He lost everything that night too."

"Elizabeth, you can't help who you fall in love with. If it's Ryder you see yourself spending the rest of your life with, then he is the man you are supposed to be with. You shouldn't feel guilty about loving someone with your whole heart."

"Oh, Drew. I love Ryder so much. But I

screwed up. I made a mistake when my memories came back. I hurt everyone, especially Ryder. I'm so lucky that he loves me enough that he was able to forgive me. I told you there was a lot I needed to explain. It's going to take a while."

"I'm not going anywhere. Whenever you're ready, Daniel and I will be there. We love you like a daughter. I hope you know that. We would do anything for you."

I sniffle, "I know. I'm sorry my anger kept me away. I threw away a lot of precious time with you and Daniel."

"Shush now, child. No more apologies."

"Thank you for taking care of me. For loving me."

"Loving you was easy," he says. "Now, I need to work on getting better so Daniel and I can walk you down the aisle."

My head pops up off his shoulder. "I was hoping, I mean, I was going to ask you both, but I didn't know how things stood between us. I would love that."

"Like I said, you're my daughter in all the ways that count. Of course, I'll be beside you for every step."

Drew and I sit and talk about what has been going on with his treatment. As hard a road as he has had to travel, the end prognosis looks promising. The treatment plan his doctors developed appears to be working, but the toll it has taken on his body is telling.

Eventually, Daniel comes to find us and helps Drew downstairs to the atrium where the boys are gathered around a circular gas fireplace situated in the middle of the room. I give Ryder, Jayson, and Julien a tour of the house while Daniel and Drew get an early dinner prepared. I take the boys to my room first, but it's the game room with the large snooker table and the theater room that grab their attention; that is, until I show them the indoor and outdoor pools, and the tennis court.

Daniel insists we eat out on the patio, the chill of the late afternoon being doused by the heat lamps situated around the marble patio table. That gives me a chance to snag him away for a private moment in the kitchen so I can tell him about my engagement. He cries which makes me cry yet again.

As evening settles along the ridgeline of Douglas firs, aspens, and oaks behind the house, we watch from the patio as the horizon glows an autumnal red. Moving inside, we settle in the great room and I try my best to explain everything that has happened since I last spoke with Daniel and Drew. I tell the two of them about my memories coming back; my trip with Fallon; seeing my house for the first time since that night and my plans to buy it and fix it up; what Maria did; the threatening text message; my vandalized Hellcat; and my most recent trip back to the hospital after being pushed in front of an oncoming car. Yeah, those last things do not go over well at all. It takes over an hour for me to belay their fears and the guys have to jump in to reassure them that I will be protected and looked after. Daniel makes them promise, against my very loud protests, that I am not to be left alone at any time. I reluctantly relent once Drew threatens to hire a bodyguard to stick by my side day and night.

We have one more day left in Seattle. One more day for me and Jayson to visit our daughter's gravesite before we leave. One more day for me to see Daniel and Drew. And then it's back home for Christmas. Even with the threat of an unknown stalker hanging over me like a dark shadow, and the possibility of Maria being brought up on criminal charges, I'm looking forward to spending the holidays with Ryder, Fallon, Jayson, and Julien. My boys. My family.

Unfortunately, I could never have prepared myself for what would happen in the coming days.

Chapter 30

Elizabeth

"Merry fucking Christmas Eve, y'all! Now get your asses up," a voice booms on the other side of Ryder's bedroom door before it opens and in strolls Fallon.

"Come on, man," Ryder groans and pulls me closer in our spooning position.

We arrived at the Cutton house yesterday afternoon and stayed up all night talking with Faith, Randy, Brea, and Jamie. Which basically meant that Faith, Jamie, and Brea yapped on about weddings, while Ryder and I sat cringing because, let's face it, no bride-to-be wants to have her wedding hijacked by well-meaning family members—even when she knows it's coming from a place of love. Perhaps eloping is not such a bad idea after all. Around one in the morning, Ryder and I were able to escape, and we fell face-first, exhausted, and still fully clothed into bed.

Fallon's ice blue eyes meet mine as he flops down on the bed beside me. "Good morning, kitten."

I grin then slap my hand over my mouth and muffle out, "Morning breath. Let me go brush my teeth."

"Fuck that. Give me a hug."

"Get your ass out of my bed and off my woman," Ryder sleepily grunts and reaches over me to shove Fallon off the side. I scramble off the bed and run into Ryder's bathroom to freshen up, thankful that I'm still in the jeans and shirt I was wearing last night. Ryder passes me on his way into the bathroom as I come out, stopping to kiss me along the way.

Feeling more awake now—even though I'm dying for a cup of coffee—I tackle Fallon where he's sitting on the edge of the bed.

"I'm so glad you're here!" I tell him, thankful he kept his promise to spend Christmas with me and Ryder. I was not going to allow him to spend the holidays by himself this year. Fallon grabs my waist and throws me up in the air to land with an *umph* on Ryder's mattress. Just like at Tatiána's house, I hop up and start jumping on it like a trampoline much to Fallon's amusement.

"Is everybody up?" I ask him between jumps. I can't see Ryder's clock from here so don't know what time it is.

"Faith let me in. They were having breakfast." Fallon eyes me, his gaze focused. "Are you going to tell Jay and Jules about that rock on your finger?"

After we landed at Raleigh-Durham airport yesterday, Jayson and Julien left to go back to their house. Ryder and I lingered a while in the airport food court, drinking coffee, and solidifying how we were going to handle telling everyone about our engagement. It was time. There was nothing holding us back anymore. So I took my ring off the necklace and Ryder slipped it back on my finger where it belongs. We're planning to make an official announcement tomorrow when all the families are here for Christmas dinner, mostly for the Jameson's benefit since Ryder's family already knows—but not before I have a chance to talk with Jayson privately first.

Fallon grabs me to stop me from bouncing. "Elizabeth, you need to tell them."

I reply honestly, "I am, Fallon. I need to handle Jayson with kid gloves, however."

"Secret for a secret, kitten," he says, taking my hand and bringing it up to his lips to kiss my ringed finger. “I’m so damn happy for you and Ry. There isn’t a better man than him, and there isn’t a more deserving woman than you. It’s about time that you have your happy-ever-after. Take it, kitten, and never look back. Don’t be afraid.”

I cup the side of his face and his icy gaze softens. “I wouldn’t have any of this without you, Fallon. Thank you for saving me. Thank you for giving my life a second chance. I always said that Ryder, Jayson, and Julien were my princes. You, Fallon, are my knight in shining armor.”

Sadness creeps into his pale blue eyes. He very nearly manages to conceal it with a cocky curve of his lips. He looks over my shoulder as Ryder comes out of the bathroom.

Fallon and Ryder do that one-armed guy hug thing in greeting and pat each other on the back. “Have you set a date yet?”

Ryder and I look at each other.

Elope he silently mouths.

Maybe I mouth back at him.

“We haven’t had a chance to talk about much of anything yet.”

Fallon touches my arm. “How was Seattle?”

His concern moves me and reminds me yet

again how glad I am that he's in my life now. When I'm old and sitting on my porch swing rocker on the patio of the house Ryder and I build together, I will look back on this past year and shake my head at the foolishness of my younger self. I wasted so many years in high school being afraid of this misunderstood man, being afraid of my immense love for Ryder, being afraid to disappoint those I loved. So many wasted years. So much pain and trauma. So many mistakes. But life is not a linear path. It's filled with trips, turns, falls and bumps, heartache, grief, joy, and love. And then there are our choices. Our choices have meaning. They make an impact. They hold repercussions. Choices alter reality and decide the future. I spent most of my life avoiding making a choice. Afraid to stake my own path. Letting others take the lead as I weakly followed. Whatever destiny the Fates have planned for me, I'm ready. I want it. I want this life that I've fought so hard for. Sacrificed so much for. I want it all.

"It was what I needed. It was healing." I don't say anything more to Fallon. I know he gets me; gets the importance of seeing my daughter's gravesite and the closure I needed.

He smooths a hand down my messy bed hair and barrels for the door. "I'm fucking starving and Faith made sausage with biscuits and gravy."

Ryder pulls me onto his back and wraps my legs around his middle so he can carry me piggyback downstairs. "You know how much that woman loves feeding you."

"Your family has always been good to me," Fallon replies, lost in a past that I've been learning more and more about recently. How many times did Ryder sneak Fallon into this house to sleep overnight away from his abusive father? How many times did Faith cook breakfast for Fallon and never ask questions as to why he was there—just automatically accepted him as part of the family like she did me?

"What car did you drive here?" Ryder asks Fallon.

"Elizabeth's."

"What! It's here?" I squeal with excitement and try to punch Fallon in the arm for not telling me the moment he came in. The last time I saw my Hellcat was when the police towed it away to dust for prints. Randy was going to send someone out to tow it back to his garage once it was released.

Ryder veers left when we get to the bottom of the stairs. I duck my head to his shoulder when we walk out the front door, heading outside to the front driveway.

"Holy shit!" I exclaim and wiggle myself off his back and run over to my car. It's absolutely gorgeous. New paint job, red hubcaps to match, and a racing stripe down the middle just like Ryder's. My name has been scripted on the side under the driver's side window. I pop the hood and find what looks like a completely new engine.

Turning to Ryder and Fallon, I narrow my eyes at them. "Was that all a set-up upstairs?"

"Yep."

"I bumped you up to 880. Kept the interior the same," Randy says as he joins me under the hood.

"Mr. Cutton, it's wonderful. I'm speechless. I can never thank you enough." I wrap my arms around him from the side and give him the biggest bear hug I can.

"Sweetheart, it was my pleasure. Merry Christmas." He leans in close to my ear. "You and my boy are good for each other. He has loved you for a very long time, and I know you have loved him for just as long. The journey the two of you have taken to get to this point was worth it. Never doubt that. You have always been part of our family, Lizzie. I'm so proud of the woman you have grown up to be and even prouder that you will be my daughter-in-law."

I hug him tighter as my heart thuds against my ribcage. "You are such a good man, Mr. Cutton. You raised a one-in-a-billion son. I love him with my whole being and promise he will know nothing but happiness for the rest of his life."

Randy coughs a few times, clearing his throat from the heavy emotion our conversation has stirred. Ryder comes over to embrace his dad before wrapping his arms around my shoulders.

"Want to take her out later?" Ryder suggests.

"Yes! I've missed her. Can we go now?"

"I drove that thing here. The least you can do is let them feed me, woman," Fallon complains.

"Alright. Food first, trip to the Fields later?"

"Pop up, sexy." Ryder motions for me to jump back on for a piggyback so he can carry me inside. As soon as Ryder secures my legs around him, I give him a dozen kisses on the neck and cheek because I'm so happy. My phone dings and I grab it one-handed out of my back pocket while keeping the other hand wrapped around Ryder's neck.

ScaryGuy: Fam wanted to wait for us to get back before decorating the tree. They'd like

for you to be here.

I really need to change his screen name. I quickly go into my contacts and edit his information.

Me: Tell Freda I'd love to. Fallon just got here.

Jayson: Fuck it. It's Xmas. He can come too. I promise to be on my best behavior.

Me: I just got my car back! Ahhhhh! So freaking happy!

Jayson: U r such a diva daredevil.

Me: Let me check with the guys about later and I'll text u back after breakfast.

Jayson: <thumbs up emoji> Miss you, Liz. Merry Xmas Eve, princess. <Xmas tree emoji>

Me: Merry Xmas Eve to you too.

Oh boy. I guess my time is up. Today will be the day I tell Jayson I'm engaged to Ryder.

Chapter 31

Elizabeth

"Hurry up, slowpokes! I told Jayson we would be there at four." I'm trying my best to get Ryder and Fallon out the door but apparently the football game on television is more enticing. Grabbing the remote, I shut the TV off.

"Hey!" the guys whine at me, even Randy who is sitting back in his big old rocker recliner. I hand him the remote and kiss the top of his head. "All yours, Pops." I wink at him.

"Dinner will be ready at eight." Faith pokes her head out of the kitchen where she, Jamie, and Brea have been baking all afternoon. I helped clean and prepare the turkey for tomorrow's Christmas supper and shredded the collard greens which are now slowly cooking in a large pot filled with chicken broth and six long bacon strips. I also snapped green beans for the green bean casserole and diced Granny

Smith and Honeycrisp apples to soak in bourbon overnight for the apple crumble pie Faith and I will be making in the morning. There is nothing better than a good old home-cooked Southern meal, and my taste buds are already watering over the feast we will eat tomorrow for Christmas with the Jamesons.

"Think Jay and Jules will have the game on?" Fallon asks as Ryder helps me slip my coat on.

"I think you can count on it. Now, git." I shoo the two men out the front door and we're on our way.

"Did you just Southern sass me?"

"You bet your sweet dandy I did," I say with my best Southern drawl. That has Ryder kissing me while laughing at the same time.

"I love your sassy mouth."

I peer up at Ryder with heated eyes. "Then you're in for a treat later tonight," I tell him, which causes him to suck in a sharp breath and kiss me longer this time.

Fallen Brook Drive has transformed into a Christmas fairytale. Homes are decorated with lights, yards are full of holiday décor, Christmas-themed inflatables, and kids full of excitement that Santa will be visiting tonight. I loved growing up here. I loved having my three best friends—Ryder, Jayson, and Julien—living on the same street as I did. This street holds a lot of great memories of our youth, like us playing freeze-tag while riding our bikes, even if I would fall off my bike and skin my knees every time; my dad and Ryder teaching me how to drive; and long twilight walks with Hailey or Jayson. Nostalgia greets me with a warm embrace as we walk. I keep expecting to feel anxiety or apprehension as we near my childhood home, but I don't. Not today. Today, when I walk up to Jayson and Julien's, my old house standing empty beside theirs, I'm going to focus on the good things, the good memories.

One hundred feet from our destination, the old oak tree catches my attention. Instead of the white fairy lights adorning its branches, flashing multi-colored lights have taken their place, creating a kaleidoscopic effect against the sides of the two homes that bracket it. Jayson must have done that. I look to the left of the oak at my house. *My house.* But it looks different. Newer. A fresh coat of paint in a pale yellow adorns the outside and is accented by deep, navy blue shutters at every window. The front door is painted the same shade of blue as the shutters. The roof is new as well, the shingles a dark blue to match the shutters and door.

"Merry Christmas, kitten." Fallon takes out a thick envelope from the inside pocket of his long wool coat and places it in my hand.

"Fallon, what did you do?" My question isn't accusatory; it's filled with wonder.

"I fulfilled your wish."

I open the envelope and quickly peruse the stapled pieces of paper. Just like I feared, Fallon bought my house. Wait, it's not just Fallon's name on the documents, Ryder's name is listed as well.

Because I'm slightly speechless, it takes me a second to force out, "You both bought my house?"

Shoving his hands into his coat pockets, Fallon kicks at an errant dry leaf. "You talked about fixing your house up, making it a good place for a family again. How could I not help make that a reality for you?"

Seeing I'm about to lose it in the middle of the street, Ryder takes gentle hold of my face, his thumbs tipping it up so our gazes lock. "We wanted to give that to you. *Please* let us give this to you."

"The house will be transferred to your name as soon as you sign those papers. You can do with the house as you please, but I have a suggestion," Fallon continues. I take a steadying breath and turn in Ryder's arms to face Fallon. "I was thinking about New York. About the boys. I plan to offer their mothers jobs at Montgomery Pharmaceutical and help move them down here if they accept my offer."

"You can do that?"

"Because of my grandfather, I own majority stock. That's why Patricia and Phillip never hassle me about corporate matters. Say, for example, I suddenly leave the country with a beautiful blond in one of the private jets. As long as the money keeps flowing in and the board is happy, I can do whatever the fuck I want. That's beside the point. What I want to suggest is that you lease your house. I would cover all of the monthly expenses like rent, utilities, and maintenance."

I finally catch on. "Fallon, that's a fantastic idea! Yes! Devon would love it here."

Devon and his mom could have a good life here. A fresh start. A safe haven. Mrs. Riley, Devon's mom, is one of the women I spoke with while visiting the women's shelter in New York. She was abused just like Hailey. She's a survivor just like me. Fallon's idea is exactly what I want. It's exactly how it should be. My heart couldn't feel fuller at this moment.

I jump on Fallon, giving him a great, big hug, then kiss the shit out of Ryder. "I love you both.

Thank you for giving me this."

"Merry Christmas, sweetheart," Ryder says.

"Thank you, Fallon," I tell him with feeling.

"You don't need to—" is all he gets out before I break loose from Ryder and grab him, smacking a chaste, yet hard kiss to his lips.

"Shut up, Fallon and accept my thank you."

"Um... okay. Please don't kick my ass," he says to Ryder who bursts out laughing.

"I think it's safe to say I can let that one kiss slide—just this once. Don't make it a habit."

I'm bouncing on the balls of my feet. "Can we go inside?"

Fallon hands me a set of keys.

I text Jayson and Julien to let them know we'll be late. Ryder, Fallon, and I spend the next hour in my old home going from room to room. The inside has been completely re-done and staged like a show house. New interior paint, completely re-done kitchen and bathrooms, dark wood floors throughout. When my eyes scan my old living room and kitchen, I no longer see *Him* or the horror of that night. I see spaces filled with family, love, and happy memories to come.

After exploring every inch of my refurbished home, we cross the yard to the Jameson's. I run my hand over the swing as we pass by the tree.

Before I get a chance to knock, the front door flies open and Julien excitedly exclaims, "I'm getting married!"

Holy crap! *How did they find out*, is my first reaction until Julien shoves his ringed hand in my face. "Holy crap!" I say.

I'm about to reach up and grab Julien's hand to get a closer look when the engagement ring on my own finger starts to figuratively burn a hole through my skin. I deftly push my hand into my coat pocket and slide the ring off with my thumb, feeling guilty as hell with Ryder standing right behind me. How can I tell Jayson about my engagement to Ryder tonight when everyone is celebrating Julien and Elijah's?

"Liz, get your ass in here!" Jayson bellows from inside the house.

Julien lifts me up and carries me inside while talking a mile a minute as if Meredith has suddenly possessed him. Elijah and Jayson are sitting on the living room couch tipping back beers and have dropped back into an animated discussion. Freda barrels past her husband to kiss my cheek with a "Merry Christmas Eve," and rushes straight into the kitchen when a buzzer goes off. Ryder hangs back with Fallon, both of them handing their coats to Mitch who hangs them in the closet off the foyer.

"Liz!" two male voices shout out from the couch.

My mind is whirling as the noise of overlapping voices intensifies in the room. Today has been a day of surprises. First getting my car back, then my house, and now this.

"So, will you?" asks Elijah.

I look over at him. "What?"

Julien passes me like a football to Jayson, and memories of them doing this exact same thing in high school spring to mind, notching up my flustered confusion.

"Will you be my best man... best woman... person. Whatever. So, will you?" Elijah asks me, his big puppy dog eyes blinking at me.

Ryder comes to my rescue and extricates me from Jayson's hold and sits down with me in his lap next to the two of them.

"Mr. Montgomery, it's a pleasure to finally meet you in person," Freda welcomes Fallon, as she sets a platter on the coffee table. The smell of baked cheese and spicy sausage has my stomach growling. Freda always makes sausage and cheese balls for Christmas. "Did Lizzie see her surprise?" she asks him.

"Yes ma'am. We were just over there. And please, just call me Fallon."

"Wait, you knew?" I ask Freda incredulously.

"Knew what?" Jayson asks.

"Yes, sweetheart. Fallon called us to let us know beforehand since there would be crews working over there day and night to get everything ready."

Jayson narrows his eyes at Fallon. "What did he do?"

"Fallon and Ryder bought my house. Complete rehab. It's gorgeous. I'm surprised you didn't see the new paint and shutters when you decorated the oak tree."

"Dad decorated the tree," Julien says.

"Thank you, Mitch!" I smile at him.

He shrugs it off. "It's a bit of a tradition now," he replies.

"I honestly didn't notice the house when we arrived. Neither did Jules or Elijah. *Huh.* I'm surprised I didn't spot the change," Jayson mutters, scratching the scruff of his chin.

"Hey, back to me," Elijah exclaims. "Liz, will you be my best person?"

"I think we need to start over from the beginning. There have been four different conversations going on and my brain is having trouble keeping up." I'm sitting sideways on Ryder's lap on the sofa, and I feel Ryder's body tense when his eyes light on my naked ring finger. I bend low to whisper in his ear, "I promise to explain later."

"My boy is getting married!" Freda gushes, holding on to Mitch's side.

"Mom, you're kinda stealing my thunder here," Julien pouts, then he grins ear to ear and kisses Elijah.

"Congrats, guys," Fallon offers as he pops a sausage ball in his mouth. That man is always hungry.

Ryder reaches around me and fist bumps Julien and Elijah. "All the happiness in the world. I mean it."

"Okay, now I'm stealing Liz," Elijah declares and pops up off the couch pulling me with him as he heads into the kitchen.

When I know no one else can hear us, I ask,

"Oh my gosh! I'm so happy for you and Julien! What changed your mind?"

I'm thinking about how Elijah was going to propose last month but then he and Julien got into a fight over me disappearing with Fallon, which led to them taking a break like Ross and Rachel did on *Friends*. I knew they were working on patching things back up, but I didn't realize that it had progressed back to a marriage proposal.

"I love him, Liz. I don't want to go another day without him. Our fight was stupid. If I made you feel like I blamed you in any way, I am so very sorry. You were the first person, and the only person, for a long while who stood by our relationship from the very beginning. I won't ever forget the sacrifices you made in high school to make sure Jules and I had alone time to be together and not have to hide who we were to each other. I will always love you for that. And it would mean the world to me if you would stand by my side on my wedding day."

My hand connects with his in a high-five. "Elijah, it would be my pleasure."

"So that's a yes?"

"Of course it's a yes! Oh, do I get to wear a tux too?"

His eyes twinkle. "Liz, you would rock it in a

tux. Like a sexy secret agent."

"As long as it's not pink. Or red. Or purple."

"Jules asked Jay to be his best man but he's going to ask Ry as well. He always felt like Ry was as much his brother as Jay was."

"So cute. Like co-best men. I love it." Noticing some sugar cookies, I pick one up. Freda must have made them earlier. She's a wizard at cookie icing. I could never get the hang of it. I nibble on the trunk of a frosted Christmas tree.

"I know the Seattle trip was something personal between the four of you, but if you ever need to talk about anything, including Elizabeth Ann, I'm here for you, Liz. I hope you know that."

I've always had a soft spot for Elijah. He truly is one of the really good guys. He gave up his full ride to Stanford to help take care of Julien when I disappeared after my attack. He and I were friends even before he grew close to Julien, Ryder, or Jayson.

A cheer goes up in the other room. "Sounds like they found the football game."

"Football's never been my thing."

"I know!" I smirk. "You fall asleep after the first five minutes of every game we watch together."

"Want to start decorating the tree?"

"Lead the way, E."

Chapter 32

Elizabeth

"It was the sweetest little thing I have ever seen," I tell Faith. Freda had knitted a Christmas stocking for Elizabeth Ann that she let me hang with everyone else's along the fireplace mantle.

"Freda has always been such a good woman. My heart breaks for her, and for you, Lizzie, for your loss. You know that Randy and I would have come to Seattle to support you if you'd asked."

"I know. And thank you. It means a lot."

I rinse off the plate I just cleaned and hand it to Faith to dry. Ryder, Fallon, and I came back as promised a little before eight for dinner. Ryder, Fallon, Randy, Jamie, and Brea disappeared somewhere and left me and Faith with the dirty dishes.

Faith drops her drying rag on the counter

and places a hand on my shoulder. "Lizzie, are you alright, sweet girl? You've had a lot to deal with these past few months."

"I'm getting there," I reply with a sigh. "Ryder takes very good care of me. He's been my rock and I feel like I'm letting him down."

"Oh, honey, why would you think you've let my boy down? He loves you. You'd have to be dumb, deaf, and blind not to see how much."

"I wish Hailey and my mom were here," I say sadly. "Hailey always knew exactly what to do when I was sucked into my thoughts. Her poems would help calm whatever conflict I was facing, and Mom always gave the best hugs."

"Ann was my best friend. She was one of a kind. However, I've been told I give great mom hugs too." Faith opens her arms to me, and I stumble into them like a lost child seeking comfort. "Now, tell me what's troubling you and why you think you've disappointed Ryder."

"I've been terrified to tell Jayson about our engagement."

She runs her palm down my hair in a gentle gesture. "That's understandable. You and Jayson had a fierce, fiery young love that was ripped away from the both of you quite suddenly in the most horrific way."

"I've always loved Ryder, though. Even when I was with Jayson. You must think something awful of me for saying that."

"Sweetie, if you recall, Randy and I were front and center to everything that happened. We saw what was going on. My husband is a very smart man. He once told Ryder that you needed time to decide what you wanted and to be patient. That if you were the one he was supposed to be with, it would all work out. I can't tell you how many boyfriends I had growing up. I swore each one of them was *the one*." Faith chuckles to herself.

"But that right there is the innocence of youth. When I met Randy, that's when it really hit me. I ran home to my momma after the first time he kissed me and told her, 'Momma, I'm in trouble.' I knew right then and there that he was my forever. That man has owned my heart ever since." I love how she describes Randy as her forever, just like I do with Ryder.

"I want to be Ryder's wife more than I have ever wanted anything else. I can't imagine my life without him by my side. I just don't want anything to be ruined by the fight I know Jayson and I will get into when he finds out. I will always love Jayson, too. He's been my best friend for so long, and he was my first love. I don't want to hurt him."

"I know. I wish I could tell you exactly what will happen and not to worry; that everything will work out. But life sometimes doesn't turn out that way. It's in those times, the times that are hard, that you must stand by what is truly in your heart. Never be afraid to fight for what you want, Lizzie. If what you want is to be with my son, well, by God, fight for him. If your heart tells you to be with Jayson, then you must fight just as hard for him. If it's neither of them, then that's your right as well. It's your choice, Lizzie, no one else's."

My choice.

I reach into my pocket and pull out my ring. I slip the magnificent yellow diamond back onto my finger with a silent promise never to take it off again.

"I will always choose Ryder."

The fire is crackling in the firepit and I inhale the burned aroma of wood fire and smoke, relishing in the camaraderie of the evening. Jamie's boyfriend, Jack, arrived earlier and he's been regaling us with stories of his backpacking trip along the Appalachian Trail. Otherwise, it's just me, Fallon, and the Cuttons enjoying a break from the excitement of the last couple of days.

The night is clear, and stars pop out against the inky blackness; a waxing, gibbous moon hangs in the sky. I've noticed Brea has been quiet most of the evening. I'll make sure to spend some alone time with her later. I've been so busy with everything else that I haven't gotten a chance to talk to her much. I texted Meredith earlier today and she said she was bored out of her mind sitting around the house and being forced to talk to cousins she rarely sees and couldn't care less about. I also texted Tatiána so I'm surprised when her text comes in now since it would be in the middle of the night in Madrid.

Tatiána: Feliz Navidad. Merry Christmas, Elizabeth.

Me: Merry Xmas Eve, Tatiána!

Me: What are you doing up at this hour? You should be in bed.

Tatiána: I was hungry. I think I will be as round as a whale when the baby finally comes. I've been craving peanut butter and fried plantains.

Me: That actually sounds pretty good. Let me know what you think.

Tatiána: How is my brother doing? I'm glad you had him stay with you for Christmas.

Me: He's good. He and Ryder bought my old childhood home for me and fixed it up. We are planning to use it to house a family we met at the women's shelter in New York City. Fallon is offering jobs down here to all the women we met at the shelter. I'm so proud of him.

Tatiána: I told you that you were good for him. Thank you for opening his heart.

Me: He helped mend mine. I owe him.

Tatiána: You can never put a price on love, Elizabeth.

Me: Speaking of love...Ryder and I are engaged! <wedding emoji> <ring emoji>

I take a selfie of me and Ryder while raising my ring hand to catch the firelight glinting off the facets of the diamond. Ryder quirks his brow up at me. I kiss his stubbled jaw and continue texting.

Tatiána: Oh my! Tan hermosa! So beautiful! I hope Eduardo and I are invited to the wedding?

Me: We haven't decided on a date yet, but yes, I would love for you both to be here. Hopefully with a little one with you.

Tatiána: Only five more months to go. Te amo, Elizabeth.

Me: Love you too. Go eat and get back to bed. Merry Xmas!

"Fallon, you may want to order some fried plantains for your sister and have them delivered."

"I thought it was fried pickles."

Brea and Jamie both make gagging noises and Brea declares, "I will never get pregnant if that's what I'm going to be craving. Gross."

"Fried pickles were last week. Apparently, this week is fried plantains with peanut butter," I share with Fallon.

Brea gags again and everyone laughs.

"Got it," Fallon notes, typing away on his phone.

"Now fried pickles dipped in peanut butter is more my thing," a voice pipes up from the side of the yard.

I turn to see who it is. "What are you doing here?" I ask, surprised but happy.

Meredith pops her hand on her hip and angles her head back to where Trevor is coming around the corner. "Your boy summoned us.

Surprise!"

"It's a wonderful surprise, but I don't understand." I get out of Ryder's lap to hug Mer and kiss Trevor's cheek.

He returns it with a hello, then he turns me around. "I think your guy has something else up his sleeve."

Somehow, Ryder is now standing along with everyone else in front of the firepit, a guitar strapped over his shoulder and a pick in his hand.

"Ryder Cutton, what is going on?"

My handsome, devilish man winks at me and starts to strum the guitar. I recognize the notes of Taylor Swift's "Love Song." Freda, Randy, Brea, Jamie, Fallon, and Jack take out sparklers and light them. Ryder looks like a country-rock god with his dark hair disheveled and sticking up where the wind and my fingers have run through it today. His copper eyes sparkle with mischief, and his biceps bulge as he grips the guitar. He is the sexiest man I have ever seen. If we were at a concert and he was up on stage, I'd be throwing my panties at him. But it's the baritone of his voice that slays me. I grab on to Meredith's hand in a death grip when Ryder starts singing.

I mouth the lyrics with him as he sings but

my words falter when I find they are different from the ones I know. Ryder has changed the words to the song. His new lyrics chronicle our life together from when we were kids to today. It chronicles *our* love story. I'm trembling so hard, Trevor has to hold on to me lest I collapse to the grass. My man's words turn my legs almost liquid and cause my heart to pound so hard, I feel light-headed.

As Ryder sings, he and I slowly inch our way toward one another; that invisible gravitational force that has always existed between us bringing us together. As he gets to the ending lyrics of the song, he swings the guitar behind his back and takes a knee. I drop down on my own knees in front of him, clasping one hand over my mouth to catch the sob that tries to escape. He pulls out a diamond eternity band that matches my yellow engagement ring, takes my hand, and sings the last words of the rewritten song.

"On bended knee, I pulled out a ring,
And sang, 'Marry me, Elizabeth,
And say you're mine forever.
I'll love you every day that we're together.
You'll wear my ring and pick out a wedding dress,
It's our love story, so baby, please say, Yes.'"

"Oh my God, yes! Always, forever, yes!" Our

lips meet with crushing force, neither one of us caring at all that we're surrounded by family. *Our* family. *My* family.

I pull my mouth from our kiss and nibble my way up to his ear. "I am going to fuck you so hard tonight and we're going to come so much that neither one of us will be able to walk for a week," I whisper.

Ryder's hands clench on my back and he stands up abruptly with me in his arms. "We'll be right back," he calls out at everyone and rushes us inside the house to the sound of our friends' and family's celebratory hoots and hollers.

Chapter 33

Jayson

With the celebration of Julien and Elijah's engagement, I completely forgot to give Liz the Christmas ornament I had made with Elizabeth Ann's name on it. I knock on the front door of the Cutton home, but no one answers. That usually means they're in the backyard. I notice a black Range Rover in their driveway and wonder who it belongs to. Rounding the corner, I hear a guitar and I smile. I love to hear Liz play and sing. I'm glad she brought her guitar with her to Seattle and sang to our little girl.

As I round the corner of the house, smile on my face, with the present secured in my hand, my smile deepens when I notice the Cuttons holding sparklers. I used to chase Liz in the backyard when we were kids, the both of us holding sparklers in our hands. Her favorites were the gold ones. My steps slow when I notice Meredith and Trevor next to Liz. My feet stop when I see it's Ryder singing, not Liz. My heart breaks when I see him kneel in front of her, a ring held in his outstretched hand. And the love that has consumed me for her since childhood twists into a raging hatred toward her when I hear her say, "Yes!"

Chapter 34

Elizabeth

"I can see some things never change," I tease, leaning a shoulder against Brea's bedroom doorframe. Brea is dressed in her finest Christmas flannel pajamas. She has fuzzy Rudolph chenille socks on her feet, a reindeer antler headband on her head, and a bowl of toffee-covered popcorn in her lap, as she sits on her bed watching the Hallmark Christmas movie marathon that airs every year. It was a tradition she and Hailey would do every Christmas Eve.

"It's not Christmas Eve without Hallmark," Brea says.

"Mind some company?"

Brea tilts her head when shouts of celebration can be heard. "Sounds like things are still in full swing downstairs."

It's almost midnight but no one is eager to

go to bed yet. Faith insisted that Trevor and Meredith stay for the night, which was an offer they easily accepted. Everyone was downstairs playing the *Exploding Kittens* card game when I noticed Brea's absence, so I came upstairs to find her.

Brea shifts over and pats the side of the mattress next to her. I hold up a finger, showing her the reindeer antler headband I had been hiding behind my back. Once I secure it to my head, I jump on the bed to join her, grabbing a fistful of popcorn and shoving it into my mouth. My headband has tiny jingle bells attached to the antlers and Brea flicks them a few times.

We're both lying on our stomachs. Brea bumps my side. "I have to confess, I never knew my brother had it in him."

"What? Being romantic? Knowing how to sweep a girl off her feet?"

"Yeah." She giggles.

"Oh yeah," I sigh. "He definitely has it and then some."

Brea lays her head on my shoulder, causing our headbands to clash and my jingle bells to rattle. "I'm so glad you're back, Lizzie. I missed you." Brea pauses. "I miss her so much."

"Me too, Brea. Every day. It's okay if you want

to talk about her."

Brea's eyes fill and become glassy. "I don't want to upset you, Lizzie. I don't want to bring back bad memories for you."

I rub her arm and kiss the top of her head. Brea has grown up so much since my senior year of high school. She and Hailey were attached at the hip from the moment they first met and shared their love of American Girl dolls.

"The only memories I have of Hailey are good ones, Brea." I pause. "Brea, I know you have a lot of questions, especially about that night. It's going to be very hard to hear, so why don't we leave that conversation until after the New Year and enjoy this cheesy, romantic movie. I'd like to think that Hailey is watching it with us."

We sit in silence for a while and watch the movie. It's sweet, sappy, and simple. Classic Hallmark. I play with her hair, braiding it loosely then finger-combing the braids apart. I remember Hailey used to do this to Brea's hair just like she would brush my hair to soothe and relax me when we talked. Brea's coloring is similar to Ryder's—dark hair, light brown eyes a shade darker than his, tanned skin. Brea is gorgeous, like her brother; she's gentle and kind like him too.

"Do you have a boyfriend yet?"

"Oh my God, no. Boys are douchebags."

I'm a bit surprised. "Brea, you're a senior in high school and you're telling me you've never had a boyfriend."

"You haven't seen the asshats that go to my school. I wouldn't date one of them for a million dollars. Besides, I have bigger things to do than worry about dressing up on a Friday night for a date."

"Like what?" I pull one braid in her hair apart and re-do it.

"I want to go to college and study psychiatry."

I don't have to ask why to know it's because of what happened to Hailey.

"I'm proud of you," I tell her.

"I'm really excited that you're going to be my sister-in-law."

"Me too." I tickle her side.

She plays with my engagement rings. "Ry did a great job. These are absolutely stunning. Why two? I thought the solitaire was the engagement ring and the band was for the wedding."

I pull my teeth over my bottom lip. "Well, tonight was his second proposal."

"You said no the first time?" Her voice raises an octave.

"No, *he* said yes the first time. I asked him to marry me. Just blurted it out like a crazy person. Come to find out, he had already bought me the ring and was going to propose. I beat him to it."

"Ahh, so tonight was him giving you a proper proposal."

"No, he already did that after he said yes."

Brea rolls over onto her back. "You guys are so weird."

I bop her nose with my finger. "Tonight was your brother making a grand romantic gesture," I sigh dreamily. "Ryder never stops amazing me. I love that man so much."

"He loves you back just as much, Lizzie. I hope one day I'll find someone that loves me that way."

Deciding now would be a perfect time for it, I roll off the bed intending to grab the present I made for Brea that I stashed in Ryder's room across the hall. "I want to give you one of your presents now."

"Breaking with Christmas tradition, are we?"

My family always opened our presents to each other on Christmas Eve and left Santa's presents for Christmas Day. The Cuttons wait to open everything on Christmas morning.

Brea takes the box from my hand and carefully opens it, lifting the top off and peeling back the red and green tissue paper. "Lizzie, this is just, wow. This is wonderful. Thank you." She one-arm hugs me and kisses my cheek. I scanned in all of Hailey's poems from the scrapbook I found in the boxes from my closet. The ones that triggered my memories to come back. I used software online to make a hardcover book of them for Brea.

"Merry Christmas, Brea."

She reads a few of the poems, turning the pages of the book reverently. "It's like she's here."

I want to tell her that Hailey will always be with us, but I decide to let her discover that on her own as she reads my sister's beautifully crafted words. *Merry Christmas, Hales. I love you.*

It's another hour before I leave Brea's room. Ryder poked his head in a little while ago to see what we were up to. After bidding Brea a good night, I head downstairs to find it dark and empty. The light from the Christmas tree is the only illumination in the room. As children, Hailey and I would lie underneath our tree and look up through the branches, telling each other what we wanted Santa to bring us. I touch one bristly branch, the scent of pine strong. I smile when my fingers trail across, then gently lift, a star-shaped ornament that has Ryder's name written sloppily in the penmanship of a child. I remember when we made these together in class in the third grade.

Lost in my thoughts, I don't hear Trevor until he steps up beside me. "Sorry." He chuckles when I startle.

"Where is everyone?"

"Meredith crashed hard and is passed out in the guest room. Ryder and his dad are out back at the firepit."

"And Fallon?"

Trevor takes one hand out of his pocket and rubs it back and forth across his neck. "We've been talking on the front porch."

I turn my head, arching my eyebrow, unable to hide the half-smirk that curves my mouth. “Talking?”

“Yeah. I opened ‘the door,’” Trevor finger quotes, using the phrase I said to him at the café.

“Did he walk through?”

Trevor barks out a quiet laugh. “Very reluctantly. But it’s a start.”

“Thank you, Trevor. I will consider it a Christmas miracle. He needs you. I think you need him too.”

“Elizabeth, there’s something I need to tell you.”

“Okay.”

“Not tonight, though.”

“Then why bring it up?”

“Because I seem to have a big fucking mouth and no filter.”

“Trevor—” My phone rings and vibrates in my back pocket. Taking it out, the screen shows that it’s Jayson. “Hold that thought,” I tell Trevor and swipe to answer.

“Jayson?” My ears are met with heavy breathing, then the sounds of something smashing in the background. "Jayson?" I repeat and hear another crashing sound like the shattering of glass. "Jayson! Can you hear me? What's going on?" Trevor frowns down at me and I turn my back to him.

"I remember the first time I saw you. Crooked tiara in your hair and that blue dress you wore, your hair braided in pigtails." When he speaks, his words are slurred and thick.

"Jayson, are you drunk?"

Another crash and a low groan. "Yes, I'm fucking drunk!" he shouts, and I almost drop the phone. "Why is my goddamn hand bleeding?" he says then starts laughing. Not a happy laugh, but one filled with a bit of mania.

"Jayson! Are you injured? What the hell is going on? Where are you?"

Heavy breaths punctuate his already garbled words making it difficult to understand. "Shit. I think I broke your window."

My window? "Are you in my house? Jayson, please tell me what's going on. Is Julien with you?"

"Waiting. Waiting. All I've done is wait. My whole life. It doesn't matter anymore. Fuck!"

I'm already grabbing my coat and heading out the door with Trevor hot on my heels. An ominous feeling deep inside of me spirals up. Something's terribly wrong. I break out into a run as soon as my feet hit the front porch.

"Kitten, what the hell?" I hear Fallon shout as I run down the walkway to the street. "Trevor, where's she going?"

"I don't know what's going on. Jayson called her."

"Get Ryder!" I yell back at them, not breaking my fast sprint down the street.

All the morning runs with Julien have paid off and I'm in front of my old childhood home in less than a minute. I've kept the phone connection with Jayson open, but other than mumbled words and crashing sounds, he hasn't said anything else to me. The Christmas lights on the oak tree are still lit and I look up to notice my bedroom window is smashed. A few jagged pieces of glass remain and reflect the colored lights from the tree. *Shit*! I don't have the keys to the house that Fallon gave me earlier. Without hesitation, I jump up and catch a low branch, allowing the memories of the hundreds of times Jayson, Julien, and I climbed this tree to guide me. Once I'm high enough, I step out onto the small ledge under my window and climb in carefully, avoiding the broken glass still attached to the frame and the broken pieces littered across the floor.

My bedroom is steeped in darkness, but the light from the tree outside is enough for me to see Jayson hunched on the floor. His knees are raised and his gaze is fixed on the blood that is dripping down his fisted hand. I rush over and kneel beside him, taking off my jacket and pressing it to his fist.

"Jayson, what happened? What are you doing in here?"

As if under a trance, Jayson looks dazedly at me, a wane smile touching his lips. He reaches out and slides the knuckles of his uninjured hand down the side of my face. "Liz?" His lips quiver, but before I can react, his silver eyes blacken with rage and his hand clasps the back of my neck, jerking my head forward. Pain radiates down from the base of my neck and I yelp.

"Jayson! Stop it! Let go!"

Standing up abruptly, taking me with him, he shoves me away with a sudden push and I fall backward on my ass. He sways a few times before steadying himself, using my jacket to wipe his bloody hand.

Fury like I've never felt before rushes through me, singeing every synapse in my body. This house is where my family was murdered, where I was stabbed and almost died. I will not allow anyone else to hurt me here. I rise up slowly from the floor with a strength I never knew I possessed.

Fallon shouts my name from below the window, cursing up a storm when I don't answer. I'm too busy staring Jayson down.

"I don't know what's going on and I don't care how drunk you are right now, but if you ever touch me like that again, I will break every finger in your hand," I snarl.

"You've already broken my heart!" he yells, pounding his injured fist on his chest.

I try not to allow the rage I feel right now overshadow my need to stay calm and figure out what's going on and what's causing Jayson to lash out like this.

"I know I broke your heart. I never meant to hurt you, Jayson. Please talk to me."

"You said yes! It's supposed to be me!" he howls. "You were mine! I loved you! My whole life, I have loved you! And you said yes to *him*!" he screams, getting in my face and yanking my hand up to show me my engagement ring.

Jayson must have seen Ryder propose tonight. When was he there?

The bedroom door starts shaking as Fallon pounds on it. "Elizabeth, unlock this goddamn door right now!"

"Fallon, I'm okay," I tell him when Jayson starts pacing in front of the bedroom door, stumbling a bit, his eyes never leaving me. I watch him warily, readying myself in case he tries to grab for me again. The man in front of me is not my Jayson. He's not the boy I grew up with. The boy I fell in love with.

"You loved me," he growls.

"I did love you."

"Your memories came back, and you were supposed to come back to me. You did come back to me. Then you left. You left me again. For Ryder. For Fallon."

"I left for myself," I counter. "I needed to heal. I needed to make a choice."

"Choice! Let's talk about fucking choices. You chose *me*, Liz! I am the one who climbed through your window that night. I was the first man to kiss you, to make love to you. You told me you loved me first. Me! Not Ryder! You took my promise ring. We talked about getting married and starting a family. My wife! My kids! Not Ryder's!" he chokes out, then madly swipes at the tears clinging to his face. Turning around, he punches the wall leaving a fist-sized hole behind. *Holy shit.*

Shouts from outside filter up through the broken window.

"She won't answer her phone!" Ryder shouts, clearly panicked.

I hear Fallon yell something and then the sound of feet pounding up the stairs.

As calmly as I can, I say, "Jayson, I'm sorry. I truly am. You're right about most of what you said. I did love you. I did have all my firsts with you, and I would never change any of it. I don't know what would have happened to us even if *that night* never happened, even if I never had amnesia. Jayson, things were already changing for me after our fight. I went to see Ryder after you kicked me out of your house. I made a decision that night. A choice. I chose him, Jayson. Just like I choose him now. And I'm not going to apologize for it anymore. Yes, I loved you. How could I not? You had been my everything since I was six years old. But you knew I loved Ryder too. You manipulated me that night when you came through my bedroom window. You knew Ryder was going to tell me that he loved me."

"I hate you," he spits, stopping his pacing in front of me, his eyes like swirling liquid mercury.

"No, you don't. You're hurt and you're angry."

"I would have given you everything. Everything. And you threw it away. You threw me away for him!"

Jayson's hand flies out and grabs me by the throat, pushing my back against the wall he just punched. Fallon did something similar at the resort in Iceland when he was trying to convince me of his darkness. I saw right through Fallon, just like I see through Jayson now. He's drunk and he's hurting and lashing out.

"I will always love you, Jayson. But my heart, my life, and my choice all belong to Ryder."

I told him I would break his hand if he touched me in anger again. I wrap my fingers around the wrist of the hand that's holding my throat and twist.

Jayson regrips and slams a bruising kiss on my mouth. "You chose wrong, princess. And I hate you for it. I hate you for choosing him."

A crash sounds behind me as the bedroom door flies open and Jayson is ripped away from me.

"Don't you fucking touch her again!" Julien

tosses Jayson across the room and faces down his twin brother. "What the fuck is wrong with you?"

"Did you know that she's marrying Ryder? They got engaged tonight?"

Julien flinches slightly at his brother's accusing glare. "I didn't know, but you and I both knew it was coming."

Ryder and Fallon rush over to stand in front of me, forming a wall to prevent Jayson from grabbing me again.

"Fuck you!" Jayson hurls the words at Julien, then bores his eyes into me. "You say you choose Ryder over me? Well, I hope you fucking choke on it, Liz. I'm not going to stand around and watch him live the life that was supposed to be mine. So fuck you both!" Jayson yells. He shoves past Julien and storms out.

Ryder turns around and enfolds me in his arms as I finally break into giant, racking, ugly sobs. I just lost my best friend, the boy who was my first love, the father of my child.

Fallon rubs up and down my back as Julien puts his arm around me and Ryder. "Liz, it's going to be alright. He'll regret every word he said to you."

"No, he won't," I cry, knowing that this is the

end of my and Jayson's story. There's no coming back from this for us.

Chapter 35

Christmas Day

Ryder

Merry Fucking Christmas morning, I think to myself, channeling my inner Fallon. What a godawful mess. What was supposed to be a happy time filled with family and friends is now just one big depressing fiasco. I brought Elizabeth back to the house and put her in my bed. I held her all night as she sobbed brokenly. Her jagged, mournful whimpers cut me deep, and I felt useless because I was helpless to comfort the woman I love. She cried so long, she literally passed out from exhaustion.

Meredith, Brea, and Jamie took over for me and have been watching over Elizabeth while she sleeps so I can explain to my distraught parents what happened. Fallon and Trevor are livid and want to find Jay and beat the shit out of him. Julien called a little while ago. Apparently, Jayson left this morning. Like packed a suitcase, hopped in his truck, and disappeared. Jayson told his parents he wasn't coming back for a while. He's not going back to CU. Freda is hysterical.

"You know I can track down that motherfucker," Fallon announces, throwing his phone down on the couch where Trevor is sitting.

"It's Elizabeth's choice on what to do, so let it go for now."

"Do you think he would have really hurt her?" Trevor asks. We all look at each other. Coming into the room and seeing Jayson put Elizabeth in a chokehold—my fists curl into tight balls just thinking about that. I will forever be grateful to Julien for stepping in and protecting her.

"God, Trevor. Before last night, I would have sworn on my life that Jay would never do something like that to her. But, fuck..." I stop, looking down at the floor, not able to finish.

"He's not getting within ten feet of her ever again," Fallon spouts at his brother.

"I want to agree with you, Fal, I do. But it's not our decision. If he comes back and she wants to see him, that's her call. But she won't be alone with him in the room if I have anything to say about it."

"Damn straight, she won't."

The front doorbell rings and I go to open it. I'm expecting Julien and Elijah. He said that they were going to stop by and check on Elizabeth.

As soon as I open the door, I let out a string of curses. Can this day get any worse? It's not even noon yet.

"What the fuck do you want? You're not even supposed to be here," I tell my unwanted visitor. Venom and loathing coats every word out of my mouth.

Maria takes a step back, her shoulders hunched over. "Please, I'd like to speak with Lizzie. I heard you both were in town and there's something I need to talk to her about."

"Hell no, Maria. You have been nothing but a complete bitch to Elizabeth. You're also in violation of your restraining order, so if you don't leave right now, I'm calling the police. Actually, Fallon is inside. Perhaps I should let him deal with you."

Maria's brown eyes whip up to mine, pleading. "Please, Ryder. I'm not here to cause any trouble. I swear. I just need to speak with Lizzie. *Please*. It's important."

I stare hard at the girl I used to date. The girl who used to be Elizabeth's best friend. The best friend who betrayed her. The girl who posted those indecent and very fake pictures of Elizabeth online. "No."

"Ryder, please. I'm only in town for today visiting my parents before I have to go back to Charlotte."

"I said no, Maria."

A hand touches my back and Elizabeth comes around my side. I wrap a protective arm around her. Her eyes are swollen and red-rimmed, the purple bags below them weighing heavy against her pale skin.

"Maria," Elizabeth greets her monosyllabically.

"Are you sick? You look awful."

Elizabeth scoffs and stares numbly back at her once best friend.

"I think it's time for you to go now," I tell Maria, backing up with Elizabeth, preparing to shut the door in Maria's face.

"No! Wait! I need to speak with you, Lizzie. Please," she pleads once again.

I can see Elizabeth is pondering the request

by the way she chews on the inside of her cheek. She exhales loudly. “Fine. Come in.”

Maria follows us nervously into the living room.

“Oh hell no. Get the fuck out.” Fallon rushes forward as Trevor stands up from the couch. Fallon is stopped in his tracks when Elizabeth plants herself in front of him.

My mom runs around the corner from the back hallway. “What is going on now?” She stops when she sees Maria and looks at me. Maria looks like she’s about to change her mind and bolt out of the house since she’s clearly outnumbered and surrounded by hateful glares.

“Maria said she needs to talk to me,” Elizabeth replies. She turns to Maria and bluntly states, “You have five minutes.”

Maria reaches a shaking hand to the back of a chair to steady herself. “I’m sorry.”

“I’ll bet you are, you freaking psycho,” Meredith says from the entryway.

“Let me finish,” Maria snaps then backs down immediately when she sees the fire raging in Meredith’s eyes. Brea, Jamie, and Jack walk down the stairs and stop when they see Maria. The room is now filled with family and friends. We stand united with Elizabeth in front of Maria.

Maria swallows thickly, scanning the faces of each person. Going back to Elizabeth, she swallows again and clears her throat. "I guess I'll get right to the point."

"That would be best," Elizabeth tells her.

"Lizzie, I'm sorry for what I did. But I shouldn't have to go to jail because of it."

"Maria, you picked the wrong day to come plead your case. I'm tired and not in the mood."

"We used to be friends. Please help me. I can't go to jail. My life will be ruined. Your lawyer won't even discuss a plea deal with mine. I could get a hundred twenty days in jail, Lizzie. I swear to you in front of these people that I will never come near you again. You will never hear from me, ever. I'm *begging* you. *Please*, Lizzie."

Elizabeth holds up her phone. "Just so you know, I'm recording every bit of this conversation. You've broken your restraining order, and your attempt to get me to drop the charges against you is illegal. Before I send this to my lawyer, do you have anything else you want to say to me?"

"Damn, kitten. I love it when your claws come out." Fallon grins at Elizabeth and her lips twitch in response.

Elizabeth stares at a silent Maria for a quick beat, then turns around to go back upstairs when Maria doesn't say anything.

"Marshall! It was Marshall," Maria frantically blurts out and drops down into the chair, her hands over her face. "Marshall and I have been dating since senior year. Since the prom. After I saw you at the party, I was so angry." She looks at me now. "All I ever wanted was for you to notice me. For you to want me like you wanted Lizzie. It wasn't fair. So yeah, I posted the pictures."

"What does Marshall have to do with it?" I ask her.

"He lost it after Lizzie beat him at the Fields. She humiliated him again in front of everyone and he couldn't take it. He was the one that messed up her car. He was the one who pushed her in front of the car. But I had nothing to do that. I wasn't even there! I was in Charlotte! I never knew he would take it that far. When he told me the next day, I broke up with him."

Everyone in the room starts shouting, but it's Fallon's declaration that has us all abruptly shutting up.

"I'm going to kill that fucker!" Fallon shouts, and Trevor has to restrain him from lunging at Maria who jumps out of the chair and shrinks back in terror at his aggressive move.

"Maria, he pushed her in front of a moving car. She could have died!" I yell at her.

"I know! I know! I'm sorry. I didn't think Marshall would do anything like that! I'll agree to testify against him if I can get a plea deal. Whatever you need me to do. Please Lizzie! I can't go to jail even for a day!"

"You are still such a conniving bitch." Elizabeth turns on her. "You're as guilty as he is. The only difference is that you're willing to throw Marshall under the bus to save your own pathetic ass. How could you be so cruel? You knew what happened to Hailey, to my mom and dad, to me! They loved you and were good to you. I lost my family, Maria! I almost died! I was in a coma for months and had no memory of my life when I came out of it. None of that mattered to you. All you cared about was your own jealous spite. What the hell is wrong with you?"

Maria lowers her head and shakes it from side to side. "My life will be ruined," is all she whispers, still not acknowledging the facts Elizabeth placed before her. Was Maria ever her friend? Did she care at all about Elizabeth? Does she even have a conscience? A soul?

"Your life is already ruined, and you have no

one to blame but yourself," Elizabeth retorts.

My dad moves from where he's been silently watching from the kitchen. Unable to listen anymore, he yanks Maria up from the chair. "You're not welcome in my home. Get the hell out."

"I'll call Mr. Worthington and tell him to make the deal. Your full confession and testimony against Marshall and I'll agree to drop the charges *if* Marshall is officially charged."

Several shocked eyes raise up in confusion in the room. "Baby, don't let her get away with it. She deserves everything that's coming her way."

"It's Marshall we need to make sure gets taken down. Look at everything he's done to our family. He hurt Julien, he started the fight at Fallon's party that could have ruined your lives, he tried to run you off the track when you guys raced. He was the one who destroyed my car. He was the one who pushed me into the street. Marshall should spend the rest of his life behind bars. Her?" She points at Maria. "Yes, what she did was despicable, but if she can help us bring down Marshall, then I'm willing to pay the price by giving her leniency."

Elizabeth goes to Fallon's side. "Besides, she knows what he'll do if she ever does anything to us again," she says, looking up at Fallon. He gives her a slight nod of the head and wraps his arm around her waist, pulling her to his side.

"Fallon, call Mr. Worthington and have him make the deal. And you—" She looks at Maria. "You know I have a recording of everything you just said. I have a room full of witnesses. After all this is done, I never want to see you or hear from you again."

Maria backs up until she's a foot from the front door. "Thank you, Lizzie."

"Don't you dare thank me. Do the right thing for once in your life. We're done here," Elizabeth tells her and walks back upstairs with the other girls and Jack right behind her.

I meet Maria at the door.

"Ryder, I'm sorry."

My gaze snaps to hers. "No, you're not. I will never believe a word out of your mouth. Get this in your head: I never loved you. I never could love you. I pity you. Oh, and one last thing. You were right. You never could measure up to Elizabeth. Now, stay away from my *fiancé*." I emphasize the word, knowing it'll get a reaction.

Fallon must be rubbing off on me because I get great joy in watching Maria's face crumble as I slam the door shut on her and lock the deadbolt loudly into place.

Chapter 36

Elizabeth

I feel the bed dip and my body pulled backward as Ryder molds his chest against my back, one of his legs going between mine, and one of his hands wrapping around to splay a possessive hand flat on my stomach. I twist my head to capture his kiss, rolling over to snuggle deeper into his warmth. I love how it feels when our naked skin touches. I'm not in the mood for words or gentle platitudes. I don't want anyone else to ask me how I am feeling or if I am okay. I want to lose myself in Ryder, and let his touch heal my wounded heart.

"What do you need, sweetheart," he murmurs against my lips, his other hand roaming up and down my arm and back in a manner that is as seductive as it is soothing.

"Just you, Ryder. I just need you."

"You've got me, baby," he promises, and I give

myself over to him. Completely.

Ryder worships me with his touch while placing open-mouthed kisses along every inch of my sensitized skin. He blazes a path down my quivering stomach, devastating me in a delicious way until he reaches my mons, dragging a finger through my folds to my bud that is throbbing and needy for him. He holds down my hips, anchoring me in place as my torso tries to arch off the bed, my breathy moan a testament to the pleasure he's giving me. No sooner do I begin to tumble down from the high of my first orgasm, Ryder amps me back up again, spreading me wide and licking me until I'm falling once more.

Boneless, quaking, and thoroughly replete, I urge Ryder back up so I can kiss his full lips that are slick with my arousal. He settles on top of me just the way that I love. His heavy weight pressing down on me is exactly the thing I need right now. We spend what seems like forever like that, more than content to relish in our leisurely exchange of kisses. Something so simple, yet it is everything.

I wrap my arms around Ryder's neck, inhaling the heated muskiness of his skin, and I'm instantly calmed. I give a small shove to his shoulder and he rolls with me so that I am now on top. I rub myself back and forth over his rigid length, my hands positioned flat on his chest. I ease myself down, taking him inside of me, and squeezing my internal muscles until he grunts. My smile is wide, and I do it again. Those gorgeous brown eyes hood with desire and he sits up to take one of my nipples in his mouth, steeping me in sensation. I moan again, low and long.

We take our time. There is no rush to the finish for us tonight. Ryder makes love to me, cherishing me like only he can. My friend, my lover, my forever. I climax for a third time, the sweetness of the rolling waves that consume me make me feel weightless and floaty. As I'm free-falling back down from the high of endorphins, Ryder thickens and pulses inside of me. I seal our mouths and drink in his release, capturing the sound and vibrations with my tongue.

Still seated securely inside of me, he holds me close to his chest and finger-combs my long hair. I feel the stickiness of his release and make a contented sigh. Ryder has always taken me bare. The likelihood of me getting pregnant is low while on birth control, but every time we make love, I always wonder whether our love has created life inside of me. I burrow closer into him and run my index finger in small circles on the top of his shoulder.

"How many children do we want to have?"

Ryder considers my question thoughtfully. "In my dreams, I've always seen us with a big family."

"You've dreamed about our children?"

He pecks the tip of my nose. "Well, yeah. I've been dreaming about our future together since I was nine years old. What about you, babe? How many kids do you want?"

I scrape my fingernails feather-light up and down the side of his face, feeling his day's-worth of stubble, liking how it tickles my fingertips. "Three or more. I would like nothing more than a bunch of cute little mini-Ryders pitter-pattering about."

"You want all boys? God help us." He chuckles, the rumble of it jostling me around on his chest and sending me into a fit of giggles.

Catching my breath, I say, "Just think, we could have our own little racing crew."

"That's actually not a bad idea."

"Boys or girls. It doesn't matter to me as long as they're all half you and half me."

"We're going to have such a good life, baby."

"I'll be married to you. It's going to be a fabulous life. Did you want to try to start a family soon or wait?"

Ryder takes his time in answering. "I want you to have your dreams, Elizabeth."

"Our dreams," I argue.

"Our dreams," he concedes. "If you want to finish college and medical school first before starting a family, that's fine with me. If you want me to knock you up tomorrow, I'm down with that too." His grin is downright lascivious. I punch his chest and kiss him silly.

"The only thing I really want is you, Ryder. Everything else is just the whipped cream with a cherry on top."

"Ditto."

We lie in our intimate bubble stroking one another. I may have dozed off for a minute if I'm being honest.

"Do you think he'll come back?" I ponder aloud.

"I don't know, sweetheart. For you, I hope he does. If he doesn't, I would think he would definitely come back for Julien and Elijah's wedding."

Freda and Mitch came over with Julien and Elijah this afternoon. We all sat down and had a long talk. Jayson called his parents earlier today and spoke with them. He told them that he wasn't going to come back home anytime soon. He doesn't know where he'll end up and he said that he was going to let the road take him wherever it leads; he needed time to figure out what to do with his life; one without me in it. Freda and I cried together for a long time. I was sure that she and Mitch would blame me, even hate me, but they don't. They're heartbroken over how things ended; not only because their boy is gone, but also because they always expected me and Jayson to eventually marry. They ended the conversation by telling Ryder and me they loved us and congratulated us on our engagement.

Before leaving, Julien gave me a letter from Jayson, one he apparently wrote before he left. I've been too scared to open and read it.

My thoughts are interrupted by a light knocking on Ryder's bedroom door. It's past one in the morning, so my first thought is that it's Fallon.

Ryder slips on a pair of boxers and pads over to crack the door open. "Hey, man. What's going on?"

I hear Trevor ask if I'm awake and decent. I slip out of bed and throw on the clothes I left hanging over the bathroom doorknob. Then I join Ryder.

"Hey Trevor. I'm up."

"Fallon needs you guys."

I step out into the hallway. "Is something wrong with Fallon?"

Trevor's breath catches a few times. "His father… my father… Fallon just got a call. Both his parents were killed tonight. Their Cessna crashed in Maryland soon after take-off. That's all I know right now."

"Take us to him."

I don't know what to expect when we find Fallon. His relationship with both his parents —if you could call them that—was basically non-existent, and what was there was filled with years of abuse and hatred.

We follow Trevor outside to the back patio where Fallon is sitting on the steps in the dark. I go over and drop down beside him. He looks over at me like a little boy who is lost in a world that has been turned upside down and doesn't make sense.

"They're gone, kitten. Should I feel bad that all I feel is relief about that?"

I gather him in my arms, and he rests his head on my chest. "You have a right to feel whatever you are feeling, especially about them."

Ryder and Trevor join us on the steps. Trevor places his hand on Fallon's knee. "I've got you little brother. I've got you."

Chapter 37

Elizabeth

We're at the Montgomery mansion in Highland helping to box things up and doing what we can to make things easier for Fallon. Ryder and I postponed our New Year's trip so we could be here for him. Trevor has really stepped up in the big brother role, and—along with Mr. Worthington and a slew of other lawyers and business partners—has been helping Fallon navigate what needs to be done. The long list includes funeral arrangements, maneuvering Fallon to step in as interim-CEO of Montgomery Pharma, and dealing with the hoard of press and paparazzi that have descended around Fallon like vultures eager to pick the scraps off of bones. He's holding on by a bare thread as more and more responsibilities get heaped at his feet. I know it's only a matter of time before he either explodes or implodes. And I refuse to allow Fallon to slide back into that dark place. He saved me and brought me back from the brink. I hope I get to return the favor for him.

"Babe?" Ryder calls me from somewhere within the expansive mansion.

"In the kitchen!" I answer, adding more turkey slices to the hoagies I'm making for everyone.

The last time I was in this kitchen was at Fallon's party in high school. Not the memory lane I want to skip down at the moment. That party was all sorts of fucked-up—from the big fight with Marshall and his football goons, to Jayson getting slipped a roofie in his beer and me finding him half-naked in bed with Jacinda later that night, to Ryder coming through my window in the middle of the night, then lastly to visiting Jayson in the hospital the next morning.

"I always forget just how big this place is." Ryder walks in and comes over to give me a kiss before swiping a piece of turkey and eating it.

"Hey!" I smack his hand away, then I add some lettuce and fold the two halves of the hoagie roll together and hand him the completed sandwich.

"Thanks, babe. I was starving," he mumbles with his mouth full.

"Fallon sent the staff home for the next couple of weeks, which means no chef-prepared meals. I've made him a few things he can just zap in the microwave or eat cold." I open the kitchen's huge luxury refrigerator and show him the stacks of Tupperware I prepared. "So, what have you guys been up to?"

"I've been in the study with Fal looking over some business papers with him."

"See? All those business classes you're taking are paying off already. Maybe Fallon will offer you a job." I grin at him.

"Hell no. I like working on cars, not wearing a suit."

"But you look sexy in a suit," I reply dreamily, an image of him in his prom attire popping to mind. God, he looked so good that night. I snack on a dill pickle spear while daydreaming and Ryder's heated gaze watches me.

I pop the pickle out and wag it at him. "What is it with guys fixating on women eating phallic-shaped foods like pickles, bananas, or popsicles?"

"It's food porn, babe. No guy can watch and not imagine his woman's lips wrapped around him like that."

"Makes sense, I guess," I reply with a shrug, then lick the juices off the side of the pickle before biting into it just to rile him up. I'm rewarded for my efforts when he has to adjust himself. "I promise to take care of that later," I tell him, my eyes zeroed in on his crotch.

"Babe."

I look up. "What?"

Ryder throws his trash away and leans over the granite counter island. "Trevor left a little while ago to take care of a few personal things. You know, I don't think he's acknowledged to himself that it's his dad who's gone too."

"He really didn't know Phillip that well. I know he said they talked and all, but that man was a shit father. I'm glad that Fallon is letting Trevor help. They're going to need each other."

"Fallon also needs food. He hasn't eaten since you forced that bagel on him this morning."

"Point me the way to the study and I'll take Fallon his lunch."

"Across the foyer, down the hall, third door to the left."

"Got it. I'll be right back." I pick up the plate I made for Fallon, snatch a bottle of water from the fridge, and give Ryder a pickle-infused kiss that has him emitting a deep belly laugh.

As I walk down the long hallway, I slow to look at the various portraits and paintings hanging on the walls. If I didn't know any better, I would swear two of the paintings are authentic Monet's, which means they probably are. On a side table against the wall sit a few framed photographs. One of them is a family photo that I stop to look more closely at. Fallon was adorable when he was a little boy with his scraggly blond hair and crooked smile. A smile that was hiding the punches and bruises from his father. The older boy with the blank, dead eyes must be Peter, the older brother Fallon told me about. Chills race down my spine at the sight of him, so I quickly look at the two adults in the photograph. Fallon's parents.

I'm not a vengeful person and I consider myself to have strong morals, but I'm not sorry that they're dead. The abuse Fallon endured by their hands for years, the things his mother did to Peter, the scars his father left on Fallon… I'm glad Fallon is free of them. I honestly don't know what kind of person that makes me, but after everything I've been through—seeing my parents' blood pooling around them and their dead eyes staring at me while I was forced to watch *Him* stab and rape my sister—it changed me. I would never think myself capable of taking another life, but I would gladly take *His*.

Some monsters should never be allowed to exist on this earth.

Wait.

The violent thud of my heart slamming against my breastbone has me picking up the framed photograph for a closer look. My eyes narrow and focus like the aperture of a camera lens. White noise fills my ears until I hear only the sound of Hailey's whimpers, and the gurgling of choked blood as it pools in my mouth as *He* removes the knife from my side. The butterfly tattoos on my upper torso that cover my knife wounds erupt into a painful fire like acid burning through flesh. Heterochromatic eyes, the brown and blue from my nightmares, look back at me from the picture.

Fuck, fuck, fuck! Ohmygod! No!

"I knew I was on borrowed time before you'd eventually find out."

I jump so violently at the sound of Fallon's voice that I drop both the plate of food and the picture frame. They fall in slow motion and smash to the floor, the sound they create traveling through me like the boom of cannon fire.

Fight or flight. Adrenaline and red-hot rage infuse my blood. *Fight or flight.* I turn to face my new nightmare, every muscle in my body vibrating. *Fight or flight.*

I choose to fight.

"You lied to me!"

Fallon stands five feet from me, hands in his pockets, those ice blue eyes never wavering from my accusatory green ones.

"I wasn't lying when I said *He* would never hurt you again," he says, but all I want to do is smack him.

"You knew all this time and you lied to me!"

"I did what I had to do to protect you," he says softly, those blue eyes looking down at the floor then back up at me again; however, this time, when he looks at me, he tries to smother the fear in his eyes with a stony expression. I watch as those sly-blue eyes darken into fathomless voids of nothingness. No emotion, no feeling behind them—just vacant and empty. But, like him, it's all a lie.

The fine hairs along my skin raise and I take a step forward. Ryder comes running down the hallway, calling my name, and I turn to spear him with a look that tells him to stay back.

"Please," I beg him, holding my palm up to tell him to stop, which he does, concern apparent on his gorgeous face. He flicks his worried gaze from me to Fallon, but, thankfully, he keeps his distance. I snap my head back around to Fallon and take another step closer to the liar in front of me, wishing so badly that I could beat the rest of his excuses out of him.

"Bullshit! You did what you had to do to protect your brother."

"That's what you think? After what he did to me, to you, to your family? You think I would protect that evil son of a bitch? You are so naïve, kitten. You have no fucking clue! You never did!"

"You're a heartless bastard, Fallon! Everything out of your mouth is a lie!"

Fallon rushes forward the remaining three feet, Ryder cursing him as he approaches me, but I stand my ground. I will not run away or flinch. I'm facing the truth of my nightmare.

"You forget, kitten. I warned you that I was one of the villains in your story. I fucking warned you that I would destroy you. I told you that you would hate me."

"Tell me everything," I demand. "I deserve to know the truth."

"Tell her," Trevor says from behind me. He must have just come back. His sudden presence has my head spinning. How does Trevor know? "We should have told her a long time ago. She deserves to know."

I feel like my body is on a swivel as I turn around again. "You knew? You've been lying to me too?"

So many things become clear. Trevor's sudden appearance at the beach the day we first met. How, even though he's a senior, he wound up in my English Lit class for freshman and sophomore years. How he's always been overly protective of me. All the times he told me he needed to tell me something important.

"Fallon, tell her, or I will."

"Fuck you!" Fallon rails at him, grabbing the sides of his own head.

"Was it Peter?" I shout back at him, needing to know for sure. Needing the truth. "Tell me, Fallon! Was it Peter that night?"

Fallon stumbles over and slams his back into the wall as if it's the only thing that can hold him upright. His desolate pale cerulean eyes hold me prisoner as he nods yes.

My bottom lip trembles. Peter killed my parents. He killed Hailey and caused Elizabeth Ann's death. He stabbed me and left me on the floor to die. The weight of finally knowing who was responsible for that night eases its relentless grip on my soul and I take a deep breath.

Knowledge is power, Fallon used to say. I missed the clues, the signs. I should have started to put the pieces together when Fallon told me about Peter. About the night his brother came into his room with a knife. *The goddamn knife*. How Peter straddled him and stabbed him. How Fallon spent weeks in the hospital recovering. All the times Fallon promised with *absolute* certainty that the man from that night would never hurt me again. The clues were there, right in front of my face, but I never saw them. *Don't you see, Elizabeth? Open your eyes and see.*

I feel Ryder edge carefully up against my back. Automatically, without thinking, I lean against him, reaching back with one hand until I feel his hand grip mine. *Breathe, Elizabeth. You aren't alone. The monster is dead.*

A new question creeps in. "Ryder, did you know?" I twist my head around so I can see his eyes.

"No," he softly answers me. *Thank fucking God*. I sink back into him, needing him to help hold me steady.

"Peter was obsessed with you," Fallon begins, and his words cause bile to boil up into my esophagus.

"Like you?" I snarl accusatorily at him.

A flittering of pain briefly replaces the emptiness in his eyes until he shuts it down. "It was my fault. I was the reason he noticed you. Because I was interested in you... wanted you." He scoffs. "But you're right, kitten. I was obsessed with you too. Perhaps I'm no better than my brother after all. Perhaps my fascination with you is what led him to you like a lamb to slaughter."

"What are you saying, Fallon? Was Peter stalking me? Did you stand by and watch and do nothing?"

"Peter could never get close to you. You were always surrounded by Jay, Ry, and Julien. I tried to protect you from him on my end as best I could."

"You did a fucking piss-poor job of protecting me then," I hurl at him, motioning to where the scars are on my side.

"At some point, when Peter failed to get near you, that's when he set his sights on your sister."

I'm sifting through every thought, every word, every moment of my life, thankful for once that I have my memories back. As I do, I realize that Fallon has always been in the background protecting me. He also protected the boys I love. He made sure that the video of the fight with Marshall never saw the light of day so Jayson, Ryder, and Julien wouldn't get into trouble. He got Marshall kicked off the Highland High soccer team after he intentionally injured Julien during a game. He made sure Jacinda left me alone in high school after her stunt with Jayson at the party. He has always stood by Ryder and has been there for him when I couldn't. He threw himself in front of me to protect me after I punched Marshall for running Ryder off the track during a race at the Fields. Fallon took me in and helped me heal when my mind was shattered with returning memories that I didn't know how to handle. He flew Ryder to Barcelona, bringing the man I love back to me. He bought my parents' house to fulfill my dream. Fallon has been protecting me in his own way for years. And I never saw it.

Open your eyes and see.

"When Peter got his claws into Hailey, I was horrified, but also relieved. He filled his obsession on you with her, and I figured that, as long as she occupied his attention, you'd be safe. I was wrong."

"Peter was the older guy that Hailey was secretly seeing?" I need confirmation. I need to hear him say it.

"Yes."

"You let your psycho brother touch my sister

and didn't do anything about it?"

Fallon doesn't answer me. My body again tries to propel forward as my anger churns higher and higher. Ryder holds on to me, not allowing me to leave his side.

"Did you know he was abusing her? All the bruises and burn marks on her body were from him? Answer me, Fallon! Did you know?" I scream.

"No! No, but I knew what he was capable of, so I should have realized what he could do to her."

I tilt my head back into Ryder's chest and howl at the ceiling, my whole body releasing the turbulent energy of my internal anguish.

"You allowed that monster to hurt my sister. Where is Peter, Fallon? So help me God, if you are hiding him or shielding him, I will kill you myself. Where is he?"

As if being hit over the head with a club, Fallon slides down the wall to fall heavily on the floor, his hands clenched on both sides of his head, his knees raised, and his body folding into itself in an upright fetal position. "He's dead! Peter can't hurt you anymore! He's dead, Elizabeth. I killed him!"

I turn around and collapse into Ryder, racking sobs convulsing from my chest. *He's dead. The monster is dead. Fallon killed him. Fallon killed his own brother. For me.* The silence that pervades the hallway is thick, the only sounds penetrating through the stillness are my hiccupping cries and Fallon's ragged breathing. Ryder murmurs something in my ear, but I can't hear him because Fallon's hushed explanation holds me hostage.

"I was here that morning. Patricia and my father were in Europe. I was here when Peter came in, soaked in blood, still holding the knife. His car was still here so he must have run the entire distance from your house to here. Jesus Christ, there was so much blood. He was covered in it. The smell of it. I'll never forget the smell. For a second, I thought he was going to kill me, like he tried to before. He told me what he did. He cried, Elizabeth. He fucking cried. He said he killed our light; he destroyed our sunshine. I didn't know what the hell he was talking about. And then he told me everything. He told me what he had done. He begged for forgiveness. He pleaded with me to help him. To save him."

Fallon presses his hands together as if in prayer. "He dropped the knife. The one he just confessed that he used to kill your family. The one he used on you. I stared at it on the floor as Peter rambled out every horrific fucking detail of what he did. He kept repeating over and over that you wouldn't see him. That he asked you to see him. To notice him. He said he didn't mean to hurt you, but you kept fighting him. He said Hailey had to die because she wasn't you. He only wanted you. He had to have you. He would never give you up. I don't remember how I came to hold the knife in my hand. I never remember picking it up off the floor. All I remember is the distorted smile on his face when he impaled himself with it, and him thanking me." Fallon shudders and wails out, "He thanked me for it! I was holding the knife that killed my brother and he thanked me for it. What kind of monster am I?"

Peter used Fallon to kill himself? How many times is Fallon going to have to shoulder the weight of his family's crimes?

Trevor walks around me and Ryder and goes to Fallon, easing himself down to the floor in front of his sibling. He cups his hand around the back of Fallon's neck and looks at me. "Fallon called me. I had only recently learned that we were brothers. That my father was his father. My mom was gone, and I had no one. He asked for my help and I didn't hesitate. I came right over. Fallon was holding Peter in his arms. The look on Fallon's face when I walked in." Trevor swallows thickly, shaking his head.

"Fallon told me what Peter did. What happened after." Trevor implores me with his blue gaze, so much like Fallon's, wanting me to see the truth of that night. "I couldn't allow Fallon to be arrested for something that wasn't his fault. Peter used Fallon as a means to an end. It was my decision to hide the body. I bundled Peter in one of the rugs from the great room. I carried his body out back to the lake on the property. I helped cover up his death. I got Fallon to erase the security camera footage. We were lucky in the fact that the staff had been given time off while Patricia and Phillip were out of town, so nobody was here at the house."

"So you see, Elizabeth, it's not just Fallon and Peter that have blood on our hands. And I'm sorry. So very sorry for my part in all of this and everything you've gone through because of it. I didn't know who you were at that time. My mom was gone, and I had a brother who asked for my help, so I did. I couldn't lose anyone else."

More than a year has passed. Why has no one asked questions? Isn't anyone curious as to the sudden disappearance of Peter? Then I remember what Fallon told me in Barcelona. Peter was lost a long time ago. He would disappear for extended periods of time, months or longer, while on drug-induced benders. His mental illness made him unpredictable and unstable. Peter was a sociopath. He was constantly in and out of rehab. His family had everyone thinking Peter was just one of the hired help. The only person who would have noticed his absence would be the mother who abused him his entire life, and I doubt very highly that she would have reported him missing. What a fucked-up family. How did Fallon survive this place?

I'm able to find my voice, but it's gruff and raw from crying. "I don't understand something, Trevor. If you helped Fallon and held onto this secret with him, then why have you and Fallon always been at each other's throats? Why act like you hate each other? Why didn't Fallon want you anywhere near me?"

Trevor helps Fallon stand up. He braces an arm around his waist in support until Fallon is able to steady himself. Fallon rolls his shoulders back and stares at me unapologetically. "I didn't trust Trevor not to tell you. I also didn't want any of the evil from that night to ever touch you again. All I ever wanted to do was to protect you from the darkness. Keep it away from you. But in the end, I failed you in every way."

I walk over to Fallon and face the man who slayed my nightmare. I didn't know what I would say until the words tumble out of my mouth. "Thank you."

Fallon didn't kill Peter; he only held the knife that Peter used to kill himself. What happened with Peter was not Fallon's fault.

"Thank you, Fallon," I tell him again. His face morphs from expressionless to utter shock and disbelief. I'm pretty sure that Ryder and Trevor have similar expressions on their faces.

"What?"

"Thank you, Fallon."

"Elizabeth, no."

I smack his face. Hard. Once. Twice. Three times. He stands there and takes it. Tears leak from his eyes and a violent red blooms on his cheek where I hit him. I may be grateful that Peter is dead, but Fallon knew what his brother was capable of and he didn't protect Hailey. *Neither did I.* I saw her bruises. I saw the marks on her body. I didn't fight hard enough for her. I never pushed her to explain. Hailey was always there for me, and when she needed me the most, I was nowhere to be found. Fallon failed my sister. He failed my family. But so did I.

There must be something terribly wrong with me for me to be feeling the way I am right now. I should feel upset, anger, maybe even horror or revulsion. I do and I don't. I'm livid and heartbroken about what happened to my sister and to my parents because of a psychotic madman's obsession. However, I also feel a sense of peace. Calm. The monster who took everything from me, including my memories and my unborn child, is dead.

"I can't deal with you right now," I tell Fallon, turning away.

I need time to process this. I need to get out of here. I can't be in here any longer.

Fallon's hand reaches out to me, and it about tears me apart when I hear his broken plea. "Kitten... *Elizabeth*, please. I'm sorry. Please forgive me."

To deal with all of the emotions that are overwhelming me, I actually laugh; the sound of it strange to my ears. "Fallon, what happened to Peter is not your fault. He killed himself. I'm glad he's dead."

Trevor tries to say something, but I hold my hands out in front of me like a shield.

"Please, stop. Whatever it is you want to say will have to wait. I need time to think things through. The only thing I can tell you right now is that you and Fallon shouldn't have to suffer any more for Peter's transgressions. To be honest, none of us should. He's dead and

I can finally breathe easy again knowing that. Let him stay buried," I tell them.

Buried and gone, no longer able to hurt anyone anymore. "Ryder, please take me home now."

Chapter 38

Elizabeth

"Thank you for bringing me here."

It's past midnight, so officially it's New Year's Eve. Ryder and I should be at Wintergreen, dreaming about running up and down the slopes, making love in front of the fireplace, having snowball fights, planning our wedding, and watching the New Year's Eve fireworks from the porch of our rental cabin that night.

"If I said this Christmas and New Year's sucked, would you be upset?" Ryder's response is to hold me tighter as we lean on the hood of his car.

After leaving Fallon's, we went back to the apartment. My mind was too restless, however, so I asked Ryder to bring me to the hill overlooking the college town. Ryder had told me that this was his quiet place. A place of solitude and peace that he would come to just to think and be alone. It's the place he brought me after our first date, and we danced together under the moonlight. It is also the place he brought me after we proposed to each other. That was the night we held each other as the snow fell all around us. Tonight, however, the sky is so crystal clear that it seems like you can see every star in the Milky Way, regardless of the city lights below.

"Momma? Dad? Hailey?" I speak up to the stars, "I hope you can hear me. I need you to tell me what to do. I'm so lost right now. What do I do? The man that took you from me is dead." I blow out a frustrated breath and watch as it forms frosty clouds in front of my face. I'm cold inside, but it's not because of the freezing temperatures of the night surrounding us.

"Babe, they hear you. They're here with us," Ryder says, resting his face beside mine while rubbing his hands soothingly up and down my coat-wrapped arms.

"Ryder, what should I do?"

Peter is dead. The man who killed my family is dead. Shouldn't I feel ashamed that I'm not upset about that? A good person wouldn't wish for the death of another person, let alone be relieved by it. What kind of person does that make me to not feel remorse for the fact that Peter is dead? I blink a few times to clear away the tears that gather and cling to my lashes.

"I can't tell you what to do, sweetheart. I can be here for you. Stand by you. Support you. But ultimately, whatever decision you make, whatever choice you make, should be yours and yours alone. What does your heart say? What is it telling you?"

My heart feels both broken and lighter. My heart is grieving for what Hailey endured at the hands of Peter. It suffers for Fallon because he has to live with the fact that his brother used him to take his own life. My heart breaks for Trevor because he was caught in the middle of this whole awful mess while trying to protect the brother he had only just found. But my heart also feels lighter knowing that the monster is forever and truly gone. It feels freer knowing that some form of justice has been served.

My heart is also conflicted. Will I be able to live with myself knowing what really happened? How the man who saved me sacrificed a part of his own soul to protect me from his brother? And what about Ryder? Will he be able to live with the secret, or will it be something that slowly festers and gnaws away at him, taking bits and pieces of him away little by little?

I reach my arm back and cradle Ryder's head with my hand, tilting my face to the side and back so I can see his beautiful copper eyes. "I would never forgive myself if I made a decision that you accepted out of your love for me, but ultimately could not live with."

I watch closely as Ryder digests my words. He slowly loops me around so that I'm sitting on the hood of the car and he is on his knees in front of me. He lays his hands on the tops of my thighs and I reach down to smooth my hands across his forehead until my fingertips spear into his thick, soft hair. We stare at each other for a very long time.

"If you want to know how I truly feel about it..." He draws in a slow, hard inhalation. "All I can tell you is—I will never forget finding you on the floor of your kitchen, blood soaked through every part of your clothes, hair, and skin. Your lungs struggling to gasp for breath, your beautiful sage green eyes losing their light. I watched the love of my life dying right before me as I held her in my arms. I felt like I was dying too. I wanted to die with you. I wanted you to take me with you. So if it makes me a cold-hearted bastard for being glad that Peter is gone, then so be it. I will happily live with that for the rest of my life as long as I get to have you—alive and happy and healthy."

But will Fallon be able to live with it? I wonder.

"And yours. I will always be yours, Ryder."

Ryder sits back on the hood and I settle in his lap.

"I think everyone has suffered enough. It's time to move on with our lives. It's time we start to live again. No more shadows creeping up behind us. No more worries about the monster. I want to live, Ryder. I want those dreams of our future. I want Fallon to find peace and happiness. I want Trevor to have a relationship with his brother. I want Jayson to heal. I want Julien and Elijah to have their happy-ever-after."

Just then a meteor streaks across the night sky. *A light in the darkness.* Isn't that the comparison Fallon made about him and me?

I make a decision. It may not be the right decision, but it is the right one for me. What happened to Peter will remain buried. It's time we move forward and look to the future with no regrets blocking our way.

"Are you ready to start our life together, Mr. Cutton?"

"Life with you is the only life worth living, baby."

Epilogue 1

Seattle

June 13

Elizabeth

It's been over five months since everything came out about Peter. I'm standing at the gravesite of my daughter in Seattle. Today is her birthday. I wanted to come out here alone first to spend time with Elizabeth Ann. Ryder is at the house with Daniel, Drew, Julien, and Elijah. Like the first time when I came here six months ago, they'll all join me later today.

"Hey, baby girl. Mama's here," I tell Elizabeth Ann as I lay a blanket on the grass in front of her gravestone. Once I smooth the blanket out, I put on some gardening gloves and start to weed the flower bed that surrounds the base of the statue. Several swallowtail and Painted Lady butterflies flutter from flower to flower in search of nectar.

"Ryder, your uncle Julien, Elijah, Daniel, and Drew will be out here later, but I wanted some time alone with my sweet girl. Your Grandma and Pawpaw Jameson weren't able to come with us this time, but they promise to make a special trip to see you soon. A lot has happened since I was last here," I tell her, wiping the dirt off my bare legs and flinging my garden gloves back in the bag I brought with me.

The day is nice and temperate, if a bit breezy. Strands of my long, blond hair come loose from its ponytail and plaster to the side of my face and neck. "Ryder and I set a date for our wedding. By this time next year, I will officially be Mrs. Ryder Cutton. We're getting married at the botanical gardens where Ryder took me on our first date."

I lay down on my stomach and kick my bare feet up in the air, my torso propped up on my elbows. I tell Elizabeth Ann about Peter and how Fallon delivered justice for us and our family.

I haven't seen Fallon in months, not since I last spoke to him. I have to admit, I miss him. He hasn't texted me or tried to call. Fallon is still trying to protect me, but this time he thinks he's protecting me from himself. A week after New Year's, I asked him to meet me. I wasn't even sure he would show up, but I should have known better. Fallon has never let me down.

"Kitten, I'm so sorry."

"Shut up, Fallon," I sob and throw my arms around him. He stiffens, his body locking ramrod straight. Perhaps he was expecting me to still be angry or blame him. Perhaps he thought I would hate him like he kept saying I would.

"Thank you," I whisper against his cheek.

I feel him begin to tremble against me, but I don't let him go.

"You always told me that I would wind up hating you. You said that you were my nightmare, the villain. You're not, Fallon. You're my hero. I don't know how fucked up that may sound. I must be fucked-up to think it. Never feel a minute's regret for what happened. Thank you, Fallon, for protecting me. For being the justice I needed for my family, for my daughter, and for me."

I kiss his cheek and allow my eyes to roam his face, taking the time to memorize every feature of the man who saved me from the devil and from myself. I will never regret my decision to run off with him and travel around the world, nor will I ever regret a single day I spent with him.

"My life is waiting for me. You brought me the closure I needed to move on. If you need forgiveness for something that wasn't your fault, then I

gladly give it to you. Peter killed himself. He's the one responsible for his death. You're the hero of the story, Fallon, not the villain. You deserve to be happy. You deserve to live a fulfilling life with no regrets and no guilt."

I press my lips to his forehead and let them remain there for a moment. "I love you, Fallon Parker Montgomery. Thank you for saving me."

I've talked to Ryder a lot about Fallon, and about what happened with Peter. I'm at peace with how things ended. I have my closure. For all intents and purposes, justice was served.

Speaking of justice, the DA accepted Maria's plea deal and Marshall was arrested. He made bail and was awaiting trial, but the Fates stepped in yet again and delivered their own form of judgment. Marshall was killed by a drunk driver last month. I allowed the charges against Maria to be dropped anyway. I did it for me, wanting that part of my life to be over.

On a happier note, Meredith has started dating Bryce, Sara's brother. I always thought Trevor would have been a good match for her, but he remains steadfast in his bachelorhood. Even though Fallon has been absent from my life and I miss him dearly, Trevor and I still see each other regularly on campus and on the weekends. Trevor has become a part of our piecemeal family and he helps fill the gap for

Julien with the loss of Jayson. Trevor has also stepped up for Fallon in a big way. Fallon split his company stocks with him so he could be on the board and help direct the future of Montgomery Pharma. Turns out, Trevor is really good at business, which I find funny for someone who majored in marine biology.

Devon and his mom moved into my house two months ago, and Mrs. Riley is working at Montgomery Pharma as an executive assistant. Devon is thriving and happy. He joined the junior varsity basketball team at our old middle school, and Ryder and I went to one his games. I foresee Devon playing professional basketball one day.

I sit up and cross my legs, lifting my guitar from beside the blanket and situating it in my lap. I sing a few lullabies to Elizabeth Ann and a new song I wrote for her called "Butterfly Kisses." I place the guitar down and reach inside the bag to pull out the book I brought with me. As I'm about to open *The Adventures of Winnie the Pooh*, a pair of booted feet appear in my peripheral vision.

I shield my eyes with my hand and look up.

"Hey you," I'm able to say, even though my heart is galloping like a herd of runaway horses.

Jayson sits down beside me on the blanket.

"Sorry I'm late."

Despite the promise we made to each other, I wasn't expecting him to show up today. He looks different now. He's thinner but still muscular. His brown hair is longer and it curls around his ears, and he has grown a short beard. It looks good on him.

"I'm glad you're here. I was getting ready to read her a story." I hand him the book.

I lean back, close my eyes, and listen to the cadence of his deep voice. I miss his voice. I miss my friend.

When Jayson finishes the story, we unearth the lockbox we buried here months ago. I hand him my letter to her, and he places mine and his inside the box and re-seals it. Jayson buries it again, then sits an old-fashioned stuffed bear on the base of her gravestone. He stands up and looks across to the horizon. I watch him as he takes a deep breath in and exhales it out slowly.

I stand as well and am the first to speak. "I'm sorry, Jayson. I'm so sorry for hurting you."

"I think we've been hurting each other for a while, ever since I climbed through your window that night and kissed you for the first time."

"A part of my heart will always love you."

"But it will never be enough. I'll never be able to forgive you for choosing him and not me. I'm having to figure out how to start a new life without you. It's been hard to do. I'm still finding my way." He pauses. "Have you read the letter yet?"

It's hard to speak since my throat is tight as tears stream down my face. "I've been too afraid to," I admit. "Where have you been?"

"Around." He pivots and bends down to kiss my cheek. "Goodbye, princess."

I watch him walk away through tear-clogged eyes. After a few feet, he stops and turns slightly in my direction.

"I love you, Liz," he says over his shoulder, and disappears down the slope of the hill.

Epilogue 2

One Year Later…

Elizabeth

"For fuck's sake!" Meredith yelps, sucking on the thumb she just burned with the curling iron.

I burst out laughing.

"What's so funny?"

"Hailey said and did the exact same thing when she was fixing my hair for prom." I giggle.

"And stop laughing or else you'll tear up and ruin your makeup. *Again.* I'm almost done, so sit still."

"Says the girl who spends half the time acting like a squirrel on crack and can't stand still for two seconds."

Meredith twirls my hair around the heated barrel one last time and spritzes it with holding spray. “Alrighty. There. I’m done. What do you think?”

I look in the full-length mirror and can’t stop the smile or the tears from forming. Thankfully, I’m able to wipe them away and avoid another makeup catastrophe. Meredith has worked her voodoo hair magic on me once again. She has my long blond hair cascading down my shoulders and back in long waves. Tiny butterflies are pinned throughout my long lengths, giving me an ethereal aura and making me look like a fairy princess. It reminds me of prom night when Hailey clipped tiny red flowers in my hair.

“Meredith, it’s gorgeous. You, my bestie, are a hair genius.”

She rubs her manicured fingers against her dress front and blows on them. “Don’t I know it, babe,” she says with a waver creeping into her voice when our eyes meet in the mirror.

“If you start crying, I’m definitely going to make a mess of my makeup.”

I look at my wedding gown that’s hanging from the large armoire. Just like when I asked Ryder to marry me, I decided to go a little unconventional. The dress is traditional white and floor-length, but the sides are cut out to reveal my butterfly tattoos. I’m not hiding them anymore. They are a mark of who I am and the woman I have become. Strong. Fierce. Capable. A survivor. The bodice is a halter that ties in a bow at the back of my neck. The waistline is embellished and the front splits almost to my navel.

Faith came in earlier and gave me a pair of yellow diamond earrings that match my engagement ring. Something new, she told me.

"Your hot as hell man is not going to be able to keep his hands off you today."

"I should hope not!" I answer before adding, "I know I won't be able to keep my hands off him. Ryder in a tux is just…" I shiver, thinking about how good he looked in his prom tux.

Meredith starts laughing. "Hey, no baby-making in front of the congregation."

"Knock, knock," Freda's voice calls from the doorway. "Permission to see the bride before the wedding?"

"Of course. Get in here," I tell her.

"Oh, Lizzie. You are so beautiful."

"Thank you. Meredith gets all the credit."

Freda takes my hand. "No, sweetheart. You have always been beautiful, inside and out, just like your mom. Ann would be so proud of the woman you have become. I know I could never take Ann's place, Lizzie, but you have always been a daughter to me, and to Faith too. We're both here for you."

I blink back more tears at the mention my mom. I miss Mom and Dad and Hailey so much, especially today—the day I'm going to marry the love of my life.

My half-grin wobbles. "I know, and I love you both dearly for it." I hesitate to ask her, but I need to know. "Is he coming?"

Freda's face falls for a second before she composes herself. "No, sweetheart, he isn't. I'm so sorry."

It's what I expected, but I had been holding out hope, nonetheless. Jayson hasn't come back and from what Julien tells me, he doesn't plan to. He's been hopping from one state to the next, never holding down a job long enough to get settled.

"Have you heard from him recently?"

"He doesn't call often, but when he does, he sounds good. He's in California now."

I don't say anything more because there really isn't anything left to say.

"I'm going to let you finish getting ready,

honey. I love you, Lizzie."

"I love you too, Freda."

As soon as Freda leaves, Meredith turns to give me a hug. "Well, that was a bit sad. We still have time yet. Why don't we bust out the champagne?"

"You are not getting me hammered before I have to walk down the aisle. And I'm not having you drunk at my wedding. You get a little too touchy-feely," I remind her.

"I can't help that I'm an affectionate girl when I'm drunk."

I remember the day I went to her dorm room after I got back from my trip with Fallon and Ryder when she got tipsy and literally tackled me on the bed and hugged me to death. I have appreciated her kind of craziness in my life. Meredith has been a true friend. I look over at the table where my purse sits. "Actually, Mer, can you give me a minute? There's something I need to do in private."

"Yeah, no prob. I'll pop out and check on everything."

"Thanks. I mean it. Thank you for everything. If you see Julien, can you tell him that I want to see him. Oh, and also, let Daniel and Drew know that I'll be ready in thirty."

"Do I need to grab a pen and paper for this?"

"Sorry. Remind me why I didn't hire a wedding planner again?"

"Hey, we've got this. Everyone has been helping and pitching in. At least it's kept everybody busy and out of your hair, otherwise they'd all be in here with us. That would be bad, so count your chickens as a blessing."

"I don't even know what that means, but okay. And no quickies in the coat closet with Bryce."

"Well, hell, Elizabeth, how do you do that?"

"I know you. So keep his pants zipped and your dress immaculate until after the wedding."

"I can wait until the reception. I figure there are plenty of places in the gardens to hide behind foliage and give my man a hand job," she titters and skips out of the room.

I take a second to gather myself, then walk over to the side table where my beaded clutch is lying. I unhook the clasp and take out the envelope from inside. It's the letter Jayson wrote to me the day he left. I haven't had the courage to read it yet, but something inside of me this morning told me today was the day. I tear open the envelope, pull out the folded sheet of notebook paper, and go to sit down on the chaise lounge next to the window.

Dear Princess,

God, where do I start? I guess the first thing I should say is, I'm sorry. I said some awful things to you that came from a place of heartbreak and anger. I don't hate you. I never could. I hate that I won't be the one waiting for you at the end of the aisle. I hate that you won't be the mother of my children. I hate that I will never be able to make love to you again. I hate that I will never wake up to you in my arms. I hate that you chose Ryder. But I don't hate you.

But what I most regret is that night. I'll never forgive myself for what I did. I wish I could blame it on being drunk, but that would be a coward's way out. I am so sorry for hurting you that way. I hope one day you can forgive me for ever laying a hand on you in anger.

Everything is so fucked-up. I don't know what to do with my life anymore. I had everything planned out. You and me forever. The girl I fell in love with from the first moment I saw her. The girl that has been my heart and soul since I was six years old. I don't know what to do, Liz. I don't know how to live a life without you.

So I'm leaving. I need to figure out what to

do with my future. I need to figure who I am. I don't know when or even if I'll come back. Perhaps never. It'll be too hard to see you and not have things the way they used to be. To know that they never will be because you'll be married to Ryder. He's a good man. He was a good friend. He deserved so much better than I gave him in our friendship. Just one more thing I'll always regret.

The part of my heart that I gave you is forever yours. Be happy, princess. Know how much you are loved. By Ryder, by Julien. By me. I love you and I always will.

Your once upon a time prince,
-Jayson

There's a knock on the door and Julien walks in. "Hey, Meredith said you wanted to see me."

I hold the piece of paper against my heart. "Julien," I cry, and he rushes over to me, lifting me up in his arms.

"Hey, shhh, shhh. If Meredith comes in here, she'll kick my ass if she sees your makeup is ruined. And I'm really afraid of her even if she is tiny."

I blubber out a half-hearted laugh. "I read Jayson's letter."

"Well, that's depressing as shit."

I hand him the letter and go check to make sure I haven't caused too much damage to my eyeshadow and mascara.

Julien reads the letter and comes to stand behind me, wrapping his hands around my waist. "No more tears. He wouldn't want that for you today."

"No more tears," I agree and compose myself, placing the letter back inside my small purse. "Let's get me dressed and down the aisle. I have an amber-eyed man I want to marry. Just think. In six months, we'll be doing this for you."

"We're getting old."

"Bite your tongue, Julien Jameson. Help me with the gown?"

"It'll be my pleasure."

"Get your man-hands off that wedding dress, mister. That's my job," Meredith scolds him as she runs in and smacks his hands away. "Everybody is here. It's showtime!"

Julien grumbles something about being attacked by a rabid chihuahua.

"She dressed yet?" Trevor asks as Julien passes him at the doorway.

"Meredith is about to help her with the wedding dress. You better get in and out before Meredith goes nuclear."

"Hey, firecracker! Put all weapons down and step away from the wedding dress."

"Oh, for fuck's sake. Do the men in your life not understand that a wedding is about to take place, and a bride cannot get married until she has on her wedding gown?" she responds with exasperation.

"You can come in, Trevor. I'm decent."

"Wow! Damn, wildcat. You clean up nice," he says, taking in my hair and makeup.

I roll my eyes at him. "How's my future husband doing?"

"About to haul ass back here and throw you over his shoulder."

Meredith fluffs my hair. "Hot damn! I love it when you guys go all alpha male."

"Ignore her," I tell him.

Trevor gives me a kiss on the cheek. "Ry told me to tell you that it is considered cruel and unusual punishment to make the groom wait to see his bride the day of the wedding."

"But I saw him last night after the bachelor-bachelorette party."

Meredith jumps in with her usual play-by-play. "Oh, we know. I think most of the hotel heard the two of you last night. I wanted to thank you for that, by the way. Your audio porn turned Bryce on, and he fucked me on every surface of our hotel room. Would advise against taking a UV light in there is all I'm saying."

I about bust a gut laughing, but poor Trevor starts choking. "Christ, woman. As one of your former fuck buddies, I did not want that as a visual in my head."

Mer pops her hip out like a diva. "Hey, you passed all this yumminess up. Can't whine and complain about it now."

I'm cracking up at the two of them. "I love you guys. But if you don't stop making me laugh, I'm going to pee my pants."

"And there's my cue to leave," Trevor says. "You look gorgeous, wildcat. See you out there."

"Why are you not dressed yet?" Elijah exclaims at me, breezing into the room.

Meredith glares at him. "Because every-damn-body keeps coming in here. And you, as her maid of honor, should have been in here helping me. Come here and give me a hand with her dress. I need someone tall."

"Yes, ma'am. Where do you want me?"

"Luckily, we can get this sucker on her bottom up and not mess up her hair. Elizabeth, strip. It's not like Elijah will care seeing you in your bra and panties since he's not into girls."

True, I think and take off my robe.

Elijah whistles. "If I was into girls, I would say you're one sexy bride," he says.

"You can still say it," I tease him. "I tell Mer all the time how pretty she is."

"Please. That's a given," she says.

Meredith asks Elijah to help her hold the wedding gown. With a little metaphorical elbow grease, I shimmy the gown up and Meredith begins the task of making sure it's tied, buttoned, and snapped into place. It molds to my figure and feels so soft and smooth on my skin that I sigh out loud.

Meredith helps me slip on my low-heeled beaded silk sandals. "I'm getting married," I squeal when I turn around to look in the mirror to get the full effect.

Elijah cups my cheeks. "You are so getting married! Holy shit, this dress is fucking gorgeous!"

Mer cuts in with, "I call dibs on it for my wedding even though you're like ten feet taller than I am, so I'll have to alter the shit out of it."

Elijah motions at my gown with his finger. "You will definitely need to alter the shit out of it as that cut down the front is going to show a lot more than your belly button," he tells her.

Meredith just shrugs with an impish smile.

I breathe in and out, taking one final look at myself. Meredith touches up my lipstick.

"Okay. Time to marry my man," I tell them.

As soon as I step out of the room, Daniel and Drew meet me, each taking an arm.

"I've never seen a more beautiful bride," Daniel says, kissing my temple.

Drew cradles my cheek and smiles. "Life, love, and happiness, sweetheart. Live it, breathe it, and never take it for granted."

We decided on an early evening wedding at the botanical gardens since the sun sets late during the summer. We wanted to capture the sunset as we said our vows. The grounds are gorgeous. Flowers are in bloom, so fragrant and sweet, and all of the foliage is filled out and lush in green. There are archways covered in purple wisteria vines that lead to where Ryder and I will say our vows. It's beyond breathtaking. I try to take everything in, see every detail, absorb every smell and sound, but the moment the quartet begins to play the music that will lead me down the aisle, I can see nothing but the man waiting up ahead.

Ryder is devastating in his all-black satin peak lapel tuxedo jacket and black dress shirt. His hair is styled with a side-part giving him that panty-dropping rock star look I absolutely love. But it's the emotion in his golden eyes that captures me. It's the look of a man who is completely and whole-heartedly in love with his woman. My emotions match his as I gaze adoringly at him, remembering the first day we met.

"So what do you like to read?" I ask Ryder.

He shoves his hands inside the pockets of his jeans and shrugs his shoulders again. I decide to try a new tactic. I grab a My Little Pony picture book from the shelf and hand it to him.

"I'm sure you must like magical horses. Who doesn't like talking rainbow unicorns?"

I try to act very serious when I say this, but the horrified look he gives me when I place the book in his hand is just too funny. It gives me the encouragement I need to continue teasing him.

"What about this one?" I say, handing him When the Crayons Quit. "Crayons get such a bad

rap. Everybody is like 'Oh, crayons are for babies. Colored pencils are for big boys and girls.'"

I keep shoving books at him until he gives in to my silliness and plays along.

"Nope. These books are way too mature for me. Do they have The Hungry Caterpillar or books about the American Girl dolls? The ones about Josephina and Felicity are my favs."

I look at him in shocked horror. "You know the names of American Girl dolls?"

"Yeah. Like I said, they're my favorites."

I walk over to the American Girl book section and begin to take a couple off the shelf before Ryder clutches his stomach and bends over laughing hysterically.

"I'm just messin' with you, Elizabeth."

My breath hitches as I approach the boy I grew up with who is now the man that is my everything. *I love you,* I mouth.

Not as much as I love you, he mouths back.

As I reach Ryder, Daniel and Drew shake his hand before each kissing my cheek.

"You are stunning," Ryder says, breathing me in.

"You are and have always been the most handsome man in the room."

"I don't think I'll be able to wait until tonight."

"Meredith mentioned a coat closet that could come in handy later."

"Babe," he groans.

"I love you, Ryder Cutton."

"I love you back, sweet Elizabeth."

I hand my bouquet to Elijah and place my trembling hands in Ryder's larger ones, linking our pinkies together. He's my anchor. My home. My sweet copper-eyed daredevil.

"You are one ballsy son of a bitch," I tell Ryder, shaking my head, a huge smile exploding across my face.

"So you liked it?" he asks about the front flip he just did on his motorbike trying to show off for me.

"Loved it," I breathe.

Ryder reaches for my hand and links our pinkies together.

I look over at Julien and Trevor. I turn to smile at Elijah and Meredith. I gaze out into the congregation. My gaze wanders over the new faces we have added to our group this past year. Our family. My family. I see Daniel and Drew, Faith and Randy, Freda and Mitch, Bryce, Trevor, and Sara, Brea, Jamie, and Jack, Tatiána, Eduardo, and their two sons. I smile at Devon, Seamus, Trevaughn, and Butch. My eyes finally land on one man I wasn't expecting but am so very happy to see.

Fallon. He came. He's here.

Fallon gives me that cocky-as-sin smile of his. The smile I beam back at Fallon in return is huge.

"He wanted to be here for you today," Ryder whispers at me.

Best wedding present ever.

The minister clears her throat and I give my whole attention back to the man I'm about to marry. The man who I'm going to spend the rest of my life with. My heart explodes with a thousand suns worth of love as Ryder lifts my hand to his lips, then flips it over and presses another kiss to my palm.

"Forever and always, baby," he tells me with tears in his eyes.

"Dearly beloved, we are gathered here today..."

"Punch it, Big Daddy," I tell Ryder, loving every inch of his new Dodge Challenger Hellcat. He presses the accelerator, and we speed down the road.

"So, where are we headed?"

"You're the first to get a ride in her, so where do you want to go?"

"I'm the first? Not even your dad?"

"Nope. I wanted it to be you. I knew you'd appreciate her."

"If it's a her, then you just destroyed my dreams of marrying it." I give a mock pout. "Okay, maybe not. She is gorgeous. Aren't you just gorgeous, Stella," I coo as I pat the dashboard.

"Stella?" Ryder's eyebrow kicks up with mirth.

"Yeah, Stella. A sexy name for a sexy car," I reply, all serious.

"I, Ryder Randall Cutton, take you, Elizabeth Penelope Fairchild, to be my lawfully wedded wife..."

"Your turn."

"I'm sorry, what now?"

"Your turn," he says, putting the car into neutral and getting out.

"No, Ryder! I can't!"

"Yes, you can."

"Are you crazy? I'll probably drive it off into a tree!"

"No, you won't."

"Yes, I will."

"Elizabeth, get into the driver's seat."

"Nuh uh. Nope. No way. You can't make me."

I cross my arms, shaking my head no like a two-year-old. Before I know what's happening, Ryder has my seat belt unfastened and me hoisted up and over his shoulder as he walks over to the driver's side.

"Ryder, what the hell?" He's perched on the branch of the old oak tree that leads to my bedroom window.

"Hey, Elizabeth. Do you mind waiting to yell at me until I get inside? I hate to admit that I'm a little terrified up here."

"Ryder, aren't you afraid of heights?"

"Yep,"

"Oh, crap. Oh, okay. Here, take my hand."

"...for better, for worse, for richer, for poorer, in sickness and in health, to love and to cherish, till death do us part..."

"Do you feel it, Ryder?"

The pull that always brings us back together. The attraction. The need. The desire. The love.

"I do."

"Will it always be like this?"

"Want to tell me what's going on? I'm assuming that's why you're here." Ryder looks at me.

Holding the bottle with my left hand since my right hand is still too sore from punching Marshall, I tip the water back and look at him. I mean, really look at him. He looks good. Strong and vital and so damn handsome. I never allowed myself to really see him before. Not just the superficial things I'm attracted to like his golden eyes I know have flecks of green in them that are the same green as my eyes. Or the way his muscles bulge when he crosses them over his chest like he's doing now. Or the cupid's bow on his full top lip. His tanned skin or his devastating smile I am lucky to be the recipient of often. No. Those are only superficial qualities.

What I see now, perhaps truly for the first time, is how Ryder always stands by me and supports me no matter what. How he has gifted me with his love and with his heart and not once expected anything in return. How he must love me so much, he was willing to give me up to Jayson and still remain my best friend even though I know it must kill him every day to see us together. I see all the years we've shared, all the times we keep finding our way back together, how even though I love Jayson so very much, my heart has always belonged to Ryder.

"I, Elizabeth Penelope Fairchild, take you, Ryder Randall Cutton, to be my lawfully wedded husband..."

"This song is one you wrote me. You gave it to me the night of our senior prom. I have played it and practiced it over and over the past year, putting it to memory, hoping that one day I would see

you again and play it for you," Ryder tells me.

"I wrote this?" I ask because the amnesia has taken all of my memories away, the last eighteen years of my life are gone. Wiped clean. But somehow, by some miracle, small pieces of memories of him remain.

My chest heaves as I breathe in and out, and Ryder starts to play my song on his guitar. His fingers glide across the strings and ruts, and not once does he look away from me. The song I wrote for him is heartbreaking in its melody. The ebb and flow of the musical notes are filled with longing. I must have written it about us. The music is our story. As I sit cross-legged on the piano bench, I close my eyes and begin to hum the tune. Do I remember it? A vision of Ryder and me dancing cheek-to-cheek surfaces, and I'm transported back to a time where longing and love flowed between us.

"I really need you to kiss me right now, Ryder."

"…for better, for worse, for richer, for poorer, in sickness and in health, to love and to cherish, till death do us part…"

"I love it when you call me that."

"What? Baby?" Ryder cocks his brow at me.

"Yes."

"I'll make sure to use it more often then."

I place my hands delicately yet forcefully on the

sides of Ryder's face, turning it so we are eye to eye. "I love you, Ryder. I hope it's not too soon for me to say it, but I need to. I feel so much for you. It's scary, thrilling, and overwhelming at the same time. But I need to say it. I need you to know. The day in the student center when you found me, I had a memory of you that night. I remembered you holding me. I remembered you telling me that you loved me, and I remembered saying it back."

"Elizabeth, I have loved you since the day we met. I have loved you for a lifetime. I loved you before, I love you now. I will love you always."

"I see you got my message." I pull my tank top off and throw it across the room. Ryder's hungry gaze roves across my upper torso and down to my bare breasts before making a slow perusal down my stomach.

"That I did." He lifts his shirt off and drops it, letting me get my fill of his golden, tanned skin and defined pectorals.

"I missed you today." I pull my shorts down and kick them to the side. No underwear.

"Not as much as I missed you." Ryder pops the button on his jeans and sheds them in one movement. He went commando today.

"How did dinner go with Daniel?" he asks as his copper eyes linger on my lips, my butterfly tattoos, my pelvis, then drift slowly down my legs and back up again. My legs almost give out from the sensual visual inspection he's giving me.

"Dinner was good." My hands twitch with the urge to touch him. I bite my lower lip. "Going to tell me what that was all about today with Fallon?"

Ryder swoops in and lifts me up. "Later. First, I need to fuck you."

I curl my arms around his neck, so giddy with love and lust that I am about to combust, my body burning to ashes from the heat being generated between us.

"I love you, Elizabeth."

"I love you too. Now shut up and kiss me," I demand, tugging the hairs on the back of his head.

"Yes, ma'am."

"Elizabeth and Ryder would like to share a few words with one another..."

"Open the door, baby."

"What?" My ears pick up a faint noise coming from the front of the house.

"Open the door, Elizabeth."

I hear the noise again. I jump off the sofa and run as fast as I can to the front door. I fling it open like the house is on fire. And standing before me, looking handsome as sin, is Ryder Cutton. The man I love more than anything. The man I want to spend the rest of my life with.

My body starts shaking uncontrollably and I drop Fallon's phone. He can afford another one.

"How?" How did he find me? I've missed him so much.

Ryder gives me that heart-stopping grin, his amber eyes liquid with unshed tears. "There's my girl."

"You marked me last night," I tell him, pointing at the love bite on my neck. "So, I'm marking you. I'm claiming you. You're mine, Ryder, just as I am yours."

"I have always been yours, Elizabeth."

By the powers vested in me by the state of North Carolina, I now pronounce you husband and wife. Ryder, you may now kiss your bride."

I lift my head and taste his sweet lips, a tiny tear escaping caused by his beautiful words. I pull back and cup his face, wanting so badly for the dreams of our future to come true. The words I have kept to myself escape out of me. "Marry me. I know this is unconventional and maybe a little unexpected, but I have known in my heart since I was nine years old that I love you with everything I have in me. You have been my best friend, my protector, the man who has always stood by me no matter what. You were patient and waited for me. And not even near-death and the loss of my memory could keep my heart, my soul, from finding its way back to you. Ryder Randall Cutton, will you give me the honor of spending the rest of your life with me as my husband?"

"On bended knee, I pulled out a ring,
And sang, 'Marry me, Elizabeth,
And say you're mine forever.
I'll love you every day that we're together.
You'll wear my ring and pick out a wedding dress,
It's our love story, so baby, please say...'"

Yes.

Epilogue 3

Thirty Years Later...

Elizabeth

I'm sitting outside a café in Venice watching the gondolas float by in the canal. It's one of those summer afternoons where you think the sky couldn't get any bluer and the sun couldn't get any brighter. It's one of those perfect days you cherish because you know tomorrow may bring rain. The waiter stops in front of me, and I look up to see him holding a tray with a glass of red wine on it.

"Complimenti del signore," he tells me and nods over to the man sitting a few tables over. The man tips his head and salutes me with his wine glass.

"Gigli grazie, ma no grazie," I reply to the waiter. He nods and takes the glass of red wine to the man at his table. The man looks over at me and frowns. I shrug with a smile and go back to drinking my coffee. My phone dings and I look to see who it is. My oldest son, Marcus, texted me a picture of himself with his two siblings, Christopher, my youngest son, and Charlotte, my only daughter. They're with Julien and Elijah at the beach. Julien and Elijah bought a beach house on Topsail Island and the kids are spending the week with them, along with their two adopted sons, Grant and Nicholas, while I'm in Italy.

Ryder and I have three wonderful, gorgeous children. Marcus, our oldest, is twenty-five, followed a year later by Christopher, and then Charlotte who will turn seventeen next month. Charlotte will become an official twelfth grader in August, and like her father and brothers, plans to attend CU after graduation. She is so smart and has the kindest heart of anyone I know. Ryder always says that she gets that from me. Several years ago, Marcus asked Ryder if he could help run the garage. Just like his dad, Marcus loves cars. He's basically a little mini-me of his father. Christopher also followed in his father's footsteps and got his MBA, then joined his brother at the garage. Marcus goes the repairs and custom work, while Christopher runs the business side of things.

And business has been good. When Ryder took over Randy's Custom Auto from his father, he expanded the business and made it even more successful than it already was. About fifteen years ago, he also bought the Fields from Mr. Jacoby's grandson and turned it into a proper Motocross track where several sanctioned events are held every year.

I finished medical school and worked in research at the cancer center at Duke. I decided I was more interested in the research side of things, rather than becoming a practicing physician. I took early retirement two years ago.

When Christopher was born, Daniel and Drew moved to North Carolina to live closer to me and the kids. Even in their mid-sixties, they are still stars in the technology world and are both currently in London speaking at a tech conference. I'll meet up with them on my way back to the States when my tour of Italy ends.

A couple of weeks ago, my children surprised me with the gift of a two-week trip to Italy. They packed my bags, drove me to the airport, gave me tons of kisses and hugs, and then shoved me to the security gate and told me to have some fun. Fun has not been part of my life for over two years. It's been thirty-one long, lonely months since I lost my beloved husband to acute myelogenous leukemia. But those thirty-one months will never compare to the decades of happiness and love that

Ryder showered me with every day. We never took a single day with one another for granted. We filled every second with love and laughter, happiness and joy. We made a beautiful life together which became even better once our children were born.

I do see Jayson once a year when we both visit Elizabeth Ann's gravesite on her birthday. He and I sit on a blanket and talk to our little girl. We read her stories, sing her songs, and bury the letters we each write to her. We cry and hug and then Jayson walks away, returning to the life he finally made for himself in California. I don't think he'll ever be able to forgive me for choosing Ryder. I wish things could be different between us, but there's only so much heartbreak one person can endure. I don't blame him. I never did. Jayson eventually married a woman he met in San Francisco. They have one child, a girl named Bethany. I hope he's happy. I hope he knows deep down how true my love for him was. Even now, after so many years, I feel the loss of his friendship as keenly as I do Hailey and my parents. Jayson was my first love and that will never change.

But Ryder was my forever love. I miss my husband beyond expression. I miss his golden-amber eyes and the way his smile would leave me breathless. I miss the deep sound of his voice and how my heart would skip a beat every time he called me *babe* or *sweetheart.* I miss his kisses and the way his arms would wrap around me and hold me tight like he would never let me go. I miss his smell and the scruff of his stubble. I miss the feel of his muscled body against mine as we made love. I miss falling asleep in his strong arms and waking up to his handsome face grinning at me, his eyes filled with love every time he looked at me. I miss the way he held me when we danced under the moonlight. I miss the sound of his voice when he sang to me. I miss the way he would kiss my tears away. I miss his laughter. I miss the way he loved me with every part of his heart. My soul will forever yearn for my husband every day for the rest of my life.

Before I was coerced into my trip to Italy, my children sat down and talked to me. Marcus said, "Mom, it's time. You need to start living again."

Christopher added, "We love you so much, Mom. We will always love Dad. We know he would want you to find happiness again."

My sweet, angel girl cupped my face in her hands and whispered to me, "Go be happy, Mama. You have so many more next times to live."

A couple's laughter a few tables down breaks me from my thoughts. My hand reaches down and touches my heart locket, the one Jayson gave me in remembrance of our daughter, Elizabeth Ann. I finger my wedding bands. The yellow diamond engagement ring, the eternity band my precious Ryder gave to me after singing his version of "Love Song," and the one he gave me the day he took my hand and made a vow to love me forever and I repeated that vow back to him. I will always love that man.

I close my eyes and silently talk to Ryder like I do every day. "Hey, baby," I tell him. "Do you recognize where I am? It's the café you took me to when we were in Venice. I still can't believe you flew halfway around the world to find me. I love you, handsome. I miss you."

A breeze floats around me and I can feel Ryder's warmth envelop me. He's always with me no matter where I am. I hear his voice in the wind as he whispers back to me, "You are the love of my life, sweet Elizabeth. But it's time for you to move on. You have so much love to give. Remember what Julien used to say about how you had an infinite capacity for love? You have so much more life to experience. Enjoy the adventure, sweetheart. I love you, baby. It's time."

I take in a shuddering breath and wipe away the tears that have gathered around my eyelids. As I'm reaching for my coffee, a shadow falls across my table. The hairs on my arms raise and my skin erupts in tingly goose bumps.

"Hey, kitten."

A smile spreads across my face until my cheeks hurt. I turn in my chair to see Fallon standing before me.

"Hey you," I reply, excitement and giddiness exploding inside of me. After over two years of feeling the numbing loss of my husband, the joy I'm feeling right now is almost too painful to bear.

Fallon comes closer and extends a hand to me. I take it. It's warm and strong. He pulls me up to stand in front of him, then steps into me so our bodies press together. His arctic blue eyes linger over my face in a gentle embrace as they trace across my features, taking in every part of me. My lips, my green eyes, my long blond hair that I refuse to cut because Ryder loved to tangle his fingers in it, and lastly, my smile.

"Secret for a secret, Fallon."

Fallon breathes me in like I am his oxygen. "I stayed away as long I could, kitten. I couldn't wait any longer."

"How did you know where I was?"

"You know I have my ways," he replies, giving me that cocky smirk I remember so well.

It's been twenty-nine years since I've seen him in person, and he still looks the same as the day I last laid eyes on him—the day I married Ryder. When Fallon left, he started a nonprofit for battered and abused women then traveled the world helping those in need while Trevor took over as CEO of Montgomery Pharma. Fallon never sent me an email or tried to contact me through social media. Instead, he wrote to me and Ryder every month he was gone. Three hundred and forty letters in all. I still have every one of them in a chest that Ryder bought me at a flea market in Virginia. Whenever one of Fallon's letters would come in the mail, Ryder and I would snuggle together on the bed and I would read it out loud. I'm proud of all the good Fallon has done in the world. All the people he has helped and families he has rescued. I'm not the only one who changed after our adventure together. Fallon may have saved me, but I think I saved him in return.

Fallon's family grew too. He had joked with me once that it wouldn't surprise him if he had a dozen half-siblings scattered about. He wasn't too far off. I've had the pleasure of getting to know each and every one of the Montgomery siblings. Fallon never did marry or settle down as far as I or his family knows. He's never said anything in his letters either.

"Your turn. Secret for a secret, kitten," he whispers, his voice shaking with emotion as his thumbs rub gentle circles across my cheeks.

"I've missed you," I tell him.

He cocks his head in that special way he did whenever he looked at me, and I laugh as tears slide down my cheeks. Fallon tilts my face up and kisses away every tear with his lips.

"Are you ready for another adventure, Elizabeth?"

"Absolutely," I beam at him.

And then Fallon kisses me. For the first time, I kiss him back.

"I love you, Elizabeth Penelope Fairchild Cutton."

I smile and Fallon kisses me once more, then tangles our fingers together. We walk hand in hand under the bright blue Venetian sky toward the Bridge of Sighs. Legend says that couples who kiss under the bridge as the St. Mark's Campanile bells ring will have a love that lasts for an eternity. I should know. It's where Ryder kissed me in the gondola.

The End...

...of Ryder and Elizabeth's love story.

Sign up for my NEWSLETTER and receive a special bonus scene of Elizabeth and Ryder, and a special announcement. I'll give you a hint: #FallenBrookForever

Reviews are like finding a pot of gold at the end of a rainbow. I read each and every one. If you enjoyed this story, don't forget to leave a review on **Amazon** and **Goodreads**. They help authors like me reach more readers like you and share my stories.

That Girl

***That Girl* is a Contemporary Romance Writers 2021 Stiletto Finalist and a Chesapeake Romance Writers 2021 Rudy Finalist!**

I was that girl; the one from a broken home who lived on the poor side of town. He was that guy; NFL football quarterback and Mr. Popular. He told me he would never leave. He lied. Now he's back. But I'm not that girl anymore.

Aurora St. Claire is that girl. The one who excels at academics. The one from a broken home who lives on the bad side of town. The one with an alcoholic mother who couldn't care less if she existed. The one with an abusive older sister who would give her bruises instead of hugs. The one who keeps to the shadows, trying not to be seen.

Sometimes the best families are the ones you create, not the ones you are born into. Aurora never knows what a true family is like until she has one suddenly thrust upon her at the age of eighteen. It takes a single revelation from a stranger to change her life forever.

Then, JD Hallstead comes barreling into her life. He is everything she never thought she wanted, but everything she craves. That is, until the day he destroys her and leaves her heart to burn to ashes in his wake. What is the adage? The flip side of love is hate. Well, her hate burns bright, and it has a name: Jackson Dillon Hallstead.

JD Hallstead is that guy. The one who is Mr. Popular and Quarterback King of Highland High. The one voted class president and most likely to succeed. The one who girls go crazy over and guys want to be. The one with a controlling, abusive father who will go to any lengths to keep his son in check. The one with the secrets.

Aurora is the girl JD has secretly crushed on for years. It takes a friend's tragic death to bring Aurora and JD together. It takes JD's secrets to tear them apart. Aurora tells JD everybody leaves. He promises her he never will.

He lied.

Now, JD will do anything, fight anyone, give up everything, to get Aurora back. Aurora said JD broke her heart. Who better than him to put it back together?

But the thing about secrets is that they always come back to haunt you. The question is: How far will JD go to protect the woman he loves before those secrets destroy them all?

Available on Amazon.

Julien

***Julien* is a Contemporary Romance Writers 2021 Stiletto Finalist!**

Soccer center forward for Fallen Brook High. Best friends with Elizabeth Fairchild and Ryder Cutton. Twin brother of Jayson Jameson.

We all know the story. Boy meets girl. Boy falls in love with girl. It's a tale as old as time.

Well, it was until I met ***him***.

My name is Julien Jameson, and this is my love story.

Julien is Book 1 in the Fallen Brook M/M Duet

Series, a spin-off of the Fallen Brook Series. Julien chronicles Julien Jameson's love story from his point of view. It is a coming of age, LGBTQ, M/M, bisexual novel that takes from childhood through high school and contains mature sexual content and foul language.

Book 2, ***Elijah***, is the conclusion to Julien's love story and takes place during college and beyond.

Reader's Warning: The duet series is intended for mature audiences ages 18+ due to sexual and mature content. All sex is consensual.

If you have read the Fallen Brook Series, you are already familiar with the fictional towns of Highland and Fallen Brook, North Carolina, and the characters of Elizabeth Fairchild, Ryder Cutton, Jayson and Julien Jameson, Elijah Barnes, and Fallon and Trevor Montgomery. ***Julien*** is Julien Jameson's love story told from his point of view and parallels events from the Fallen Brook Series.

If you enjoy contemporary story lines with a twist and some OMG moments that are packed with lots of high-heat, emotion, and love, this series won't disappoint.

Fallen Brook M/M Duet Series

Book #1: Julien

Book #2: Elijah

CLICK HERE to read bonus chapters in Julien's point of view (from All Our Next Times)!

Tattoo Confessions

(A letter by the author - unedited)

Dear Reader,

Thank for you for coming on this incredible journey with me. As I wrote the Fallen Brook Series, I realized two things while writing Book 2 (Paper Stars Rewritten).

Thing #1: I decided to let go of all my preconceived notions on how I originally planned to write Elizabeth's story and allowed my thoughts to wander and change. I thought it made the story more organic and better that way. When I first came up with the story in my head, Elizabeth was going to end up with Jayson at the end. As Book 1 (All Our Next Times) ended and Book 2 began, I came to understand that Ryder was the perfect man for her. Then along came Fallon. I fell in love with his cocky a-hole ways, so made him a focus in Book 3 (Broken Butterfly) to guide Elizabeth on her journey of self-discovery. That's when it hit me – Thing #2.

Thing #2: Without me noticing it, I was

sneaking in bits of my life into the story. Some readers might not understand why I ended the story the way I did, or why I had the various relationships between Elizabeth and her boys change. That's life, folks. All the twists and turns, all the decisions and choices you make, can change your life in unexpected ways. How you imagine your life to be or how you wish it will turn out is not always what you actually get.

Elizabeth's life was much like mine. My first real, true love I met when I was young. We made plans to get married. He gave me a promise ring just like Jayson did Elizabeth. We were with each other for ten years. But during those ten years, we both changed. We were young when we first met and had so much life yet to experience and live, and after ten years, I realized that he wasn't the man I should marry. He was possessive and domineering like Jayson was with Elizabeth. He clipped my wings when I wanted to fly.

Then, I met a man in my senior year of college. He and I instantly gravitated toward one another and became fast friends. After I graduated college, he moved an ocean away, but we remained friends even though thousands of miles separated us. After my relationship ended with my first love, I fell in love with my college friend and we have been happily married for the past sixteen years (add another five years of dating before he proposed). So, it made sense to me that Elizabeth could love two men but only one of them would be her forever love.

You're probably asking, "If Ryder was her forever love, then why did you kill him off at the end?" My answer is once again, that's life. We have no guarantees that anything lasts forever. People change, loved ones get sick, friends move away, our children grow up and create lives of their own. When I thought about how Book 3 should end, all I could hear in my head was Fallon saying, "Hey, kitten," in that cocksure way of his. Fallon was such an important part of Elizabeth's story and I wanted him to be a part of her life at the end. I wanted to give them a chance to explore that connection they made while on their world adventure. I wanted Elizabeth to have her forever love with Ryder, and then I wanted Elizabeth to fall in love again with Fallon.

Who knows if I'll ever write Fallon and Elizabeth's story. It may be something I come back to at a later time. My first inclination is to write Julien and Elijah's story. What do you think? (Update: By the time Broken Butterfly releases, there is, in fact, going to be Julien and Elijah's story! The Fallen Brook M/M Duet Series!)

Until then, enjoy life and live for love. Don't forget to check out ***That Girl: The Montgomerys (A Fallen Brook Standalone)***, my new standalone novel coming out in October 2021.

Remember all those hypothetical half-siblings Fallon made a joke about to Elizabeth? Aurora's story is up first in ***That Girl***, with Harper's story soon to follow in ***Wanderlost***. Julien Jameson will also get his own book, which is aptly titled, ***Julien***.

Now for my thank yous. Thank you to my wonderful beta readers, The Beta Girls: Lisa, Landi, Julia, Kelly, Maegan, and Rita. You guys kept me in stitches and gave me much needed laughs and support as I wrote this series. Lisa, seeing as you were very vocal about being Team Ryder, I hope that the wedding and ending of the series made you happy–well, except for the epilogues which made people cry. I won't tell anyone.

Thank you to Paul for his fabulous proofing skills and for giving me a guy's perspective. I know more about drifting cars now that I ever thought possible! Thank you to my son for always being my sounding board when I wanted to discuss storyline ideas. You gave excellent suggestions. Thank you to Ellie at My Brother's Editor for her excellent copy-editing skills, kind words, and emojis to show me how happy she was that Elizabeth and Fallon met up at the end.

Thank you to all the Jennifers (there are several of you!) and Kelly, Maegan, and Rita for your enthusiastic support of this series. You are why I write! I hope you enjoyed the dedication. And thank you, Reader, for coming on this journey with me and supporting independent authors like myself.

Don't forget to sign up for my NEWSLETTER to receive updates on new releases, sign up for a chance to win free stuff, and receive bonus scenes not in the books.

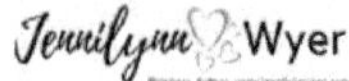

Also by the Author

Under Jennilynn Wyer (New Adult & College, Contemporary Romance)

The Fallen Brook Series

#1 All Our Next Times

#2 Paper Stars Rewritten

#3 Broken Butterfly

The Fallen Brook Boxed Set with bonus novella

The Montgomerys: Fallen Brook spin-off series

That Girl* [Aurora + JD]
* A Contemporary Romance Writers 2021 Stiletto Finalist
* A Chesapeake Romance Writers 2021 Rudy Finalist

Wanderlost [Harper + Bennett] (Available for Pre-order and releasing February 22, 2022)

Fallen Brook M/M Duet Series

#1 Julien*

* A Contemporary Romance Writers 2021 Stiletto Finalist

#2 Elijah (Available for Pre-order and releasing August 22, 2022)

Kingdom of Chaos (Reverse Harem)

#1 Savage Princess (Releasing March 21, 2022)

#2 Savage Kings (Coming Soon)

#3 Savage Kingdom (Coming Soon)

Under J.L. Wyer (High School & Young Adult)

The Fallen Brook High School Young Adult Series - a reimagining of Fallen Brook for YA

#1 Jayson

#2 Ryder

#3 Fallon

#4 Elizabeth (Available for Pre-order and releasing January 25, 2022)

#5 Hailey (Standalone – Coming 2022)

YA Standalones

The Boyfriend List (Coming 2022)

About the Author

Jennilynn Wyer the author of the Fallen Brook Series. She is a two-time Contemporary Romance Writers Stiletto Finalist and a Chesapeake Romance Writers Rudy Finalist. She is an author of steamy and emotional Young Adult, New Adult and College, and Contemporary Romantic fiction. She lives with her family in the Gulf States, is married to a Brit, and you can usually find her in her favorite reading spot, e-reader in hand, with the latest romance novel. Her Teen and Young Adult books are written under the pen name of J.L. Wyer.

She is an active educator, researcher, and environmental scientist who enjoys lecturing, teaching, and sharing her love of science with students and the public.

Her Fallen Brook High School YA Series

under the pen name, J.L. Wyer, was inspired by readers who wanted their teenagers to be able to enjoy the characters and story. The YA series is the result and is a reimagining of the adult Fallen Brook Series suitable for a teenage and YA audience aged 15+.

Connect with the Author

WEBSITE | EMAIL | FACEBOOK | INSTAGRAM | TIKTOK | TWITTER

GOODREADS | BOOKBUB | AMAZON | NEWSLETTER

SUBSCRIBE TO MY NEWSLETTER
for news on upcoming releases,
cover reveals, sneak peaks,
author giveaways, and other fun stuff!

email: jennilynnwyerauthor@gmail.com

Printed in Great Britain
by Amazon

87684598R00373